I,
JESSICA

MARTIN GUNN

Matador
9 Priory Business Park,
Wistow Road, Kibworth Beauchamp,
Leicestershire. LE8 0RX
Tel: 0116 279 2299
Email: books@troubador.co.uk
Web: www.troubador.co.uk/matador
Twitter: @matadorbooks

ISBN 978 1800462 656

British Library Cataloguing in Publication Data.
A catalogue record for this book is available from the British Library.

Typeset in 11pt Minion Pro by Troubador Publishing Ltd, Leicester, UK

Matador is an imprint of Troubador Publishing Ltd

It may be that our role on this planet is not to worship God, but to create him.

Arthur C. Clarke

Everyone who is seriously involved in the pursuit of science becomes convinced that a spirit is manifest in the laws of the universe. A spirit vastly superior to that of man.

Albert Einstein

CONTENTS

CHAPTER ONE

A FORCE OF NATURE

Jackson, Hinds County, Mississippi
August 2018

The warehouse job had been a good one, with plenty of exercise and good pay. But alas Natalie Young's ability to compete with the men and beat them at their own game made her eminently unpopular. Eventually, her position became untenable and with great regret from the foreman, he was forced to let her go. Not wanting to draw attention to herself, Natalie left without a fuss.

Two years earlier she had a future; now she found herself isolated with no family or friends to fall back on and a dead-end job. For over eighteen months now, Natalie had been on the lam keeping as low a profile as possible. A fugitive who had committed no crime other than simply existing.

There was of course Wesley, the only person with whom she had struck up any kind of friendship. Natalie had met Wesley in a diner when she first moved to the area in the spring of the previous year. He had tried to hit on her, but since it was obvious that he was a good deal older, twenty years older as it turned out, Natalie initially wasn't interested. Until, that is, he used his usual chat-up by casually slipping in the line, "I'm a pilot", at some point in the conversation. Suddenly he had her attention. Here was a person who might just be useful if ever she needed to make a quick getaway. Natalie found herself performing a fine balancing act of keeping him on a leash just long enough to keep him at arm's length, but just short enough to keep him interested. Wesley was no fool though, and despite being flattered by Natalie's attention, there was a part of him that was irritated by the fact that he was almost certainly being used.

Staring out of the large plate glass window, she squinted as the sun peeked out from behind a dark cloud. The mini mart where she finally found some kind of employment was particularly quiet that morning – no, deserted would be more apt. As she idly twirled her finger around the hair in front of her right ear, Natalie looked up from the dormant cash register in front of her and noticed a spider industriously spinning a web in a top corner of the glass. Then she glanced across to the other top corner. There was a six-inch crack which she was certain had lengthened since the day before. Natalie had mentioned the crack to the manager weeks ago, but true to form he had done nothing about it. Outside in the street she observed a few people going about their business and she hadn't seen a car for some time.

God, she was bored.

Her manager came into view so she motioned for him to approach her.

"I'm sure that crack has gotten worse," she stated, pointing up to the corner.

"I've reported it," confirmed the manager, glancing up with concern. "I'll chase up maintenance to get it fixed."

Looking at her watch, Natalie stood up and stretched her legs.

"Can I take my break now? It's not exactly busy."

The overweight middle-aged man looked at his watch also. It was 10.34am.

"Sure," said the manager nodding and looking around at the vacant store. "I'll get Paige to cover for you."

"Cover what exactly?" she cajoled. "The place is dead."

Natalie moved away from the till and was forced to squeeze past the manager who deliberately stood his ground.

What a douchebag, she thought as she smelt a faint hint of stale sweat.

"Be back in fifteen minutes," he called to her as she made her way to the front of the shop, picking up a small bottle of soda as she went. Helping oneself was forbidden, but Natalie cared little for her job and even less for her reputation.

Outside in the street, Natalie breathed deeply. The air was warm and humid and it seemed to her like a storm might be brewing. Twisting the top off the soda bottle she took a long swig. Then, as she took a second gulp, Natalie stopped with the bottle still to her lips. Some distance away to her left she heard a car door open and a woman's voice giving orders like an officer marshalling her troops. The voice sounded familiar. In her peripheral vision she noticed three men in dark grey suits fan out from a black Chevrolet Traverse SUV with blacked-out windows, parked several hundred feet up the street. The four security agents separated into pairs and began entering shops on either side of the street. She recognised them immediately.

"Fuck," she muttered under her breath. "Spooks."

Without hesitation Natalie turned and re-entered the shop, hastily making her way to the back where she picked up her coat, purse and crash helmet before exiting the rear of the store to where her scooter was parked. As she started up the bike, Natalie looked behind her. Nobody seemed to have noticed her leave, so she placed the helmet on her head and sped off before she was spotted.

Fifteen minutes later two men entered the mini mart and approached Paige at the till. She looked up to see the men, in dark grey suits, white shirts and black ties. Both men were wearing dark sunglasses and an earpiece in their left ear.

"Who are y'all," she joked nervously, "the Blues Brothers?"

"We need to speak to whoever's in charge, ma'am," was the impassive reply to her jibe.

"What's going on here?" enquired the store manager as he noticed the strangers standing ominously over Paige.

The two men turned around; one of them removed his sunglasses and spoke.

"Are you in charge here?"

"I sure am. Can I help you?"

"And your name is?"

"Jared Suitor," replied the manager somewhat unnerved. "Who are you? FBI?"

Ignoring the question, he produced a photograph and handed it to Jared.

"We are looking for this girl. Does she work here?"

"Look, before I answer any questions, I'm going to have to see some identification."

The two strange men looked at each other in a brief exchange of exasperation. Then the one doing the talking opened his jacket to reveal a large handgun nestling in a shoulder holster. Even though the gun was partially obscured, Jared recognised a Colt Anaconda .44 Magnum when he saw one.

"This is the only badge I carry," replied the man, frowning. "Now look at the photo."

Jared did as he was told and glanced at the picture. The image was of a pretty young girl with blonde hair cascading down over her shoulders.

"Well, it could be," mused Jared as he rubbed his chin in thoughtful contemplation. "Paige, come here a minute."

Rolling her eyes, Paige stood up and approached the three men.

"What do you think?" enquired Jared, passing her the photo.

"Hey, that's Natalie," exclaimed Paige, glancing at the

picture. "She has a black pixie cut hairstyle now but that's definitely her."

"She should be back from her break," observed Jared. "Have you seen her?"

Paige simply shrugged and shook her head.

"Find her now," barked the man with urgency.

Five minutes later, Paige strode up to the men excitedly.

"I've just looked out back. I think she's left – her scooter's gone."

"Right, we need her address now," shouted the man in anger, frustrated that she had evaded them. The other man was speaking into his sleeve as Jared hastily moved into his office to pull up Natalie's employment file on his computer.

"The rest of the team is heading this way," announced the second man.

"Good, we have her address," he announced triumphantly. "This time we've got her."

***

Pulling to a halt with a screech of brakes to the side of her apartment block, Natalie parked up and bounded at great speed to the top of the stairs to her front door and stepped in. Moving directly to her bedroom, Natalie pulled a knapsack out of the wardrobe and checked its contents. The two passports were there plus the remainder of her depleted savings, which now amounted to around $5000 in $100 bills. The fact that her cash was gradually diminishing, however, was fast becoming academic. With great haste she changed out of her work uniform into jeans, a T-shirt and sweatshirt, then proceeded to pack clothes into her knapsack.

Picking up her pay-as-you-go cell phone, she tapped in a contact. Natalie knew that Wesley was flying out today but wasn't sure when. She prayed that he was still at the airport. The phone rang and Natalie was relieved to hear his cheery voice.

"Hey, Natalie," he greeted. "Wasn't expecting to hear from you."

"Wesley," responded Natalie, "look, have you got room on your plane? I need to get out quick."

"Err… I guess." Wesley's voice showed bemusement and concern. "What's wrong, are you in trouble?"

"There's no time to explain now," urged Natalie. "Can you take me?"

"I'll have to change the passenger manifest," mused Wesley. "You'll need your passport."

"No problem," replied Natalie. "I'll be there as soon as I can. Please don't leave without me, Wesley, I'm counting on you."

"Okay," Wesley found it difficult to refuse Natalie anything, "but don't be too long. We've brought the flight forward. There's a storm brewing."

Buckling up her knapsack and carrying it into the small sitting room, Natalie's heart jumped into her mouth as a sharp rapping came at the front door.

"Yes?" she enquired through the closed door, stalling for time.

"Are you Natalie Young?" came a woman's voice from the other side.

"Who wants to know?"

"Let us in," came the somewhat exasperated reply. "You know who we are."

Refusing to open the door, Natalie's mind was racing; she needed an escape route. Before she could formulate an idea, however, the door was kicked open to reveal two people in dark grey suits. One man and one woman.

"Katrina Hart," sneered Natalie. "So, you finally caught up with me. What kept you?"

"The CIA may be efficient," she said, "but America's a big country. And you didn't make it easy."

"Sorry for the inconvenience," sneered Natalie again.

"Are you going to come quietly this time," said Miss Hart, smiling, "or are we going to have to take you by force? I have more men outside."

"I'm getting right out," declared Natalie, "to where you'll never find me."

The man drew his .44 Magnum, to show that they meant business, and brandished it at the girl.

"Put it away," mocked Natalie. "You're not going to use that phallic symbol, you need me alive."

"She's right, Anderson," sighed Hart, "holster it. There's a better way."

Producing a Wattozz stun gun from inside her jacket, Miss Hart checked that it was set to high and shot projectile one into Natalie's stomach. The girl felt a sting, then as a jolt of electricity shot through her whole body, she recoiled. The girl pulled it from her skin and grinned. Miss Hart shot the second projectile at Natalie's torso, sending her backwards against a wall. She slid down seemingly unconscious.

"Bring her," ordered Miss Hart.

Anderson crouched down to pick Natalie up under the arms, and as he lifted her, Natalie's eyes opened wide. She punched the man hard under the chin, sending him flying across the room. He fell against a cabinet, knocking a television onto the floor, then rolled over onto his front unconscious. Realising that she was in a compromising position, Miss Hart began to back off. Natalie jumped her at the bedroom door, swung her round and flung the CIA agent over her shoulder. The woman hit the wall with a thud and dropped onto the bed. Pausing to make sure that she was okay, Natalie heard the dazed woman groan.

"I didn't ask for this," asseverated Natalie. "I didn't ask for any of it."

She picked up her knapsack and made her way back down the stairs to ground level. As she exited the building, Natalie saw a black SUV parked up close. The door was opening so she ran over at lightning speed and kicked it shut again, putting a deep dent in the panel. Before the two men inside could respond, she crouched down, grabbed the sill and heaved. The SUV flipped over on its side with a clatter of metal and shattering glass, causing the passenger to fall against the driver in a flurry of arms and legs.

Dashing around the side of the building, Natalie put on her helmet and sped off towards John Bell Airfield, from where Wesley operated. Looking up at the sky, Natalie frowned; the clouds were looming black and the air was oppressive. With the knapsack secured on her back, Natalie took out her cell phone, removed the SIM card and snapped it in two. Then she dropped the phone down a drain. Kick-starting her bike, she gave one last look up at the apartment window to see Katrina Hart stagger to the window and then sped off towards the airfield.

Five minutes later, the two CIA agents exited the building to see the SUV lying on its side, the door open and one man struggling to clamber out. Katrina looked around in consternation.

"Damn that girl," she shouted. "Smith, get on to the local police station, we need two patrol cars here pronto."

Hart started thinking on her feet. Where would Natalie be going? She hinted that she might be leaving the country. The scooter wouldn't get her far, especially with a storm brewing. They needed to check out the nearest airfield. Again, Miss Hart looked up to the threatening sky; the dark clouds were glowing with lightning and large drops of rain were beginning to fall. She held out her hand as water began to splash off her palm.

***

The backdrop looked ominous as Natalie sped into the airfield; the weather front coming in from the north looked like a black shroud hanging over the horizon as far as the eye could see. The journey had taken longer than normal, as she decided it prudent to take the back roads.

With great relief she recognised the gleaming white Cessna Citation Jet CJ3 with its high tailplane and twin turbofans, the passenger plane belonging to Wesley. Thank God he was still here.

Wesley stepped down from the portside door of the aircraft, just aft of the cockpit, just in time to see Natalie screech to a halt inside his hangar. As she parked up,

Wesley strode over, eyebrows raised, wondering what it was all about.

"What's going on, Nat?" he asked with genuine concern.

"Am I good to go?" replied Natalie, ignoring the question.

"Yeah you just need to go through passport control," he revealed, "then we can take off."

"Where are we headed by the way?" she asked as an afterthought as they walked over to the main building.

"I'm on a humanitarian flight to Venezuela with a doctor and supplies," he confirmed, looking up at the brewing torrent. "We'd better get on board asap."

Natalie gave him a kiss on the cheek.

"Thank you," she said, smiling. "You're a sweetheart."

"You're not going to tell me what this is about, are you?"

"It's better you don't know, really," she beseeched. "You'll just have to trust me."

With the formality of passport control sorted, they finally stepped into the aircraft to see a woman in her late forties strapped in and waiting patiently for take-off.

"This is Natalie Young," introduced Wesley. "She will be joining us for the flight."

"Pleased to meet you," said the middle-aged woman, smiling. "I'm Dr Abigail Sanders."

"We'd better get in the air. This rain is really starting to come down now," advised Wesley, looking up at the clouds.

Soon the aircraft was up in the air, just as the storm turned into a torrential downpour with violent thunder and lightning. The plane banked and turned south, and

Natalie was able to glance out of the windows to see the airfield getting ever smaller. Two small grey dots could just be discerned moving at great speed and were about to enter the airport. She had made it – just.

As the Cessna levelled off to a cruising height of 35,000 feet, Natalie pondered her destination. It occurred to her that South America might be a good place to disappear. Suddenly she was snapped out of her reverie by the doctor. Natalie had deliberately sat as far back in the plane as she could, to avoid as much interaction as possible. Dr Sanders had to twist herself round to face the new passenger.

"Are you on some kind of hiking vacation in Venezuela?" she enquired, trying to make light conversation.

"Something like that," retorted Natalie unhelpfully.

Natalie turned away to look out of the window, making it crystal clear that she was not interested in talking. Dr Sanders got the message, sat back in her seat and closed her eyes. Neither passenger spoke for the rest of the journey.

Sooner than she expected they were passing over the coastline of Venezuela and for miles all that Natalie could see was rainforest. As a mountain range came into view the plane began to descend and bank sharply to port, making its final approach into Santa Elena Airport. The twin-engine aircraft touched down, taxied into a parking area and halted.

Before Wesley could say anything, Natalie unbuckled her seatbelt, opened the port door, jumped the short distance to the ground and looked around at her surroundings. The airport was small, with one runway and nestled close to a line of mountain slopes. The sky was a bright azure blue with cumulous clouds idly drifting by.

Natalie felt the warmth of the sun on her face as it peeked out from behind a cloud.

"Where are we exactly?" enquired Natalie as Wesley stepped down from the plane. "I need to get my bearings."

"Well, that mountain range is the Serra do Sol Raposa," advised Wesley, pointing east. "Beyond it is Guyana."

"And south?"

"Just beyond this airport is the border with the State of Roraima."

"Where?" enquired a puzzled Natalie.

"North Brazil," informed Wesley. "I trust you've got a map and compass?"

Nodding, Natalie thanked and hugged him, then Wesley walked back to the aircraft to talk to Dr Sanders. Eventually he turned back to Natalie but she was nowhere to be seen. He looked all around him and walked out to the runway and scanned beyond to the border with Brazil. She had simply vanished. *Well, this is going to take some explaining*, he thought. Wesley frowned, sensing that he was never going to see the girl again. After a long curious look at the jungle to the south, Wesley turned his attention back to his aircraft and the doctor.

Following a track which soon brought her into a densely forested area, Natalie stopped to mop her brow; jeez it was hot. After a few hours' hiking, she sat down on a large fallen tree and took a swig from her water bottle. Turning her thoughts to the people that she had left behind – especially Nathan and Jessica – Natalie felt a well of emotion rise up in her. Not wanting an emotional goodbye, she had slipped away when Wesley was distracted. She resolved that this was going to be the last leg of her journey. No one would find her this time. The CIA and the United States Air Force could go to hell.

***

The rain lashed the windows of the air traffic control tower at John Bell Airfield and Katrina Hart looked out in dismay, knowing that all flights were now cancelled. After checking with passport control, she confirmed, much to her chagrin, that Natalie had managed to escape on the last flight out. Hart's expression matched the sky. Both were full of thunder.

Twice now the bitch had gotten the better of her, and now that she had disappeared into the interior of South America, Katrina felt it was time to admit defeat. Natalie had proven to be her nemesis. She wasn't looking forward to facing her boss. It could mean demotion. But what the hell, maybe it was time to go back to a desk job. Apprehending the girl was always going to be a tall order; after all, how do you compete with a force of nature?

CHAPTER TWO

THE PRINCIPLE OF PARSIMONY

Oakland, East Bay, Near San Francisco, California August 1986

Looking down at her three-month-old baby, Dr Laura Phillips frowned. The child was cradled in her arms as she sat in a chair and bottle fed the infant. Breastfeeding wasn't an option for her, not because she wasn't capable, but because Laura simply didn't feel a strong attachment to a child conceived in such traumatic circumstances, and felt no inclination to try. Her resentment was profound, knowing that she was going to have to put her career on hold for the foreseeable future. It didn't help that she had to watch her husband, David, go off to work doing the job that she loved too. At least he had honoured his promise though: to stick by her. Laura did at least feel grateful for that.

"Is this it?" she murmured, looking down at the rosy-cheeked girl drinking prodigiously from the bottle. "Is this my life for the next fifteen years or more?"

Studying the innocent face staring blankly back at her, she frowned again.

"Why don't you ever cry? Babies are supposed to cry, aren't they? Perhaps I should be grateful. At least when you are asleep, I can forget about what that bastard did to me," she cooed incongruously.

As the child fell asleep, Laura stood up, walked over to the cot set up in the dining area of the sitting room and tucked the infant in. Laura looked at her watch: just gone 11am. Should she do some ironing or take this moment to get some much-needed sleep? Inwardly she jeered at her options, at how her life had become so mundane. Alas the decision was taken away from her by an insistent knock at the door. As she opened the door, Laura was greeted by four men, all conservatively dressed in black suits, white shirts and black ties.

"Yes?" she enquired with raised eyebrows. "Can I help you?"

"Sorry to bother you, ma'am," replied one man at the front. "We are following up on the interview that you gave to an FBI officer earlier this week."

She assessed the men standing in front of her. They were all early to mid-thirties, tall, slim – athletic looking even – and of average looks.

"I told him everything I know," confirmed Laura, slightly irritated by this intrusion. "Why don't you speak to him?"

"We just want to make sure that nothing has been overlooked."

"And who's 'we', might I ask?" Laura was beginning to get a little nervous. "Are you FBI too? If so, I will need to see some identification."

The man stepped forwards and put his right hand inside his jacket, but instead of an ID card he produced a handgun, forcing his way into the house and grabbing Laura's right arm. The other three men calmly followed him in and closed the front door behind them.

"What is this? What are you doing?" exclaimed Laura, frightened now. "Let go of me."

Laura was manoeuvred to an armchair and forced to sit by two of the men, now standing menacingly behind her. The first man sat opposite on the couch, whilst the fourth took the opportunity to check out the bungalow.

Placing his gun back in its shoulder holster, the first man leant forwards to address her.

"A counterintelligence officer of the FBI, Colin Bolman, came to see you on Tuesday, is that correct?"

"He said he was FBI," confirmed Laura, still flustered by this intrusion, "but he said nothing about intelligence. Counter or otherwise."

"Did he ask you about the work you did on a drug last year?"

"Well, yes he did," recalled Laura, "but I couldn't add anything that wasn't reported at the time."

"So, you didn't hold back any information on how to replicate the drug?"

"No – no, of course not," she protested.

"And you didn't keep any of the drug for yourselves?"

"We tested the drug on rats before we handed it over to that… that Nazi," declared Laura. "It didn't do anything but kill them, horribly. We were under pressure to get results. We just handed over everything and that was that. We wanted to distance ourselves from the whole thing."

"That didn't work out too well for you, did it?"

"No," agreed Laura sullenly.

"And what about your husband, David? Do you think it's possible that he held back some of the drug?"

"No, he wouldn't do that," confirmed Laura. "We both agreed to hand it all over. I trust him implicitly."

"Would it be possible, do you think, to synthesis the drug from scratch?"

"No, definitely not," urged Laura. "There was something weird about its composition. We couldn't identify it. The only way we could replicate the drug was with a sample of the drug itself."

The sound of a baby came from the back of the room and with a look of surprise on his face Laura's interrogator stood up, walked over to the cot and brought the child back to the couch.

"Give her to me," exclaimed Laura, surprised at her strong feelings of anxiousness.

"Relax," he assured her, sitting down and cradling the infant. "She won't come to any harm, just so long as you cooperate. What's her name?"

He made the assumption on gender by the pretty pink patterned romper suit that the baby was wearing.

"Her name is Jessica," fretted Laura.

At that moment, the fourth man re-entered the room holding up a plastic bottle of pills – Laura's prescription to help her sleep. The first man nodded and the fourth retreated to the kitchen with the pills.

Laura's daughter was wriggling in the man's arms and he smiled as he put his left forefinger into the baby's hand. The infant still had the Palmar grasp reflex and instantly the child's fingers gripped tightly round his finger.

"Ouch!" He grimaced in pain and extricated his finger. "That's one hell of a grip she's got there."

Laura stared blankly back at him, anxious to relieve him of the baby.

The man in the kitchen returned with a glass and moved to a drinks cabinet in the dining area.

"What's your poison, Mrs Phillips?" he enquired.

"Excuse me?" asked a nonplussed Laura.

"Drink," he clarified.

"Um, gin, I guess," she confirmed, still a little puzzled.

He took the tall tumbler and filled it to near brimming with gin, stirred the contents vigorously and passed the glass to Laura.

"You honestly expect me to drink this?" exclaimed Laura.

"Are you familiar with Occam's razor?" enquired the first man with a smile.

"Of course I am," confirmed Laura, showing her indignation, "I'm a scientist. It's often confused with the principle of parsimony."

"Then you know that when confronted by a set of circumstances, the simplest explanation is often the correct one."

"If you say so," countered Laura, knowing that this was a somewhat oversimplification. The irony wasn't lost on her.

"Drink, Mrs Phillips," insisted the first man. "Drink the whole tumblerful."

"I… I can't," stammered Laura, taking a sip. "It's too much."

One of the men behind her took the glass and brought it up to her mouth. Laura took a big gulp then began to cough and splutter as he forced her to drink more.

"Please, stop," she begged, coughing strenuously. "I can't do it."

The first man gave her an implacable stare and motioned to the other man to assist. He pinched Laura's nostrils together and pulled her mouth open whilst his accomplice poured the gin steadily down her throat. A few minutes later the glass was empty and Laura was left coughing and panting for breath.

"In God's name, why?" she summoned up eventually, wiping her mouth with her hand.

"Later today you will be found in bed," the first man explained, "some pills and a bottle of gin by your bed. The simplest answer will be that you committed suicide."

The alcohol and strong sedatives were already starting to take effect as Laura's head started to loll unsteadily from side to side. Standing up with the baby the first man walked to the main bedroom door.

"Bring her in here," he ordered.

Laura was carried into the bedroom and placed on the bed. She was almost unconscious by now and they had no trouble removing her jeans and sweatshirt. Finally, in just her undergarments, the duvet was pulled over her and the rest of the incriminating evidence carefully staged on the nightstand.

"It's a shame," lamented the fourth man, "she's really quite beautiful."

"Yes," agreed the first man, "but we couldn't allow her to live. She is too unpredictable. We need to keep what she knows under wraps."

"What about her husband?"

"Our orders were explicit. The woman only."

After checking everything was in place just as it should be, the four enigmatic men swiftly exited the bungalow, like thieves in the night. No one saw them arrive and no one saw them leave, as Laura drifted off deeper and deeper into a coma.

***

The trepidation Dr David Phillips felt as he pulled up onto the drive seemed to increase with each passing day. With Laura's mood swings getting worse and more erratic, he found himself in the unenviable position of not knowing what he would be walking into when he opened the door. At least today he had good news. After years of hard work, he had finally been offered a professorship at the University of California, Berkeley. And with a possibility of tenure sometime in the future, at least David's professional life was looking up.

Picking up his walking stick from the passenger side, David carefully stepped out of his car. With the support of the stick he gingerly put weight on his left leg. Even after a year his knee was still painful from the gunshot wound inflicted on him by von Brandt. All their woes could be attributed to that psychopath. But then would Laura have agreed to marry him if circumstances had been different? David preferred not to think about it. He opened the front door and stepped inside.

"Hi, Laura," he greeted cheerfully. "I've great news."

There was no reply, but immediately he could hear a baby crying in the bedroom. David moved as fast as he could to find Laura asleep in bed and the baby in its cot, clearly in some distress. What the hell was going on? How could she sleep through such a noise? Sitting on the side of the bed, David tried to shake the comatose woman awake. Frowning, he finally noticed the pill bottle on its side with a few tablets scattered around. Next to that was a bottle of gin and an empty glass.

"Oh Jesus, Laura, what have you done?" he bemoaned.

Ignoring the child, he grabbed the phone and dialled 911 for an ambulance, then moved over to the cot to console the crying infant. As he held her close, it occurred to David that this was the first time he had ever needed to soothe the child. Realising he was going to need someone to look after the baby he picked up his stick and hobbled round to a neighbour's house in the hope that they could look after her. By the time David returned from next door he could hear an ambulance siren down the street.

The next hour was something of a blur as David found himself driving home in a daze. He had arrived at the hospital just behind the ambulance, only to be informed by the paramedics that they couldn't find a pulse and all attempts to revive her had failed. Laura was proclaimed dead on arrival.

***

Keeping an eye out for David's return, the woman from next door saw his car pull up onto the drive. David opened the front door to the house just as his neighbour walked up the drive carrying the baby, who was sleeping in her arms.

"How is she?" enquired the middle-aged woman with great concern.

"She's gone," exclaimed David in disbelief. "They couldn't revive her."

After half an hour of consoling, the woman finally left, leaving David to his own thoughts. *How could a day that started out so well end so badly?* he thought. Eventually he limped over to the cot and picked up the child who was now awake and gurgling quite happily. Sitting back down on the couch, David held the child up in front of him. She beamed a rosy-cheeked smile back at him, oblivious to recent events.

"Well, Jessica," he sighed, "it looks like it's just you and me now."

As grief welled up inside him, David pulled his stepdaughter close and began to shake as tears rolled down his cheeks.

***

Hollywood, Los Angeles, California
August 1986

If it had been up to Ian Swales, they would not have been here at all. Being a Yorkshire lad born and bred, he would have quite happily spent their honeymoon back in the UK in glorious Blackpool. But alas no, his new bride, Linda, had insisted they splash out on a fortnight in LA, in one of the hottest months of the year. In an attempt to avoid the crowds, they had breakfasted earlier than usual and now at 8am had just slipped off the Hollywood Freeway and were making their way up the slope of Mulholland Drive in a hire car that Ian was still struggling to get to grips with.

"Do you think we will get a good view from up here?" enquired Linda excitedly.

"Dunno," said Ian with a shrug. "It should be – it is a viewing point."

Even at this time of the day, the temperature had risen to twenty-one degrees Celsius and, unlike Ian, Linda seemed to revel in it.

The incline was initially straight, but very soon the pair encountered a series of hairpin bends as the road snaked its way higher. On their right the road was flanked by a rock wall partially covered with trees and shrubs. To their left, the terrain dropped away, giving them an elevated view of the city below. After another straight incline, they turned another hairpin bend and the early morning sun, still low on the horizon, hit them in the face.

"There it is," exclaimed Linda, squinting and pointing at a brown sign mounted onto a small stone wall.

Indicating left, Ian pulled across the road and entered the small car park of the Jerome C. Daniel Overlook.

"It looks like we've got the place to ourselves," commented Ian, parking up.

"Come on," enthused Linda, opening the door and scrambling out. "Bring your camera."

Doing as he was told, Ian grabbed his camera bag and followed Linda up the path which led to the viewing point. The path had about fifty steps and, as they reached the top, the pair paused to catch their breath.

The viewing point was a small circular structure with a stone wall built to around waist height, and as they leaned over the wall, the pair could survey a panoramic vista stretching out before them.

"Look down there," said Ian, pointing in a south-easterly direction. "That must be the Hollywood Bowl."

"Where's the sign then?" asked Linda with a frown.

Scanning his gaze round to the left, Ian saw the freeway they had recently exited, busy now with rush hour traffic, until finally he found what he was looking for.

The Hollywood Sign could be made out in the distance across the valley and perched on the side of a hill.

"Over there." He squinted as he looked in a north-easterly direction.

"But it's miles away," complained Linda. She was hoping to get some pictures of them both next to the iconic landmark.

"We could get closer," advised Ian, "but it would involve a hike up a steep track and you know you hate that sort of thing. Let's take some snaps now we're here," he continued, "and I'll see if we can find a better vantage point."

Placated for the time being, Linda nodded as Ian took his SLR camera from its bag and began taking pictures.

"Take a picture of me with the sign," insisted Linda.

Ian did as he was told but the wide-angle lens served to push the sign further into the background. Ian removed the lens and delved into his camera bag, pulling out a long zoom lens. He attached it to the camera and aimed at the sign.

"Are you going to take one of me then?" asked Linda impatiently.

"Wait a minute," he replied, slightly irritated. "I just want to see how close in I can get with this lens."

Whilst Linda stood with her arms folded and pouting, Ian aimed his camera at the sign, and zoomed in as close as he could get. The huge letters came into sharp focus, filling his viewer. Ian didn't press the button to take a snap, however, he just stood there staring at the sign.

"Well, take a picture then," admonished Linda.

Eventually Ian lowered the camera in shock and stared blankly at his wife.

"What's the matter?" she enquired with a little concern.

"There's a man hanging from the sign."

"What!"

"From the 'O'," he confirmed. "There's a man hanging from it."

"Which one?" she asked dubiously.

"Next to the 'W'."

Linda grabbed the camera to look for herself. Indeed, a man in a dark grey suit, white shirt and tie was suspended from the letter.

"Shit," she exclaimed. "We need to get to a phone and report this."

Ian nodded his agreement and hurriedly they made their way back down the steps to the car park. Soon they were heading back the way they had come looking for a pay phone.

***

Just over an hour later, Lieutenant Felix Wilson and his partner Detective Sharon Howard were making their way up the tortuous track which led to the Hollywood Sign. They pulled into the LA Central Communications Facility, parked beside two police squad cars and stepped out. Putting his hand up to his brow to shield his eyes from the bright sunlight, Lieutenant Wilson gazed at the tall slender steel tower tapering to a point at the top and festooned with communication dishes. He had seen the tower many times from the valley below but not this close.

"I guess the officers are all down at the sign," commented Detective Howard as she endeavoured to focus his attention on the job at hand. Already she was making her way out of the enclosure.

"I guess," he agreed pensively, then, snapping out of his reverie, caught up with Howard as she was just exiting the facilities entrance.

"Hell of a place to kill yourself. Smacks of showboating, don't you think, sir?"

"Well, if you are going to showboat, this is the town to do it in," he countered, still deep in thought. "As for suicide, let's keep an open mind."

After a short walk the detectives were overlooking the rear of the sign some fifty feet down amongst the scrub and bushes of Mount Lee. Four police officers were down at the sign, staring up at the body and wondering what to make of it. With great care Wilson and Howard made their way down the steep slope to the sign as one of the officers approached them.

"An ambulance is on its way, sir," he advised.

"Good," said Wilson, nodding. "What have we got here then?"

"Suicide, sir," stated the officer as they walked round to the front of the sign and looked up at the man dangling above them.

"These letters are bigger than I realised," observed Lieutenant Wilson.

"Forty-five feet tall to be precise," boasted the officer. "They were erected in 1923 and originally spelled out Hollywoodland – up until 1949, that is."

"Well, aren't you a mine of information," declared Wilson with a hint of sarcasm. "Who called it in?"

"A couple of Brits, here on their honeymoon."

"You mean British?" affirmed Wilson. "And they came up here?"

"No, sir," advised the officer. "They saw him from the other side of the valley."

"But that's miles away," declared Wilson, looking in the general direction in which the officer was pointing.

"Long-lens camera," confirmed the officer. "We took a statement and we know where they are staying, but I can't imagine they'll have any more to add."

"Hmm – maybe," agreed the lieutenant cautiously.

Wilson walked around to the rear of the sign where Detective Howard was studying the scene. A rope had been tied off at the bottom of the scaffolding that supported the letter and stretched up and over the top of the sign.

"He must have tied it off first before climbing up," assumed Howard, "though I wouldn't want to do it. These signs are really high."

"Yeah – he might have slipped and hurt himself,"

replied Wilson sarcastically. Then as an afterthought he added, "They are forty-five feet high to be precise."

"Well, aren't you clever," retaliated Howard, annoyed at the derisory comment.

"We can't assume anything at this juncture," mused Wilson, ignoring the jibe.

"You don't believe in Occam's razor then?" proffered Howard. "You know, the simplest explanation is usually the truth."

"I know what it means, Howard," asserted Wilson irritably. He'd had enough of being patronised, especially by a junior officer.

Turning to the uniformed cops Wilson continued,

"Get him down and up to the road."

As the men lugged the dead weight up the slope, the ambulance arrived. Hastily a gurney was removed and the dead man placed unceremoniously onto it. Wilson noticed that his suit was well tailored as he began to search the dead man's pockets. Eventually he found a small black wallet in the inside jacket pocket. He opened it up and sighed.

"Colin Bolman," he read, showing the ID to his partner. "He's FBI."

"Counterintelligence," exclaimed Howard with raised eyebrows. "Well, that complicates things."

"That's not all," added Wilson. "If this is suicide, where's his car? This is a long dusty road. Are we expected to believe that he walked up here lugging a heavy rope? Look at his pants, his shoes, there's no dust or dirt on them. No way has he done any walking. Someone brought him up here."

"So, you think this is a homicide?"

"Yeah, staged to look like a suicide."

As the body was taken away in the ambulance, the police officers walked back to their cars. Wilson contemplated the crime scene as they drove back down the track. Whoever did this, he surmised, didn't try too hard to make it look like a suicide, almost as if they didn't care. There was a certain arrogance about it and that bothered him.

"Thank God Occam's razor is the exception rather than the rule," opined Wilson, glancing at his partner, "or you and me would be out of a job."

***

Arlington County, Virginia
August 1986

Darren Garner woke up a worried man. The previous day CIA headquarters was buzzing with news of the death of Rosie Hoskins, especially amongst the typists who knew her better than most. She had been found in an alleyway after a night out, mugged and strangled. The significance of her death immediately became apparent to Garner and he decided to take today off. He needed to think. Eventually Garner came to the conclusion he needed to contact the one man he could trust.

***

"What is it?" enquired Hazel with concern. She had noticed her partner's expression as he placed the phone on its cradle.

Liam Slater sat down on the couch and put his hands to his cheeks. Initially he was annoyed at being contacted; he had just returned from a tricky assignment in Cuba and was looking forward to some rest and recuperation. Garner sounded agitated and insistent though, and Slater felt obliged to see him.

"That was Darren from work," he replied eventually. "He wants to meet up."

"But you've only just got back," complained Hazel.

"I know, I know," agreed Slater. "He sounded worried, I'd better go and find out what he wants."

Just under an hour later, Slater was walking through Marcey Park, about five miles south east of where he lived and close to the Potomac River. The track was flanked either side by dense deciduous trees preventing the strong summer sun from penetrating too deeply. Eventually he spied a wooden bench, with Garner sitting patiently awaiting his arrival. They had used this bench as a rendezvous point in the past, whenever they needed to be away from prying eyes and ears. Slater could tell as he approached that something was seriously wrong; Garner looked worried. He sat down on the bench and turned to his case handler.

"What's this all about, Darren?" he queried, deliberately avoiding any preamble.

"Have you heard about Rosie Hoskins?" offered Garner.

"Rosie," mused Slater. "Isn't she one of the secretaries back at headquarters?"

"Yeah," confirmed Garner. "Christine Kaplow's to be precise."

"What about her?"

"She was found the night before last murdered in an alley. It looks like a straightforward mugging on the face of it."

"Poor girl," muttered Slater. "And you think that being a secretary to the director of operations is significant?"

"There have been other deaths linked to this one that affect you and me."

Slater raised his eyebrows; suddenly Garner had his full attention.

"Firstly, Laura Phillips has recently been found dead."

"What, the biochemist?" exclaimed Slater. "How?"

"The verdict was suicide," continued Garner, "but two days earlier Colin Bolman had been to see her and he was next seen hanging from the Hollywood Sign in LA. It looked like another suicide but the LAPD haven't ruled out homicide."

"What was Bolman doing there?"

"I suspect he was trying to find out more about Operation Solar Eclipse," surmised Garner. "The report we passed to the FBI was a heavily redacted one."

"What could she tell him?"

"Well, obviously she knows about the Infinity Serum, not to mention the time machines."

"And they were both killed for what they know," reasoned Slater, "but what about Rosie?"

"She typed up the Solar Eclipse documents that were handed out at the briefing. Don't you see? Everyone who is linked to this operation is slowly being bumped off."

"That puts you and me in the frame too," exclaimed Slater excitedly. "Have you any idea who is doing this?"

"The only other person who has a vested interest in this is Kaplow herself," pointed out Garner. "It has to be her, there's no one else left."

Garner turned to look at the field agent.

"Look, Slater, I'm scared, if we don't…"

Slater was stunned as he heard a dull thud and blood splattered from Garner's right temple; then a spray of red exited his left temple as a high velocity bullet passed through. Without hesitation, Slater dashed behind a tree just as another bullet splintered bark off the edge, grazing his right arm. He looked over at his beleaguered colleague. Garner had fallen forwards off the bench and was now lying on his side, a pool of blood leaking from the fatal wound and soaking into the track.

Pressing his back against the tree trunk, Slater contemplated his next move. He knew that he had to get back to his car or die. The sniper was using a silencer and could sit in the trees all day if need be. Fixing his stare on a clump of trees opposite, Slater made a dash for them. A bullet zipped past behind him as he just managed to outrun his assailant. Another dash moving from tree to tree and two more near misses found Slater out of direct line of fire. With no more bullets being shot he made a final sprint for his car. As he fired up the engine, the first thing that sprang to his mind was Hazel. If they had gone looking for him, she could be in danger.

It took nearly ten minutes before he found a public telephone booth. Slater screeched to a halt, jumped out of his car and started dialling rapidly. The phone rang the other end.

"Come on, Hazel, pick up," he uttered in near panic.

"Hello," came a cheery reply.

"Hazel, it's me." Slater was close to panicking. "Don't ask…"

"Hold on, Liam, there's someone at the door."

"No, wait," pleaded Slater.

Hazel had already put the receiver down and moved to the door. Pulling down on the latch, she opened the door to see a well-dressed man in a black suit, but before she could say a word, he lifted his handgun and put a bullet in her head.

Slater heard the sound he knew to be a silenced gun and then someone collapsing to the floor.

"Hazel!" he shouted in anguish, but he knew it was too late.

On the other end of the line, Slater heard the receiver being picked up and then the sound of faint breathing. For a few seconds he and the assassin listened to each other in silence, until finally Slater hung up and moved swiftly to his car. He knew exactly what to do next.

After abandoning his car in a public car park, Slater found a taxi cab and made his way to Washington DC Union Station. The plush railroad building with its ornate arched ceiling was bustling with travellers going about their business. Slater dashed directly to the storage locker area; he scanned the wall of grey metal doors and found the number he was looking for. Pulling out his keys Slater opened the locker door, dragged out a black rucksack, then made his way to the toilets where he locked himself into one of the cubicles. Sitting down he placed the rucksack on his knees and unzipped the main compartment. Everything was there – $50,000 in cash, two passports, a

Glock 17 handgun and several boxes of 9mm parabellum ammunition. The CIA agent had prepared for such a situation as this. He leaned back and ran the past few hours through his mind. How could his life change so dramatically in such a short space of time? It's not as though he was on an assignment. It suddenly dawned on him that his right arm was hurting. After removing his jacket, he inspected the wound. Luckily it was superficial, so he found a handkerchief in his rucksack and wrapped it around the wound and tied it up securely. Hazel came into his thoughts and he had to stifle a cry of anguish and wipe tears from his eyes. This wasn't the time to mourn, that would have to come later. Now he had to get moving.

Very soon he was boarding a train to Cleveland, from where he would board another train to head out west and disappear.

***

The Great Falls, Potomac River, Virginia
August 1986

The white water roared and snaked past the jagged rock formations throwing up spray as it thundered down the Potomac River Falls. Christine Kaplow watched the sight absentmindedly from 'Overlook Two', one of three viewing points in the vicinity. It was mid-morning and her agreed appointment was overrunning. Kaplow looked at her watch impatiently; her left hand was shaking slightly and she had to steady it with the right to read the time.

Fifteen minutes late. Where the hell has he got to?

Christine Kaplow was a tall slender woman in her early forties. Shoulder-length brown hair framed a face of average good looks, partially hidden by large dark-lens sunglasses. The grey trouser suit that she wore was expensive and her demeanour emitted style and class, befitting of someone in her position.

Eventually, she spotted a tall man walking casually towards her in a black suit and also wearing dark sunglasses. He approached Kaplow.

"You're late," she hissed irritably. "I don't like being kept waiting."

The man removed his glasses and remained reticent, giving neither an explanation nor an apology.

"Speak to me," demanded Kaplow; she was anxious for news.

"Everyone's been taken care of except Slater."

"This isn't what I wanted to hear," she replied, making no effort to hide her disdain. "He's potentially the most dangerous of them all."

"He's gone to ground," added her accomplice. "Finding him is going to be difficult."

Kaplow sighed in exasperation.

"As long as he's out of play, does it matter?" he continued. "Surely we have more pressing objectives."

This simply wasn't good enough for her. She formed this group and financed it from a slush fund which only she had access to; no one knew of its existence except her. Sensing this man was trying to manipulate her, Kaplow became angry, having learned early on in her career that she had to be tough to survive in a world dominated by alpha males.

"I pay you to get results," Kaplow barked. "I created you, I can easily dispose of you. No one is indispensable."

"We'll keep looking," he assured her.

"What about the drug?"

"Still nothing," he replied. "We tried Laura Phillips but I am certain that she hasn't any. We could go after her husband."

"No, leave him," asserted Kaplow. "It would look too suspicious if anything were to happen to him as well."

This was not good news; Kaplow's interest in the drug was initially motivated by vanity and greed, but recently her priorities had changed. Having recently been diagnosed with early onset of Parkinson's disease, Kaplow hoped that the drug would reverse it.

"Have you assigned yourself code names yet?"

"Yes," he declared, "mine is Jude."

"Any particular reason?"

"We have all taken a name of one of the Apostles."

"Not Judas then," Kaplow remarked sarcastically with a sneer.

Jude's indifference to the slight showed with an impassive expression. He turned back to view the rushing water of the Potomac River.

"I want Slater dealt with," she threatened as a parting shot. "Remember what I said: no one is indispensable."

Kaplow walked away and Jude turned to watch her go. A few minutes later he followed and just as Jude reached the edge of the car park, he heard Kaplow switch on her ignition. The car exploded in a ball of fire so powerful it lifted the vehicle off the ground. Jude felt the blast and the heat as the car became an inferno.

Casually he walked past the blaze as bystanders began to run around in panic, women screaming. Further down the car park he opened the door to a black Range Rover and stepped into the passenger seat.

He nodded to Matthew in the driver's seat, who immediately started up the engine and slowly moved away, then out onto the main road. Jude pressed a button and the dark tinted window slid down. Glancing to his right, he saw thick black smoke billowing into the sky.

"Perhaps I'm Judas after all," he uttered dispassionately to himself as their car drove through the smoke drifting across the road.

"Did you say something?" enquired Matthew.

"Yeah," sneered Jude. "Nobody's indispensable."

CHAPTER THREE

TOMORROW AND TOMORROW AND TOMORROW

CIA Headquarters – Langley, Virginia
September 1986

Two men in brown overalls walked out of Christine Kaplow's office carrying boxes, just as Alex McInnes walked in. He looked around the bare room and sighed. Then he walked over to the window and gazed out over a small, partially full car park, and beyond to a large expanse of deciduous trees which wrapped themselves around the complex. There was just a hint of yellow and orange amongst the greenery to suggest that summer was nearly over.

McInnes eventually turned away, sat down at the empty desk and leaned back in his chair. He was a tall slim man in his early forties, wearing an immaculate grey suit and white shirt. His thinning grey hair covered a long, hawk-like face with a slit for a mouth which rarely broke into a smile. With large rimless spectacles, the overall impression was of a stern schoolmaster and the only hint of whimsy in his personality was the paisley tie that he wore neatly tied in a Windsor knot. He was an ambitious man and made no secret of the fact that he aspired to one day be director of operations. The trouble was, he didn't expect it quite so soon. Kaplow's violent death had shaken his resolve and it forced him to consider whether he actually wanted the job after all. But then, he rationalised, the recent slew of deaths had been identified as being related to the Solar Eclipse operation of the previous year and, since he knew very little about that, he relented and accepted the position that he had always coveted.

The tall man was snapped out of his reverie by a rather plain woman in her mid-fifties wearing a frumpy tweed skirt and white blouse buttoned up to the neck. She stood in the doorway and smiled warmly. Immediately McInnes snapped forwards on his chair, as though he expected to get scolded for slouching.

"Your belongings are on their way up, Mr McInnes," chirped Alma Cook. "Would you like a coffee?"

"That would be nice," McInnes replied and waited patiently for the steaming beverage to arrive.

Alma had been his secretary for what seemed like forever and he was more than happy to bring her along with him because, what she lacked in glamour, she more than made up for in efficiency. Frankly he sometimes wondered how he would manage without her.

Whilst he drank his coffee, McInnes busied himself personalising his office. After placing some books on shelves to his left, he sat down and began positioning various paraphernalia meticulously on his desk – in and out trays to his left and a picture of his wife and two daughters to his right. In front of him he placed a writing pad which he took great care to align with the edge of the desk. Finally, after placing some files neatly in the bottom right drawer, he pulled out the drawer above it, which seemed to show some resistance. A sharp tug and it fully extended, and he was able to place some pens and other stationery inside before closing it again. As he pushed the drawer in, however, it suddenly stopped halfway. He tried again, a little firmer this time, but to no avail. Frowning, McInnes knelt down and pulled the drawer completely out of the desk and looked in to see what was causing the obstruction. What he saw was a small red notebook which had once been gaffer-taped to the underside of the deck and was now dangling precariously by one piece of tape. McInnes reached in and retrieved the book, then sat down to examine it. After ripping off the grey tape, he leafed through the book and frowned. Then he reached over to the intercom and pressed down a switch.

"Alma," he advised, "I'm not to be disturbed for the next half hour."

"Very good," came the curt reply.

***

At 10.59am, McInnes glanced at his watch. He had arranged a meeting for eleven that morning and was anxious to get started. Just as he reached over to his intercom to find out if there was any sign of him, the device sprang to life.

"Mr Garret Sanderson is here to see you, sir," his secretary chirped cheerfully.

"Send him in, please, Alma," replied McInnes, concealing his relief.

There was a knock at the door followed by the emergence of a man in his late twenties. He was tall, slim with short fair hair, wearing a well-tailored dark grey suit, with a light grey button-down shirt and pale green silk tie. The good-looking man exuded an air of arrogance, virility and self-confidence. In that moment, McInnes took an instant dislike to him.

"Special Agent Sanderson," he greeted, extending his hand with a smile.

McInnes stood up and shook his hand, then offered for him to sit down opposite his desk. The two men sized each other up for a fleeting moment, then Sanderson spoke.

"So, what can the Intelligence Branch of the FBI do for you?"

The CIA director smiled candidly and decided to get straight to the point.

"I'm sure you must be aware that we have had four deaths within the agency recently. Two of which were administration staff. Plus, a member of FBI Counterintelligence of course."

"I am familiar with the death of Bolman," mused Sanderson with his right hand rubbing his chin. "It seemed more like an execution if you ask me. Four of your people, you say. Any clue as to who's behind it?"

"All I can say for sure is that all the victims were directly or indirectly involved with a covert operation which was wrapped up last year."

"Are we talking about Solar Eclipse?" offered Sanderson.

"You know about that?" queried McInnes with raised eyebrows.

"I know of it," corrected the FBI agent. "I saw the file passed to us by your good selves but it didn't tell us much. The document was heavily redacted don't forget."

McInnes nodded grimly. He hoped the lack of cooperation wasn't going to force a wedge between the two agencies. Especially now that he needed them.

"The problem is," declared McInnes, "we have no idea who is behind this. Someone, for whatever reason, is trying to eradicate all knowledge of Solar Eclipse and almost succeeded."

"Almost?"

"One of our field agents got away and has gone into hiding," continued McInnes. "A man called Slater."

"And you want us to find him?" interjected Sanderson, trying to second guess the reason for this meeting.

At this point McInnes shifted uncomfortably in his chair, then he unlocked the top left drawer of his deck, to remove a small red hardback notebook and a map.

"No, he is the least of my concerns at this juncture," confessed McInnes, placing the notebook and map in front of him. "The day I moved into this office, I found this notebook hidden under this desk. I can only surmise that it belonged to Christine Kaplow."

"What's in it?" asked Sanderson, leaning forwards, his curiosity piqued.

"Some crazy stuff that doesn't make any sense," confided McInnes. "Some crap about time machines and some drug she wanted to get hold of."

Leafing through the pages, McInnes stopped when he found what he was looking for.

"Here she has a list of all the people who were killed off except Hazel Collins. In hindsight it reads like an execution list."

"Who is she?" enquired Sanderson.

"Collins worked here in archives," confirmed McInnes, "but more interestingly, she was Slater's partner. They lived together. I suspect it was a simple case of being in the wrong place at the wrong time."

"Whoever this person is," mused Sanderson, "they are ruthless."

"I think it might be persons," corrected McInnes, nodding. He turned a few more pages in the book and stopped.

"There are six names on this page, "he continued. "I have no idea who they are and all checks that we have done on them have produced nothing. To all intents and purposes, they don't exist."

"You think they are the killers."

"Yes," declared McInnes.

The director turned over the page and looked at the FBI agent.

"This is the final entry," he declared, showing the page to Sanderson. "It is two sets of numbers which is obviously a map grid reference."

"I assume you have checked it out," commented Sanderson rhetorically.

"It's a warehouse close to Dulles International Airport, about twenty miles west of here."

He took the map and opened it out and pointed to an area, where he had placed a red cross in felt tip pen.

"The warehouse is here," confirmed McInnes, pointing to the cross. "It needs to be checked out. It's just possible that this facility is the hideout of these six men."

"Where does the FBI come in?" Sanderson was frowning suspiciously.

"We need you to check the place out."

"Why?" offered the special agent coolly. "This is your mess not ours."

"Look, we have an unknown terrorist group at liberty and killing at will." McInnes was leaning across his desk with voice raised. Sanderson had him rattled. "You know we have no jurisdiction on American soil. The FBI have the authority to make arrests and we need to act on this and fast."

"It didn't stop you with operation Solar Eclipse," stated Sanderson somewhat sullenly, refusing to be intimidated by this outburst.

"That's because it was part of an ongoing operation which dated back three decades. Besides, it wasn't so much an arrest, more a clean-up operation."

Sanderson sat back in his chair and became reticent. Eventually, he stood up and said, "I'll talk to my superiors and get back to you, though they may take some convincing."

"I would appreciate an answer at your earliest convenience," uttered McInnes after regaining his composure. He stood up and shook the young man's hand.

The agent simply nodded, and as a parting shot turned and remarked, "You do realise that this book implicates Kaplow and, ultimately, the CIA."

The director of operations did not reply as he watched the FBI man leave his office. He sat back down as the door closed and he was alone with his thoughts.

Yes, don't I know it. Whatever Kaplow was up to, she got herself murdered for it.

***

The Great Falls, Potomac River, Virginia
September 1986

The roar of the Potomac River thundered past in a relentless barrage of grey and white water as the veil of twilight descended on 'Overlook Two'. The sun had just disappeared over the horizon somewhere beyond the river, and Jude stubbed a cigarette out on the ground and leaned over the rail to look down at the torrent below him. He glanced to his left as a tall figure in a dark overcoat approached and stood at his side.

"Isn't this where you took out Kaplow?" the shadowy figure declared.

"So what?" challenged Jude.

"So, isn't it a little risky coming back here so soon?"

"Look, Sanderson, you said you have something for me," barked Jude, irritably, ignoring the question. "That's what we pay you for."

"Yeah, well, fifty grand isn't enough for what I've got," stated Sanderson. "I want more."

Jude turned and faced him and the FBI agent suddenly felt nervous.

"I have information that's going to save your bacon. But it's going to cost you another fifty."

The head Apostle didn't like being held to ransom by this weasel, but he felt he had little choice.

"That's not a problem," reassured Jude, producing a thick wad of notes in an envelope from his inside pocket.

"You've brought money with you?" exclaimed Sanderson to his astonishment.

"I've met your type before," commented Jude dispassionately. "They always want more. Now tell me what you've got. It had better be good."

"I had a meeting with Kaplow's replacement earlier today, a man called McInnes," Sanderson confided. "They're on to you."

"How?"

"It would seem Kaplow kept a book on you, hidden in her desk," advised Sanderson. "Where you're holed up and a bunch of other stuff. Much of it made no sense."

"What kind of other stuff?"

"I dunno, drugs and something about a time machine. Shit like that," snapped Sanderson. "I think she must've been having a nervous breakdown."

"Perhaps," smirked Jude. He knew differently.

"You've got to get outta that warehouse asap," urged Sanderson. "An FBI SWAT team are raiding it at dawn."

Jude nodded grimly, his mind racing.

"That's got to be worth the extra, I'd say." Sanderson had a smug tone to his voice.

"I've been ready for this contingency for some time,"

assured Jude, collecting his thoughts together.

"Just make sure you're gone," urged Sanderson, pressing the point home. "I shall be part of the raid tomorrow."

Handing Sanderson the envelope, Jude shook his hand and watched as the FBI man walked away. Jude followed shortly afterwards and as he reached the car park, he heard Sanderson turn on his ignition. The car roared into life and Sanderson switched on his lights before moving away. As his red tail lights disappeared into the night, Jude walked to his Range Rover and stepped in. He turned to Matthew and said, "We have work to do."

***

The doors of the warehouse slid open and allowed the Range Rover to pull in without having to stop. Jude jumped out and turned to James who was closing the doors behind him.

"Everyone on the mezzanine in five minutes," he barked.

James simply nodded and walked away.

Five minutes later four Apostles were sitting at an eight-foot-diameter wooden table up on the mezzanine floor. The men were Simon, James, Thaddeus and Bartholomew. They all wore black suits, white shirts and black ties – and looked for all the world like executives waiting for a corporate meeting to commence. Very soon Jude entered carrying a batch of dark red wallets, followed by Matthew carrying a tray with a bottle and six shot glasses. The tray was placed in the centre of the table and the two men sat down. Without hesitation Jude began to pass around the wallets to each member of the group, retaining one for himself. The men looked down at their wallets to confirm the name inscribed upon it. Jude looked up, his face expressionless and resolute.

"Gentlemen," he proclaimed, looking around the room at each man in turn, "alas our time here is over, our cover has been compromised. Both the FBI and CIA are on to us and these premises will be raided at dawn. We all knew this was a possibility but I must confess I didn't expect it quite so soon."

The five men glanced at each other, then fixed their attention back on Jude.

"In your wallets, you will find a passport with a false name, $1000 in cash and plane tickets to Geneva. We will all be taking different flights and different routes. When you arrive, book into a hotel and we'll meet at the address also in your wallet two days later. Is everyone clear on that?"

A murmur of confirmation rose from the table as Matthew passed the shot glasses round and opened the bottle.

"If anyone has any doubts, any misgivings, now is the time to state them."

Looking around the table, Jude saw five impassive faces, all five men resolved to their fate. Jude stood, picked up the bottle and began filling each man's glass in turn to the brim.

"This whiskey is a Reservoir Wheat," he exclaimed, "a particularly fine Virginia brew which I have become rather fond of."

He stood at his seat and raised his glass. The other men followed suit.

"Well, gentlemen," he said with a smile, "to the future."

"To the future," echoed the other five and they all knocked the dark brown spirit down in one.

***

As the first rays of light of a new day began to make their presence felt and forced all nocturnal activities scurrying into the shadows, three armoured personnel carriers of an FBI SWAT team thundered down the road towards their target.

Garret Sanderson sat in the rear of the lead vehicle contemplating the three men sitting opposite, and the two either side of him. He felt smug and for good reason. Having convinced his superiors it would be a good idea if he participated in this mission, he reasoned that any suspicion of his betrayal, if there were any, would be mitigated by his presence. To him it was the perfect cover. With the knowledge that the warehouse was going to be empty and a $100,000 in cash, he was sitting pretty, plus he knew, unlike the rest of these grunts, that this operation was going to be a breeze.

The signal came from the driver that the convoy was fast approaching its destination, and Sanderson and the other five men pulled gas masks over their faces and secured the straps of their helmets, MP5 submachine guns firmly held vertically between their knees. Sanderson felt the personnel carrier swing sharply into the compound and braced himself for the impact. The vehicle rammed the locked steel doors of the warehouse, sending them flying inwards, then continued on into the building, stopping just inside.

The rear doors opened and all six men spilled out onto the ground. Sanderson saw the other two vehicles stopped just outside, their occupants already covering the periphery of the building, in an effort to secure the grounds and prevent an attempted escape.

Several smoke grenades were lobbed into the warehouse to give cover and as the white smoke filled the cavernous space, the leader extended his left arm out to his side, to indicate line abreast formation, and the six men began to fan out wide, aiming their weapons and scanning the area in front of them. The men split into three fire teams and two men on each side moved to the edges of the building. Those on the left approached makeshift living quarters and those on the right encountered the stairs to a mezzanine level.

As Sanderson moved forwards a dark vehicle began to manifest itself through the clouds of smoke. It was a black Range Rover, and as he looked over the hood, he could make out two other Range Rovers creating a triangle in the centre of the space. Sanderson moved back to the side of the car and opened the passenger door. The first thing he noticed were several wires running from a black device and draping out over the ground, disappearing into the smoke. A red LED was silently counting down and now displayed the number four.

"Oh, sweet Jesus," implored Sanderson as realisation hit him.

Seconds later the whole warehouse exploded in a ball of fire, blowing out doors and windows and parts of the roof. Most of the men outside were killed instantly by the blast. Those who survived were thrown back, their uniforms torn, exposing gaping wounds and burns.

The inferno raged, licking the morning sky and giving off thick black smoke which threatened to block out the sun. When the emergency services arrived only three men were found alive behind the warehouse.

Eventually a civilian car pulled up and two FBI agents got out and walked as close as the fire fighters would allow. All they could see of the team was two personnel carriers on fire, with one blown over on its side. As footsteps approached from behind, the two FBI agents turned around to see a tall well-dressed man walk up beside them.

"Can we help you?" enquired one. "This is a restricted area."

McInnes looked at the two men with disdain, almost contempt. They must have been at least ten years his junior. He pulled out his leather identification wallet and presented it.

"This went south real quick," he uttered. "Any survivors?"

"Three of the team survived," advised the agent grimly. "Our man didn't make it."

Nodding, and with nothing else to add, McInnes turned slowly and walked back to his car. He opened the rear door and sat down next to another man who had been watching intently.

"Dumb fuck got himself killed," asseverated McInnes. "This whole thing stinks."

"No shit," exclaimed the man. "It looks to me like someone tipped them off. This gang is still out there."

"I'm fully aware of that, Slater," declared McInnes. "All the more reason for you to come in, so we can protect you."

"No, this is just a flying visit," insisted Slater decisively. "If I've still got a contract on my head, I'd prefer to look after myself."

Before the CIA boss could respond he slipped his left hand into the inside pocket of his coat and pulled out an envelope.

"My resignation," he offered, passing the missive to McInnes.

His boss was about to speak but Slater cut him short and stepped out of the car.

"You're making a big mistake, Slater," he barked through an open window.

"I don't think so," replied Salter, who turned on his heels and moved briskly away.

The director slumped back in his seat, wound up the window and sighed in exasperation.

"Back to headquarters, sir?" came a voice from the driver's seat.

"Yeah," muttered McInnes sullenly. "Get me outta here."

***

Geneva, Switzerland
September 1986

Turning off the Promenade du Lacon on the southern side of Lake Geneva, Jude began to stroll down the Jetée des Eaux-Vives, the long pier which served as a harbour for dozens of small boats. Further down the pier was the spectacular Jet d'Eau with its eruption of water shooting ninety metres into the air and descending at an oblique angle in a tumult of cascading spray and mist. The early evening sky was a darkening blue, with barely a cloud to be seen, and Jude, noticing a chill in the air, put his jacket back on.

It was the first time in a while that he was without a weapon and he felt vulnerable. He wondered if the other five had made it okay. They were the closest thing to family that he'd ever had and the only people that he trusted implicitly.

Hailing from Texas, Jude was a product of an alcoholic father and a promiscuous mother. He ran away from home at an early age when the beatings became intolerable. Living off his wits he quickly became streetwise, his education being the school of hard knocks. With no one else to worry about but himself he became extremely self-sufficient and fiercely independent. And, with one alias after another, he could barely remember his real name. This kept him not so much below the government's radar but off it completely – a status making him a useful asset to Christine Kaplow when she began to undertake her nefarious activities. He had no time for sentimentality; women were something he used and then discarded at will. His five cohorts were from similar backgrounds and all created from the same mould. In the years they had been together, the team had forged a strong bond which had hitherto stood them in good stead.

Jude looked at the blue face of his Omega Chronometer watch; it was nearly 9pm and time for him to make his way to a rendezvous at the Metro Hotel. He walked through the hotel, and found the staircase which took him up to the rooftop lounge. It was nearly dark now and the lounge was doing brisk business. Luckily a group stood up to leave, enabling Jude to secure a table.

The view of the vast lake was one of the best in town. Beyond the iconic fountain, hundreds of lights of all colours lit up the northern edge of the lake and reflected in the inky black water as it arced its way round to the east. Directly below, one could just make out the trees and lawns of the Jardin Anglais, the English-inspired park with its ornate fountain at the centre.

In no time at all a curious man came striding down the path between tables looking left and right, clearly looking for someone. He was an amiable-looking man with his thinning hair cropped short and an impressive handlebar moustache. His clothing was no less eccentric: a tweed jacket, green cross-hatch country shirt and dark green bow tie. His plus twos matched his jacket and plain knee-length green socks terminated with brown brogues. The man exuded charm and confidence, looking for all the world like an English country gentleman. So, it came as no surprise to Jude when he stopped abruptly at his table and grinned exposing a row of tobacco-stained teeth, that he had an upper-class English accent.

"I say," he spluttered, "are you Jude, perchance?"

"Yes," replied Jude, "and you must be…"

"Dr Osborne," announced the man, cutting Jude off. "I'm frightfully sorry if I'm late. I hope you haven't been waiting long."

"Not at all," placated Jude, shaking the man's hand.

"Well, now we're here," retorted Dr Osborne, "let's order food and drink."

Jude wasn't particularly hungry but the doctor was insistent. He caught the eye of a waiter and, without looking at the menu, began to order. It was clear that he came here regularly.

"We'll have the beluga caviar on toast and smoked salmon and cucumber with a cream cheese dip with dill," he announced cheerily, "and to wash it down we'll have the Krug Brut '81."

"Very good, sir," said the waiter and walked away.

The waiter arrived with the bottle of champagne and two flutes, and soon after that the food arrived. Dr Osborne tucked in heartily and encouraged Jude to do the same.

"When are we to meet the rest of your men?" enquired Osborne between mouthfuls.

"I have arranged for them to meet me tomorrow morning around ten at your establishment," advised Jude.

"Excellent," exclaimed the doctor. "That couldn't be more perfect. We'll get down to brass tacks the moment they arrive."

Jude nodded nervously; the moment of truth was getting nearer.

"You can stop at our facility tonight," continued Osborne. "We have a spare room for you."

"That… would be ideal," hesitated Jude apprehensively.

Close to midnight, the two men were winging their way around the northern coast road in the doctor's two-tone cream and red Austin-Healey 3000. His driving was rather reckless for Jude's liking and he put it down to the two bottles of champagne which they had consumed.

Eventually he turned into a drive and parked outside a modern building that had the look of a small hospital.

As they entered the building through automatic sliding doors, Jude noted a bright, clean environment with a few people sitting relaxing, and further down the corridor a nurse was wheeling a patient back to their room.

"What is this place exactly?" enquired Jude, slightly unnerved.

"This is a euthanasia clinic," Osborne replied, sensing Jude's unease. "Don't be alarmed, this is just a front for our more… err, exotic activities which you will be benefiting from."

Dr Osborne finally showed Jude to his room and bid him goodnight, leaving the Apostle with his thoughts.

As he lay in his bed, he hoped that the others would arrive promptly tomorrow. He hadn't suffered from this level of anxiety since he was a small boy, so tried to put all thoughts of tomorrow out of his head.

Safety in numbers, he thought, *safety in numbers.*

***

By 9.30am, Jude was up and breakfasted. He wandered out of the main entrance past a family gathered around an ailing relative. The image unnerved him and he couldn't put his finger on the reason why.

Dismissing the thought from his mind, he lit a cigarette just as Dr Osborne came over and stood beside him.

"Enjoy it," he said, smiling. "It will be your last one."

"What will happen?" enquired Jude.

"Complete oblivion," advised Dr Osborne. "Like a dreamless sleep."

"I trust the money has cleared your account?" asked Jude.

"My dear boy, everything is quite in order," replied Dr Osborne, blithely as ever.

Just before ten, two taxis arrived and five men alighted. Jude walked over and greeted them, pleased that they all had made it okay. Then he introduced them to the doctor.

"Well, gentlemen," he announced, clapping his hands together, "I think it's time to get down to business."

The doctor led them back inside and down a different corridor, which terminated with an elevator door. He pressed a button and the doors slid open.

The seven men stepped in and the doors closed behind them.

"This lift gives access to the first and second floors," he advised, then he produced a card from his coat pocket, "but when I insert this card in here, we will have access to the basement level."

Osborne inserted the card and pressed the basement button. Immediately the elevator began to descend, stopping seconds later with the doors sliding open to reveal a laboratory environment and several technicians in white lab coats.

The six men stepped out and began looking around them. Dr Osborne followed behind, smiling, knowing that they were impressed.

"Come, gentlemen," he gestured, steering them to an anteroom, "we will need to do a few checks on you all before we can start the procedure."

"When will it proceed?" enquired Matthew.

"All being well in twelve hours' time," said Osborne with a smile. "I don't envisage any problems."

Several hours later, Jude and his men were given a clean bill of health and were supplied with a tight-fitting white latex body suit. Their hair had been cut short to enable the integral hood to fit closer.

The six men were led out into the main lab area. They looked around the walls and saw banks of doors with green LED lights adjacent to each, all with numbers counting down.

"It looks like a high-tech morgue," commented Jude, staring at the doors, doubtfully.

"For some it is," replied Osborne, unfazed by the comment. "Not everyone makes it. You must understand that cryogenics is still in its infancy and a satisfactory outcome cannot be guaranteed."

"What are our chances, do you think?"

"Fifty-fifty, I would say," declared Osborne, appraising his customers. "You all look pretty fit."

"Fifty-fifty," repeated Jude. "That's just great."

Osborne checked each man out individually to ensure their outfits were fitted correctly.

"Excellent, you're nearly ready," he announced.

"Who else have you got down here?" enquired James somewhat naively.

"No names, no pack drill, as I'm sure you can appreciate," uttered Osborne, "though you will be in excellent company."

Walking over to a bank of lights he continued,

"In here we have a Russian colonel, and in this one we have a British aristocrat, allegedly accused of murder. They are still looking for him."

Jude raised his eyebrows and Osborne felt the need to justify himself.

"We pass no judgements here," he advised. "We are scientists and leave that to the judiciary."

"Now, gentlemen," announced the doctor, clasping his hands together and becoming more businesslike, "are we ready?"

"Yes," confirmed Jude, looking at the other five for their confirmation.

"Then there is no more to be said," quipped Osborne.

He led them over to six drawer-like compartments which were fully extended from the wall. Each man was shown to a drawer and helped to lie down on his back. Then technicians busied themselves attaching cables and wires. Finally, masks were placed over their faces.

"The process is very quick," comforted the doctor. "You won't feel a thing."

Each drawer withdrew back into the wall at the press of a button and the freezing process began.

"How long should I set the timers for?" asked one of the technicians.

"Thirty years," chirped Dr Osborne with a smile and marched away to the elevator.

The technician tapped on a keypad on each compartment in turn and green LED numbers appeared and began to click over. The thirty-year countdown had begun.

CHAPTER FOUR

THE GIRL OF MY DREAMS

Downtown Berkeley, Near San Francisco, California September 2016

Squinting to his left through blurry eyes, Professor Nathan Harrison slipped off the bar stool and staggered unsteadily towards the jukebox. The bar which he had chosen to call home for the evening was mostly filled with students. For most of the evening, he had been bombarded by songs which he considered dreadful, so Harrison had decided to choose something more to his liking. He reached the jukebox and used it for support as he scanned the list of what was on offer. Eventually he found something acceptable and put a quarter in the machine and pressed a few buttons. By the time he was installed back on his stool the song had begun.

"This is more like it," he drawled as the song reverberated out of the speakers. "ZZ Top – 'Beer Drinkers and Hell Raisers'. Not that crap we've been listening to all night."

"Well, you're drinking beer," observed the barman with a big grin. "I sure hope you're not going to raise some hell."

Harrison simply grinned inanely and took another guzzle from his beer glass. He wasn't in the mood for talking, a trait, he thought, which would have stood him in good stead earlier in the week.

"To hell with it," he announced to no one in particular, finishing his glass, and setting it down harder than he intended.

"Same again?" offered the barman, taking his glass.

"Sure, why not," slurred the professor.

The barman poured him another beer, and as he passed it across commented,

"A lot of the people in here seem to know you."

"Yeah," agreed Harrison, talking absentmindedly into his glass, "they're from Berkeley University – probably."

The barman dubiously looked over at some students sitting round in groups and wondered whether they were old enough to drink.

"So, are you a tutor there then?"

"I'm a professor of palaeonto... palaeon..." He stumbled in his inebriation. "I dig up old bones."

"Cool," retorted the barman as he moved away to serve another customer.

Harrison looked behind him and scanned the room. Several students acknowledged him with a nod and a smile; he in turn grinned and raised his glass to them, then swivelled back to the bar.

The professor was well liked by the students. He was easy-going, good-natured and approachable, making him very popular on campus. His enthusiasm for palaeontology was always apparent and filtered down to anyone who attended his lectures. Unfortunately, his enthusiasm had got the better of him recently when he had announced quite naively to the faculty that he and some of his students on a field trip during the summer holidays had discovered a dinosaur with a bullet hole in its spine, and that he was going to write a paper on his findings and publish it. The news was met with such mirth that he decided not to mention the human remains and their own unique irregularities. When it finally dawned that Harrison was in fact in deadly earnest, the mood changed to one of derision and the threat that if he pursued such an outrageous hypothesis any further then he could look for employment elsewhere before he brought the university into disrepute. Jessica had been no help either. He had looked to her for support, only for her to chastise him for making the find public. She was furious that he had not consulted her first, telling him that if he wanted to ruin his own reputation and risk his career, well that was up to him, but to leave her out of it, pointing out that there were times to speak up and times to just keep your mouth shut. The fact that her father, David, seemed to know something about the skeletons cut no ice with her and she refused to discuss the debacle with him any further. Frustrated and humiliated, Nathan uncharacteristically sought solace in the bottom of a glass and now was getting steadily wasted in the process.

Whilst holding on to a half-empty beer glass as though his life depended on it, Harrison barely noticed as a group of students approached from his right.

"Professor Harrison?" enquired a blonde-haired girl in the group. "Is that you?"

Harrison turned towards the voice with heavy eyelids. He recognised most of the people in the group, but could only remember the name of the girl who had just spoken to him. It was Sophie Hunter, one of the brighter students in his class.

"Man, Sophie, he's hammered," laughed one of the guys behind her.

"Shut up, Jason," admonished Sophie. "He needs help."

"Well, if it isn't the girl of my dreams," drawled Harrison, struggling to keep his balance on the stool.

"I think we'd better get you home," said Sophie with a frown. "Help me get him out of here so I can hail a cab."

"But, Sophie," protested one of the girls, "it's your…"

"Forget it," interrupted Sophie. "I can't leave him here like this."

Two of the guys supported the professor as he was manhandled out of the bar, whilst Sophie walked up to the kerb to try and flag down a taxi. The fresh air hit Harrison like a brick wall and suddenly he felt nauseous.

"I'm going to be sick," he announced.

One of the students looked around and saw a side alley with a few trash cans against the wall.

"Quickly get him over here," he barked.

Harrison was dragged over to the bin and no sooner had the lid been lifted than he vomited violently into it. Having eaten very little that day it was mainly fluids.

"Jeez, that's gross," said one of the guys wincing, holding him there.

"That's better," sighed Harrison, standing up straight.

"Here, wipe your chin," offered one of the girls, handing him a paper tissue.

"Look, I'll be okay," assured the professor not too convincingly. It was beginning to dawn on him what was happening and suddenly he was embarrassed.

"I've got a taxi," announced Sophie, and Harrison was escorted over.

"I don't need this," Harrison protested again. "Go and enjoy yourself."

"Just get in," ordered Sophie, who was beginning to lose her patience.

Harrison was bundled into the back of the cab and Sophie followed in after.

"Are you coming back?" enquired one of her friends.

"I don't think so, it's getting late anyhow," replied Sophie, looking at her watch. "I'll catch up with you tomorrow."

"Where to?" demanded the cab driver, and Sophie looked at Harrison for an address. He slurred a reply and the driver realised that he was drunk.

"Hey, you're not going to be sick back there?" he cautioned.

Sophie shot Harrison a look of confrontation and the professor shook his head sullenly, then closed his eyes.

"What brought this on?" Sophie muttered quietly to herself, watching her teacher lolling about beside her as the taxi cab weaved its way through the busy evening traffic.

Getting the professor up the stairs to his apartment proved to be a nightmare and, after fumbling with his door keys, they were finally inside. Sophie checked in a few rooms, found Harrison's bedroom and dropped him unceremoniously onto the double bed. As she took his shoes and socks off, Harrison came to again and he glanced at Sophie. She unbuttoned his jeans and slid them down his legs before tucking him under the duvet.

"The girl of my dreams," he muttered, turning over and falling immediately into a deep sleep.

Sophie sat on the end of the bed and studied the man whom she not only admired but found herself attracted to. On the last night of the summer expedition, she had slipped into his tent and given him a peck on the cheek. Now she was in his apartment and the man was comatose, damn it. With a heavy sigh she closed the door and found a spare room to bed down for the night.

***

The following morning, Harrison woke up with a start. Initially he panicked until it dawned on him that it was Saturday. The late summer sun was streaming through the blinds endeavouring to penetrate the alcohol-induced malaise from which his brain was currently suffering. He squinted and groaned, then turned away from the inexorable light. As he lay there, it became apparent that the shower was running. Who it might be was anyone's guess and Harrison began to rack his afflicted brain over the events of the previous evening in the hope that it might provide him with the answer. Memories of the previous night slowly began to filter through, and between the many blanks he remembered being put into a taxi and being sick. Harrison hoped it wasn't in that order. There was someone else there with him, but who was it? Slowly an image of Sophie's disapproving face came into his mind and he winced in abashed embarrassment. Sliding out of the bed, Harrison stood up and realised he was wearing only his boxer shorts and a shirt. Putting that thought out of his mind for the moment, he padded to the bathroom door and knocked.

"Is that you, Sophie?"

"Yes," she announced. "Give me a minute, I'm nearly done here."

Realising his mouth was dry and tasted disgusting, Harrison continued into the kitchen and filled a pint glass with water from the tap. Just as he was finishing off the last drops, Sophie exited the bathroom with nothing more than a towel wrapped around her torso. She was running a brush through her wet hair, when she caught a glimpse of Harrison.

"How are you feeling?" she enquired with a big smile.

"I've felt better," confessed the professor. "I hope I didn't make a complete idiot of myself last night."

"Not one of your finest moments," she replied with a chuckle.

Sophie was an 'only' child and the product of two ambitious parents who were attorneys at law. Lacking the time to spend with her, she was fostered out to boarding schools and summer camps respectively, to minimise the time required to spend with their offspring. Rather than undermine her, however, this neglect gave Sophie a self-assuredness and confidence which was lacking in most of her peers, and to assuage their guilt, her mother and father had a tendency to indulge her every whim. So, when she insisted on taking a degree in palaeontology, they were appalled their daughter had not chosen a subject that they considered more suitable. Believing it to be a flash in the pan, however, they acquiesced in the hope that she would soon get bored and move on. Unfortunately, they didn't know their contrary daughter at all and not only did she enjoy the subject but excelled in it too. This behaviour, which her parents considered to be nothing short of perverse, was Sophie doing what she had learned to do best: getting on with her life without them.

At a loss for what to say next, Harrison became self-aware standing there half-dressed feeling gross and almost certainly looking it; he felt completely undignified. Sophie, however, was the exact opposite. Even with her wet hair slicked back over her scalp and no makeup, she was still stunningly beautiful, her demeanour sunny and cheerful without any hint of self-consciousness. Just as the silence was about to get awkward, she spoke again.

"Why don't you go freshen up and I'll get some breakfast going."

"No breakfast for me," countered Harrison, "but coffee would be nice."

Whilst he was in the shower, Sophie heard the muffled trill of a cell phone ringing. She sauntered into the bedroom and finally located it in the front pocket of Harrison's jeans. The screen displayed the name 'Jessica' and Sophie pressed the green symbol.

"Hello," she chirped cheerily.

"Oh," came the astonished voice of Dr Jessica Phillips. "Is Professor Harrison there?"

"He's in the shower at the moment. Can I take a message?"

"Err... no," replied Jessica, her voice faltering. "I'll leave it for now."

Hanging up, Jessica found herself rather perturbed at this turn of events and it surprised and confused her. Why should she care if Nathan had a woman stay over at his place? It's not as though she was romantically interested in him, surely.

Fifteen minutes later, Harrison vacated the bathroom having showered, shaved and brushed his teeth. He entered the bedroom wearing nothing but a towel wrapped around his waist and the first thing he saw was Sophie sitting up in the bed with the duvet pulled up over her ample breasts and a cup of coffee in her hand.

"There's a coffee on the side there for you," she said, beaming and indicating the nightstand.

Harrison picked up the cup and took a large gulp. He glanced dubiously at the beautiful girl in his bed, frowned then sat on the edge.

"Are you naked under there," he asked somewhat naively.

"That's for you to find out," replied Sophie, leaning over and grinning lasciviously.

"I'm very flattered," he said, grimacing, "but you are a whole mess of trouble that I can well do without at the moment."

"Is that the thanks I get for looking after you last night?" declared Sophie, pretending to be offended. "And on my birthday too."

"Damn, and I ruined it for you. I'm so sorry," fretted Harrison. "How old are you?"

"Twenty-one," she chimed, "so I'm not a kid anymore."

"No, you're not," replied Harrison with a wry smile.

"I thought I was the girl of your dreams," she teased.

"What?" exclaimed Harrison, taken completely off guard. "Why do you say that?"

"You kept telling me last night. What did you mean?"

Harrison had no recollection of saying anything like that, but he knew exactly what he meant by it and couldn't possibly tell her the truth.

"You shouldn't pay any attention to that," he lied. "It was just the drink talking."

"Oh," replied Sophie succinctly, nodding her head.

"Look, you'd better go and get dressed," announced Harrison decisively. Though it pained him to say it.

"That reminds me," recalled Sophie, "you had a phone call when you were in the shower."

"Really, who?" queried the professor.

"Don't know," she said, shrugging with indifference. "Someone called Jessica."

"Jessica?" he repeated rhetorically. "What on earth does she want?"

Picking up his cell phone, Harrison walked into the sitting room and tapped in her number. The phone rang and the familiar voice of Jessica answered.

"Hey, Jessica," he greeted breezily. "You rang me earlier, are you okay?"

As Harrison listened to her, he could tell that she was distressed, then he said, "Look, I'll be there as soon as I can."

Sensing that something was wrong, Sophie had slipped out of the bed and proceeded to get dressed. Harrison did likewise and they both exited their rooms simultaneously.

"What's going on?" enquired Sophie with a look of concern.

"That was Dr Phillips," he replied. "She's at the hospital."

"*The* Dr Phillips?" asked Sophie wide-eyed.

"Yes," confirmed Harrison. "Her father's had a heart attack."

Harrison found his wallet and handed Sophie some notes.

"Look, get yourself a cab, I need to go," he urged, giving her a peck on the cheek. "And thank you for last night."

"It was nothing," retorted Sophie sullenly as she watched Harrison leave the apartment, "literally nothing."

Sophie hadn't bargained on the professor turning her down. Being rebuffed was something she wasn't used to. She wasn't so easily put off, however, and had no intention of giving up on him.

***

Alta Bates Summit Medical Center, Berkeley,
San Francisco East Bay Area, California
September 2016

Dr Jessica Phillips sat in the family room, close to the intensive care unit, impatiently waiting for news. She looked up as the door opened to see Professor Nathan

Harrison walk in with a look of concern on his face. He sat down next to her and gave a sympathetic smile. Jessica smiled back wanly.

"How is he?" enquired Harrison.

"I don't know," said Jessica with a shrug. "I haven't heard anything since they took him through."

"What happened?" asked Harrison.

"Well, I popped round to see him as I usually do on a Saturday," she replied. "I have my own key so I went in. When I called him there was no answer. I found him on the floor in the bathroom unconscious."

Harrison studied the woman in front of him as she spoke. Jessica was wearing black loafers with tassels, faded blue jeans and a lacey white top hanging loosely off her shoulders. Her jet-black hair was tied up in a ponytail and the fine bone structure of her face, with its piercing green eyes, was partially obscured by the large black-rimmed spectacles, which she always insisted on wearing. Harrison had never seen her dressed casually before; Jessica always seemed to be dashing here and there in a lab coat, usually holding some document or some such. For once she looked human and, for the first time, vulnerable. Harrison warmed to her, realising that despite her standoffish behaviour she was a very lovely-looking woman.

"How long have you been here?" he enquired.

Jessica looked at her watch; it was 11.37am.

"I'm not sure," she said, frowning. "Probably a couple of hours, I guess."

"I phoned as soon as I got your message," assured Harrison.

"I hope I didn't ruin your date," commented Jessica. She didn't really care that much, she just wanted to bring the subject up.

"Date!" exclaimed the professor. "No, that's not what it was. It was Sophie Hunter, one of my students."

Jessica shot him a glance of disapproving surprise.

"Aren't you in enough trouble?" she hissed.

"Nothing happened. I wasn't capable even if I wanted to," replied Harrison, going on the defensive. "I got smashed... very drunk at a bar last night and she kindly got me home. She slept in the spare room."

"Very noble of her, I'm sure," commented Jessica sullenly.

"She did try it on this morning though," said Harrison with a grin, hoping to lighten the mood, "but no, I was strong and turned her down flat."

"It must have been very difficult for you," uttered Jessica, making no effort to hide her sarcasm.

Harrison had no answer to that, she was absolutely correct; it *had* been difficult and frankly he was proud of himself for showing such restraint, though he decided to keep this fact to himself.

"Is this a regular thing for you, getting drunk in bars?"

"No, not really," he muttered glumly. "I guess I was just feeling sorry for myself. You know, over this business with the skeletons."

"Well, you've only yourself to blame for that," she admonished. "It was a crazy thing to do. It was obvious that they wouldn't believe you."

"Your dad knows something about them," stated Harrison, changing tack.

"I know," said Jessica, frowning. "I tried to broach the subject but he refuses to talk about it."

"He seemed to recognise that facial reconstruction you did. And what was that about the gun? He seemed to know it was a... what was it? A Walther P38."

"The more I quizzed him about it, the more stressed he became," replied Jessica, still frowning. "I wouldn't be surprised if all this business didn't contribute to his collapse."

They both fell silent, suddenly reminded of why they were here. Harrison looked over at the glum expression on Jessica's face as she stared blankly at the floor. Gently he placed his hand on hers for reassurance but immediately she whipped it away.

"I'm sorry, I didn't mean..." stumbled Harrison self-consciously.

"No... I wasn't expecting..." She struggled with the sentence, annoyed with herself for reacting in such a way. Then she changed the subject. "When are we going to hear something?"

Jessica burst into tears and Harrison put his arm around her. Jessica relented, leaned into him and allowed herself to be comforted. It seemed like forever when the door finally opened and a doctor and a nurse entered the room and sat down opposite them. They had sombre expressions on their faces.

"I'm afraid your father passed away ten minutes ago," advised the doctor. "We managed to revive him for a short period but he had another massive heart attack and we couldn't save him."

Jessica, consumed with grief, put her hand to her

mouth and began to weep. Harrison hugged her as the medics looked on helplessly.

"We did everything we could," interjected the nurse, as if this would help.

"I want to see him," Jessica insisted finally, standing up.

"Of course," replied the nurse. "If you would like to follow me."

The nurse led them both into the intensive care unit and over to a bed where Professor David Phillips lay motionless and peaceful. Harrison had always liked Jessica's father and respected him immensely, both professionally and personally. For Jessica the loss of her father was going to leave a gaping hole in her life. A void that would be difficult, if not impossible, to fill.

***

By mid-afternoon, Harrison was driving Jessica home when he suddenly became acutely aware that he was famished. He hadn't eaten all day and desperately needed some food in his stomach.

"I think we should get some food," he asserted. "I don't know about you but I'm starving."

"Okay," came the curt reply.

Jessica looked distracted and Harrison wasn't convinced that she had actually taken in what he had just said.

"How about a Chinese takeaway?" he offered.

Jessica nodded and continued to stare blankly out of the window. The world outside the car seemed to be going about its business, clearly oblivious to the extraordinary event which had just taken place. Jessica felt as though she was trapped in a bubble, detached from the passing of time and reality, with only her thoughts to remind her of her very existence.

Before she realised it, they had pulled up outside Jessica's apartment building and Harrison was opening the door for her and carrying a bag of food. Inside he got straight down to dishing up the steaming rice and chicken chow mein. He brought the two plates to the dining table, while Jessica, looking disconsolate, watched with disinterest.

"Please sit down, Jessica," he implored through mouthfuls of food. "You must eat."

"Would you like a beer?" she offered, deliberately changing the subject.

"God, no," protested Harrison, "I'm on the wagon for a few days at least. Some water would be nice though."

Nodding, and with the faintest hint of a smile, Jessica went to the kitchen, filled two glasses with water and returned to the table and sat down opposite him. She watched with her head leaning against the palm of her hand as the professor ate heartily. After taking a few mouthfuls, she started idly playing with her food, deep in thought.

"This is all my fault," she declared eventually.

"How do you work that out?" asked an incredulous Harrison.

"If I hadn't invited him to see my results on the skeletons, he would never have known."

"That's nonsense and you know it," he countered. "David was bound to find out sooner than later. Maybe I'm to blame for bringing them back and wanting to publish the results."

"Thank you for coming today," she offered, changing the subject.

"I had a lot of time for your father," Harrison replied, "and I thought you would need some support."

This comment made her ashamed that she hadn't shown more support for him when the faculty were baying for his blood.

Presently Jessica took their plates into the kitchen, and Harrison took the opportunity to look around the apartment. It was meticulously clean and tidy, with comfortable furnishings but very little to suggest that a woman lived there. The closest thing to an ornament was a photo of her father on the mantelpiece.

Eventually Jessica returned from the kitchen with a tray of cups and a cafetière full of coffee. She set them down on a coffee table and moved to a drawer, and opened it. Her thoughts took her back to the day they had discussed the two finds with David. Pulling out a piece of paper, Jessica sat down next to Harrison on the couch.

"Quite a striking face, don't you think?" mused Jessica, holding up the printout of the reconstructed skull of Gustav von Brandt.

"The students called him Captain Hook because of the missing hand," said Harrison, smiling, hoping to lighten the mood.

"Do you suppose he shot the dinosaur?" she offered. "I know it sounds ludicrous."

"Do you think the *Dilophosaurus* bit his hand off?" countered Harrison. "That's equally ludicrous."

"That *is* ludicrous!" mocked Jessica, laughing out loud. "We would have found the hand in its stomach."

"Assuming the thing swallowed the hand, that is," countered Harrison.

"I guess we'll never know," she declared, "not without a time machine."

"A time machine," jeered Harrison, chuckling and nudging her gently.

"Don't laugh at me," she replied, nudging him back. "How else would we find out? And besides, he had to get there somehow."

Harrison became aware of how close they were sitting together and, on an impulse, he leaned in and gave Jessica a peck on the lips. She pulled back in surprise.

"I'm sorry…" he beseeched. "I didn't mean to…"

Before he could finish the sentence, however, Jessica moved forwards and kissed him back full on the lips. Their caressing became more passionate and Jessica held him tight.

"We should stop this before it gets out of hand," announced Harrison, pulling back. "I should go."

"Please stay," pleaded Jessica, holding him close again. "I don't want to be alone tonight."

"Are you sure?" He hesitated.

Jessica nodded and gave him a warm smile. It occurred to Harrison that he had never seen her smile in such a way before.

***

On his way home the following morning, Harrison reflected on the previous days' events. It was the first time in his life that he had had offers from two beautiful women, turned one down and made love to the other. He was feeling quite justifiably smug with himself, though he was now exhausted and needed a rest. Jessica had proven to be insatiable and not as gentle as he had expected. When it came to making love, he had always prided himself on being tender and considerate, but his efforts were stifled with every move. At one point, Harrison was on top and before he knew it Jessica had manoeuvred him round and under her with such speed and dexterity that he could only wonder at the strength that would be needed to execute such an act. The experience had scared him a little and he wasn't sure whether he wanted to repeat it. Bumping into Jessica on Monday, as he usually did, could be awkward but that problem would have to wait. Right now, all he was interested in was getting his head down for a few hours' sleep.

CHAPTER FIVE

REVELATIONS

Sunset View Cemetery and Mortuary
El Cerrito, North of Berkeley, California
October 2016

After overhearing a man in a group of mourners say that he hated funerals, Nathan Harrison considered why this fact needed to be clarified. It presupposed that there might be people who actually liked such dour events – a notion he felt hard to believe, since he hated them with a vengeance. The last thing Harrison needed was to be reminded of his own mortality and the short life which we have on this planet.

It was a pleasantly warm overcast day as Harrison stood at the graveside at David's funeral, and he took a moment to look around him. He was halfway up a gentle slope that dropped down past a myriad of headstones to San Francisco Bay. The summer fog which blighted the vista in the summer months had gone and the view was clear. Harrison could see the mudflats of the Albany Marine Park and, further out, Alcatraz Island. The Golden Gate Bridge shimmered on the horizon, marking the entry point to the Pacific Ocean and beyond. The turnout had been exceptional, which didn't surprise him, knowing how well liked and respected David was, even though he had been retired for nearly ten years. Jessica stood opposite him adorned in a black dress suit, simple cream silk blouse and black medium-height sling-back shoes. With her lush long black hair cascading down past her shoulders, Harrison thought that she looked chic, elegant and completely bewitching. What made it all the more beguiling was the fact that he knew she wasn't even trying.

As the minister continued with the sermon, Harrison thought back to their night of passion and how he dreaded seeing Jessica at work the next day. He needn't have worried, however, as she had taken compassionate leave. That was ten days ago and this was the first time he had seen or spoken to her since.

Jessica looked over to where Harrison was standing opposite her and frowned. She couldn't understand why he hadn't contacted her, and was now feeling hurt and confused. Being the only man that she had slept with, Jessica was unsure of the convention in these situations. Should she call, or should he? She was hopeless when it came to relationships, which was one of the many reasons she tended to steer clear of them.

The service became more protracted and Jessica zoned out, no longer hearing the minister's solemn intonation. Then a voice came into her head, seemingly from nowhere.

"Jessica." The voice spoke in a calm manner as if it was right next to her.

She looked around her, slightly startled at the sound of her name.

"Jessica!" the voice repeated with a little more urgency.

As her agitation increased, Harrison began to notice.

"Jessica, I know that you can hear me," stated the voice. "Look over to the tree line and nod slowly."

Doing as she was told, Jessica looked up the slope to the tree line above them some 150 yards away and zoomed in with her hawk-like eyesight on a middle-aged man in a dark grey overcoat. His hair was silver, as was his full beard, and he was holding a pair of binoculars.

"We need to talk," he urged. "I have important information that you need to know. Can you meet me at Sack's Coffee House on College Avenue tomorrow morning at eleven? Nod slowly if you agree."

Moving her head slowly up and down, Jessica became aware that Harrison was staring at her quizzically. As self-consciousness got the better of her, Jessica began to pay more attention to the proceedings, but as she stole a glance up to the tree line again, the man was gone.

The rest of the day was long and emotional as well-meaning friends and family tried to give some comfort, but all Jessica could think about was this strange man who insisted on meeting her. Who was he and what did he have to say? It was early evening when the last stragglers drifted away and Jessica walked out of the French windows onto the patio, to get some air, deep in thought.

"A penny for them?" enquired Harrison, walking up beside her.

She glanced slightly to her right and then looked straight ahead again.

"So, you've finally decided to talk to me."

"I'm sorry," he replied, feeling slightly ashamed. "I didn't mean to be a stranger."

"It's no matter." Jessica's tone was dismissive. "I was too busy organising the funeral."

Harrison decided to change the subject.

"What happened at the graveside?" he asked. "At one point you were behaving very oddly."

"I was burying my father, how else was I to behave?"

She couldn't tell him that she listened to a man talk to her that no one else in the congregation could have possibly heard. Jessica knew that her hearing and eyesight were good, but no one had ever put it to the test like this. The stranger intrigued her and she was curious as to what he had to say. There was no question; she would be meeting this man tomorrow.

***

Jessica paused at the entrance to the coffee house, gently sighed, gathered herself together and looked at her watch. The minute hand ticked over to the number twelve indicating that she was bang on time. She opened the door and entered. Inside, the café was moderately busy and she scanned the room looking for the mysterious man. He was to be found sitting away from other customers in a secluded corner. The middle-aged man saw her immediately and beckoned her over with a welcoming smile. The young woman approached, then sat down opposite and studied him with a frown.

"My, but you're the image of your mother," he announced, hoping to make Jessica feel more at ease.

"You knew her?" enquired Jessica with slightly raised eyebrows.

"Yes, we met the year before you were born," the man confirmed. "Let me introduce myself. My name is Liam Slater and I used to work for the CIA."

A waitress arrived and Slater ordered another café au lait and Jessica ordered a pot of Earl Grey tea.

"What did the CIA have to do with my mother?" riposted Jessica.

Slater sat back in his chair. The moment had arrived which he had played out so many times in his head and now he was struggling to find the words. Jessica sensed his unease and it made her nervous.

"I have information to tell you," he began finally, "information that you are not going to like. But you need to know."

"I'm listening," replied Jessica, looking up at the waitress who placed their order on the table.

The grey-bearded man stirred his coffee pensively as he watched the young woman pour herself a cup of tea.

"Have you any idea how extraordinary you are?" he announced finally.

"Everyone is unique in their own way, aren't they?" she countered in a matter-of-fact manner.

"Yes," agreed Slater, "but I said extraordinary and I mean that in the true sense of the word."

Jessica looked at him nonplussed.

"For starters," he continued, "why do you wear those glasses? We both know that you don't need them. You were able to see me yesterday as if I was standing next to you."

Jessica sighed and removed the large black-rimmed glasses, placed them on the table and looked at Slater intently.

"Look at me," she demanded. "Is this the face of a thirty-year-old?"

Slater studied her features; it was true her face looked more like that of a girl in her mid to late teens.

"So, you wear plain-lens spectacles to make you look older," he concluded, "or at least to disguise how young you look."

"I have always been conscious of the fact and it worried me that I might not be taken seriously professionally if I didn't look the part."

"There have been others with your, err… abilities, but you are the first to be born with them."

"How did *they* get them then?" enquired Jessica.

"They injected a drug known as the Infinity Serum."

"If I was born like this," puzzled Jessica, working it out in her mind, "that must mean that either my mother or my father would've had to have injected it. And I know my father didn't have any special abilities."

This was crunch time for Slater; he knew he couldn't delay this moment any longer.

"There's no easy way to tell you this," he agonised with a deep frown, "but I'm afraid David Phillips was not your father."

Jessica stared blankly at him motionless in shock. She wanted to shout at him for his impertinence, tell him he was a crazy old man, but something in the way he had said it, his expression, made her realise, no matter how much she hated to admit it, he was telling the truth.

"And my mother?" she uttered eventually.

"Laura is… was your mother," confirmed Slater.

"Who was my father then?"

"He was an SS officer by the name of Gustav von Brandt."

"SS!" exclaimed Jessica. "But that's the Second World War, isn't it? He would have been an old man in 1985."

"I know it's hard to believe but not only did he inject the drug, he travelled to 1985 in a time machine."

"Hold on a minute," she gasped. "Are you trying to tell me that my real father was a time traveller?"

"Possibly the first," said Slater, nodding, "though we can't be sure."

"And my mother had an affair with him."

"Well, not exactly," hesitated Slater.

He let his reply sink in and watched as the implication dawned on Jessica's face.

"He raped her," she hissed incredulously.

"I'm sorry," consoled Slater, dipping his hand into the inside pocket of his coat. "This is a photo of him taken around 1943 or 44.

Slater passed the photo to Jessica who looked at the image and took a deep intake of breath as the shock hit her. She put her left hand to her mouth and her right hand shook as she held the photo. Here was the man that she had been studying, wondering about, these past few weeks. The man whose face she had reconstructed on her computer. The skeleton which she had dated to the Jurassic period. Everything suddenly made sense. The fillings in his teeth. He was a time traveller. She had joked about it with Nathan but it was real, there was no other explanation.

"You recognise this man?" enquired Slater, leaning forwards.

Jessica simply nodded, still with her hand over her mouth.

"How?" asked an incredulous Slater.

"Well, a friend… colleague of mine… a palaeontologist," stumbled Jessica, "found this man's remains on a dig a few months ago in Arizona. He was complete except for his right hand."

"How can you tell it's him?"

"I reconstructed his…" Jessica paused, remembering that she had a printout of the face in her purse. Opening out the folded piece of paper, she continued, "This is an image of his face after I reconstructed it."

Looking from one image to the next, Slater's jaw dropped. There was no doubt in his mind: this was von Brandt.

"How old would you say his remains were?"

"I dated them to around 195 million years."

Slater couldn't help but smile; their theories were correct. He had travelled to prehistoric times. That meant that the other time machine and von Brandt's were sent safely out of harm's way too. He could only surmise what happened to Hitler and Bormann.

"Jessica, you must keep all that we've discussed to yourself," urged Slater. "People have killed to get this drug or information on it. I myself had to go into hiding for fear of my life."

This fact brought him to his next revelation.

"You have always been told that your mother committed suicide. She never really recovered fully from being raped, and that was given as the reason. But I know for a fact that she was murdered for what she knew."

"What did she know?" said Jessica, frowning.

"She and your father… David replicated the Infinity Serum. Can you imagine how valuable that would be to our, or any, government? It would be unthinkable for it to get into the wrong hands."

Jessica nodded in confirmation, and went thoughtful for a moment.

"I carried out a DNA test on the remains and there was something strange in the results. It couldn't be identified."

"That would be the drug," confirmed Slater. "Your parents couldn't identify it either. Though reports from other sources have suggested that it is extraterrestrial."

"Are you suggesting that I am part alien?" Jessica gasped.

The ex-CIA agent was at a loss as to how to respond; he had no idea. Finally, he began to shift in his seat.

"I've told you everything you need to know," he concluded, standing up. "I'm sorry if it has come as a shock."

"Will I see you again?" enquired Jessica.

"Who knows what the future holds," came the curt reply.

Jessica stood up also and shook his hand, then something occurred to her.

"Infinity Serum?" she asked. "Is it called that because it prolongs life?"

"Yes," replied Slater sheepishly, placing some dollars onto the table, "and as for your next question, I have no clue."

The enigmatic man slipped out of the door and disappeared, leaving Jessica wondering just how long her life had been extended by.

***

If anyone had asked Jessica how she got from the coffee house to her laboratory at the university, she couldn't have given an answer. Her mind was in a daze, a whirlpool, awash with thoughts and emotions that hitherto she had managed to keep suppressed.

She was angry and confused, but mostly she was angry. At David, the man she now knew to be her stepfather, for not telling her the truth. Angry at Laura, her mother, for her weakness and not being there when she needed her greatly. But most of all she was angry at her biological father, for raping her mother and creating her, Jessica, not out of love but something much more malevolent. Slater's divulgence made her question her very own right to exist, in human form, and certainly not as some kind of super-human, alien hybrid.

As she stood leaning against the door to her outer office, Jessica collected her thoughts together and breathed in deeply. She booted up her computer and brought up the file which contained the facial reconstruction. After studying it one last time, she deleted the file and the two backups that she had created.

Then she walked over to a drawer and picked up a clear slender tube about four inches long and removed the swab. She held the stick firmly and wiped it around the inside of her cheek, making sure to rotate the tip as she did so, to ensure that she obtained a good sample. After preparing the sample in the next-generation DNA sequencer, she set it up to run overnight and went home.

That evening, Jessica had a restless night's sleep and when she looked in the mirror the following morning her eyes were puffy and red. She selected a pair of glasses with a slightly darker tint and left about mid-morning for the university.

Walking briskly into her laboratory, she checked the sequencer, which had finished its task. She immediately booted up her computer anxious to check the results. Eventually the electropherogram was displayed on the screen and she was able to compare it with von Brandt's. Leaning back on her chair, Jessica sighed. It was a perfect match. There was no doubt: this Nazi *was* her father.

After a while she stood up and walked over to a shelf, pulling out a box containing the remains of her father, Gustav von Brandt. Slowly one by one, she painstakingly placed the individual bones in their correct place on the table. Finally, she pivoted and took a ball pein hammer from a drawer, turned back to the table and without hesitation, Jessica brought the hammer down with all her might on the top of the skull. With a crack splinters flew off in all directions. Then she continued further down the remains, hammering and smashing each bone, getting more and more frenzied as she let her inhibitions go. Eventually, out of breath, she released her grip on the hammer and it dropped to the floor. Dust began to settle and Jessica surveyed her handiwork. The remains had been obliterated and lay strewn all around the lab as dust or small fragments. She laughed out loud, humourless and manic, but it soon subsided into sobs, her body shaking as tears ran down her cheeks.

Hearing the commotion further down the corridor, Harrison came bursting in, surprised to see Jessica back at work. He surveyed the chaos in the laboratory.

"Jessica!" he exclaimed. "What the hell?"

She just stared blankly, then turned her back on him.

"What's going on here?" he asked, looking at the obliterated bone fragments scattered all around. "What have you done?"

Jessica remained silent and as Harrison moved round the table to confront her, she moved over and sat back down at the computer. Harrison picked up the hammer and looked at her completely perplexed.

"Why?" he cried out.

"This is why," she replied, indicating the computer screen with a nod of her head.

Harrison walked over and peered at the screen.

"The skeleton's DNA profile," she announced, and then scrolled down, "and this is mine. A perfect match."

"No way," exclaimed Harrison. "What made you do a comparison?"

"I met with someone yesterday," she sniffed, "a man, and he told me a whole mess of things. And he is correct. That box of bones was my biological father."

This was all too much for Harrison to take in right now; he looked around the laboratory.

"I think we had better get this place cleaned up," he announced finally.

It took several hours to get the lab back to some semblance of order, but by late afternoon it was looking presentable, the fragments of bone and dust put back in their box and placed on the shelf. Jessica moved over to the computer and began tapping.

"What are you doing now?"

"Deleting the DNA results," she replied without looking round.

"For God's sake, why?" Harrison strode over to her but he was too late.

"It's a long story," she declared. "I'm exhausted. Can we talk tomorrow?"

"Sure," confirmed Harrison. "I have a free day tomorrow. Shall I come over to you?"

Jessica nodded and powered down the computer. She turned and gave him a weak smile but Harrison just turned on his heels and left.

By the time Jessica arrived home, there was mail in her letter box. She leafed through it as she opened the door and entered her apartment. Jessica stopped and studied one letter in particular. It looked like it was from David's solicitors. She threw it on the couch. After two days of crap, she'd had enough. It would have to wait until tomorrow.

***

After another restless night, Jessica finally got her act together by mid-morning. She placed a mug of tea on the coffee table, then sat on the couch and took a bite out of a piece of toast. Out of the corner of her eye she caught a glimpse of the letter from David's solicitor, lying there beckoning her. Putting down her plate, she picked it up and was about to prise open the envelope when the doorbell rang. Flinging the missive casually onto the table, Jessica padded over to the intercom. It was Nathan, so she buzzed him in and walked back to finish her brunch.

Harrison walked into the sitting room and was astounded to see Jessica lounging on the couch wearing light blue silk pyjamas, a cup of tea in her hand. This new, nonchalant Jessica was going to take some getting used to. He, on the other hand, was ill at ease and although he wasn't as angry as the day before, he wasn't smiling either.

Jessica gave him a hesitant smile.

"Good morning, Nathan," she greeted, getting up from the couch. "Tea or coffee?"

"Coffee," he replied, then remembered his manners, "please."

Harrison sat down in an armchair opposite the couch and Jessica returned shortly bearing a steaming cup of coffee. She sat down on the couch with a fresh cup of tea and considered the man in front of her.

"Are you still cross with me?" she asked.

"Could you blame me if I was?" he replied.

"I don't really see why," Jessica countered. "The human remains may be sensational but they have no archaeological value whatsoever."

"They are... were proof," he corrected with indignation, "that modern man was around during the Jurassic period."

"No, Nathan, it proves that *a* man was around during that time," Jessica's voice was slightly raised, "and how were you going to explain it? The man had dental fillings! It's lucky you didn't mention him when you made the *Dilophosaurus* public or you might well have been looking for another job right now."

"It was quite a coincidence finding those bones," mused Harrison.

"Yes," agreed Jessica, "and I would still be living in blissful ignorance if you hadn't."

"You looked half crazed when I entered your lab," he countered, trying to regain some moral high ground.

"Do I come across to you as someone who's irrational?" she reasoned, "Given to wild, impetuous behaviour?"

Harrison couldn't think of a more level-headed person, at least up until recently. He put her uncharacteristic behaviour down to grief.

"What prompted it then?"

Jessica put her mug down and gathered her thoughts.

"Remember I told you yesterday about a man I met with in a café?" she began. "Well, he claimed to be ex-CIA and I had no reason to disbelieve him. He seemed to know all about me."

For the next half hour, Jessica recalled everything that Slater had imparted to her and Harrison listened intently, becoming more and more astonished with every divulgence.

"So now do you understand why we need to destroy the remains? We won't be safe until they are gone."

"This is too much to take in," blustered Harrison. "Time machines, Infinity Serums, rape and murder, it's insane."

Jessica produced a folded-up piece of paper from her purse and handed it to the professor.

"You recognise this, don't you?" she said.

"Of course, the facial reconstruction."

"Look at this." Jessica handed him the black and white photo of the Nazi officer.

"My God," gasped Harrison. "It's the same man."

"His name was Gustav von Brandt and *he* is my biological father," she confirmed. "He was also a captain in the SS."

"That means you share his DNA," mused Harrison, "DNA which you couldn't identify. DNA we came to the conclusion is extraterrestrial."

"I haven't had a day's illness in my life," confessed Jessica, "and I am only just beginning to discover the powers that I have. I only wear these glasses to cover up how young I look."

Harrison sat back and became pensive and Jessica suddenly remembered the envelope that she was interrupted from opening. As she suspected, it was a letter from David's solicitors, requesting that she make an appointment.

"Excuse me while I make a quick phone call." She stood up and walked into the kitchen.

Harrison heard her making some arrangements for the afternoon.

"That was David's solicitor," commented Jessica. "He wants to discuss his estate with me."

It didn't go unnoticed with Harrison that she had referred to her father as David.

"He was... is your father, you know," he offered. "David didn't have to raise you after your mother died. He deserves that at least."

"I know," agreed Jessica, "but I wish he had told me the truth himself. This was a hell of a way to find out."

"I guess he was just trying to protect you."

"Yes, but from what?" declared Jessica. "We have no clue what we are dealing with, or why."

"So, what is your lifespan now?"

"I sensed that Slater wasn't telling me the whole story," fretted Jessica, "but I'm pretty sure that's the one thing he couldn't tell me."

"You do realise that telling *me* all this implicates me as well."

Jessica stood up and placed a hand on his shoulder and smiled the way a mother would to a child.

"My dear," she simpered with a patronising tone, "you were implicated the moment you dug up those bones."

She left Harrison to ponder that thought, whilst she padded off to the bedroom to get dressed.

***

The clock on the wall ticked over to 3.20pm and Jessica tutted louder than she intended, causing the middle-aged lady opposite her, behind the desk typing, to look up and glance down her glasses in a disapproving manner. She had agreed a meeting for 3pm and since she wasn't used to the vagaries of such arrangements, was beginning to get impatient. As far as she was concerned, if an appointment is agreed for a specific time, then she should be seen at that time exactly.

Jessica arrived looking as businesslike as possible, wearing a light grey trouser suit, white cotton blouse and black leather loafers. For the first time, she chose not to wear her spectacles and applied cosmetics to make herself look older. She was so pleased with the results that she considered dispensing with the glasses altogether. It left her wondering why she hadn't considered this course of action sooner.

A door opened and two men, both in their early fifties, appeared, shook hands and one left the office. The other, a tall overweight man with thinning grey hair, glanced over at Jessica and smiled kindly.

"Miss Phillips," he said, "would you like to come through."

Still annoyed, Jessica barely acknowledged the smile and walked past him into the inner sanctum of Jonathan Beale's office. The solicitor sensed her irritation; he had seen it so many times before.

"I'm so sorry to keep you," he implored. "Please, take a seat."

The room was furnished with oak wood panelling, with two walls given over to a vast array of books from floor to ceiling. A large antique oak desk with a maroon leather top stood at one end, and Jessica sat opposite and watched as Mr Beale busied himself looking for her documents. Papers on the desk were set out in an orderly fashion, reinstilling some confidence in Jessica that his tardiness had shaken.

"Please accept my condolences, Miss Phillips," he declared. "I knew your father well. He was a fine man."

"Thank you," muttered Jessica. "I presume my… father left a will."

"Indeed he did," observed the solicitor, leafing through pages in a folder. "Everything is very straightforward. As he was your legal guardian, he has left the whole of his estate to you."

"Legal guardian! You mean he adopted me legally."

"Indeed so," replied Mr Beale. "Were you not aware?"

Jessica shook her head. She was taken aback and slightly embarrassed that she didn't know this fact. Why hadn't David told her?

The next half hour was taken up with legal formalities until finally the solicitor removed a white envelope from the bottom of the folder and passed it to Jessica.

"In here is a key to a safety deposit box. We were instructed by your father to hand it over to you after his passing. The box is in the Wells Fargo Bank in Sausalito just north of the Golden Gate Bridge."

"Yes, I'm familiar with the town."

"There is also a letter of introduction from myself, which you must present on your arrival along with some sort of photo identification. I took the liberty of making an appointment for you for 11am tomorrow. Is this convenient?"

"Yes," she said, nodding.

"Well, Miss Phillips," said Mr Beale, smiling as he stood up and shook her hand, "that concludes our business. The transfer of the property into your name is in process and a cheque for all monies coming to you will be sent in due course. If there is anything I can do to help you further, please don't hesitate to ask."

Later that afternoon, Jessica was back in her apartment looking at the key and wondering what could possibly be so important that David needed to hide it away.

***

Wearing the same trouser suit from the day before, Jessica pulled up in a car park, walked through the small Viña del

Mar Park, with its ornate elephant statues, and stood at the kerb of Bridgeway, Downtown Sausalito, waiting for a gap in the traffic. On the other side of the road opposite her was the Wells Fargo Bank. The building was small but elegant, being built from light grey stone and furnished with three tall arched windows.

At exactly 11am she walked up to a desk and made herself known. A young woman smiled and went to find the member of staff written on the piece of paper Jessica had presented. A well-dressed man in his late thirties eventually came over to Jessica and offered his hand.

"Miss Phillips," he said, beaming, "we've been expecting you. My name is William Howe. Please, come this way."

Jessica followed the man over to a desk and they sat down.

"I believe you are here to open a deposit box of your late father," Howe said rhetorically.

"Yes, I have this letter from his solicitor," she confirmed, passing it over with her driving licence, "and here is my photo identification."

The man studied both and finally announced,

"They all seem to be in order. Have you got the key?"

Delving into the side pocket of her jacket, Jessica produced the key and passed it over to him. He looked at the number and passed it back. Then he pulled open a drawer, grabbed a key of his own and stood up.

"This way if you please," he proffered.

Jessica was led down a flight of stairs into a vault with a vast array of small silver doors of various sizes lining three walls. Her companion walked straight over to a door three inches by ten inches and placed a key in one of the slots.

He then invited Jessica to do the same with her key. The door was swung open and William Howe pulled out a tray with a closed top, carried it into a private room and set it down on a table.

"Let me know when you are ready to return it. Take all the time you need." He smiled and left the room.

As the door shut Jessica lifted the lid and peered in. What she saw was an envelope and a shallow white plastic box about five inches wide and eight inches long. The box had two heavy-duty red rubber bands wrapped around its width, which she hastily removed. Then she opened the lid and looked inside. In front of her were four compartments lined with grey foam. Nestled firmly in each compartment was a glass phial with a black plastic cap, each measuring 75mm by 19mm in diameter. Picking one up, Jessica studied the curious object and held it up to the fluorescent light above her head. A clear liquid could be discerned, that to all intents and purposes could be water. Jessica doubted that David would have gone to such trouble to store water, so she carefully placed the phial back in the recess in the foam compartment, closed the lid and placed the box in her bag along with the letter.

An hour or so later, she was back at her apartment and studying one of the phials again. There seemed to be a wax seal around the top, but when she turned the cap, it unscrewed easily.

Pouring a little onto some paper, Jessica observed the reaction. Nothing.

She sniffed it. Still nothing. Gingerly touching the liquid with her forefinger, she tasted it. Having no taste, it would be easy to conclude at this point that it *was* water.

After replacing the cap, Jessica put the phial away and turned her attention to the envelope. Inside were three A4 sheets of paper stapled together in the top left-hand corner. The top sheet began '*My darling Jessica.*'

Jessica began to read with great interest.

If you are reading this, it is because I am no longer with you. You will probably know by now that I am not your real father. That man died the year before you were born. I'm sorry that I didn't tell you the truth, but the longer I left it, the harder it became to do so. I did, however, adopt you and I want you to know that I loved you as though you were my own child. When your mother committed suicide, I devoted my life to you.

You will also have in your possession a box with four phials of liquid which looks like water but believe me when I say, it isn't. This liquid is a longevity drug which has come to be known as the Infinity Serum. Your real father injected this serum and has passed it on to you genetically. In its present state it is lethal. The accompanying pages describe how to replicate the serum and a formula for working out the correct dosage per individual. Subsequent tests on pigs and one human were successful, though I cannot stress enough the importance of administering the correct dosage. All the information required is in these pages.

I can't honestly say what motivated me to keep some of the serum back; I think perhaps that I couldn't bring myself to let go of such a wondrous thing. Be warned, though, whatever you do with the serum, people will kill to get their hands on it.

I do hope that you find some happiness and contentment in your future life because knowing that this serum is embedded in your DNA, your future will be a long one.

All my love. Your father, David.

Jessica put her hand to her mouth and tears rolled down her cheeks. She realised that David was unaware of her mother's murder. Either that or he was trying to keep the truth from her, though this she felt was unlikely. Jessica looked at the phials in front of her and picked one up again. Holding the phial up to the window, Jessica looked at the serum in a new light. And who was this person who had taken the drug? Should she try and seek them out? After all, they had much in common.

After eating a light meal of chicken and salad, Jessica set about studying, with great interest, the process for replicating the drug and the formulae set out by her father for administering it. She weighed herself on the scales in the bathroom and worked out exactly how much serum she would need to take – in theory – if she needed it. To her amazement, she estimated that in these four phials was enough serum to inject around 500 people. Jessica sat back on her couch and contemplated the phials lying in their box on the coffee table in front of her. Why did her father keep them? What exactly did he expect *her* to do with them?

Her thought processes became wistful, until she suddenly realised that it was getting dark. Jessica looked at her watch: 21.37. It was later than she realised. Feeling composed enough to contact Nathan, she picked up her phone and selected Harrison's number. As he answered, she cradled a phial in her left hand.

"Hey, Jessica," came the cheery voice of the professor. "Erm… how are you?"

Jessica noticed a certain hesitancy in his voice.

"Could you come over, Nathan?" she asked, rolling the phial around absentmindedly in her hand. "I have something to show you."

CHAPTER SIX

SCHOOL'S OUT

Smolensk, Union of Soviet Socialist Republics
August 1946

No matter how much Kiril Yelagin tried to put the war behind him, the devastation of his home town was a constant reminder. The Nazi occupation of the city in 1941, as it pushed on towards Moscow 250 miles further to the east, had resulted in its almost total destruction. It pained him to see so many familiar places, so many landmarks and so many memories reduced to rubble. As he walked home Yelagin looked around in despair, dispirited by the suffering and wondering if the city he grew up in would ever be brought back to its former glory. After leaving the army, Yelagin managed to secure a job in a factory turning out machined parts *ad nauseam* on a lathe. He had no idea what the components were and didn't much care. At this point in his life all he cared about was bringing in a steady income so that he could support his wife and growing family. He walked up several flights of stairs to his apartment and put his key in the door.

"Is that you, dear?" called his wife, Elvira.

She waddled out of the kitchen smiling, holding the small of her back with her left hand and a glass of vodka in the other.

"Of course," said Yelagin with a smile, then downed the drink and embraced his heavily pregnant wife. "Who else would it be?"

Elvira ignored his logic and gave him a kiss.

"Dinner is in twenty minutes," she announced. "Go and look in on your son."

Yelagin opened the door to the bedroom, where baby Mikhail, the product of a passionate weekend whilst he was on leave in 1944, was fast asleep. Glancing back across the hallway he could just make out his wife laying the table for dinner. She was nearly due and it brought home the fact that they were going to need somewhere bigger to live.

His wife called him through to eat and as they began, there came an insistent knock at the door. Yelagin gave out a heavy sigh, placed his knife and fork back down on the table and walked through the hallway to answer it. The persistent knocking continued, making Yelagin angry.

"Alright, alright," he shouted, "I'm coming!"

As he opened the door, Yelagin was confronted by three men. One in front wore a bright blue and red cap, a khaki jacket, dark blue trousers and knee-high black boots. Behind were two armed guards, standing ominously faceless in the shadow of twilight.

"Kiril Yelagin?" enquired the visitor, displaying his identification. "My name is Captain Sasha Grekov."

"Ministry of State Security!" gasped Yelagin. "What does the MGB want with me?"

"You will have to come with us."

"Now?" exclaimed Yelagin. "I was just sitting down to eat."

The officer stepped in uninvited and walked into the hallway.

"You will need to pack clothes for three to four days," he said with an impassive expression. "Please, do it now."

"What's going on?" fretted Elvira, beginning to panic. "Kiril?"

"Mrs Yelagin," implored Grekov, "do not alarm yourself. Your husband is not in trouble. We need his... err expertise."

Elvira wasn't convinced but went to help her husband pack. Shortly, Yelagin returned with a small suitcase, trying to pacify his distraught wife.

"Don't worry," he soothed, "I'll be back before you know it. If you have any problems, go to your mother's."

He kissed her and was escorted away to a black Gaz-11 sedan waiting at the bottom of the stairs. Yelagin was seated in the back with one of the guards, whilst Grekov sat in the front passenger seat. The car moved off to the outskirts of the city and soon entered Smolensk-Severnyy Airport about two miles north of the Dnieper River. In the darkness Yelagin could just make out an olive green

Lisunov Li-2 transport plane waiting on the runway. The image brought back memories of the war and Yelagin didn't like it one bit. He was immediately escorted to the plane and all four boarded. Just as they sat down and clipped their seatbelts in, the plane began to taxi into take-off position. When they were in the air, Yelagin looked out of the widow to see three Lavochkin La-9 single-seat fighters flying in close formation.

"Why the escort?" he shouted, leaning forwards. "We're not at war."

"We're taking no chances."

"Where are you taking me?" shouted Yelagin again over the noise of the engines.

"Poland," replied Grekov succinctly.

Poland! What on earth do they want with me in Poland? he thought.

Yelagin sat back and said no more for the five-hour-plus journey. Eventually they landed at Copernicus Airport just south of Wroclaw, Poland.

"We are going to stay here for the rest of the night and carry on to our destination first thing tomorrow."

"When are you going to tell me what this is all about?" glowered Yelagin.

"You'll find out soon enough," replied an unhelpful Grekov. "I'll show you to your billet."

After a restless sleep, Yelagin and Grekov, now without the guards, were driving southeast. The weather was warm, and since Yelagin knew it was a waste of time asking any more questions, sat back and enjoyed the ride. The route took them through miles of countryside until eventually they passed a few houses and Yelagin sat up. He recognised this place. And then he saw it, the structure which would haunt him for the rest of his life: the concrete henge.

"This is Germany, surely," asserted Yelagin.

"It was until the German border was pushed back after the war," stated Grekov. "We're in Poland now – just."

"Obviously you know about my involvement here last year," declared Yelagin, "but I was not the commanding officer. So why pick me?"

"We searched for Major Dementyev and his family," replied Grekov, "but they have disappeared without a trace."

They passed the concrete henge on the left set back some distance, still in the compound, and continued on. Yelagin thought about his comrade in arms and how they had both survived the war. It was a concern of Dementyev's that he, like so many others, might fall victim to one of Stalin's purges. Yelagin just hoped that he and his family managed to get to somewhere safe before that happened.

After a short distance the car turned into a field and in front of them stood a large khaki tent. Yelagin looked at Grekov for an explanation.

"It's a field hospital," announced Grekov, opening the door.

Nonplussed, Yelagin did likewise and Grekov paused to brief him.

"There are twenty-seven casualties in there," he stated with a grim face. "Some are dead, all are dying. I warn you now it is not a pretty sight."

They were handed a precautionary mask at the entrance and the two men entered the tent. Lined up on both sides were beds with men, women and children. All lying very still and silent. A doctor and three nurses were attending to patients as the two men scanned around them.

"My God, what is this?" exclaimed a horrified Yelagin.

He was staring down at a man of about thirty, who stared back with lifeless, sunken eyes. His cheeks were sunken also and his hair was reduced to a few wisps around the crown. The skin stretching over his frame had an ashen pallor. The most shocking thing, however, was the degeneration of the body and limbs which were withered almost to the bone and the way all the veins protruded in a black network of lines from head to toe.

"How long has he been dead?" asked Yelagin.

"He's still alive," corrected a nurse, "but not for much longer, I fear."

"Are they all like this? Is it contagious?" he blurted.

"Yes, they are," confirmed the nurse. "We cannot help them because we don't know what it is. And no, you are quite safe from infection. This is some kind of poisoning."

The overall image reminded him of the Nazi concentration camp atrocities, only much worse, if that were possible. As he scanned around the tent, staring wildly at the unfortunate casualties, Yelagin felt the need for some air and made a swift exit.

"Cigarette?" offered Grekov, who had just lit one for himself.

Yelagin nodded and took one; Grekov proffered his lighter. They both inhaled deeply as the nurse stepped out of the tent. She looked exhausted.

"He's gone," she said. "Can you spare one of those for me?"

Grekov gave her a cigarette and lit it.

"How many is that now?" enquired Grekov.

"He's the sixteenth," she replied grimly. "The rest will be dead in the next forty-eight hours."

"What has caused it?" asked Yelagin.

"We don't know for sure. Autopsy results will hopefully reveal some answers," advised Grekov, "but it is possible something has got into the water supply. This is the only area affected. Water samples are being tested now."

"Let's get out of here," insisted Grekov. "We've seen enough."

They walked back to the car and drove out of the field. Yelagin watched as the nurse stubbed out her cigarette and walked forlornly back into the tent.

"What now?" asked Yelagin.

"I'm taking you to the research base."

They sat in silence as the car continued up the road to the entrance of the base. The car halted and Grekov showed his identification to an armed Russian guard. The man saluted and allowed them through into the complex. The site wasn't quite as Yelagin had remembered it. The two hangars were gone and all that remained was a large concrete apron and the henge, which seemed just as mysterious as it did the previous year. Grekov pulled to a halt and they both alighted from the car. The sun was shining brightly and the air pleasantly warm, which seemed to Yelagin to be completely at odds with what he had just witnessed.

"I've read the report of your raid," said Grekov, "but I want you to talk me through what happened."

Yelagin walked the captain through the raid, how they breached the fence and what happened when they approached the henge.

"A man dashed out of the hangar which was once here," he said, pointing, "and ran over to the henge. His speed was incredible. Almost inhuman. We shot at him but not one bullet found its target."

"What happened next?"

"Well," replied Yelagin, nervous now, "he accessed a strange vessel. A bell-shaped craft. It began to spin, then rise up high into the air and... well, it just disappeared."

"You witnessed this a second time?"

"Yes," confirmed Yelagin reluctantly. He was concerned where Grekov was going with this. "Tempelhof Airport."

"And you had no idea what was going on here?"

"No," asserted Yelagin with all the conviction he could muster, "the Nazis managed to burn everything useful before taking cyanide capsules. Though the whole complex had a sinister feel about it. Frankly it gave me the creeps."

This was no exaggeration on his part and Yelagin wasn't best pleased to be back.

"So, you found nothing which could have possibly caused this outbreak?"

Yelagin shrugged. What could have possibly caused such an atrocity? He certainly didn't see any evidence of it. Grekov said nothing. Deep in thought, he wandered up to the henge.

"Just disappeared, you say?"

Before Yelagin could reply, they were both distracted by a man in uniform running and calling to them excitedly.

"What is it?" said Grekov, frowning.

"Quickly, sir," he panted. "They've found something."

Hurriedly they followed the guard back to the area where Hangar A used to be. All that remained was the concrete at ground level and steps that descended to the basement. The guard led them down and along a dimly lit corridor. In contrast to the temperature outside it was cool and damp.

Yelagin stopped at a side opening where the metal door had been pulled wide open and back against the wall. It was badly damaged.

"I presume you had to blast your way in here."

"No," corrected Yelagin, "this door was ripped off its hinges by someone – a Polish worker we think – who then blew this room up along with himself."

"No man could have done that," replied an incredulous Grekov.

"No ordinary man, perhaps," agreed Yelagin, "but as I said, strange things occurred here. We have no idea what he was determined to destroy, or why he had to die with it."

They continued further down the corridor, passing a few cells until the guard stopped at another side opening and gestured for them to enter. The room was well lit and occupied by a scientist in a white lab coat.

"Ah, Captain, you're here," greeted a forty-year-old man with a shock of greying hair. He eyed Yelagin suspiciously.

"This is Kiril Yelagin," announced the captain. "He was part of the operation that captured this base last year."

"Pleased to meet you," imparted the man, relaxing and shaking his hand vigorously. "Professor Levkin Antonovich. It's a shame you couldn't secure it intact."

"Their defences gave them enough time to destroy everything," reasoned Yelagin. He didn't much care for this line of enquiry.

"Quite so," said the professor with a smile, sensing that he had struck a nerve. "I'm sure you did everything you could."

"What have you found, Professor?" asked Grekov, determined to stay on topic.

Antonovich led them over to where a heavy concrete hatch had been slid away to reveal a hole in the floor about a metre square and a metre deep. He shone a torch into the hole, which was lined with Bakelite.

"What are we looking at?" enquired a nonplussed Grekov as he stared into the empty compartment.

"Look! Over there in the corner where the lining is cracked," he replied, "that silver residue gleaming in the fissure."

"What is it?" said Yelagin, frowning. "It looks like mercury."

"That's what I thought at first, but it doesn't react to a metal detector like mercury, nor does it react to a Geiger counter. And since mercury is the only liquid metal we know of, I can't imagine what it might be."

"Do you think it might be the source of the poisonings?" asked Grekov.

"Highly likely," agreed Antonovich. "Now we know what to look for, we can check during the autopsies. We must obtain a sample."

The professor jumped into the compartment and took out a fountain pen from his breast pocket. Then he bent down awkwardly in the cramped space and hooked some of the silver liquid onto the end of the cap. He studied the substance as it clung to the plastic body.

"Fascinating," he observed as he placed the pen on the floor and clambered out.

Professor Antonovich picked the pen up again and began to twist and turn it in all directions. Then he held the pen up vertically. The silver liquid ran down the plastic body in a thin line and onto the professor's thumb and forefinger.

"Ahh!" shouted Antonovich in panic, dropping the pen.

He examined the two digits on his left hand which had come into contact with the liquid.

"Ah you alright, Professor?" exclaimed Grekov. "Did it hurt you?"

"No, it just gave me a shock," said the professor, grimacing. "I'm fine."

"Wait… look!" bellowed Yelagin.

The tips of the two digits were beginning to dissolve and drip silver liquid onto the floor. The three men stared aghast, the professor clearly in shock.

"What is happening?" was all that he could utter as he saw his thumb and forefinger disappear. The liquid was now moving up his hand consuming the rest of his fingers. "I feel no pain."

The three men and the guard stood rooted to the spot, uncertain of what to do. The silver liquid began steadily creeping up past his wrist and was partway up his forearm when the professor became frantic.

"Please," he implored as fear took a hold of him, "do something."

"What can we do to stop it?" cried out Yelagin, coming to his senses.

"There's only one way to stop it," shouted Grekov. "We'll have to amputate further up the arm."

Remembering that he'd seen a fire bucket with an axe hanging above it on the wall back down the corridor, he ran out of the room. A minute later Grekov was back with the axe and a slither of wood. The professor's left arm was now dissolved just below the elbow.

"Take off his coat," ordered Grekov.

Yelagin and the guard carefully removed the lab coat and laid the professor on his back.

"Professor, I want you to bite down on this," he urged, putting the wood into his mouth. "I am going to take your arm off just below the shoulder."

Before the professor had a chance to protest, Grekov raised the axe and swung it down hard on the limb. It came away in one with very little blood and the professor screamed out in agony, biting the piece of wood in half. Grekov pushed the remainder of the afflicted arm aside with the axe blade and they watched as it was completely consumed.

"We need to get him to the field hospital, quick," urged Grekov.

"Wait," shouted Yelagin, examining the wound, "we haven't stopped it. The liquid is further advanced on the inside."

The three men looked on in dismay, knowing that they had failed to stop the flow.

"I'm sorry, Professor," said Grekov, grimacing, "we've done all we can."

"I'm in no pain now," said Antonovich weakly and smiled. "In fact I feel…"

His sentence was cut off abruptly as the liquid reached his heart. He lay there motionless, his eyes staring at the ceiling. The three men stepped back and watched as silver patches began to appear all over his head. Pin pricks at first, then getting bigger until they joined together and his head became a silver blob, his features sinking into it. In less than five minutes, the professor and all his clothes had been converted into this lethal silver liquid. It sat on the floor's surface and slowly coalesced into a globule about the size of a small dog.

"Look," shouted the guard, "his coat has dissolved."

The other two men swung round to see a much smaller globule and close to it four plastic buttons.

"It doesn't seem to like plastic," concluded Yelagin, looking from the buttons to the pen which was still intact.

"We need to get back to the field tent quick," urged Grekov. "Those medics are in danger."

"What are we going to do with the bodies? We don't dare let the medics examine them."

"We have no choice," continued Grekov. "Dig a pit and burn them."

Two days later Yelagin turned to look out of the rear window of the staff car to see thick black smoke rising up into the summer sky. They had done everything they could and now they were leaving. The contamination had been traced to a well the victims were using and the whole area was cordoned off.

To Yelagin's amusement, Grekov had sworn him to secrecy. After all, who would believe such an insane story? Grekov had claimed that the silver liquid had all been disposed of. He didn't believe a word of it, though he had the good sense not to dispute the fact.

By the end of the third day the Gaz-11 sedan pulled up

outside the apartment block and a weary Yelagin got out. Grekov wound down the window and leant forwards.

"Remember what I said," he warned. "Keep this to yourself."

"Don't take me for a fool," remonstrated Yelagin. "I have kept my mouth shut about this whole affair from day one. And besides, who would believe me?"

Satisfied, Grekov motioned for the driver to move off and Yelagin was left to ascend the steps to his apartment. He put the key into his front door and opened it. His wife gave out a gasp of surprise and delight then ran to give him a hug.

"Thank heaven you're back," she bawled, bursting into tears and kissing his cheek.

He held his wife tightly, relieved to be home. Neither was sure who was comforting whom more.

"He hasn't put in an appearance yet then," said Yelagin with a grin, caressing her stomach.

"No," said Elvira, smiling, "*she* has been waiting for you."

Yelagin laid back on his bed and waited for sleep to consume him. It didn't come immediately, however; he just couldn't get the horrific images out of his head.

***

Geneva, Switzerland
September 2016

Dr Monique Bellegarde, along with five technicians in white lab coats, stood in front of a wall of doors as they watched the green LED counters on six compartments count down to zero and sound off an alarm. With a satisfying clunk the doors unlocked and the six attendants each wheeled a gurney into place as the drawers slid open automatically.

A whiff of white vapour emanated from the open chambers, to dissipate and reveal the bodies of the six men who had been incarcerated thirty years earlier. Without hesitation each man was disconnected from his life support and laid on a stretcher.

"Quickly," urged Dr Bellegarde, "into the recovery room."

The six gurneys were wheeled into an adjoining room and Dr Bellegarde checked their heartbeats with a stethoscope.

"Pulses are low, as is their core temperature," she announced. "They will be dehydrated. Set up a saline drip and cover them with a thermal blanket. Drop the temperature ten degrees, they must warm up gradually."

After satisfying herself everything was in place, Dr Bellegarde walked to the door and turned to the chief technician.

"Check them every fifteen minutes," she ordered, "and let me know when they are *compos mentis*."

Jude's eyes opened and, blinded by light, closed again, then flickered open and squinted until he became accustomed to the bright white ceiling above him with its diffused lighting. He could just about discern a voice somewhere out of his line of sight, then a woman in her mid-thirties was peering over him, shining a small torch into his eyes. As his pupils contracted the woman smiled.

"Welcome back to the future, Mr Jude."

The woman spoke with a strong French accent and Jude studied her face. A short black pixie cut hairstyle framed a face of slightly heavy features that one would consider handsome rather than beautiful. The mouth was wide with full red lips and her eyebrows were also black and left to grow naturally. With bright brown eyes and dark lashes, she was striking, despite the fact that she wore no makeup whatsoever.

"How long have I been awake?" croaked Jude, clearing his throat.

"No more than ten minutes," replied Dr Bellegarde. "Do you think that you could sit up?"

Nodding, Jude attempted to push up with his arms and he suddenly became aware of the pain in his limbs.

"You will experience pins and needles in your extremities until your circulation is back to normal," she advised, lifting the bed up behind his shoulders for support.

"No shit!" said Jude, wincing.

After five minutes of discomfort the doctor smiled again.

"Do you think you could try and stand for me, please?"

He swung his legs round and gingerly slipped off the gurney. Immediately he began to buckle, but the doctor and a technician caught Jude under his arms and guided him over to an awaiting bed.

"You will all have suffered significant muscle atrophy," she said, frowning. "We will have to initiate a regime of exercises to get you all fit again. Starting tomorrow morning. I would like you all to rest and take some food for now."

"What year is it?"

"2016," replied Dr Bellegarde. "September 22nd to be precise."

"Thirty years, of course."

"One thing that I ask all my clients," she intimated, "did any of you dream?"

Jude's thought processes were still in disarray as he tried to rack his brain for memories. He vaguely half remembered a childlike dream where he was with his mother and father. It was a happy illusion, full of hope and missed opportunities, but as the fog began to sweep from his mind and he became more lucid, the dream seemed to be swept away with it, leaving nothing but a merciful void in his consciousness.

"If I did, I've got no recollection of it," replied Jude eventually, who then looked at the others. They all shook their heads in agreement.

"It's probably for the best," she offered. "Could you imagine a thirty-year-long nightmare? It could drive a person insane."

She left all six to recover and take a light meal and drink. Then they lay back and closed their eyes. Jude wondered after such a long sleep why he felt so tired, but before he could dwell on the fact, he and the other five drifted off into a fitful slumber.

***

The following morning, the Apostles awoke to find a wheelchair each beside their beds. Light grey tracksuits were draped over them, with plain white espadrilles supplied for their feet. At 8.30am they were all helped into a shower cubicle with a seat so that they could wash away thirty years of grime. After dressing and breakfasting the six men were wheeled into a small anteroom where Dr Bellegarde sat patiently waiting for their arrival.

"Good morning, gentlemen," she announced breezily. "The next month will be a strict regime of exercise and learning. You need to build up your muscle strength and so much has happened in the last thirty years. Politically the world has changed significantly, as has technology. First of all, though, do you have any questions?"

"Where is Dr Osborne?" enquired Jude. "I realise he must be in his seventies by now."

"He retired to Canada," she stated, "and is now a silent partner, having no active say in the decision-making here."

"Who is the president of the United States?" enquired Matthew.

"You will probably be surprised to hear that the current US president is black and his name is Barack Obama," replied the doctor, expecting this question. "He is the fourth president since you were put under."

"Republican or Democrat?"

"Democrat," she advised. "He was sworn in for a second term in 2013."

Dr Bellegarde stood up and passed a folder to each of them.

"These folders contain a history of the last thirty years, for you to study in your leisure time, but for now we need to get you up to speed on current technology."

For the rest of the morning the Apostles were astounded as they learned about the progress in computer technology, the internet and cellular mobile phones.

"The first cell phone was available in 1987, and looked like this." Dr Bellegarde held up what looked like a black brick with an aerial. "It was called the Mobira Cityman 900."

The men looked at each other.

"Now," she continued with a wry smile, and holding up a smartphone, "they look like this and are more like mini computers."

"My God," gasped James, realising that there was so much for them to learn. By lunchtime their brains were suffering from an information overload and by the afternoon, all were glad to get down to some straightforward physical exercise.

After his evening meal, Jude sat on his bed and opened the folder that the doctor had given them. It was a potted world history since 1986. He read assiduously, and was surprised to learn about the collapse of the Berlin Wall in 1989 and the subsequent decline and breakup of the Soviet Union. As he continued to read, Jude was particularly shocked at the attack on the World Trade Center just over fifteen years before. Jude came to the conclusion that there was one aspect in which the planet had not changed in thirty years, and that was the world is still a very dangerous place.

One month later, with their fitness restored and a solid grounding on what to expect when they returned to the United States, Dr Bellegarde approached Jude a few hours before their departure. He was dressed in the clothes in which he'd arrived, now freshly laundered.

"Will we look out of place in these clothes?" he asked.

"Trends become fashionable then unfashionable," she smiled, adjusting his tie, "but style is timeless. You all look fine."

She dipped into the right-hand pocket of her lab coat and produced an envelope.

"Dr Osborne asked me to hold this and pass it to you when you are about to leave."

"What is it?" enquired Jude, examining the missive with his name written on it.

"I don't know," she replied, frowning slightly, "but he was most insistent that I didn't forget."

"Thank you," he said absentmindedly as he began to slide his forefinger along the top.

Dr Bellegarde had walked away and Jude opened up the letter and began to read.

My Dear Fellow,

If you are reading this then you obviously survived your hibernation.

The reason for this message is I would like and urge you to come and visit me in Canada. I have something to show you, the importance of which cannot be stressed more highly. It is something I think you might be better placed to deal with.
You will find my address on the reverse of this letter.
Come alone.

Kind regards
Dr Osborne

Jude flipped over the letter to find an address for Oak Point, Manitoba, Canada. He reread the letter and after some thought called all the Apostles together.

"There's going to be a change in our schedule," he advised. "We are not all going to the States tomorrow. Matthew and I will be going to Canada."

"I trust there is a reason for this," said Matthew, frowning.

Jude passed the letter over for them all to read.

"What's it all about?" asked James.

"I have no clue," said Jude, shrugging, "but he is most insistent, so I am going to find out. The rest of you can establish a base back home."

"It says in the letter to come alone," stated Thaddeus.

"Yes, it does, doesn't it," replied Jude, "but since I don't know what I will be walking into, I think it would be better to cover our backs."

An hour later two taxis arrived to take them to the airport and, after saying goodbye to the staff, Jude addressed his men.

"Well, gentlemen," he said, smiling, "school's out. It's time for us to get back into the big bad world.

***

Oak Point, Manitoba, Canada
October 2016

As Jude turned off Provincial Trunk Highway 6 towards Oak Point in his hire car, he expected to be able to see Lake Manitoba. The land for miles around, however, was flat and given over to agriculture, and, unfortunately, autumnal trees dotted around conspired to block his view. The day had started with a clear blue sky and Jude had expected the car to be covered in frost, but to his surprise the steady dry wind which tended to blow constantly on these flat prairie lands had kept the frost at bay.

He eventually turned off the road near the centre of Oak Point and into a long drive which culminated with a large brick British Colonial Georgian house with large white-framed windows and three dormers in the pitched roof.

Gravel crackled on the drive as the car pulled up to a halt, and Jude got out and pulled his overcoat around tightly as he braced himself against the chill of the wind. Hurriedly he walked up to the front door, sheltered by a portico supported by two fluted Doric pillars, and rang the bell. As he stood impatiently in the freezing breeze, the door was finally opened by a stout old lady about five feet tall and a wisp of grey hair tied back in a bun. She stared blankly at the stranger in front of her, then eventually uttered with a frown,

"Can I help you?"

"I'm here to see Dr Osborne," replied Jude. "I hope this is the right house."

"What do you want?" she chimed suspiciously.

"He left a letter some years ago for me to contact him when I am able," stated Jude producing the letter from inside his coat pocket.

The old lady rummaged in an apron tied around her waist and found her spectacles. After placing them firmly on her nose, she squinted at the letter.

"Please, step into the house," she invited, eventually.

Jude didn't wait to be asked twice and entered into a large hallway. He looked around him. The place must have been quite grand at one time, but now looked somewhat dilapidated.

"Wait here, I will go and see if he will receive you."

She sauntered off and disappeared into the drawing room and Jude could hear an indistinct exchange of words.

"Bring him in, bring him in," ordered Dr Osborne impatiently, and the old lady, whose demeanour had warmed slightly, motioned for Jude to enter.

"My dear fellow," he gushed as Jude walked in, "how marvellous to see you at last. I'm so glad you heeded my letter. This is my sister, Tabatha. Would you like a coffee or would you prefer something stronger?"

After shaking hands with Tabatha, Jude stooped slightly to shake hands with the doctor who was sitting in a wheelchair with a green tartan blanket over his knees.

"Something stronger would be nice," said Jude with a smile.

The doctor wheeled himself over to a cocktail cabinet and opened the door and removed two tumblers.

"I have a rather fine collection of single malts here," he confided. "Please, come and choose one."

Jude scanned the cabinet and chose a ten-year-old bottle of Ardbeg.

"Ah excellent choice," announced Dr Osborne, taking the bottle off Jude and pulling the cork stopper. With an unsteady hand he poured two generous glasses and passed one to his guest.

"I'm guessing you are wondering what has happened to me?" he continued. "Muscular dystrophy, old chap. It's quite bad, I'm afraid, and will only get worse. Alas I can no longer walk."

"I'm sorry to hear that," replied Jude, when he eventually managed to get a word in.

Dr Osborne wheeled himself closer to the open fire and Jude sat down in an armchair adjacent to him and watched as the old man picked up a poker to stoke the fire. He prodded the embers with more vigour than was needed, as if to prove to himself, at least, that his health was not deteriorating. The fire crackled back to life and they both basked in its comforting warmth.

"Ironic, don't you think?" mused Dr Osborne, when he saw Jude watching him intently. "I am an ideal candidate for the euthanasia clinic, but I haven't got the courage to go through with it."

"Perhaps it takes more courage to live," replied Jude. It felt like he was throwing a rope to a drowning man.

"Perhaps," sighed the doctor, sensing that he was being humoured.

"Why am I here?" asked Jude. "As much as I am enjoying sharing a whisky with you, I am curious to know what is so important."

"I have something to show you…" the doctor replied, "… give to you, if you'll take it."

Pivoting his wheelchair round, the old man wheeled himself over to a cupboard and removed a wooden box about six inches cubed and a file. Then he returned to the fire.

"Do you remember when you first arrived at the clinic all those years ago, I mentioned a Russian colonel who was interned?" he said, finally. "His name was Zykov Ilyich. He stole this box and defected when the Soviet Union collapsed."

"Was?" The past tense didn't go unnoticed on Jude.

"He was contracted from 1985 to 1995. Alas he didn't

make it," pondered the doctor, with genuine regret. "As we warned everyone before they committed themselves, the technology was not foolproof and his age went against him."

"What did he die of?"

"It's hard to say, we simply couldn't revive him."

Jude studied the contents on the doctor's lap with great curiosity. *What is the old goat holding?* he wondered.

"This box and this file were all he left behind," continued Dr Osborne, "and with no next of kin to send it to, I appropriated it."

Jude felt that this was a euphemism for taking something which wasn't his, but couldn't be bothered to argue the point. The doctor wheeled himself over to a table, placed the box on it and removed the lid. With both hands he carefully pulled out a clear perspex cube which sat snuggly in the box and placed it on the table. Standing up, Jude walked over to inspect the object closer.

"What am I looking at?" he enquired with a frown.

"Notice the silver fluid-like substance at the bottom," observed Dr Osborne, picking up the cube and twisting and turning it in his hands.

Jude watched as the liquid, about an inch deep, sloshed about inside.

"It's mercury, surely," he surmised.

"Wait here," said the doctor enigmatically and manoeuvred himself over to the window. With a flourish he drew the curtains over the large window, causing the room to be immersed in semi-darkness.

"Look at it now." He smiled triumphantly as he approached the table again.

Turning his head back to the cube, Jude was astounded to see the silver liquid had formed itself into a sphere the size of a tennis ball and was floating.

"What the hell!" he exclaimed.

"I know," said the doctor with a smile. "Fantastic, isn't it."

"It has to be a trick," challenged Jude, standing up and looking at the cube from different angles.

"Pick it up," encouraged Dr Osborne. "Twist and turn it. Give it a shake."

Jude did just that and noticed that no matter how much he turned the cube, no matter how much he shook it, the silver sphere remained central, never touching the sides, seemingly defying gravity. Eventually he placed it down on the table.

"Do you know what it is?"

Dr Osborne shook his head and a cloud seemed to come over his usual cheery demeanour.

"I'm afraid not," he bemoaned, picking up the file. "There are some clues in here but alas it is all in Russian. I have managed to translate some of it, but I have struggled to make sense of it all."

"What does it say?" Jude's curiosity was piqued.

"It talks of a small village in Poland called Milkow," Dr Osborne began. "Some people there were falling seriously ill and dying mysteriously in 1946. It would seem this liquid was retrieved from the site and was determined to be the culprit."

"So, it's dangerous then," concluded Jude, looking at the hovering silver ball with a new respect.

"Apparently there was some sort of research base

there during the Second World War. The file refers to a man running at great speed and entering a bell-shaped object. This object raised off the ground spinning until it eventually vanished."

"Vanished?" exclaimed Jude. "You mean it exploded."

"No," corrected the old man, "vanished, never to be seen again."

"I guess there were witnesses."

"A company of Russian paratroopers who raided the complex."

"Who compiled this report?" asked Jude, scanning over the pages uncomprehendingly.

Taking the folder off him, Dr Osborne began leafing through the sheets of paper.

"Here we are," he announced, holding one sheet up. "A Captain Sasha Grekov. He was there with another man, a Kiril Yelagin, who witnessed the vessel take off in 1945 and was also at the site just after the war when the deaths were investigated."

"What do you think might have happened to it?"

"I have given this some thought," pondered the doctor. "Have you ever heard of the Einstein-Rosen bridge?"

Jude shook his head.

"You probably know it as a wormhole."

"I've heard of wormholes in space," confirmed Jude.

"Well, it just might be possible that this vessel traversed some kind of wormhole enabling it to travel through space and time."

"Isn't that a little speculative, not to mention implausible?"

"Yes, it is rather fanciful, I agree," mused Dr Osborne,

"but alas it's the only logical explanation that I can come up with. If you have a better one, I would be happy to consider it."

Jude pondered for a moment, then asked,

"What do you intend to do with this thing?", picking up the cube and examining it closely again.

"I want you to take it," urged the doctor. "Frankly the thing scares me. I wish I'd never taken it but I simply couldn't leave it behind."

"What can I do with it?"

"From the first moment I met you," said the old man, smiling, "you struck me as a very resourceful young fellow. You are much better placed to deal with it than I am. Will you take it?"

Dr Osborne looked up at the enigmatic man expectantly; Jude kept him on tenterhooks for longer than was necessary until he finally said, "Yes."

A short while later, Jude was on his way back to the hotel where he'd left Matthew. The drive gave him time to reflect on his meeting. He glanced across at the wooden box on the seat beside him and thought about the doctor's theory. It wasn't the first time that he'd heard time machines being mentioned and tried to remember who had referred to them.

Who was it? he thought, then it dawned on him. *Yes, it was that creep Sanderson. He said it was in some book kept by that bitch Kaplow. Maybe there is something in it. Worth checking out anyhow.*

An hour later he was back at the hotel. Matthew was waiting for him in the foyer area, talking on his cell phone.

"How did it go?" enquired Matthew.

"Not here," gestured Jude, "it's too public. Did you contact the others?"

"Yeah I've just got off the phone with James, they are back in LA looking for a suitable headquarters."

"Good."

Once back in their room, Jude grabbed a bottle of bourbon and poured himself a half tumbler full. Matthew did the same as his cohort told him about the meeting with Dr Osborne.

"It's unbelievable," babbled Matthew, staring intently at the cube, "but what the hell are we going to do with it?"

"More importantly," corrected Jude, "how the fuck are we going to get it over the border into the States?"

"Yes, it is a little bulky to hide," mused Matthew, re-examining the box. He stood up. "Leave it to me, I've got an idea."

Matthew put his coat on and made for the door.

"Where are you going?" asked Jude.

"Out to buy some rubbers and a plastic funnel."

CHAPTER SEVEN

THE NEW FRONTIER

The Rocky Mountains, Colorado
July 1995

The stony track was just how he'd remembered it. A little steeper perhaps, but that was almost certainly down to the fact that General Sterling Chambers hadn't been here for nearly fifty years. After two hours of steady walking, the sixty-two-year-old stopped to catch his breath. He unbuttoned his jacket and loosened his collar before taking a handkerchief and wiping the sweat from his face. Even at this lower level the view was magnificent. The slopes were adorned with Douglas firs and wild flowers bloomed in abundance. In amongst the rocks and shrubs were yellow

Blanket flowers reflecting the light of the sun, bright pink Parry primrose and Colorado columbine with its delicate purple and white petals. And as the general scanned further into the distance, the mountain range seemed to stretch out forever, disappearing into a shimmering haze of blue sky and sunshine.

General Chambers was typical for a man of his age: his tall slim frame had given way to a heavier-set stature, though by no means could he be considered corpulent. His dark brown hair was now almost white, standing out in stark contrast to his tanned clean-shaven face, with piercing blue eyes that rarely blinked and could stare down anyone who he felt was out of line.

By the age of twenty-three he was cutting his teeth as a fighter pilot during the Korean War flying F-84 Thunderjets and then later in the mid-sixties piloting F-4 Phantoms during the Vietnam conflict. By the time his flying career was over Chambers had seven kills to his name, downing two Lavochkin La-11s in Korea along with three MiG-21s and two MiG-19s downed in Vietnam. Thus, he attained the status of ace. His one regret was that he never fulfilled his ambition to become an astronaut. Having been passed over on numerous occasions, instead he had to settle for a steady rise up the ranks within the US Air Force.

After a further ninety minutes of walking and scrambling, Chambers was relieved to finally see what he was looking for: a log cabin. It wasn't quite how he'd remembered it though; in his mind's eye he recollected a picture-perfect cabin and not the slightly run-down shambolic shack which stood a short distance up the slope above him. Maybe it had always been this way and he had over-romanticised the cabin, after all, it was the memory of a child, and he knew as well as any that memories cannot always be trusted.

Apart from a wild turkey hanging in the veranda the place looked deserted. He cautiously approached the cabin, but stopped suddenly as he felt a force against the small of his back. Instinctively he raised his arms up. Despite the thickness of his jacket, he recognised the pressure of a twin-barrelled, twelve-bore shotgun.

"Look, is this really necessary?" he gasped, trying to look behind him. "I'm out of breath, middle-aged and unarmed."

"Who are you and what do you want?" came the voice from behind.

"Well, if you remove that blunderbuss from outta my back and let me sit down, I'll tell you," complained the general. "It's playing havoc with my lumbago."

The gun was released from the general's back and he turned around to face his assailant. The man in front of him wore faded blue jeans, a red plaid shirt and, covering that, an olive-green hunting jacket open at the front. His dark hair and full beard were beginning to grey. The man was clearly on edge and the general chose his words carefully.

"Ah," he said, with what he hoped was a reassuring smile, "Liam Slater. The very man I am looking for."

"How did you find me?" said Slater, frowning.

"Educated guess," said Chambers, shrugging. "I came here a few times when I was a kid. I know your dad came here with my father years ago, but how do you know about it?"

"My mother told me about this place."

"Yes of course," remembered Chambers, "Sara. I recollect her coming up here once. Is she still alive?"

Slater simply nodded and continued to hold the shotgun up, pointing in the general's direction.

"I was sorry to hear about your dad," continued Chambers. "He was a brave man."

"I never knew him," countered Slater. It pleased him, though, to have this confirmed by a military man.

"Yep, that sure was a terrible thing," mused Chambers. "Look, I'm going to go and sit on that step over there and take the weight off my feet. I would sure appreciate it if you'd stop pointing that scattergun at me."

Observing the four silver stars on each of the epaulettes on the general's shoulders, Slater decided to relax a little and lowered the firearm.

"You have me at a disadvantage, General," declared Slater. "You know my name, but I don't know yours."

"General Sterling Chambers," he replied, offering his hand, "US Air Force."

Slater shook his hand and sat down on the wooden step next to him. He sat in silence looking out over the valley, keeping the shotgun close at hand.

"I don't think I'll ever get tired of this view," noted Slater.

"I hear you," confirmed the general, "but don't you think it's time to come back into civilisation?"

"Staying away from civilisation is what's kept me alive," advised Slater. "For all I know there's still a contract out on me."

"You won't have to worry about that," assured Chambers. "Where you're going has to be one of the most secure places on the planet."

"I didn't think this was a social visit," commented Slater churlishly, now that it had been made clear that his presence was required.

"I'm getting too old to be doing this kind of thing for fun," said Chambers, wincing, standing up and stretching his back.

"Do I get to know where?" probed Slater. "And do I have a choice?"

"The answer is no, and no," confirmed Chambers, "though you'll find out soon enough."

"I'd better stow my weapons away then," said Slater, standing up and entering the cabin.

He returned a few minutes later as the roar of a helicopter came from behind the cabin. A dark green Sikorsky HH-3E breezed into view and hovered close to the two men.

"Right on cue," said the general with a smile, "the Jolly Green Giant."

Slater looked at the general with a puzzled expression. He had expected to be walking down to ground level.

"I'm not walking back down," exclaimed the general. "Walking up was bad enough."

"Why didn't you arrive by chopper?"

"I just wanted to prove to myself that I could still do it," said the general, grimacing, regretting the decision.

Slater chuckled and followed him to the chopper, which had dropped a rope ladder. The two men clambered aboard and the helicopter banked away. During the ascent, they were able to see the Rockies in all their splendour as the aircraft cleared the peaks. After a while they had left the Rocky Mountains behind them, and the no less magnificent canyons of Utah and Arizona came into view. Slater realised that they were heading west and pondered on their destination. *It couldn't be Area 51, surely,* he thought, *could it?*

After a flight which lasted several hours, and at the very limit of its range, the helicopter began to descend. Peering out of the window Slater saw an air base below him. The chopper landed and the two men stepped out into the California heat.

"This isn't Area 51," announced Slater.

General Chambers winked and smiled, then led him over to a building.

"Let's eat," he insisted. "I don't know about you but I'm famished."

"Is this our final destination?" bellowed Slater, looking around him. A flight of three General Dynamics F-16 Fighting Falcons were powering up and beginning their taxi to the runway.

"All in good time," replied the general enigmatically. "We'll get our heads down here tonight and I'm sure all your questions will be answered in the morning."

***

Edwards Air Force Base, Kern County, California
July 1995

The deafening roar of a Northrop Grumman B-2 flying wing woke Slater up and he squinted through the curtains to see the huge dark grey experimental stealth bomber take off and disappear from view. He looked at his watch; it was 08.33. Padding off to the bathroom, Slater took a shower. He had forgotten what it was like to have such conveniences and revelled in the hot jets of water. Afterwards he wiped steam from a mirror over the sink and looked at his reflection. His unkempt hair and bushy beard looked out of place on the base. There wasn't much he could do about his hair right now, but at least he could shave his beard off.

When Slater finally found the canteen, General Chambers was there waiting for him. He did a double take as he saw his beardless guest approach and motioned for him to sit down. They made an odd-looking pair: the well-groomed middle-aged man in uniform and the slightly dishevelled younger man in jeans, white T-shirt and green plaid shirt unbuttoned at the front.

"Making yourself look human again," said Chambers, grinning.

"Just taking advantage of the facilities," replied Slater helping himself to coffee.

A waitress walked over to their table with pen and notepad poised in readiness to take Slater's order.

He looked over at the general's half-eaten bacon, sausage and eggs with relish and looked up at the waitress.

"I'll have the same, please," he said, pointing to the general's plate. The woman nodded and disappeared.

"What do you know about Edwards Air Force Base?" enquired the general, getting down to business.

"Very little," confirmed Slater, sipping his coffee, "apart from the first Space Shuttle landings here."

The waitress placed a plate in front him and Slater began to eat with gusto. Chambers waited patiently for his guest to finish eating and as Slater wiped a dribble of yolk from his chin, the general continued.

"This base has been a proving ground for experimental aircraft since the Second World War. I'm sure you must be familiar with the rocket-powered Bell X-1. The first aircraft to officially break the sound barrier in 1947."

"I saw a weird wing thing take off this morning," mused Slater. "That was really impressive. What was it?"

"That," advised Chambers, "is one of the many classified development projects undertaken at this base. Not all of them at this particular site though."

"It would be nice if you could tell me what this is all about," retorted Slater sullenly, leaning back on his chair.

"Follow me," announced Chambers, standing up. "It's time for you to find out."

Slater followed the general out onto a tarmac apron where the Sikorski helicopter was waiting for them. He was handed a lanyard with his identification attached and Slater slipped it over his head.

The chopper rose into the air and Slater noticed it moving in a north-easterly direction. He hoped this journey was going to be shorter. After about thirty minutes, Slater was relieved to feel the helicopter beginning to descend. It landed on a rough track close to an awaiting yellow ochre Humvee. The two men alighted from the aircraft and the stifling heat hit them like a brick wall. Slater looked around him; the area was rocky, barren and arid. Following the general's lead, Slater approached the vehicle, and a soldier dressed in desert camouflage approached and saluted. He checked Slater's identification, and nodded.

"Welcome to Death Valley, sir," he announced. "Best not linger, it's nearly fifty degrees out here."

It was cooler inside the Humvee but not by much since it didn't have air conditioning. They continued along the track for a while until it appeared as though they were approaching a near-vertical slope. Slater doubted whether the Humvee could negotiate such an incline, when a large rectangular section in front of them cracked open and two halves parted, exposing a gaping hole in the hill. Without even slowing down the vehicle entered and drew to a halt. Slater was astounded; the doorway, which was now closing, was completely invisible. And now as he stepped out, he looked around in amazement. The room was cavernous and well lit. He observed several trucks of various sizes and people milling about, some in uniform, others in lab coats.

"What is this place?" enquired a wide-eyed Slater.

"This is AirForce Plant 52," proclaimed General Chambers, enjoying Slater's reaction, "and what is more, it doesn't exist."

"Of course," acknowledged Slater, with a slight hint of sarcasm, realising he had been brought to an installation which was highly classified. "I was certain that you were taking me to Area 51."

"We leave Area 51 to the media and conspiracy theorists. The real work gets done in places like this," confided Chambers. "Follow me, I'll show you why you're here."

With great curiosity Slater followed Chambers over to an elevator. He pressed a button and they entered. The general pressed another button and they descended five floors and stopped. The doors opened and they stepped into a short corridor that led to a steel door. Chambers entered a six-digit code and the door opened with a click. They walked through onto a steel gangway attached to a wall on the right and steel railings to the left. After walking halfway along, Chambers leant over the railings and gestured down into a massive underground vault below them. Slater glanced down and was completely taken aback by what he saw. He turned to Chambers in a mixture of shock and disbelief.

"Holy shit!" he blurted out. "What have you done?"

"Impressive, don't you think?" pronounced Chambers, a big grin on his face.

Below them stood twelve highly polished silver bell-shaped vessels about five metres tall, with the US Air Force insignia and a large black number on the side. Twelve *Die Glocke* time machines all grouped together like eggs in an eggbox.

"Follow me," invited Chambers as he walked to the edge of steel steps which would take them down into the vault.

Slater duly did just that, his mind in a daze. All he kept thinking was, *What have the stupid bastards done?*

They approached the time machines and General Chambers watched as Slater walked around the vessels deep in thought. He slid his hand over the shiny reflective surface as the memories of his time in the bunker raced through his mind. The fight on the parapet where he watched them rise from their silos. Where he came so close to losing his life.

"It's called Project Phoenix," declared Chambers with pride. "I'm sure you appreciate that allusion."

Slater understood all too well. He gave the general a withering look.

"Why?" he exclaimed.

"Why not?" retorted Chambers. This wasn't the reaction he was expecting. "Better us than anyone else, don't you think?"

"Nobody should have these, not even us," corrected Slater. "They will bring nothing but grief. I thought they were all destroyed. How did you do it?"

"We salvaged enough parts from the debris to reverse engineer them."

"Are they operational?" enquired Slater.

"This one is," confirmed Chambers, opening the hatch of a *Bell* with a large black number One above it.

Peering in, Slater could see that it was fitted out and looked perfectly serviceable.

"You are aware that the timer modules were sabotaged," advised Slater. "It was in the report."

"We didn't at the time. The report we saw was heavily censored," said the general, frowning, "but we knew the boy Scott Anderson designed them and he built a timer for us. He is a remarkable young man, he had it all committed to memory."

"You can't use them," urged Slater. "The timers are out by a factor of ten thousand. There's a good chance you'll never see it again."

"We've tested one already," confirmed Chambers. "It returned when expected."

"The boy must have removed the dubious circuitry, enabling the machines to operate predictably," acknowledged Slater. "So, you've tested it successfully then?"

"Not quite," said Chambers, frowning.

A metallic clanging sound emanated from above them and Slater glanced up to see a tall slim man in a light grey suit walking across the gangway above them, looking down and smiling. Slater recognised him instantly, a little older but there was no mistaking the director of operations for the CIA.

"Liam!" greeted Alex McInnes, beaming. "It's been a while."

"McInnes," replied Slater, taken aback. "What are you doing here?"

Slater bounded up the steel stairs with Chambers following steadily behind. He strode across the walkway and McInnes offered his hand, with a smile which revealed the fact that he was still enjoying his surprise appearance. A lacklustre handshake from Slater betrayed the fact that he was not best pleased to see him.

"Call me Alex, after all you're not CIA anymore." McInnes leant over the railings and looked down at the *Die Glockes.*

"You do realise this is madness," exclaimed Slater, gesturing to the twelve craft, "though I shouldn't be surprised that the CIA are involved."

"As soon as we discovered that the things could be reverse engineered," explained McInnes, "there was no way that we wouldn't be. You of all people should realise that."

"Aren't you concerned about the consequences of using these things?"

"Time travel is the new frontier, Liam," retorted McInnes. "This technology is out there now. Better that we have it, don't you think?"

Slater glanced across at the man. Being in his early fifties now, his hair was much thinner and his face was engraved with lines around the eyes, which looked dull and tired. His mouth had a downward slant, suggesting that his tenure at CIA headquarters had taken its toll. The ex-CIA agent chose not to answer the question; he had to admit that there was some logic to what he was saying. But Slater was damned if he was going to give voice to it.

"What did you mean by 'not quite' when I asked you if they were tested successfully?" reminded Slater.

"This way," instructed Chambers, and along with McInnes, led Slater out of the hangar and back into the short corridor. At the other end was another door where General Chambers stopped and produced a key. He unlocked the door and entered with McInnes, their guest following close behind. What Slater saw was a small room with a few chairs facing a large television screen. Below it sat a VHS player. Chambers walked over to a safe and began punching in a number combination. He opened the door and retrieved a VHS cassette, which he inserted into the player. All three men sat down to watch as the general pressed play on the remote. The screen came to life with images of men standing around, shaking hands.

"This is the research team meeting for the first time," declared Chambers.

The picture changed to a small group of people and a younger man. Slater recognised him as Scott, a little older perhaps, but still just as awkward. He was standing close to his mother and staring at the ground. The images changed again; this time a desert scene was shown with the unmistakeable image of a *Die Glocke* glistening in the sunshine.

"This is the first flight of *The Bell*, two months ago in the Nevada testing ground," commented Chambers.

Slater watched the all too familiar site of *The Bell* as it began spinning until it rose up and disappeared with a thunder-like crack. He glanced over at the general and then the CIA man.

"The first flight was operated remotely to return a quarter of a mile east one hour later."

The video suddenly jumped to *The Bell* reappearing again, on time and on target.

"Since this flight went so well," continued Chambers, "we decided to use a test pilot."

A man in his early forties could be seen dressed in an astronaut suit holding a helmet under his right arm and being escorted to the time machine.

"This is Major Tim Watson," confirmed Chambers. "He volunteered to be the first American time traveller."

"Or guinea pig," countered a sceptical Slater.

Both men ignored the comment as they watched the test pilot being helped into the vessel. He strapped himself in, put the helmet on, and technicians closed the hatch. The scene changed to a safer distance as the time machine rose up into the air and disappeared. Then, as before, it showed the machine returning.

"We used exactly the same settings," Chambers' voice was edgy now, "but when we opened the hatch…"

The film showed the hatch opening to reveal the test pilot slumped forwards in his seat. He was pulled out by two technicians and laid on the ground. The pilot's helmet was carefully removed to expose the man's face. His eyes were closed and a trickle of blood had run down from the corner of his mouth. Medics set to work to try and revive him.

"What happened?" enquired Slater.

"He was dead," revealed Chambers. "Everything went smoothly, as you saw, but for some reason he didn't survive the trip."

"Do you know what caused it?"

"The film shows the autopsy done immediately afterwards," said McInnes, pointing at the screen. "Results showed that his heart… well, there's no other way to put it, exploded in his chest."

The screen displayed an unrecognisable bloody mess being lifted from the hapless pilot's chest cavity and placed into a stainless-steel bowl.

"Needless to say, all tests were cancelled," continued McInnes, "and that's when the decision was made to find you. For someone who wanted to drop off the grid, you didn't exactly make it difficult."

"To be fair," reasoned Slater, "the general did have insider knowledge. Though how on earth can I help?"

"You spent more time at that installation than anyone," replied Chambers. "Is there anything you can think of which might shed some light on why those Nazis could survive the flight and our man couldn't?"

"I only know of three people who used them," mused Slater. "Only one I can say for sure survived a trip, when he travelled from 1945 to 1985. Unfortunately for him, he ended up in the distant past. We can thank Scott Anderson for that."

The general sat back and exhaled a gasp of exasperation, and fell into deep thought.

"This is disappointing," sighed Chambers. "You are our last link to the Nazi base. Involving the men from Delta Force simply isn't an option."

Picking up the remote, Slater rewound the tape and watched the *Die Glocke* take off and reappear again. Perhaps McInnes was right. Better to have this technology in American hands. The possibility of, say, Russia getting their hands on it didn't bear thinking about. He turned and looked at General Chambers and then at Alex McInnes.

"That's not strictly true," he announced eventually. "There is one other."

"Who?" enquired McInnes with raised eyebrows.

"Dr Maxwell Copeland," replied Slater.

"That creep," sneered Chambers. "He's a complete waste of time. We got nothing from him."

"I think we should talk to him again," suggested Slater. "Nine years of incarceration may have made him more receptive."

***

ADX Florence, Supermax High Security Penitentiary, Fremont County, Colorado
July 1995

After flying into Colorado Springs Airport, Slater and Chambers transferred to a small US Air Force Hughes OH-6 Cayuse helicopter waiting for them and headed south. Out of the starboard side, the Rocky Mountains could be seen in all their majesty, standing like a massive silent sentinel, and Slater couldn't believe he would be returning quite so close to what he had called home for the last nine years.

They soon passed over the town of Penrose and then the small town of Florence, until eventually the high-security prison known as 'The Alcatraz of the Rockies' came into view. The facility was less than a year old but already had a fearsome reputation, not least because of the miscreants, many of them terrorists, who were incarcerated there. Most, if not all, never to see the light of day or the outside world again.

As the small chopper came closer, Slater observed the twelve-foot-high razor wire perimeter fence interspersed with seven tall circular light grey gun towers. They flew lower into the compound and a large white 'H' on a circular pad came into view and the chopper set down on it. The two men stepped down to be greeted by a white SUV. A guard dressed completely in black, a semi-automatic rifle over his shoulder, got out and approached them. He checked their IDs and the two men were driven into the prison and ushered into a waiting room. A guard opened the door, entered and smiled.

"The warden sends his compliments but is unable to meet you today due to other commitments," advised the tall stout man in light blue shirt and dark blue trousers. "He sends his apologies but couldn't rearrange his schedule at such short notice."

"That's not a problem," replied Chambers, "as long as a meeting has been set up."

"I'm afraid there is a problem," said the guard, frowning. "He will only see one of you, namely Mr Slater."

"What!" exclaimed Chambers. "Why?"

"He says he has an aversion to military men and uniforms," said the guard with a shrug. "We know he's playing games, but as far as he's concerned, he has nothing to lose."

"Uniforms are kinda tricky to avoid in this place, don't ya think."

"It's him or nothing," urged the guard.

"It's not a problem," countered Slater. "I can handle it."

"We'll give you an earpiece and watch the interview from another room," said the guard. "Try to keep the interview formal and as short as possible. Do not pass anything to him. Do not take anything from him. Do not lean forward across the table. Above all, don't let him needle you. And if he does, don't show it."

Fitted with an earpiece, Slater opened the interview room door and entered. The room was stark, with no more than a table and two chairs. Sitting on the other side of the table was a man in his early fifties wearing khaki trousers and a khaki V-neck top over a white T-shirt. Both his wrists were restrained by handcuffs, linked by a chain which looped through a short rail which was bolted to the table top. His forearms rested on the table with his hands clasped tightly together. He sat bolt upright with his eyes closed. Slater sat down opposite the man, who didn't flinch. The ex-CIA agent studied the man opposite him. He was of average height and build, with a long face and pointed features; his hair was a mousy light brown with only a hint of grey, which was tied back in a ponytail. Round spectacles sat on the bridge of his nose and he continued to sit stolidly resolute with his eyes closed.

"Dr Maxwell Copeland," declared Slater, keen to get the interview started.

The prisoner slowly opened his eyes and gave Slater a steely stare.

"Good afternoon, Liam," drawled Dr Copeland with a refined English accent, and a wry smile. "I can call you Liam, can't I?"

Slater was taken unawares; he expected the man to be German.

"Before we begin," continued the doctor, "I would like you to remove the earpiece."

Slater hesitated and then reluctantly plucked the device from his right ear and placed it on the table.

"You look haunted, Liam," simpered Copeland. His eyes narrowed, as if trying to penetrate Slater's very soul. "No, hunted would be more apropos. Who's hunting you, Liam?"

"If I knew that I wouldn't have needed to disappear," countered Slater.

"Ah the dog-fox went to ground," said Copeland, smiling. "You and I aren't so different. It would seem we are both living out our lives in splendid isolation."

"Except mine has a better view."

"I didn't know it was a competition," commented Copeland. "I have everything I need, it's all just a state of mind."

Slater gave a non-committal shrug.

"Who are you, Liam? You're clearly not police," probed Copeland. "You're not wearing one of those cheap off-the-peg suits, so you're not FBI. That only leaves the CIA."

"Ex-CIA," corrected Slater.

"Of course. We are both survivors."

"How was it that you managed to stay alive?" asked Slater. "You were the only survivor."

"I kept my head down – played dead," declared Copeland. "I had no intention of being martyred for the cause. Especially a lost cause."

"How did an Englishman end up with a Nazi terrorist group?" pressed Slater.

"You consider me a terrorist," contended Copeland, "I'm a physicist, with no political agenda. The Nazis' ambitions were of no interest to me."

"What were *your* ambitions then, Dr Copeland?"

"I have none. Science has no ambition nor conscience. Its *raison d'être* is to simply seek out the truth."

"And what was the truth in this instance?"

"In this instance, to see how viable time travel really is."

"Weren't you worried about the damage to the timeline?" reasoned Slater; he was beginning to realise that this man was an amoral sociopath. "The calamity it could have caused?"

"Logic dictates that if physics allows such a device to be feasible, then wouldn't it also have to find a way to accommodate it." Copeland said it more as a statement than a question.

"But you had no idea what you were doing." Slater was struggling to keep calm.

"This is nothing new," reasoned Copeland. "When scientists developed the atomic bomb, there was a fear it might cause a chain reaction and ignite the whole atmosphere, destroying all life on the planet. But it didn't stop them."

"So, you justify your actions by tempting fate a second time."

"Do you believe in fate, Liam?" mocked Dr Copeland. "That our destiny is shaped by forces beyond our control? You could be right, but since the same forces allowed such a device to exist, isn't its effect a part of that destiny? We put the present on a pedestal. The rock on which the very foundation of reality exists. But what is it? Nothing more than a transitional state – ephemeral, as it passes from the past into the future. The present barely exists. And what of the past? That only exists in our collective memory – it cannot be trusted. As for the future, isn't that just somebody else's past?"

"And how many time machines would it take, and how much interference in causal events before reality is ripped apart and we all descend into chaos?"

"I cannot answer that," confirmed Dr Copeland, "no one can. But wouldn't it be fun to find out."

Realising that they had exhausted this subject, Slater decided to change tack. He didn't want this man to become bored with him.

"What about the drug?" enquired Slater. "The Infinity Serum, did you take it?"

"I had no involvement with the drug. If I had taken it," said the scientist smiling menacingly, "there isn't a prison on the planet that could hold me. I'm afraid you had to be part of the inner sanctum for that privilege."

"How many people used the time machines and were there any casualties?

"Ah, so you have come to pick my brains," observed the doctor. "Why should I help you?"

"Your life here could be made more comfortable if you do," reasoned Slater, "as long as your requests are not too outrageous."

Copeland thought for a few seconds and then replied,

"I would like access to books and a television. The days are awfully long, don't you know."

"I'm sure that can be arranged."

Again, Copeland sat in deep thought weighing up his options. Eventually he nodded his agreement to these terms, realising that it was the best he could ever hope for.

"There were no casualties that I know of," he mused. "Why would you ask this?"

Slater didn't answer but his reticence betrayed his thoughts.

"You've tested one!" exclaimed the scientist, showing obvious glee. "You've tested one and it didn't work. What happened?"

"The pilot died. He had a heart attack." Slater knew that this was putting it mildly, but didn't care to elucidate.

"I know of four people who used the vessels," acknowledged Copeland.

"We are aware of three. Bormann, Hitler and a man named von Brandt," confirmed Slater, "but who was the fourth?"

"I believe a Polish Jew was the first."

"What was so different about these men?" enquired Slater.

"The question you need to ask yourself is: what did they have in common?"

Infuriated by Dr Copeland's evasive cryptic answers,

Slater decided to bring the interview to an end. He picked up the earpiece and stood up.

"Remember, Liam," said Dr Copeland as a parting shot, "the inner sanctum is the key." He closed his eyes again and lowered his head as Slater left the room.

General Chambers had opened the door to the viewing room and came out to confront him.

"What the hell did he mean by that?"

"The inner sanctum," speculated Slater, "they were the drug takers. But one of the time travellers was a guinea pig. Not part of the inner sanctum, he wouldn't have taken the drug."

Then it dawned on him.

"Of course, if they used him as a guinea pig for the time machine, they would have used him as a guinea pig for the drug too." Slater grinned in triumph. "That's it. To survive the trip through time you need to take the drug."

"So they are useless without it," confirmed an exasperated Chambers.

"It's the only explanation," agreed Slater.

"No drug was found in the wreckage after the bunker was cleared out," declared Chambers. "There must be someone, somewhere who knows, surely."

Slater thought of David and Laura, and the fate which befell her. Then he thought of Jessica. In the long nights sitting up in the cabin he pondered over the infant. The fact that she was the daughter of a man who had taken the Infinity Serum. It may be nothing but he doubted it. And Slater had no desire to thrust them back into the limelight. They had been through enough.

"There's no one," he uttered finally, "no one at all."

Twelve hours later, Slater was back in his cabin. Glad to be back to some kind of normality. Chambers had wanted him to stay, but he was determined to be as far removed as possible. Going his own way had kept him alive thus far and if he was going to change his circumstances, it was going to be on his terms. Slater grabbed the wild turkey still hanging in the veranda and went inside to prepare it for dinner.

CHAPTER EIGHT

JUST ANOTHER COLD CASE

Mojave Desert, Nevada, California, Border
May 2007

The beaten-up old truck trundled along the desert road, and to Hank Miller's disgust something pink, wet and slippery slurped up his right cheek. Hot breath panted in his ear as he tried to push the mass of brown fur away from him. The truck swerved a little and Hank had to take evasive action to keep it straight. Sitting next to him was Zachary Stevens, who was trying, with little success, to keep an overexcited canine under control.

"Will you keep that damned mutt off me," Hank demanded, "before we have an accident."

"Sorry, Hank," said Zak, wincing. "He's always like this when he comes out with us."

The mutt in question was an oversized light brown Heinz 57 variety mongrel called Hendrix. The teenager dragged the dog across to sit between him and his girlfriend, Abigail Rawley. She sat pushed up against the passenger door in the cramped cabin.

"Oh, he's just overly friendly is all," replied Abigail with a big grin. "I think he likes you."

"Yeah, well I'd like him a whole lot better if he'd just calm down some."

Hank Miller was a man in his late forties who had a soft spot for Zak's mother, Mia. He found it difficult to say no to her and reluctantly agreed to take the kids out into the desert, dirt bike riding. It had recently been Zak's eighteenth birthday and his mother had bought him a Honda CRF250R dirt bike and Zak couldn't wait to put it through its paces. His mother had managed to scrape the money together to get him a 2001 model. As a single parent it was as much as she could afford. Hank had helped to get her a good deal and Zak was chuffed to bits with it.

"How much longer, Hank?" enquired Zak.

"We're nearly there," replied Hank as he looked in his wing mirror to see the ten-year-old grubby white four-wheel drive Suzuki Sidekick following behind. Zak's friend Oliver was driving with Zak's younger sister, Jasmine, sat beside him.

Oliver was following a little too close for Hank's liking, so he decided to give them plenty of notice when he turned right off the road and into the desert.

The truck trundled on for about thirty minutes before coming to a halt. The Suzuki pulled up beside it, and everyone piled out of their vehicles excitedly, to run around to the back of the truck.

"Okay, okay, hold your horses," exclaimed Hank with a big grin. "We need to slide the ramp out."

The ramp happened to be nothing more than two weathered wooden boards which Hank and the two boys pulled out and sloped to the ground. Sensing the excitement, the dog started bounding around the ramp barking.

"Will someone getta hold of that mutt," shouted Hank irritably.

"He just wants to join in," replied Jasmine petulantly, "and he's not a mutt!"

She grabbed the dog's collar and led him away from the truck.

"Come on, Hendrix," she soothed, giving the dog some fuss. "We love you even if they don't."

"Speak for yourself," said Abigail, frowning, looking down at the dog doubtfully.

By now two dirt bikes had been removed from the truck and a quad bike was being brought gingerly down the ramp. Oliver looked enviously at his best friend's red and white Honda as Zak swung his leg over the saddle.

"Dude, that is so dope," he enthused. His own bike was just a 50cc.

"I can't believe it," said Zak, nodding. "I didn't think Mom could afford one."

"She's been saving a while to get you this bike," advised Hank, "so you just look after it."

"Yes, sir," replied Zak. "Where are we going?"

Hank pointed to a ridge of hills where jagged red sandstone shimmered in the heat.

"You see that bluff over there," he declared, starting up the quad bike, "well, there's some uneven ground just as you approach it. You can practise there."

The two boys kick-started their bikes and Abigail walked over to Zak and gave him a peck on the cheek.

"Be careful," she said, smiling.

Zak smiled back and the three bikes accelerated away kicking up dust in the process. The two girls needed all their strength to hold Hendrix and prevent him from following. He barked until the bikes could no longer be seen or heard, then he went about his business, sniffing around in the sand.

The two girls sat against the rear wheel of the truck taking advantage of the shade it offered. They watched Hendrix absentmindedly mooching about, then Jasmine turned to Abigail.

"What do you think of Ollie?" Her voice was hesitant. "Do you think he's cute?"

"You think he's gorgeous," sang Abigail with a big grin. "You want to date him, make love and marry him."

"Stop it," said Jasmine with a frown, shoving her friend in mock annoyance. The film quote wasn't lost on her. She chuckled at her friend's teasing. "Yeah, I like him but he doesn't show much interest."

"Those two are as bad as each other," complained Abigail. "I'm sure I take second place to that damn bike."

Hendrix walked over to the passenger side door, sat, looked up and began barking.

"Now what?" Hendrix was beginning to get on Abigail's nerves.

"He wants his ball."

"Let him have the damn thing, if it'll shut him up."

Jasmine opened the door and Hendrix began running around with excitement. She pulled out a bright yellow tennis ball and a long tennis ball launcher.

"Hey, chill out. Let's play ball," said Jasmine, smiling. She placed the ball in the cup at one end and with a full swing of her arm flung the ball about one hundred feet. Without hesitation, Hendrix bounded after it. He returned less than a minute later with the ball in his mouth and his tail wagging profusely. She grabbed hold of the ball and tried to extricate it from the canine's mouth, but Hendrix was having none of it. Eventually he relented and Jasmine placed the ball in the launcher again, to send it even further.

"He wants me to throw it," she said, grimacing, wiping dog saliva down the side of her shorts, "but he never wants to give it back."

"Stupid dog," observed Abigail.

Very soon Hendrix was back again. This time he dropped the ball and Jasmine picked it up and placed it in the thrower.

"Look, you have a go. My arm is beginning to ache," said Jasmine, wincing. "He'll do this all day."

As Abigail reluctantly took the launcher, they heard the buzzing sound of the bikes getting nearer. A cloud of dust could just be discerned beyond a sea of shrubs. Bringing her arm back as far as she could, the teenager flung the ball as far as her strength would allow. They watched the ball fly through the air in the direction of a Joshua tree. Hendrix was on his way again, bounding out to intercept the projectile as the two girls were distracted by the antics of the bikers. It wasn't long before Jasmine realised that Hendrix hadn't returned. She squinted in the direction that he had gone and frowned. The dog had lost interest in the ball and was now circling near the tree and sniffing the ground. Then he began to excavate, and as sand flew up behind him, Hendrix's hindquarters raised up as his front paws dug ever deeper.

"What's the stupid mutt doing now?" enquired Abigail.

"He must have a scent," replied Jasmine. "He's not stupid and he's not a mutt."

They returned their gaze to the dirt bikes until both girls saw movement in their peripheral vision. It was Hendrix returning.

"Now what has he got?" said Abigail with a sigh.

"Looks like a stick," suggested Jasmine.

The intrepid canine bounded closer, and as he approached them it became clear that the stick in his mouth had four fingers and a thumb. Hendrix dropped his prize onto the sand and the two teenagers stared at it in horror. The hand was attached to the right forearm of an adult human. The skin, which had dried and shrunk around the bones, was patchy in colour – a dark tan to very dark brown, almost black. The parchment-like skin had a leathery texture and had gone black at the joints. On the forefinger was a signet ring slightly dulled but clearly gold.

"What the hell!" exclaimed Jasmine as she stared at the withered arm and then at the dog, who was looking back at her expectantly and panting.

"Oh my God, that's gross," said Abigail, wincing and putting her hand over her mouth. "I think I'm going to hurl."

Squatting on one knee, Jasmine decided to inspect the arm a little closer. For some reason it was the fact that the fingers had still retained their discoloured nails which repulsed her the most.

"The ring has an engraving on it. Initials, I think."

"Shut up," whined Abigail. "I don't want to look at it."

Jasmine stood back up again and looked over to the Joshua tree and the small mound of sand that Hendrix had created.

"What are we going to do?" whined Abigail again.

Jasmine thought for a few seconds, and then said,

"Put the dog in the truck and crack open a window, I'm going to check out that hole he's dug."

With Abigail following reluctantly a few paces behind, Jasmine made her way purposefully towards the small mound of sand. As she approached and looked over the mound, a shallow depression came into view. She didn't say anything but simply put her hand to her mouth as she gasped in shock.

In the depression was the partially exposed body of a mummified corpse. Part of the upper right chest, right arm and shoulder were displayed along with most of the head. Seconds later Abigail was alongside her and looking in. She didn't look for long, before turning away and running over to a bush. She knelt down and began to retch.

The extent to which the body had decayed was much like the arm, being well preserved, with dark tan and brown-black parchment-like skin, stretched over the bones like a drum skin. The head had lost its eyes and the lips had shrunk away to reveal a full set of teeth which were still remarkably white, making the macabre grin all the more startling. Much of the hair was still on the scalp and looked wiry and wild.

Looking over to the truck, Hank braked and saw that no one appeared to be there. He scanned the near vicinity and was relieved to see the two girls near a Joshua tree. Their demeanour looked odd to him, so he put the quad bike into gear and raced over towards them with concern.

"Where's Hank off to?" enquired Ollie, who had stopped when he noticed Hank heading away from them.

"Dunno," said Zak, frowning, "let's go and find out."

The two girls heard the quad bike pull up to a stop near them and watched Hank dismount. He noticed Abigail wiping her mouth and tears on her cheeks. As he walked up to a clearly distressed Jasmine, he glanced into the hole.

"What the fuck!" he exclaimed. "How did you find this?"

"It wasn't us, it was Hendrix," explained Jasmine. "He dug up an arm and brought it to us."

"That freaking mutt." Hank took a closer look and frowned. "We need to inform the police about this."

"He's not a mutt," shouted Jasmine and burst into tears.

At that moment Zak arrived, braking heavily and throwing up sand.

"For Christ's sake be careful, Zak," bellowed Hank. "We might have a crime scene here."

Zak swung his leg off the saddle and laid his bike on its side. As he did so the front wheel displaced some sand and two small thin glass tubes poked out about an inch by the tyre.

"Woah," barked Zak as he spied the corpse, "that is so rad."

"Fuck!" exclaimed Ollie in a hushed tone as he stepped up and peered down.

"What are we gonna do?" enquired Ollie, looking at Hank.

"There's only one thing we can do," he confirmed, "call the police. We'd better go and do it now."

They all moved away from the grave except Zak who couldn't seem to take his eyes off the body.

"Zak," shouted Hank, "come on!"

"Coming," replied Zak, snapping out of it.

He grabbed the handlebars of his bike then noticed the glint of two glass nozzles poking out of the sand by his front wheel. Reaching down he dipped his hand into the sand and scooped the two objects up. As he allowed the sand to filter through his fingers, Zak was left with two glass ampules about three inches long with a thin neck and a bulbous base. Holding one in his left hand, he turned it, then shook it. He noticed the objects were filled with a clear liquid.

"Zak!" insisted Hank, more forcefully this time. "Shift your butt now!"

Looking behind him, he saw the others a good fifty yards away. He put the ampules in the top pocket of his jacket and rode back to catch up with them.

***

The sun was low in the sky when Detective Peter Jacks watched the truck and the Suzuki pull away. They headed out west and he could feel the sun warm on his face as he

MARTIN GUNN

placed a pair of Ray-Bans over his eyes. The temperature had dropped to a comfortable twenty-one degrees Celsius, for which he was truly grateful. Jacks turned his attention to the tent which had been erected over the exposed body over an hour ago. He placed his notebook in the inside pocket of his jacket and strolled casually over to a figure dressed in a hooded white coverall.

As she pulled down the hood, Detective Lieutenant Cynthia Kiefer put the edge of her right hand over her eyes to protect them from the glare of the sun, which was now a big orange orb just above the horizon. She watched as Jacks approached in his dark blue Canali suit, white button-down shirt and grey paisley tie. With a flourish, he removed his sunglasses, folded them and placed them in his top pocket.

"Jesus," said Kiefer, wincing, "you are such a poseur."

"Yes, ma'am," chuckled Jacks. To him it was a compliment.

"Did you get much out of them?"

"Not so much," confirmed Jacks. "The dog dug up the arm and then they found the body. I think they're in shock."

"Hardly surprising, it's pretty grisly."

"How is it going in there?" enquired Jacks, gesturing to inside the tent.

"Well, if you'd put one of these damn things on, you could see for yourself," admonished Lieutenant Kiefer.

"What and mess up a $2000 suit," blurted out Jacks. "I think not."

Shaking her head in disbelief, Kiefer sighed.

"Trust me to be landed with a fashion victim."

They both watched as the crime scene investigators went about their business, then one of them stood up and walked

165

over to the detectives. The hooded figure removed a pair of safety goggles and pulled down her hood to reveal a woman in her mid-thirties. Dr Veronica Coleman shook her head to rearrange her shoulder-length fair hair, then fixed her attention on the two police officers with a grim expression.

"We've found another body," she announced finally. "You need to come and look."

She gave Jacks a look of disapproval and continued.

"We've uncovered a shotgun too."

"Stay here while the adults deal with this." Lieutenant Kiefer's tone was mocking and patronising.

"Jacks, you're such a popinjay," said Dr Coleman, smiling as she turned and followed the detective.

"A what?" retorted Jacks lamely, not sure whether he'd been insulted. "Yeah, well… one of us has got to be."

The two women stared down at the bodies lying side by side in a shallow depression. The first thing Kiefer noticed was that the sockets where the eyes would have been on the first body were nothing but gaping holes, whereas the eyes of the second were covered in skin, suggesting they were shut. Dr Coleman stood closer to the first body and knelt down. Lieutenant Kiefer followed suit.

"Both bodies are male and are remarkably well preserved," commented Dr Coleman.

"Yes, I was surprised by that."

"I take it you are not familiar with taphonomy?" asked Dr Coleman.

"No, enlighten me," said Kiefer with a frown.

"It's the study of decaying organic matter," Coleman explained, "from death, through all the stages of decomposition to eventual fossilisation. The environment which organic matter is exposed to can make a big difference to how this process manifests itself. In this case an arid climate along with a burial in sand impeded the decomposing process. The fluids within the body would have been quickly absorbed or dried out by its surroundings, thus restricting the bacteria from thriving and doing their job."

"How long do you think it would have taken to get to this state?"

"Well, it's hard to say," said Coleman, frowning; she hated having to be vague. "Maybe ten, fifteen years. But they could remain in this condition for centuries."

"At least hopefully we can identify them from their dental records," offered Kiefer.

The forensic scientist decided to move on quickly to points that she was clear on.

"You can see severe trauma to the chest," she advised, indicating the gaping hole. "There are also random cartridge pellets around the periphery of the wound. This man was killed with a shotgun and probably both barrels. He died with his eyes wide open, so he may have been taken by surprise. The gun which probably killed him has been found buried with them."

"Good, we can check it for prints."

"This will be of interest to you," continued Dr Coleman, offering an evidence bag to the lieutenant.

"The ring on the arm the dog found?" replied Kiefer, taking the bag.

"It has an inscription on it. Initials C.H. That should hopefully narrow down your investigation."

"What about the other body?"

"Ah yes," considered Dr Coleman, "this one is a little more curious, to say the least."

"Oh, how?"

"On first inspection there are no obvious signs to the cause of death," Dr Coleman pondered, "but look at his torso, it is much flatter than the other. Almost as if it had been squashed. And the jawbone, look how distorted it is. Almost as if it's been melted. I can't tell you any more about that until I get him on the slab."

"Let me know what your findings are."

Lieutenant Kiefer thanked Dr Coleman, took the evidence bag with the ring in it and walked back to where Jacks' silhouette was waiting patiently as night began to descend.

"If it wasn't for those kids coming out here," offered Jacks, "we may never have found them."

"I know," said Kiefer, nodding.

"They were really pissed 'cause they were delayed from getting home. Especially that guy Miller."

"Yeah, well, shit happens, doesn't it," snapped Kiefer and walked down to their car. She opened the door, sat down on the passenger side and glanced over at Jacks as he settled into the driving seat.

"We've got one lead at least," she said, brandishing the evidence bag, "the initials of one of the victims. We need to check our records for anyone with the initials C.H. who went missing in, say, the last fifty years."

"Fifty years!" exclaimed Jacks.

"Yeah," warned Kiefer, "that could be just for starters."

***

The clock on the kitchen wall ticked around to 18.45 and Mia Stevens frowned, then huffed in exasperation. She checked on the dinner that was simmering on the stove. Then she checked the oven.

"What's the matter, Mommy?"

Cassandra was her youngest child, being ten years younger than Jasmine. She sat at the kitchen table painting and looking at her mother curiously.

"It's that brother and sister of yours," explained Mia, "they're late."

Five minutes later the kitchen door burst open and Zak, Jasmine and Hendrix, followed by Hank, piled in.

"Where the hell have you been?" Mia implored. "Dinner's nearly ruined."

"We found a dead body," blurted out Zak excitedly. "Well, Hendrix did."

Hendrix padded over to his bowl and began lapping up water noisily. He looked at his food, ignored it and walked over to his basket and sat down panting, oblivious to the trouble he'd caused.

"We tried to call you but you didn't pick up," explained Jasmine.

Mia checked her cell phone; it was dead.

"Well, there's still the landline," she countered.

The teenagers looked at her as if she was speaking a foreign language.

"I'm sorry, Mia," said Hank, wincing, "but we had to wait for the police and give a statement."

"A body," she mused. "Do they know who it is?"

"I doubt it," interjected Jasmine. "Looked like it had been there for years."

169

"Was it a skellington?" gasped a wide-eyed Cassandra.

"It was a mummy," teased Zak in a scary voice and gesticulating his arms in a contorted manner, "and it's coming to get ya."

"Mom, Zak's scaring me," whined Cassandra.

"Way to go, Zak," admonished Jasmine, putting an arm around Cassandra. "Make things worse, why don't you. Ignore him, Cassie, he's an idiot."

Not wanting to be scolded any further by a clearly flustered Mia, Hank decided to make his excuses and beat a hasty retreat.

"Look, I'd better go," he declared, opening the kitchen door. "Sorry again for being late."

Mia approached him and leant against the doorframe then placed a consolatory hand on his arm.

"Thanks for doing this. I really appreciate it," she said, smiling. "I was just worried is all."

"Any time," Hank returned the smile. "I'll catch ya later."

Mia watched Hank walk to his car and drive off. She was aware of his soft spot for her and it made her feel guilty that she didn't feel the same way. Sometimes she worried that she might be using Hank, but the kids really liked him. Putting the thought out of her mind, Mia turned her attention to dinner.

"Okay, clear the table for dinner," she ordered, "food is ready."

"What you painting, Cass?" enquired Jasmine, approaching the table.

"A house," replied Cassie, brandishing it proudly.

"Don't we have decorators for that?" joked Zak with a grin.

"Idiot," snapped Jasmine, rolling her eyes.

Zak began removing his denim jacket and as he did so, he heard a faint chinking sound coming from his top pocket. After hanging his jacket on the back of the chair, he pulled one of the ampules out and held it aloft.

"I found these in the sand," he proclaimed.

"These?" said Jasmine, frowning, staring at the single object.

"Yeah I've got another one in my coat pocket."

"Oh my God, you idiot," censured Jasmine. "Did you find those near the body?"

"What if I did?" replied Zak sheepishly.

"Well, didn't you think you should've handed them to the cops?"

"Well… I, I didn't think," spluttered Zak. "In the commotion I forgot all about them."

"Let me see that." Mia grabbed the ampule and examined it. A loud hiss came from behind her as a pan began to boil over onto the hob, so she put it down on the table and turned to attend to dinner.

"You two, go and wash up, it's ready."

The two teenagers reluctantly walked out of the room to do as they were told. Cassie reached over the table and picked up the ampule. She looked at it, she shook it, then she held it close to her right eye.

"It looks like a genie bottle," she announced finally. "I can't see a genie in it."

"Put these knives and forks out, Cassie," requested Mia, ignoring her, whilst taking the ampule and putting it back down on the table.

Jasmine and Zak returned and sat down just as Mia

lowered a plate onto the centre of the table. The ampule was knocked out of the way and wobbled over close to Cassie and stopped near the edge.

The kids looked at the plate of food, grinned and began singing at the top of their voices.

"*Like a bat out of hell I'll be gone when the morning comes…*"

"Do you have to sing that every time I make meatloaf," sighed Mia. "It's starting to get old now."

"Well, it's an old song," said Zak, beaming.

The smell of meat brought the attention of Hendrix, who sauntered over and sat next to Cassie, the only one who sneaked him any morsels of food. He looked up panting expectantly with what looked like a slice of ham hanging out of the side of his mouth.

Eventually, everyone sat down and was piling food onto their plates. Suddenly realising how hungry they were, all three began to tuck in heartily. Cassie sneaked a piece of meatloaf to Hendrix, who gulped it down with gusto.

"You call the police up about that little bottle thing, do you hear me," admonished Mia, pointing her knife in Zak's direction, "as soon as we've eaten."

Zak nodded and continued to tuck in.

"Pass it to me, Cass," requested Jasmine. "I haven't seen it yet."

Cassie picked up the ampule and threw it in Jasmine's direction. The teenager plucked it from the air, inches from her face.

"I said pass it, not throw it. You silly girl," glowered Jasmine.

She examined the curious vessel and, just like all the others, could make very little of it.

"What do you think that fluid is?" she mused, placing the ampule back down on the table and picking up her fork.

"Could be anything," said Zak, shrugging. "Pass it back so I can put it with the other one."

Jasmine put down her fork again and flicked it over to Zak, harder than she had intended. The ampule wobbled rapidly in an arc over to Cassie who tried to stop it dropping off the edge. With a fork in her hand, however, she clumsily managed to knock it faster on its trajectory, where it dropped off the edge to be snapped up by an unsuspecting Hendrix. He yelped as broken glass cut into his gums and tongue. The innocuous-looking clear liquid slid slowly down his throat.

All four looked at the hapless dog and then at each other. Hendrix began to give a high-pitched whimper as a little blood seeped out of the side of his mouth.

"Is he alright?" shrieked Mia from the other side of the table.

"He's bleeding some," said Zak, wincing.

"Somebody, help him," cried Cassie.

Hendrix stood motionless for a few minutes as they gathered around him. Zak opened his mouth to try and extricate any broken glass.

"The bleeding has stopped," he said, pulling some jagged shards out.

Suddenly Hendrix's eyes became wide and bright. He knocked Zak for six and bounded onto the table, sending plates, cutlery and food flying. In a manic display, Hendrix began spinning around as if chasing his own tail but much faster. Then he bounded off the table, through an open door and landed in the middle of the sitting room. The family looked at each other; the jump was extraordinary. Way beyond his capability. He turned and looked at them all, almost pleadingly and then began to shake uncontrollably.

"I think he's fitting," exclaimed Mia, rushing to the poor dog's aid.

By now Hendrix had collapsed and was on his side still convulsing. Then, just as suddenly as it had started, the seizures stopped. Mia squatted next to him and started to stroke his head when she was startled by a thick dark brown liquid which oozed out of the Hendrix's mouth. She stumbled back in disgust.

"Oh God!" screamed Jasmine, putting her hands to her nose. "That smells disgusting."

Cassandra began to scream hysterically and Mia tried to calm her down.

"What's happened to Hendrix?" she bawled. "Is he alright?"

"What is that stuff?" brooded Zak. Then realising what he had brought home, cried, "How was I to know it was dangerous?"

Mia was panicking inside, not knowing what to do. She pulled her sleeve over her nose; God, the smell, it was like nothing on earth and seemed to seep into your very skin. Snapping herself out of it, Mia turned to the kids.

"You two, get Cassie upstairs and try and calm her down."

The teenagers just stared blankly back.

"Do it!" she shouted. "Now!"

When the kids were finally out of the way, Mia stumbled to the kitchen door; she coughed, spluttered and tried to fight the wave of nausea which had come over her. When she had finally got her composure back, Mia stepped back into the kitchen, picked up Jasmine's cell phone and dialled 911.

***

Since being promoted to lieutenant detective five years ago, Cynthia Kiefer had been given two cold case murders to solve. Leaning back in her chair Kiefer sighed and closed her eyes. Cold cases often remained unsolved – an unsatisfying situation for the police and no closure for anyone else. She hated them, and now she sat alone in her office lumbered with another. In her opinion raking up the past like this rarely did anybody any good. For friends and family, it meant opening up old wounds long since healed and often forgotten, and for what? To investigate a crime which she had little hope of solving. If Dr Coleman was right and these remains were hundreds of years old, there may not be anyone to interview, and no way of identifying the bodies. Dental records wouldn't help, but they did at least have the engraved ring. The detective picked up the evidence bag and examined its contents. Shining brightly through the PVC was the signet ring with the initials C.H. clearly engraved upon it. Hopefully this investigation would be short. With an overwhelming feeling of antipathy, Kiefer flung the bag onto her desk just as Detective Jacks burst in.

"There's been a 911 call from the Stevens family," he announced excitedly.

"The family who found the body?"

"Yeah, something about their dog."

"Well, can't uniform deal with it?" sighed Kiefer. She'd had enough for one evening.

"It was uniform who called it in," replied Jacks. "They want you there. It seems something odd has happened."

"Okay," said Kiefer, frowning as she stood up and grabbed her keys. She paused and thought for a second. "This doesn't need both of us, you stay here and work on those initials. I'll probably be back within the hour."

It was dark as Kiefer pulled up behind the black and white patrol car and looked across at the Stevens' residence. A number of onlookers had come out of their homes to watch as officers began to tape off the area.

Looks like the ghouls are out in force, she thought with utter contempt.

As she stepped out of her car she was greeted by a uniformed officer. He was slightly overweight, balding and approaching middle age.

"Good evening, ma'am." His manor was perfunctory. "I'm officer Walter Stokes. Me and my partner were called out here by a hysterical mother."

"Their dog," confirmed Kiefer.

"Yes, ma'am," declared Officer Stokes, "it's dead and it's not a pretty sight. If you've got some cream you can put under your nose, well, I suggest you use it. The smell is real bad."

"Trust me, officer, if such a cream existed, I would've known about it by now."

As a precaution, Kiefer reached into her glove box and pulled out a grey N95 respirator mask.

"Right," she said, smiling grimly, "lead the way."

Stokes led her up to a side door which gave access to the kitchen. About three yards from the opening, Stokes held back and let the detective continue. A yard from the entrance, the odour hit her like a brick wall. Immediately she placed the mask over her face and hooked the loops around her ears. Gingerly she entered the kitchen and made her way to the sitting room. Even with the mask on, the smell was difficult to endure. In the middle of the room lay the body of the dog with a disgusting brown goo which had oozed out onto the floorboards. She squatted and studied the sludge. What in God's name was it?

Standing up she walked back into the kitchen and picked up a cutlery knife from the floor, then returned. With the knife, she carefully prodded the sludge. Initially it gave some resistance before pushing through. The substance had formed a skin rather like a rice pudding. Kiefer retracted the knife with some sludge on the blade. It seemed to be of even consistency and colour.

"What have we got here then?"

The detective was snapped out of her concentration and pivoted to see Dr Veronica Coleman standing over her in white coveralls, goggles and a respirator. Standing up, Kiefer placed her head close to Coleman's.

"Thank goodness you're here," she said with conviction, "I need some air."

The doctor nodded and watched Kiefer leave before investigating her subject. The air outside was a blessed relief and Kiefer grabbed at the mask. She breathed in deeply, relishing the fresh cool breeze.

Officer Stokes approached her, holding an evidence bag.

"We spoke to the family and it seems the dog swallowed one of these."

"What is it?" enquired Kiefer, studying the ampule inside.

"Couldn't say, ma'am," said Stokes with a shrug. "The boy found two of them near the bodies and decided to keep it to himself. Lucky for them that the dog got to it first. Whatever it is, I'd sure as hell treat it with respect."

"Indeed," replied the detective absentmindedly, still staring at the ampule. "Where are the family now?"

"They're with a friend right now," advised Stokes, "a guy called Hank Miller."

"He was one of the people from earlier today," mused Kiefer almost to herself. "Oh and thanks, officer… Walter, isn't it?"

"Yes, ma'am," said Stokes, smiling as he walked back to his patrol car.

Ten minutes went by and eventually the forensic scientist appeared from the doorway. She was carrying an evidence bag containing a phial filled with some of the brown sludge. Removing her mask, she too inhaled deeply to rid her nostrils of the pungent aroma.

"I will need to analyse this to see what's in it," she gasped.

"I've never seen anything like it," groaned Kiefer.

"And did you notice the body?"

Kiefer shook her head.

"Just like one of the bodies in the desert, it's flat," she continued, "as though nothing is supporting the outer skin. Hopefully we'll know more after I've examined them."

Judging by what she had seen, Lieutenant Kiefer had her doubts about that. As she walked out onto the front lawn, she saw the uniformed officers talking to a journalist. The man was short, wearing a shabby beige suit, and had grey, thinning hair. Even from behind, in the darkness, she recognised him instantly.

McQuillan! How the hell did he get on to this so quick? she thought.

Striding briskly over to the three men, she interjected.

"Okay, enough," she blurted. "You'll have to wait for an official statement in due course. Just when we know what we are dealing with."

The journalist protested but, realising he wasn't going to get anything else for the moment, slinked away like a thief in the night.

As Kiefer watched the dog being wheeled out in a body bag, her cell phone rang. She looked at the screen; it was Detective Jacks.

"Yes, Peter," she greeted.

"I think I might have the owner of the ring."

"Really?" declared Kiefer. "That was quick. How far back did you have to go?"

"Twenty-two years."

"Is that all? I'm on my way back to the station now," she advised.

"Damn," she cursed. "Twenty-two years! Easily within living memory. There will be people to notify."

"Damn," Kiefer repeated again to herself as she pulled away in her dark grey sedan.

CHAPTER NINE

THE CHRONOS PROTOCOL

Evergreen, Jefferson County, Colorado
May 2007

The door opened in the Lakeside Café and Martha Berry smiled as she saw the man she expected step in and frown. After what seemed to be a winter of hibernation, activity around Evergreen Lake was beginning to awaken. The café was a little too busy for the man's liking, but after years of coming here he was used to it.

Martha had served him breakfast most mornings ever since she had worked here, and she liked him. He wasn't especially tall or dashing but he was always polite and courteous, which was more than she could say about many of her customers. Courtesy went a long way with Martha, having had to put up with her fair share of jerks over the years. She glided along the counter as he approached.

"Morning, Liam," she said breezily and smiled. "The usual?"

"Yes please." Liam Slater returned the smile, then glanced around the room. "It's getting busy in here."

"Sure is," agreed Martha. "I'm afraid your corner booth is taken today."

"Oh well," said Slater with a grimace, mounting a stool by the counter, "I'll just have to sit here and put up with you."

He grinned and winked; socialising with Martha suited him just fine.

"Don't put yourself out on my account," fretted Martha in mock indignation. "Coffee?"

Slater laughed and nodded as Martha poured him a steaming mug of the black liquid. He liked Evergreen; the place had a shambolic, nineteenth-century frontier town feel about it and ever since Martha had begun working here, he made a point of coming in whenever he could. Even though she was in her late forties, Slater found her extremely attractive. Her husband had died five years previously and, for whatever reason, they were never blessed with children. The money here wasn't great but it didn't need to be. What Martha needed, initially at least, was a reason to get up in the morning, and working in the café provided that impetus. She had a good figure for a woman her age with shoulder-length brown wavy hair framing a face that, though not stunningly beautiful, was pleasant and kindly. For some time now Slater had considered asking her out. He definitely sensed something there between them, a rapport, but was reluctant to involve her in his life and the baggage that came with it. Simply put, he didn't want to place her in danger.

In no time at all a plate of hot food was placed in front of him.

"*Bon appétit*," she said with a smile.

Slater looked down with relish at the dish. Three rashers of streaky bacon, two sausages, two fried eggs over easy and baked beans. Beside that, Martha placed two rounds of toast and left him in peace to eat.

Eventually he pushed the empty plate away and wiped his mouth with a paper napkin. Martha approached and topped up his mug, then handed him a newspaper. Before Slater could look at the front cover of *The Denver Post*, Martha leant over.

"The cinema listings are on page twenty," she hinted, beaming at him. "Do you like going to see films?"

"Sometimes," commented Slater, pretending to miss the hint. Nevertheless he leafed through the pages until he reached number twenty. He scanned down the list.

"There's a film here called *Waitress*," he laughed. "How about that one?"

"Great, just the kind of escapism I'm looking for," groaned Martha, rolling her eyes.

"Tell you what, why don't you pick one and I'll take you tonight."

Martha grabbed the newspaper and swung it round to check the listings for herself.

"There are a few here that we could see." She scanned down in concentration. "*Lonely Hearts*, *The Condemned* or *Next*, maybe?"

"Sure, any of them," agreed Slater, who wasn't bothered either way. He was just happy to spend some time with her.

Martha showed her delight by giving his forearm a gentle shake and then moved off to serve another customer. Slater grabbed the newspaper and pulled it back round to read. He began flicking backwards through the pages looking for something interesting. Eventually he stopped at page ten as his eye caught a small headline near the bottom of the page. It read: "*Two mummified bodies found in the Mojave Desert.*"

Peering closer at the article, Slater read with fascination how the bodies were found and how a mysterious liquid had killed the dog of the family that had found them. The article went on to say that the liquid was now in the hands of the police who at the time of going to press had no comment. Leaning forwards on his stool, Slater placed a hand on each cheek and began to ponder. He didn't like the sound of this one bit. After serving her customer, Martha noticed Slater deep in thought. She approached him.

"A penny for them?"

Slater glanced up, snapped out of his reverie.

"I'm sorry, Martha," he lamented, "we're going to have to take a rain check on that date."

"Oh, why?" Martha's disappointment was palpable.

"I can't say," replied Slater, slipping off the stool, "but I need to go – now."

As he moved to the door, Martha strode around the counter towards him, a look of confusion on her face.

"What's wrong? Where are you going? You can at least tell me that," she said, frowning.

"San Francisco. There's something I need to deal with."

"You will be back – right?" Martha's large brown eyes were full of tears.

"Of course," said Slater, nodding. "I can't say exactly when."

"You promise me?" insisted Martha.

"I promise," soothed Slater.

Martha gave him a hug and the ex-CIA agent walked out the door with a feeling of unease. He had no idea what he was walking into and he may have just made a promise which he would be in no position to keep.

***

Bethesda, Montgomery County, Maryland
May 2007

As Elinor McInnes absentmindedly sipped her coffee, she stared at the wall of newsprint which separated her from her husband. When it was only at weekends, she had tolerated such ignominy, but now that Alex had retired, she was confronted with it every morning during breakfast. She'd had enough. Placing her cup down, Elinor stood up and moved to the worktop. Pulling a carving knife off the magnetic strip on the wall, she ran the blade through the knife sharpener fixed to the worktop and walked back to her seat. Leaning across the kitchen table, she gripped the top of the newspaper with her left hand and with the knife in her right, slid the razor-sharp blade down the centre crease. The two halves flopped open like the parting of the Red Sea to reveal her astonished husband looking more than a little startled.

"What the hell!" exclaimed Alex McInnes, gathering the pages together.

"It's just that I almost forgot what you looked like," she replied with a sardonic grin, placing the knife back on the wall.

"Couldn't you have just said something?"

"Haven't you always said that actions speak louder than words," she reminded him, "and I think I got my point across."

The beleaguered ex-CIA director picked up the mess of pages and stood up.

"I'm going to the sitting room for a bit of peace," he complained.

"Coffee?" said his wife with a grin.

"Yes," barked McInnes, clearly rattled, then added a little calmer, "please."

Elinor filled his cup, and McInnes picked it up and began to move towards the sitting room. However, with coffee in one hand and the dishevelled newspaper in the other, it wasn't long before pages were beginning to drop to the floor.

"For fuck's sake," he muttered.

His wife simply smiled inwardly at the chaos she had caused and continued to sip her coffee.

Placing his cup back on the table, McInnes squatted down to pick up the pages, and as he did so, his attention was drawn to one particular headline. He paused there and read intently.

"What is it?" enquired Elinor, who had noticed he had suddenly become preoccupied.

"Err... nothing," replied McInnes.

He stood up and placed the page down on the table and walked out of the kitchen. His wife pulled the page across and looked at the headline: "*Two mummified bodies found in the Mojave Desert.*" She walked to the kitchen door and saw her husband enter the study and close the door behind him. Elinor knew from experience that this was his way of saying, "Do Not Disturb!"

His study was festooned with clutter accumulated over decades and it was just how McInnes liked it. The small room was like a haven – reassuringly familiar and comfortable. Its disorganised appearance, however, belied the fact that he could put his hand to anything he needed. He reached up to a bookshelf and pulled out a hardback novel, *Pudd'nhead Wilson*, by Mark Twain. Inside the dust jacket was a slip of paper with a line of letters and numbers written upon it. Removing the slip of paper, he sat down at his desk and switched on his laptop. As the device booted up, a line of applications appeared down the left-hand side and the rest of the screen filled with images of yellow folders, each with a number below it. The slip showed two digits and a hyphen, which indicated to him which folder to select. He double-clicked the folder and it opened up on the screen. An encrypted program was displayed entitled '*Central Intelligence Agency*' and below that the word '*Protocols*'. Moving down to a window, McInnes scrolled through several words until he found what he was looking for. He selected the word '*Chronos*' which then brought up a dialogue box with two buttons: '*Activate*' and '*Cancel*'. Moving the cursor over to the Activate button, he hovered for a second and then pressed it. Picking up his cell phone, McInnes scrolled through his contacts and selected a number, then waited for the other end to answer.

"General Chambers?" he asked eventually. "Are you busy? Good. I'm afraid it's time to come out of retirement."

The study door opened again and Elinor watched as her preoccupied husband emerged.

"For goodness' sake, what is it?" she implored.

"I need to report in to headquarters," McInnes replied eventually.

"Why?" Elinor enquired, looking crestfallen. "You're supposed to be retired."

The ex-CIA director embraced his wife in an attempt to placate her.

"Unfinished business," he imparted with a sigh.

The answer told Elinor nothing and she knew not to press him any further.

***

CIA Headquarters, Langley, Virginia
May 2007

This particular Tuesday morning started like any other day for Katrina Hart as she began her shift at nine o'clock. Being an office-bound operative suited her just fine. She didn't relish the potential dangers that field agents could get themselves into and was quite happy to live out their exploits vicariously through the reports she read.

Katrina signed in, and made her way over to her computer, switched on, then walked over to a vending machine to get a cup of coffee. She took a sip and pulled a face. The light brown beverage was disgusting, so she made a mental note to try the hot chocolate next time. When she returned to her workstation, the monitor was flashing with an alert. Hastily she sat down and clicked on the pulsing message. The screen stopped flashing and changed to a dialogue box which read: '*Chronos Protocol Activated*' and a list of three names. Alex McInnes, General Sterling Chambers and Liam Slater. Reaching for the phone on her desk, Katrina punched in a number.

"Get me the director of operations – urgently."

With his predecessor having been in the job for just over ten years, Lucas Foster knew McInnes would be a tough act to follow. He had only been in the job a few months and was struggling to live up to his mentor's monumental reputation.

At the age of thirty-three, Foster was relatively young to be appointed director of operations, a point he was fully aware of. He hadn't settled in as quickly as he had hoped and still at times felt out of his depth. The intercom buzzed on his desk and Foster leaned over and flicked a switch.

"Yes?"

"You have an internal call on two," replied his secretary.

"Who is it?" pressed Foster.

"Katrina Hart," she advised and knowing that the name would mean nothing to him, added, "She's an operative who works on the second floor."

"Can't someone else deal with it?"

"She's most insistent, sir."

"Okay," sighed Foster, "put her through."

The phone rang and Foster picked it up. Before he

even spoke Foster was getting irritable, expecting this to be a complete waste of his time.

"Yes, Katrina," announced Foster in a slightly patronising manner, "what can I do for you?"

"A protocol has just been activated, sir," gasped Katrina.

"Which one?" enquired Foster, sitting up straight and giving his full attention.

"Chronos Protocol," she replied. "It happened at 08.26 this morning."

"You'd better come up immediately," ordered Foster.

Five minutes later, Katrina approached her boss's office. To the right was a desk where his secretary sat. The middle-aged, frumpy-looking woman peered over the top of her spectacles in an overbearing aloof manner and said,

"You can go straight in."

Then with equal indifference turned her attention back to the PC in front of her. Katrina moved towards the door; she adjusted her attire and knocked tentatively.

"Come," came a voice from behind the door. Katrina hated it when people responded in this way. To her it was a discourteous response to a courteous act, which she considered arrogant and pompous.

The director of operations looked up to see a woman only a few years younger than himself enter the room. She looked smart in a blue-grey trouser suit and plain cream blouse which complemented her short fair hair. Makeup and jewellery were understated, giving her a professional bearing. Foster smiled approvingly and gestured for Katrina to sit.

"What's this all about?" he asked.

"I, err, don't know, sir," stammered Katrina. "Full access is above my pay grade. All I can tell you is this protocol has been activated by Alex McInnes about an hour ago and he is en route here right now. He is one of three listed on the alert."

Foster raised his eyebrows at this news. *What does the old man think he's doing?* he wondered.

"Chronos?" queried Foster with a frown.

"In Greek mythology, he's the personification of time," enlightened Katrina.

"Oh – right," replied Foster. "Well, let's see what it's all about."

He typed in his authorisation code and navigated his way into the relevant files.

Katrina watched patiently as Foster opened folder after folder in silence. Eventually he looked up and seemed more perplexed than before.

"It would seem that this protocol is to be invoked if anything crops up relating to a drug known as the Infinity Serum, or a bell-shaped…"

Foster paused, reluctant to continue.

"Bell-shaped what?" enquired Katrina, intrigued.

"Time machine," scoffed Foster, "a bell-shaped time machine."

"Well, that would explain the Chronos reference," commented Katrina. "Am I allowed to see the files?"

"It's all to do with something called Project Phoenix," added Foster.

He turned the screen so that they both could view the files and systematically he clicked on them. They stared in disbelief at pictures of debris. Damaged *Die Glockes* retrieved from the Nazi base, being picked over by men in bright yellow hazmat suits. More pictures followed of complete *Die Glockes* being handled by US Air Force staff. Another file showed a video of the time machine taking off and disappearing and then reappearing again. The pair looked at each other incredulously. Katrina was about to say something when Foster's intercom buzzed. He reached over and barked into it, annoyed that they had been interrupted.

"Yes! What is it?"

"Mr McInnes has arrived, sir," quaked his secretary. "Shall I send him in?"

"Yes, Miss Thear," Foster sighed in a calmer voice, "if you would be so kind."

The door opened and the former director of operations entered. Foster stood up and shook his hand, then moved a spare chair over next to Katrina. After introductions had been taken care of, Foster leaned back in his chair and waited for the older man to get himself comfortable. Then he became more businesslike.

"Well, Alex," he quipped, "I think you've got some explaining to do."

The mood in the room suddenly became frosty. For his part, McInnes didn't like being talked down to by someone who was younger than his daughters. Conversely, Foster was aggrieved that he was not privy to this information and felt somewhat embarrassed. Sitting to McInnes' left, Katrina was unsure what to do; her instincts were telling her to excuse herself and make a hasty exit. On the one hand she didn't want to get caught in the crossfire of a testosterone battle; on the other, she wondered whether she should be here at all.

"I can't believe I haven't got to hear about the agency's involvement in the development of a fucking time machine!" Foster looked over at Katrina apologetically for his outburst.

"As you can imagine, Project Phoenix is highly classified and revealed on a need-to-know basis," replied McInnes calmly. "This is technology retrieved from Nazis operating in Montana, twenty-two years ago."

"And it's operational!" continued Foster, still rattled, and ignoring the Nazi element for the moment. His focus was still fixated on the *Die Glocke*.

"Well, not exactly," corrected McInnes.

"But the video," said Foster with a frown, pointing at the monitor.

"What you see is a film of the... um, device leaving and returning," advised McInnes. "What it doesn't show is what happened to the test pilot."

"What *did* happen to him?" enquired Katrina.

"Check out the next file down, it should show you."

They watched as the limp body of the test pilot was removed from the vessel and the autopsy which was subsequently performed on him.

"So, as you must realise," continued McInnes, "a time machine isn't much use as a form of transportation if humans can't survive the trip."

"The project ground to a halt then?" Katrina was highly fascinated by now and wild horses couldn't drag her from the room.

"An investigation by a former CIA field agent concluded that there's a drug used by the Nazis which made human physiology more robust," commented McInnes. "They called it the Infinity Serum because it also extended the life span. All this information is there."

"This Infinity Serum, I take it we haven't got any?"

"That's why the project was put on hold," said McInnes, nodding.

"So why reactivate it now?"

"Because of this." McInnes reached inside his jacket, pulled out a newspaper clipping and passed it to Foster. After reading the report he passed it to Katrina, who fervently did likewise.

"I can't be sure," continued McInnes, "but this could be the drug we need."

"Christ, it's in the hands of the Los Angeles Police Department," exclaimed Foster.

"Exactly," sighed McInnes, relieved that he was finally being taken seriously. "They don't know what they've got. We must shut this investigation down, and quick."

"Who are these other two names listed?" enquired Katrina.

"General Sterling Chambers was in charge of development of the time machine. I have contacted him and he is heading for Edwards Air Force Base."

"And this Liam Slater?" asked Foster.

"He resigned from the agency in 1986," confirmed McInnes. "He has been in on this from the very beginning. Contacting him will be a little tricky. He has my number, but I don't have one for him."

Foster paused for thought for a few seconds and then leaned forwards to flick a switch on his intercom.

"Miss Thear, I need you to book a flight to Los Angeles now, please," he requested. "Three seats."

"Three?" asked Katrina, with eyebrows raised.

"Yes," confirmed Foster, "you're coming too."

The dutiful operative looked stunned and a little perturbed. Katrina's reaction didn't go unnoticed on McInnes.

"Welcome to the sharp end, kiddo," he chuckled, and smiled kindly at her.

***

Logan Center, Forensic Pathology Consulting Practice, Los Angeles, California
May 2007

The glass partition reflected a ghostly image of Detective Peter Jacks and Lieutenant Cynthia Kiefer as they stared down intently on the autopsies about to be performed by Dr Veronica Coleman and her assistant. Three bodies were laid out on individual stainless-steel slabs illuminated by a ceiling of panels diffused with bright light: two human corpses and those of the unfortunate dog, Hendrix. Both police officers looked on with a combination of fascination and revulsion as the forensic scientist moved towards one of the mummified bodies to make the first incision.

"I'm starting with the remains of the body you believe to be Curtis Hoyt," stated Dr Coleman. "If this crime was committed twenty-two years ago then it is no surprise that dental records are not available."

Jacks looked at his boss with raised eyebrows. Kiefer picked up on his enquiring expression.

"By law they are only obliged to keep them for six years. His dentist kept them for ten," she advised.

With great care, Dr Coleman peeled back the denim jacket, now more a black and brown than the original faded blue. An incision was made down the dark brown T-shirt which only showed hints of white. As she cut, the material disintegrated easily – a combination of shotgun damage and the fact the material was rotten. The parchment-like skin was now exposed to reveal the entry wound.

"There is a hole in the centre of his chest about 10.5cm, with several individual buckshot holes around the periphery," she commented, laying a ruler across the wound. "I would estimate that the killer was no more than ten feet away when he pulled the trigger. He would have been blown off his feet and died instantly."

Making an incision from the upper chest to the lower abdomen, Dr Coleman carefully pulled back the brittle skin, which crackled and split as she did so.

"The internal organs are remarkably well preserved apart from catastrophic trauma to the lungs and heart," she advised. "At least his death was quick."

"What about a DNA sample?" offered Jacks.

"DNA profiling didn't begin 'til at least a year later," interjected Kiefer, "so there would be nothing to compare it with." She frowned disapprovingly at Jacks; he should know this.

Dr Coleman was now leaning over the second body, scalpel in hand, again poised to make an incision.

"I believe you have identified this body as a man called Jerry Richardson."

"We think so, his fingerprints were found on the shotgun," offered Kiefer, "along with another set of prints that we haven't been able to identify."

"The prints of the killer," suggested Jacks.

"Maybe."

"There was obviously a third person there," reasoned Jacks. "Those bodies didn't bury themselves."

It was a fair point but Kiefer was keeping an open mind at this juncture. Their attention was brought back to the autopsy as the pathologist began to speak again.

"I would have expected to see some remains of the tongue," she frowned, "but there is no trace of it. Also, look at the lower jaw, the way it is distorted, throwing the teeth out of alignment."

"It looks pretty grotesque for sure," said Jacks, wincing.

"It's as if the bone has been softened or melted," added Dr Coleman.

She made an incision down the torso of the second corpse and opened the chest.

"Well, that would explain why the torso is almost flat," she announced incredulously. "There appears to be no bone structure to support it and a complete absence of organs."

"You mean that sludge dissolved them?" enquired Kiefer.

"Let's see how the remains of this dog compare."

The hapless canine was lying on its side, the distorted jaw hanging limply and matted with fur. Just like the body of Jerry Richardson, the torso was flattened.

Expecting the smell to be as noxious as ever, Dr Coleman adjusted her goggles and pulled her face mask up in the hope it would stave off the worst of it. Very carefully she made an incision down the torso and prised open the chest cavity. The smell that she had expected was mercifully absent. Before she went any further, however, she checked her gloves were not affected by the corrosive substance. She breathed a sigh of relief when she saw they were still intact. The inside of the carcass was devoid of any bone structure or internal organs. What remained glistened the same colour brown as the sludge, as she shone a torch inside.

"It appears to be inert," she said, now poking the inside gently with a scalpel, "just like the sample we took."

"So, is it your conclusion that Richardson swallowed the liquid, the same way the dog did?" offered Kiefer.

"I can't say whether it was deliberate or an accident, as in the case of the dog, but yes, I believe they both died from ingesting that liquid."

Five minutes later, Dr Coleman had removed her protective coveralls and invited the two detectives into her office. She picked up a newspaper and offered it to Kiefer.

"I assume you've seen this."

"Yeah," said Jacks, wincing, "fucking reporter named Robert McQuillan got to the family before we had a chance to shut this down."

"Not Scottie McQuillan!" exclaimed Dr Coleman. "I've had run-ins with him too. He's such an arsehole."

"Tell me about it," asseverated Kiefer. "Luckily it's only on page ten so hopefully it will go unnoticed."

"Good luck with that," replied Dr Coleman doubtfully. "If anything else crops up I'll let you know."

The pair thanked her, left the office and walked out to their car. Dr Coleman watched them as they drove off, then walked back to the autopsy theatre and reflected on the three bodies lying within. Her instincts were to have them incinerated. There was something abhorrent about this whole affair that made her uneasy. The theatre assistant approached.

"What are we going to do with the bodies?" he asked.

Dr Coleman paused for thought.

"The morgue, I guess," then added, "for now."

***

North Hollywood Police Station, Los Angeles, California May 2007

The drive back to the police station was made mostly in silence, as each officer, deep in their own thoughts, contemplated the morning's events. Before they realised it, they were on Burbank Boulevard and turning right into the front parking lot, just as a black and white patrol car was leaving.

The police headquarters was a modern-looking, but not particularly attractive building, being a mish-mash of various shapes and jagged angles. The overall impression was of something neither aesthetic nor functional. If the intention was to unsettle any visitor, then the construction was a veritable triumph.

Lieutenant Kiefer made a beeline for her office, only to be intercepted by Police Deputy Chief Tyrell Garcia. He was a tall, overweight, middle-aged African American, with a bullish personality who didn't suffer fools easily. His rise up the ranks had not been an easy one and he didn't believe in giving anyone a free ride. Whatever their colour or creed. Being cantankerous was something he saw as a virtue, a trait which he'd inherited from his grandmother.

"Lieutenant!" barked Deputy Chief Garcia as he leaned out of his office doorway. "A minute of your time."

She stopped in her tracks, closed her eyes and sighed to herself, before turning to confront her boss with a smile. This is exactly what she didn't want. Kiefer had been avoiding him for a few days now. At least until she had some results.

"Yes, sir."

"Don't be going anywhere this afternoon, I'm going to need you here," he insisted. "Is that clear?"

"Sure. Any particular reason?" She was expecting to be grilled about the morning's events, but noticed a look of concern on his face.

"You'll find out soon enough."

"What about Jacks, do you need him too?"

Garcia looked doubtfully over at Jacks who was putting a comb through his hair.

"No," he said, trying to hide his disdain, "we won't be needing him."

Slumping down in her chair, Kiefer picked up the phone on her desk and punched in a number. The other end answered.

"Jacks," she requested, "bring everything in that we've got on the case and let's see what sense we can make of it."

Jacks opened the door with a small pile of buff files in his hand and sat down opposite his boss. Without waiting for her to speak, he opened the older dog-eared folder and began sifting through the leaves of paper.

"This is the file from the original investigation in 1985," he commented. "It started as a missing person report."

"Who?"

"A Miss Kimberley Richardson," confirmed Jacks. "She hadn't reported in for work for three days, so a patrol car was sent to her home. After an inspection of the property, they spied her through a bedroom window, in bed and appearing to be asleep. When the officers tried to rouse her, she didn't respond. The girl had been dead for about three days."

"What was the cause of death?"

"Autopsy revealed that she had soapy water in her lungs," continued Jacks. "The tub in the bathroom was full of water and it was conjectured that she drowned in it."

"So, someone was there when it happened or found her like that," mused Kiefer, "then, carried her to the bedroom and placed her in a sleeping position. That's the act of someone who cares. Or at least a mark of respect."

"The second set of prints on the shotgun," added Jacks, "the set we couldn't identify, was also on a tumbler in the lounge. Our mystery man poured himself a bourbon."

"They came in, found or killed her," reasoned Kiefer, "put her to bed then helped themselves to a drink."

"And then drove her VW Beetle into town and abandoned it. My guess would be early the following morning," concluded Jacks.

Lieutenant Kiefer stood up and blankly stared out of her window, deep in thought.

"What about the desert scenario?" she pondered eventually.

"Curtis Hoyt's pickup was found about a quarter of a mile away abandoned," Jacks replied, "which backs up the theory that he is one of the bodies."

"What was he doing? Stalking Jerry Richardson and our mystery man?" pondered Kiefer. "He must have thought the sound of his truck would give him away."

"It seems logical, except it didn't work," reasoned Jacks. "The killer was waiting for him and caught him off guard."

"What were they doing there? And what is the connection between Hoyt and Richardson?"

"The only connection he has to Jerry Richardson, that we know of, is that he once dated his daughter, Kimberley," confirmed Jacks.

"Who was almost certainly murdered at their bungalow."

"Yes."

"And this strange liquid," declared Kiefer, "what is it? Where did it come from?"

"All we can say is someone was prepared to kill for it," concurred Jacks, "and may still be out there."

"Yeah," agreed Kiefer, "a dangerous man."

"Look, type this all up," she said, finally, "and then take your lunch break."

"What about you?" asked Jacks, gathering the files together and standing up.

"I'll send out for something. The chief wants me to stay in the office."

"Why?" said Jacks, frowning.

"He didn't say," Kiefer replied, "but I'm sure I'll find out soon enough."

***

The only thing that betrayed the fact that the two dark blue SUVs travelling south on State Route 14 were United

States Air Force, was the white USAF letters printed discretely on the tailgate. In the back of the lead vehicle sat Katrina Hart and Lucas Foster, whilst the SUV following contained Alex McInnes and General Sterling Chambers. The retired CIA man glanced at his cohort in dismay. The general didn't look a well man. His eyes were sunken and the sparkle seemed to have left them. He had lost at least 20lbs in weight; the hollow cheeks and ill-fitting uniform gave this away all too clearly.

"I've got prostate cancer," confirmed Chambers as he interpreted the withering look on McInnes' face.

"I'm sorry to hear that, General," he sympathised. "How bad is it?"

"Just as bad as it can get," confirmed Chambers with a coughing fit. "It's spread over my body. There's nothing they can do."

"You didn't have to come, you know."

"I couldn't waste an opportunity to see this thing through," Chambers replied, "even if it kills me."

"Were you able to contact Liam Slater?" asked McInnes. "He might be of some use. He keeps me at arm's length."

"No," said Chambers, wincing and shaking his head, "he has my number. I'm hoping he'll be in touch."

"It would seem he keeps everyone at arm's length," observed McInnes.

In the lead SUV, Katrina Hart sat in silence for most of the journey, once small talk with her boss had been exhausted. It had become a little awkward, so she spent most of the journey looking out of the window in an attempt not to make eye contact. She still didn't know why she was here, but had to concede it made a change from her regular routine. It was mid-afternoon when she saw the sign which read '*North Hollywood Police Station*' come into view as they turned right into the parking lot. At last she could get out and stretch her legs.

In her office, Lieutenant Kiefer became aware of some commotion occurring outside. She stood up and walked over to the partition and discretely prised open two slats of the venetian blinds with her forefinger and thumb. Police Deputy Chief Garcia was standing at his office door shaking hands with four strangers. To her they looked a motley mixture: two old men and a younger man and woman around her own age. She was particularly intrigued by the frail old man in the blue uniform and what possible reason he could have for being here. Garcia motioned with his hand for them to enter his office and then turned his attention to the lieutenant. Immediately she whipped herself away from the window and sat down just as her boss entered. If he noticed, he didn't show it, but gazed at her with a solemn look.

"My office," he ordered, "now – please."

"What's it all about?" fretted Kiefer. She was racking her brains wondering whether she'd done something wrong.

"I think we're both about to find out," confided Garcia.

The four strangers glanced round as Kiefer and Garcia entered the room. Garcia closed the door behind him and sat down at his desk. Kiefer stood awkwardly wondering where to sit until her boss gestured to a chair to the right of his desk. She sat and studied the four people across from her, only making eye contact with the young woman, who tried to avoid hers. Apart from the old man in a USAF uniform, nothing gave away who they might be. All four were introduced to the lieutenant, who dutifully shook hands with them all.

Lucas Foster, who was closest to her, took it upon himself to take the initiative and speak first.

"I shall get right to the point. As director of operations for the CIA, I need to inform you that the case you are currently working on, relating to this newspaper article," Foster pointed to the page of newsprint laid out on Garcia's deck, "is of great interest to us. And, without beating about the bush, you must cease and desist from any investigation pertaining to it."

"What!" exclaimed Kiefer, looking at her boss for support. He was equally surprised. "This is bullshit! Why?"

Slightly ruffled, Garcia put a hand up to quell her outrage.

"This is highly irregular," he protested. "What possible grounds…"

McInnes put his hand up to cut him short. After his replacement had jumped in with both feet, he decided a more diplomatic approach might be more conducive.

"Deputy Chief," he drawled with what he hoped was a winning smile, "you have inadvertently stumbled into something of great national security. This leak to the press has compromised top secret work and we need to contain it before it gets out of hand."

By referring to this imposing man opposite him by rank, McInnes hoped that he would be flattered and respond to a little respect. Garcia, however, was no fool, and sensed when he was being soft-soaped.

"Okay, so what happens now?" Garcia's manner was calmer; he realised that they weren't going to win this one.

"We will be confiscating everything," revealed Foster.

"But we're close to solving this case," appealed Kiefer.

"No you're not," advised McInnes. "The man you are seeking is dead. He died years ago."

Chambers gave a slight scoff at this understatement. Kiefer and Garcia gave him a puzzled look.

"We will need all the information going back to 1985, any physical evidence, plus all three bodies," confirmed McInnes, "the drug in particular. We will need to appropriate all samples found."

There was a stony silence until she saw her boss's big brown eyes boring into her.

"There is only one other sample," she uttered petulantly.

"Where is it now?" asked General Chambers.

"Locked in my drawer," replied Kiefer. "I haven't processed it yet."

"Would you be so kind as to get it?" requested McInnes.

Standing up, Kiefer sidled behind the four visitors and left the room.

"Needless to say, all computer records will have to be deleted under our supervision," proffered Foster.

Garcia nodded glumly. There was no more point in protesting any further.

As Kiefer exited the office, Jacks was waiting to pounce.

"What the hell's going on?" he spluttered, trying to keep pace as Kiefer strode to her office.

"We're off the case."

"What? How? Why?" he spluttered again.

"CIA are taking it off us," she replied. "National security. And don't ask, I have no clue either."

Leaving Jacks dumbfounded she entered her office and returned with two plastic bags. One containing the ampule and the other containing the signet ring.

Walking past the gaping-mouthed Jacks she ordered,

"Gather up all the files on this case and bring them to me." She watched as Jacks didn't respond. "Now would be a good time."

Leaving him to get on with it, she re-entered the room and passed the evidence bags to McInnes. The only visitor in the room whose authority she acknowledged. McInnes studied the objects for a moment, then, satisfied, passed them to Katrina, who placed them in a briefcase.

"Have you checked the area to see if any more of these ampules are buried at the site?" asked Katrina.

"Yes," confirmed Kiefer, "after the bodies were removed, we excavated a large area of the crime scene and found nothing."

Minutes later there was a knock at the door and Jacks opened it sheepishly to pass through all the files they had on the case.

"This includes the latest which I've just finished typing up," he muttered.

Kiefer gave him a withering smile and took the documents. Garcia simply nodded.

"Where are the bodies now?" asked Chambers.

"Autopsies were only carried out this morning," confirmed Kiefer. "They will either be with forensics or in the morgue. I'll check."

"Good," declared McInnes. "We will make

arrangements for the remains to be picked up tomorrow. And if you could be available to oversee the transfer that would be helpful."

McInnes looked at Kiefer for a response and she looked to her boss for instruction.

"That will be acceptable," he confirmed.

Later that day, Kiefer was sitting in her office fuming inside and fidgeting in her chair. She couldn't believe it. The one time she was getting somewhere with a cold case and it was summarily taken off her. And they seemed to know who the culprit is – or was.

Eventually she picked up her cell phone and called Dr Coleman.

"Yes, Cynthia," she greeted cheerfully.

"Where are those bodies?" Kiefer enquired, getting straight down to business.

"They're in the morgue, why?" replied Dr Coleman, sensing something was wrong.

"They are being requisitioned."

"By whom?"

"It would seem the CIA and the US Air Force," Kiefer stated churlishly.

"Why of course," responded Dr Coleman in a sarcastic tone. "Who else."

"You don't sound too surprised."

"Are you?" Dr Coleman replied rhetorically. "This case has been bizarre from the get-go."

It was a point that Kiefer found impossible to dispute.

"They will want all your records too," Kiefer advised.

"I understand," uttered Dr Coleman, still unfazed.

"Anyway, I'll be there tomorrow to oversee the transfer."

"Whatever's going on, you know, we're probably better off out of it," assuaged Dr Coleman.

"Yeah, sure." Kiefer knew she was right, but at this point in time, it felt like scant consolation.

"Thanks for the heads-up. I'll see you tomorrow then," concluded Dr Coleman.

Detective Jacks entered her office and sat down. He pulled a mock glum expression at her downcast demeanour.

"Stop it," she chuckled eventually, turning away from him.

"What now then, boss?" he enquired.

"We get down to what we do best," replied Kiefer in a much brighter tone, "real police work."

CHAPTER TEN

KILL OR CURE

*Oakland, East Bay, Near San Francisco, California
May 2007*

The flight had been a turbulent one and Liam Slater
didn't enjoy it one bit. He had landed at Buchanan Field
Airport and was now sitting in the back of a taxi which
had just entered the outskirts of Oakland. Slater was not
a fan of the constant heat in California, though he had to
concede that the spring temperature of eighteen degrees
Celsius in San Francisco was surprisingly comfortable,
and more like the temperatures he was used to. He looked
out at the overcast sky, and saw that the weather here was
more capricious than he realised. It actually looked like

it might rain. Despite this, California was not for him. He much preferred Colorado, the place he had made his home for the last few decades, where the changing of the seasons was more dramatic and marked the passing of the year.

The cab driver was wittering away but Slater barely took any notice. He was thinking of his destination, and hoped that his journey would not be in vain. The ex-CIA agent decided to visit unannounced, a habit he had established over the years to ensure his movements remained as circumspect as possible. So, as the taxi approached the address he had given, Slater was relieved to see a red Toyota Belta on the drive. After paying the cabbie, Slater asked him to wait until the door was answered. He walked up the drive to the bungalow, rang the bell and waited patiently. After a little longer than one would expect, the door swung inwards to reveal a middle-aged man supported by a walking stick in his left hand. Having been over two decades since they had last met, Slater noticed he was much greyer and had put on several pounds around the waist.

"Professor Phillips," said Slater, beaming, "it's been a long time."

For a split second the professor struggled to recognise his visitor, but as he realised who was standing in front of him, he grinned and offered his hand.

"Liam," he exclaimed, "you've hardly changed. Apart from the bushy beard, that is. Indeed, it has been a long time. And please, call me David."

It was true, Slater's mountain lifestyle had kept him physically fit and he could give a man half his age a good run for his money. The only thing that betrayed his age was the patches of white in his hair and beard. David ushered Slater into his home and the ex-CIA agent was shown through to the sitting room.

"I'm sorry to drop in on you unannounced," stated Slater awkwardly, "it's kind of the way I live my life these days."

"Not a problem," reassured David, "I rarely get any visitors. Can I offer you a drink? Coffee? Or a beer perhaps."

Slater glanced at his watch; it was 12.05.

"What the hell," he said with a smile, "the sun's over the yard arm. I'll have a beer."

David chuckled and disappeared into the kitchen, shortly to return holding a tray with two bottles of beer and two glasses. Without his cane, David's movement was shaky and Slater stood up to take the tray off him.

"Your injury still gives you trouble I see."

"I can walk short distances without a stick, but generally, yes," sighed David, "it gives me pain from time to time, especially when it's damp."

"I'm sorry to hear about Laura," sympathised Slater. On numerous occasions he had considered telling David the truth, but decided little good would come from it.

"What have you been up to all these years?" interjected David, keen to change the subject.

"Well, I quit the CIA in 1986 and have been living an almost hermit-like existence ever since," admitted Slater. "The agency still pulls me back in from time to time. I just can't seem to shake it off."

"Is that why you're here now?"

"Kind of," confirmed Slater. David's astuteness threw him off balance somewhat. He slumped back on the couch and took a long pull of his beer. Slater didn't want to jump in immediately with what he had on his mind, so changed tack.

"How's Jessica?" he asked with genuine curiosity.

"She's okay," replied David cautiously. "This is her last year at university, so I hope to see more of her, unless she decides to continue studying. There's a picture of her on the side there."

Slater glanced over to where David was pointing and he stood up, moved over to the picture and held it in his hand. The colour photograph showed a young girl with straight black hair, beautiful dark eyes and what could only be described as a Mona Lisa smile. Enigmatic, arcane and impenetrable. Slater guessed her age to be twelve.

"How old is she here?" enquired Slater.

"She's seventeen," affirmed David. He noticed his guest's surprise. "I know what you're thinking, she looks much younger, right?"

"Yes," said Slater, nodding and studying the picture once more.

"Her arrested development is purely physical," noted David. "I believe this to be due to the genes which she inherited from her father."

"What about her mental capacity?"

"Mentally I would say she is mature beyond her years." Apprehension had crept into his voice and it didn't go unnoticed on Slater. "It has been of great concern to Jessica. She is highly intelligent and knows something is wrong, or at least different. I've had to discourage her from going to see doctors. I'm afraid that they will discover just how unique she really is. Up until now I have managed to dissuade her by pointing out that she has never had a day's illness in her life."

"Really?" declared Slater. "Not even a cold?"

"No – nothing," confirmed David. "She told me much to her relief that she began menstruating earlier this year and her figure is finally beginning to develop. Jessica turned twenty-one on the 9th of this month."

"It must have made things difficult with her peers."

"She was constantly out of step with them. They teased her mercilessly and it made her very reclusive and very self-reliant." David's tone was tinged with sadness. "Jessica has no friends to speak of, and seems to prefer it that way. When she realised her intellect was way above theirs, she simply treated them all with contempt. I sometimes wonder if she looks at me that way as well."

"Do you really think that?"

"Her arrogance would be conceited if it wasn't born out of fact," imparted David. "I rue the day when Jessica finds out that, compared to her, the rest of us are mere mortals."

Slater walked back to the couch and sat down. He felt great empathy with the man sitting opposite him. They'd both had their lives inextricably altered by events of the last two decades. The legacy of von Brandt was an immutable imbroglio; who seemed forever to haunt them.

"I guess you'll have to cross that bridge when you come to it," he sympathised. "At the moment we have more pressing matters."

"I didn't think this was a social visit," declared David. "What's on your mind?"

"First a question," Slater began. "If you were going

to drop a time machine forty years into the future, where would you put it?"

"Ah, so you're admitting it *was* a time machine now?" said David, smiling.

"The time for pretence has long gone."

Sitting back in his chair, David became pensive as he ran his mind over the ramifications of landing a time machine in the future.

"Well," he said, eventually, "you couldn't guarantee what the world would look like that far into the future, so you would have to choose a place where you could be absolutely certain it wasn't going to be built on. Somewhere like agricultural land or desert."

"Exactly."

"Why do you ask?" said David, frowning.

Reaching into the inside of his jacket, Slater pulled out a newspaper cutting and passed it to David. He unfolded it and began to read, looking up at Slater once partway through in astonishment. After he had finished reading, David placed the cutting down on the coffee table. It quickly dawned on David where Slater was going with this.

"You think this is where von Brandt landed."

"The two ampules found there make for compelling evidence."

It was hard to dispute Slater's logic and it revealed what to David was another disturbing fact.

"Then he would have also killed the two men mentioned in the clipping."

"That's a fair assumption," agreed Slater. "Who knows what trail of death he left behind him. There could be more."

"That evil bastard just won't go away," complained David. "I still curse the day Laura introduced him to me."

"Yeah, well he's gone for good," reassured Slater. "We won't be troubled by him again."

"The serum!" exclaimed David, realising the implications of the story. "It's in the hands of the police. Do they know what they've got?"

"That's highly unlikely. I need to advise some people about this, if they don't know already."

"Where do I fit in with all this?" queried David, fearing the worst.

"We need that drug, David. Humans aren't strong enough to survive a time jump without it."

"I thought I was done with all that."

"I've done my best to keep you out of this, especially for Jessica's sake. But the serum has reared its ugly head and there is no getting away from it – your expertise *will* be required."

"You want me to replicate the drug, the way we did for the Nazis?"

"Yes," said Slater, nodding.

"Do I have a choice?" David asked the question knowing full well what the answer would be.

"I'm sorry," said Slater, wincing, "it's better coming from me than anyone else."

Taking a cell phone and a small tattered notebook out of his pocket, Slater found the number he was looking for and punched it into the handset. He paused as the phone at the other end rang and picked up.

"Alex," he greeted, "it's Liam Slater."

McInnes breathed a sigh of relief, and, dispensing with pleasantries, got straight down to business.

"Liam, have you seen the newspaper report about the Mojave Desert? It looks like the serum's been found."

"I know," confirmed Slater. "I'm with Professor David Phillips right now. Yeah – I'm bringing him in."

"Good," replied McInnes, "I'll organise a flight out and get back to you."

Slater confirmed and hung up. He glanced apologetically at a slightly perturbed David.

"When are we leaving?" asked David, resigned to his fate.

"How long will it take for you to pack a suitcase?"

***

Edwards Air Force Base, Kern County, California
May 2007

A special flight had been arranged in an Air Force Raytheon T-1A Jayhawk, a small twin-engine jet normally used for advanced pilot training. The 190-mile flight south to Edwards Air Force Base took less than an hour, and by mid-afternoon the two men were stepping down onto the tarmac on the last day of May. David had to squint as the sun reflected off the gleaming white paintwork of the swept wing as he descended the short steps. Waiting for them was what he assumed to be top officials. He was meeting these people for the first time: Alex McInnes; General Sterling Chambers, looking as frail as ever, and representing Lucas Foster who had made the decision to fly back to CIA headquarters; and Katrina Hart.

"It's good to finally meet you," gushed McInnes, shaking David's hand vigorously.

"You want me to reverse engineer the drug," replied David, unmoved by his enthusiasm.

"Not just replicate it," advised McInnes, "but to develop it for use on humans."

"Like the Nazis did."

"Err... yes." McInnes sensed some reluctance on David's part. "You must understand the time machine is useless to us without it. Your work here is vital."

Realising that he had no choice in the matter, David resigned himself to the task ahead. He hoped his reference to the Nazis had registered his disapproval, but if the job had to be done, he may as well throw body and soul into it. *Body and soul*, he thought. Those words seemed strangely pertinent.

"I will need a laboratory," he advised.

"That is all set up and waiting for you," confirmed General Chambers, who spoke for the first time.

"And I will need pigs," advised David. "Let's say six for starters, with a body mass index similar to the average male human."

"Why pigs?" enquired McInnes.

"I will need to test the drug on something, and the general physiology of pigs is similar to that of humans. They also have similar fat cell size and body fat distribution."

"It will be arranged," confirmed Chambers.

"Have you got access to an incinerator?" queried David. "All the injected animals will have to be destroyed. Whether they survive or not."

"That can be arranged too," agreed Chambers grimly.

"We will be transferring to another site tomorrow," advised McInnes, "where you will be carrying out your research."

"How much of the drug is available?" asked David.

"One ampule," replied McInnes succinctly.

"I'd better not screw up then," fretted David with a wry smile.

***

AirForce Plant 52, Death Valley, Mojave Desert, California
June 2007

The small convoy of Humvees trundled along as fast as the desert track would allow, and Katrina and David looked at each other. Neither spoke but were thinking the same thing: what the hell were they expecting to find out here?

"So, what's your role in all this?" asked David.

"A good question," mumbled Katrina. "I feel my presence here is a little superfluous. I guess I will observe Project Phoenix and report back to headquarters."

"Project Phoenix! Is that what they're calling it?" retorted David with a sardonic smile. "That figures."

"Things could get a little crazy around here in the coming days," added David, "so brace yourself."

"It did occur that I might be witnessing something significant," Katrina replied.

David smiled at this understatement and fell silent, just as some activity could be discerned up front beyond the two Humvees ahead of them. The rock face slid open and the convoy drove straight in and parked up in the cavernous antechamber.

The team alighted from their vehicles and grouped together as a soldier approached, stood to attention and saluted the general.

"Everything is waiting for you, sir," vociferated the soldier. "If you would all like to follow me."

Mesmerised, Katrina and David gazed around, barely looking where they were going. The antechamber was massive, spotlessly clean and very busy with staff milling about.

"What is this place?" asked David.

"Research of all kinds, of the highest classified nature, is undertaken here," advised McInnes. "Very few people know what goes on here. Even the president is only told on a need-to-know basis. Needless to say, security is extremely tight."

"How big is this place?" enquired Katrina.

"This is the top floor," imparted McInnes, "and there are seven floors below us."

They were led to an elevator and first taken down to the quarters where they would be bunking, and then McInnes took David down another level to show him the laboratory where he would be working. Opening the door to the lab, McInnes allowed David to walk in first. The room was about thirty feet square, modern and clean. David was pleased to see it was well equipped and he walked around checking the apparatus with approval. He opened a drawer and was pleased to see a good quantity of petri dishes.

"I'm going to need glass phials," he said, smiling, from the middle of the floor, "around half a fluid ounce capacity with a plastic cap. And they must conform to ISO standards. Anything less will not be acceptable."

"Understood, Professor," agreed McInnes. "How many?"

"That depends on how much serum you want me to make," mused David. "I'll leave that up to you."

"I have an identification card here for you." General Chambers stepped forwards, dipping his hand into his jacket side pocket. Two were pulled out and he selected one and passed it to the professor. "This gives you access to parts of this floor and the one above. You will need it on you at all times."

"That only leaves you to hand over the ampule of serum," concluded David, "and I can get started."

"We'll let you settle in and have it brought down to you this afternoon," declared McInnes.

"One last thing," added David, almost as an afterthought, "I would like Katrina Hart to be my assistant."

McInnes and Chambers looked at each other, both waiting for the other to take the lead. Finally, General Chambers spoke.

"I don't see a problem with that," he said with a shrug. "We'll let her know during dinner."

The two men and the soldier left David to his own devices and made their way to the door. As a final parting shot the soldier looked back and spoke.

"FYI, sir, dinner is at 1700 sharp," he advised in a solemn tone. "The canteen is on the floor above."

***

Over the next week, Katrina watched as David assiduously created phials of serum. After her initial misgivings, Katrina realised that she was of great help to the professor. His difficulty walking without a stick meant, if nothing else, she could fetch and carry for him. David's instincts to use her proved judicious. She was bright, attentive, if a little too curious for his liking. Deflecting some of her more vexatious questions was becoming problematic. By the seventh day, David carefully placed the one-hundredth phial into a foam-lined aluminium case, closed the lid and turned to Katrina.

"Put this with the other four, will you?" he said, offering her the gleaming metal case.

"Yes, Professor," she replied dutifully. "What happens next?"

"Phase Two," sighed David. "Phase One was the easy part. I knew how to replicate the serum, but administering it may prove to be more hit or miss."

"Hence the pigs," stated Katrina rhetorically.

"Have they arrived yet?" enquired David. "I've been so wrapped up in Phase One, I didn't even think to check."

"Yes, I believe they came in a few days ago," confirmed Katrina.

Later that day, the team reconvened in a meeting room to decide the next plan of action. David and Katrina were the last to arrive. The door opened and Katrina held it wide to allow the professor to limp in and take a seat. Without any preamble, David spoke.

"The serum is ready whenever you want me to test it."

"How about tomorrow?" suggested the general.

"That would be fine," agreed David. "We will need two pigs, some scales to weigh them on and an armed guard."

The group round the table glanced at each other in

surprise. Katrina wasn't expecting this. She knew the drug was dangerous but David had kept this quiet. Clearly, he was playing his cards closer to his chest than she realised.

"Armed guard?" exclaimed McInnes. "Why?"

"I've seen what this serum does to rats," commented David solemnly. "I don't want to take any chances."

"A room will be available close to the lab with everything you need," confirmed General Chambers. "Is there any other business?"

Nobody answered and a few shook their heads.

"Very well then, we shall begin testing tomorrow at 0900 hours," announced McInnes.

Everyone filtered out of the room except Slater who sat pensively with his elbows on the table and his hands on his cheeks. Katrina began to stand up, but noticed Slater's disinclination to leave. She sat back down opposite Slater and smiled nervously at him. Snapped out of his reverie, he sat back and raised his eyebrows, a gesture of silent enquiry. The girl opposite him looked fidgety, nervously playing with her fingers on the table.

"What's on your mind?" enquired Slater.

"It's the professor," she sighed. "I don't know if I'm working with a genius or a mad scientist."

"You don't need to worry about him," chuckled Slater. "He's probably the sanest person out of all of us."

"Why is he making so much of that serum?" Katrina fretted. "We've got five cases of the stuff."

"He's only doing as he's been told," defended Slater.

"Where did the serum come from in the first place? Did he create it?" enquired Katrina. "It's weird, he uses germs – pathogens he calls them – to increase it."

"Ah, so that's where the mad scientist notion comes from. I can see that," chuckled Slater again. "No, he didn't invent it. The truth is far more outrageous." He paused before continuing, wondering whether it was wise to let her in on the whole story. Then he thought, *What the hell, they've dragged her in on this, she deserves to know.* "The serum is believed to have been seized from a downed UFO that crashed in Germany before the Second World War."

Slater paused and watched her reaction, allowing the information to sink in.

"Are you for real?" she exclaimed. "You're telling me that stuff came from space. No freaking way."

Katrina was aghast at learning that they were dealing with something alien, and it showed in her expression.

"We don't know the full details, but that's about the size of it," confirmed Slater. "The exact events died with the Nazis so we will never really know the whole truth."

"Unless we use that time machine thing and go and find out," mused Katrina, recovering slightly.

"A good point," uttered Slater, "though I think that might be foolhardy. The outcome of our engagement with the Nazis was a satisfactory one, considering. We wouldn't want to jeopardise that now, would we?"

"I suppose," pondered Katrina sullenly. It seemed a good idea to her on the face of it. "You looked a little preoccupied yourself when the others left."

"Yeah, you could say that," replied Slater. "Now we're getting closer to a useable serum, it suddenly occurred to me: who are they going to test it out on, who is going to be a suitable candidate?"

"Shit, I hadn't thought of that." She noticed Slater staring intently at her. "Don't look at me. They're not pumping that stuff into me."

"Would it be so bad," reasoned Slater, "to become superhuman with an extended life span?"

Katrina looked at him, mortified at the idea.

"Don't worry," said Slater, smiling at her reaction, "I'm sure the right candidate will be found elsewhere. I don't think we will be short of volunteers who'll jump at the chance of immortality."

***

The following morning at 0900 hours sharp, McInnes, General Chambers, Slater and a young soldier by the name of Corporal Dexter Webb were waiting in the testing room for the professor to arrive. The room, similar in size to the laboratory, was sparsely furnished with a table and two chairs, plus two large slatted packing crates made of pine wood. Each crate contained a pig approximately five feet from head to tail, who took up most of the space in their confinement, thus prohibiting any significant movement. Both pigs were of the same breed, their skin tone an even pale pink, almost white, with no spots or patches.

"What breed are they?" asked the general as he and McInnes strolled over to the wooden crates.

"American Yorkshires," confirmed McInnes. "All the specimens are boars."

"They look pretty strong – burly," observed Chambers. He turned to the corporal, who was standing next to

Slater, further back against the wall. "I hope you're ready, Corporal. We don't want any mishaps, son."

"Cocked and locked, sir," replied Corporal Webb, nervously lifting his black Beretta M9 semi-automatic handgun out of its holster and checking.

"Relax, fella," soothed Slater, sensing his unease. "I doubt if you'll even be needed."

The door opened and David stepped in and held the door for Katrina, who was carrying an aluminium case in one hand and a smaller black leather bag in the other. Katrina walked straight across the room and placed both on the table.

"Good morning, gentlemen," greeted David. "My apologies for keeping you waiting. So, without further ado, let's get started. Have the animals been weighed?"

"Yes," confirmed McInnes, "the weight of each beast is marked on the crate."

"And a tarpaulin to cover the other crate?" asserted David. "I don't want to cause the animals any unnecessary distress."

"It's here behind the crates," confirmed Chambers, "just as you requested."

"Okay, let's cover one of them and get started."

One of the animals was covered over and David checked his first guinea pig's weight. On a piece of paper stapled to the front, it stated 187lbs. David walked over to the table, sat down and removed a calculator and a notebook from his leather case. He did a quick calculation and wrote some figures down in his notebook. Then he removed a plastic box containing two hypodermic syringes and a phial of serum. Picking up a syringe he pulled back the plunger to draw air into it. With his left hand, he picked up the phial and held it vertically, pushed the needle into the rubber top and squeezed the air into the phial. Finally, with the two items held vertically, he drew a measure of the serum into the syringe. Turning to the group who were watching intently, he smiled nervously.

"Okay, we're ready."

Katrina took the syringe and the team made their way over to the crate.

"I'm going to inject the serum into the rump," stated David as he took the hypodermic from his assistant.

General Chambers nodded to Corporal Webb, who took the hint and removed his Beretta out of its holster.

"I suggest you all stand back a little," advised David, "I have no idea what the reaction will be."

They all stepped back and David squirted a little liquid out of the needle, then pushed it firmly into the rump of the pig and discharged the syringe. The animal gave a slight squeal and flinched. David, as fast as his damaged knee would allow, hobbled over to the table and put the syringe down. They all stared intently at the pig for a reaction. Nothing happened for about thirty seconds and then the hapless animal began to shake uncontrollably. The fitting became severe; the convulsing caused two of the slats to break. The young officer brought his handgun up and held it shakily at the creature, just as it gave out a high-pitched squeal and collapsed – motionless. David approached the crate.

"Katrina, pass me the stethoscope."

Placing the earbuds of the scope in his ears, David pulled away the broken slats to gain access. He placed the bell on the chest of the pig and listened.

"There's no heartbeat," he sighed. "We've killed it."

"What did it die of?" enquired Slater.

"Judging by the work I did on rats twenty-odd years ago," mused David, "my guess is heart attack."

"We need to get this creature out of here," suggested McInnes.

Presently, a soldier with a pallet jack arrived and took the crate out.

"Put it in room 5b," advised Chambers. "We'll deal with it later."

Slater closed the door as the crate exited the room and Katrina removed the tarpaulin off the second crate. David checked the weight of this creature – it read 179lbs. Back at the table, he again made a few calculations and loaded the hypodermic with forty percent less serum. He made his way over to the unsuspecting animal, took the syringe from Katrina and injected its rump.

Again, for half a minute, nothing happened, then the creature began to shake. Still out of control, but less severely this time. The shaking continued for twice as long and the pig inadvertently headbutted the crate, splitting the wooden slats. Then just like the first it collapsed and lay still. Taking his stethoscope, the professor checked for a heartbeat. He listened intently, moving the bell of the scope until he found what he was looking for.

"It's alive," he announced, with great relief. "The pulse is weak but I can hear it."

"But it's unconscious," complained the general.

"Look!" exclaimed a clearly annoyed David. "This is uncharted territory for me. I have no idea how long it might take for the creature to come round, if it does at all."

The length of time it took for the pig to regain consciousness was exactly seven minutes. They all turned around surprised to see the pig get to its feet and stand motionless in the crate. Picking up his stethoscope, David squatted by the side of the crate and fed it awkwardly through the three-inch gap. He placed it where the front leg joins the torso and listened.

"Its heart is beating fast," he disclosed, "rapid even, and strong."

The creature's eyes opened to reveal heavily bloodshot whites, then with a deafening screech it leapt from its confinement, the broken slats proving to be no obstacle. David tried to extricate his arm but his right wrist was broken in the melee. Everyone around the room instinctively backed off except for the young soldier who bravely advanced whilst removing his pistol. He brought his right arm up to take aim but wasn't fast enough. The demented boar threw its weight against him, biting into the soldier's right arm just below the elbow with a sickening crunch. They both fell to the floor, the corporal in agony.

"Get it off me!" screamed Corporal Webb as the pig bit through and amputated his arm.

McInnes made a move for the exit in panic, followed by Slater.

"Don't open that door," shouted David, "we can't risk it escaping."

The pig had lost interest in the arm and was now squinting angrily at Corporal Webb.

"For God's sake, somebody…" he screamed.

Before he could finish, the creature bit down hard on his throat and ripped it out. The young soldier lay still as a puddle of red began to expand around him. The pig reared up slightly and gave out a triumphant cry, exposing teeth and gums gorged with blood and flesh.

Katrina squatted down by the table and chairs and kept very still. With a quick glance around, she surveyed the room. David was to her right, keeping low and silent beside the packing crate, nursing his broken wrist. In the centre was the pig screeching at the top of its voice. Beyond the creature was General Chambers who had backed off, stumbled and slumped down the wall, about thirteen feet away from the carnage. Slater and McInnes were to Chambers' right also against the wall. She realised that the only hope they had was for someone to retrieve the gun. David and Chambers were out of action, which left Slater and McInnes. Neither of them was in any position to take on the beast so she looked for something, anything, to distract the animal. She picked up one of the chairs and flung it as hard as she could towards the corner of the room to Chambers' left. The pig heard the chair crash into the wall and instinctively turned and leapt at it. Immediately, Katrina ran to Corporal Webb's body to retrieve the gun. Reaching across she picked up the severed arm. Katrina was kneeling in a large puddle of blood and she made the mistake of glancing at the dead young man. Repulsed by the arm in her hand, she grimaced at the gore in front of her and felt a wave of nausea begin to rise up inside. The CIA operative fought against it and ripped the Beretta from the hand, just as the pig lost interest in the mangled chair, screeched another ear-piercing cry and began to run at her, eager to reclaim its prize. Katrina backed off at speed to the table again fumbling with the gun to flick off the safety switch.

The four men watched dumbstruck, but Slater, seeing that she was in trouble, began to holler at the top of his voice.

"Over here, you evil fat bastard," he bellowed.

McInnes looked at Slater, astounded by the outburst, took up the cue and joined in. Distracted and confused, the creature turned and stared down the two men. Realising what they were doing, Chambers began to shout.

"Leave her alone, you ugly brute," he bawled.

The brute turned its attention to the general and, sensing his vulnerability, began to move in on him. By now Katrina was ready with the gun; she raised it and pointed directly at the pig.

"Back off, you bastard," she shouted with a quivering voice and then pulled the trigger. The bullet entered the creature's left rump; it gave out a squeal and stopped in its tracks just a few feet from Chambers. The others watched, stupefied, wondering what would happen next.

The creature turned in a fit of rage, fixing its attention on Katrina. Still shaking, she brought up her left hand to help steady the gun. The two adversaries stared at one another.

"Come on, you goddamn mother fucker," she shrieked in an attempt to bolster up her courage.

Facing her now, the pig made one step forwards then leapt with all its strength. Midway she let fly with three successive shots. The first missed by an inch and buried itself in the wall just above the general's head. The other two found their target: one caught the left cheek and the second between the eyes. The dead weight fell towards Katrina, but she managed to side-step the hulk as it hit the floor and slid into the wall behind her. Without hesitation, Katrina walked over to the motionless body and pumped the rest of the magazine into the dead creature. The first to respond was Slater who rushed over to calm the girl. The gun was making a metallic clicking sound as Katrina continued to pull the trigger over and over, oblivious to the fact that she was out of ammunition.

"Okay, that's enough," he soothed, relieving her of the pistol, "it's dead already."

Turning away from him and the carcass, Katrina leaned against the wall and vomited. Finally, she coughed and burst into tears. Slater hugged the traumatised girl and guided her away from the slaughter.

"Hey," he smiled, trying to comfort her, "you did good."

The others rallied round to thank her except David who was supporting his wrist and staring down with dismay at the unfortunate young man. With a heavy heart, he knelt down and gently closed the corporal's eyes.

***

Another week passed before David and the team were ready to resume tests. With his right arm in plaster, the professor relied on Katrina even more. The group reconvened to witness the administering of another reduced dose whilst six soldiers stood guard, aiming their semi-automatic M4A1 carbines constantly as David injected the third subject. The results were more positive and by the fifth attempt, David was satisfied that he had the correct formula. Finally, he typed up a report and called a meeting.

"Well, gentlemen," he announced when everyone was sitting down, "the serum is now viable. All that needs to be decided is: who are we going to choose to be the first recipient?"

"Clearly we need someone who is stable," suggested McInnes. "We don't want a repetition of what happened last week."

"Indeed," agreed David. "Extensive psychological analysis of all volunteers will have to be a mandatory prerequisite."

"There is another alternative," quipped General Chambers, glancing round the room.

The others waited on tenterhooks for the general to continue.

"You use me as the first human guinea pig."

"But you're unwell," responded McInnes.

"I'm dying, it is true," lamented Chambers, "therefore I have nothing to lose. It makes me the perfect candidate."

"If you're sure, General," cautioned David. He looked at each person in the room in turn. "Has anyone got any objections to this?"

They all shook their heads solemnly.

"Then it is decided," announced David.

"Good," declared Chambers with a grim smile, "let's see what this drug can really do. It'll be kill or cure."

CHAPTER ELEVEN

SELF-FULFILLING PROPHESY

Edwards Air Force Base, Kern County, California
June 2007

The funeral of Corporal Dexter Webb took place at Arlington National Cemetery in Virginia, with full military honours. A flight of General Dynamics F16 Fighting Falcons roared across the sky just as the coffin was being lowered into the ground. Representing the team from Edwards Air Force Base were General Chambers and Alex McInnes. Meeting the grieving parents was particularly difficult. Having been informed that he died in an aircraft accident, the unfortunate soldier's mother and father were spared the knowledge that their son's death could easily have been avoided. Lying about their son's demise, however, only exacerbated the two men's guilt.

Back at Edwards Air Force Base, David tried to keep himself busy. He too was ridden with guilt, questioning his decision to use pigs instead of rats, his logic being that pigs would yield more reliable results in a quicker time frame. In hindsight, he realised that one armed guard was wholly inadequate, especially since he had some insight into how the rats reacted. It was incredibly naive of him to think that pigs would react any differently.

Slater elected to stay at the base also. He felt it was incumbent upon him to try and placate a traumatised colleague, who was clearly not trained for this kind of operation. Katrina spent much of the subsequent days in tears and barely eating. By the sixth day, however, she seemed to snap out of it and Slater found her solemnly eating some lunch in the base canteen.

"Mind if I join you?" he said, smiling.

Katrina gestured for him to sit and Slater pulled up a chair opposite her, sat down and began to peruse a menu. A waitress sauntered over and he ordered a burger and fries, with a cup of coffee.

"I suppose I should man up and get used to this sort of thing," she stated.

"As baptisms of fire go," consoled Slater, "that was a pretty grim one. You should be proud of yourself."

"I guess." Katrina shrugged, not convinced.

"I'm not feeding you a line," insisted Slater. "If it wasn't for your quick thinking, the situation could have been a whole lot worse. Any one of us could've been killed in that room. We owe our lives to you."

"What about you? Did you ever get used to it?"

Slater thought back to the few Nazis that he had killed at the secret base in Montana and his only other adversary on a previous assignment.

"I haven't killed that many people. It's not like it is in the films," he assured, "and no, you never get used to it. The moment you become too blasé is the time to start worrying."

"How is the professor taking all this?" asked Katrina, with genuine concern.

"He took the corporal's death pretty hard," confirmed Slater, "but I've spoken to him and he seems to be coming to terms with it."

"What happens next?" enquired Katrina, changing the subject.

"Well, I guess we wait for the others to return and then continue where we left off," surmised Slater, taking a big bite from his burger.

In fact, they had to wait another four days before General Chambers and McInnes returned, and within a fortnight all five team members were back at the top-secret facility, ready to begin the next phase of the experiment.

***

AirForce Plant 52, Death Valley, Mojave Desert, California June 2007

The image stared back at General Sterling Chambers, gaunt and feeble, as he examined himself in the mirror. He barely recognised the man reflected back at him standing unsteadily in his shorts and vest. Stepping up onto the scales, Chambers closed his eyes to allay his wavering body. The cancer had taken its toll, and in a short space of time, he had lost over 50lbs in weight. Professor Phillips took a note of the reading on the scales which the general was standing on, and frowned.

"What's the matter?" asked the general. "Don't you think I'm up to it?"

"Like you said, General, it's kill or cure," assessed David. "This drug doesn't take any prisoners and there's already been one death too many."

"Yeah, but this time it's my choice," declared Chambers.

David sat at a desk in his lab making a calculation, ignoring the general's last comment. Finally, he looked over to Chambers, who was now sitting down.

"We are good to go," remarked David, "whenever you're ready. Do you want the others to witness it?"

"What's your preference?"

"To have at least one person here," confirmed David.

"Okay," agreed Chambers. "How about Slater? Besides you, he knows the most about the drug."

This seemed logical to David; he nodded his approval and picked up the phone and punched in a number. After a brief conversation with the professor, Slater put the phone down and picked up his Glock 17 handgun, checked the magazine and tucked it into the back of his waistband, then he covered it with his untucked shirt. After what happened last time, he was taking no chances. By the time Slater arrived at the lab everything was set up. A gurney had been provided, fitted with three leather straps, to restrain chest, waist and ankles.

"What are the restraints for?" enquired Slater, walking around the contraption. It looked to him like an instrument of torture.

"It's to prevent the general from injuring himself," informed David. "You saw what the serum did."

Slater couldn't argue with this but couldn't help wondering if the professor was thinking of their safety too, as they observed the reaction to the injection.

"Okay, General," requested David, "if you would take your position on the gurney, we can begin."

Climbing up onto the gurney, Chambers winced in pain and Slater helped him into position. David proceeded to strap him in.

"Tell me if the restraints are too tight."

"Could you slacken them just a little?" said Chambers, wincing.

David complied and adjusted the straps, then walked over to a bench and prepared a syringe. He returned to the gurney, hypodermic in hand and squirted a little serum from the tip.

"This is your last chance to back out," advised David.

"Do it," said Chambers, grimacing.

The professor gave a quick glance at Slater, who had backed off about ten feet; finding a vein in Chambers' emaciated left arm posed no problem. David inserted the needle expertly and injected the serum.

"How do you feel?" enquired the professor.

"Nothing seems to be…" Chambers' voice trailed off as his body went into spasms. For about a minute his fragile frame shook uncontrollably, though held confined by the straps. At the point where David thought that he might break some bones, the seizure stopped as suddenly as it had started. Chambers lay very still and appeared to be dead.

With his stethoscope, David listened to his chest. He moved the bell of the scope around, trying to pick up any signs of life.

"I've found a heartbeat of sorts," he cried out with excitement. "About one beat every thirty seconds."

"Can he survive that?" asked Slater.

"I don't know. It seems his body has gone into a coma," mused David. "The best thing we can do now is make him comfortable and see if he wakes up."

The gurney was wheeled into a recovery room and the comatose general was transferred to a bed.

"We will need a round-the-clock guard placed on him," insisted Slater.

"I agree," concurred David. "Can you organise it?"

Nodding grimly, Slater and the professor took one last look at Chambers, locked the door and left.

***

We are but nothing without our senses. Sight, sound, smell, taste and touch, all these things inform our brain which commits them to memory as a sum total of our experiences. This is the process by which our personality is formed and establishes us as unique individuals. So, to be locked into a nether world of pure darkness, impenetrably black, unfathomable and disorientating, is a kind of living death. And barely alive but for the faintest of heartbeats is how General Sterling Chambers lay on his bed in a state of semi-oblivion for over twenty-five hours. Then, without fanfare or histrionics, his eyes opened and the general was conscious. He stared at the ceiling for a short while, getting his bearings, then swung his legs round off the bed and sat up. Placing both hands over his face, he rubbed the sleep from his eyes and stood up. Chambers walked around the room. He felt good. Better than good, he felt fantastic. In fact, he hadn't felt this good in years. Still only wearing his vest and shorts, he approached the door and tried the handle; the door was locked. The two guards outside his room stepped away, initially startled, then one moved away in haste to raise the alarm. The general rattled the door to alert someone's attention and to his surprise, ripped it off its hinges. The remaining guard backed off and brought his gun up in defence.

"Woah, easy, soldier," said Chambers, smiling and raising his right arm to placate the young man in front of him. "Everything's cool."

Realising that he was still holding the door by the handle, the general somewhat self-consciously leant it against the frame.

"I literally don't know my own strength," he said, wincing. "Shouldn't you be going to notify someone?"

"Err… help is on its way, sir," confirmed the guard, relaxing a little and lowering his rifle.

Walking back into the room, Chambers sat down on the bed and waited.

"How long was I out for?" he asked the guard who decided to stay in the corridor.

"Over a day, sir," he replied, consulting his watch. "Nearly twenty-six hours, I would say."

"It only seems a second ago that I had the injection," Chambers muttered as much to himself as the guard. He scratched his head and felt his chin. Sure enough, he had a good day's growth of stubble.

The guard who dashed off returned shortly with McInnes and David in tow. The two men looked in on General Chambers, then McInnes inspected the dislocated door with raised eyebrows.

"It came off in my hands," commented Chambers in a matter-of-fact manner.

David sat on the bed beside him and checked his heartbeat, then shone a torch into his eyes.

"Your heartbeat is strong and your responses seem fine," he declared. "How do you feel?"

"I feel fantastic," confirmed Chambers. "All my senses seem enhanced. But why did it take so long?"

David stood up and walked around the room, deep in thought. Eventually he stopped, turned and looked at the general.

"My guess is," he pondered, rubbing his chin, "because of the severity of your illness, the drug took longer to repair your body. We will have to get you checked out, but I wouldn't be at all surprised if your cancer hasn't been completely eradicated."

"What's next, Professor?" asked McInnes.

"To get cleaned up and something to eat," interrupted Chambers. "I haven't felt this hungry for a long time."

After a large steak dinner, Chambers wanted to order more, but David advised against it.

"Baby steps, General, your body isn't used to such quantities of food. You may feel physically fit but your body needs building up to regain the body mass you lost over the past months."

"Whatever you say, Professor," conceded Chambers. "I'll begin tomorrow."

With strict discipline and high motivation, General Chambers embarked on an intensive fitness course. A large fully equipped gymnasium was available for use by the personnel of the base on the third level, and Chambers put it to good use. Elevated above the gym equipment was a running track which formed a full circuit of the room. The track was about ten feet wide and cantilevered out from the wall. David, the rest of the team and Chambers' personal coach watched with fascination as the man who was once so close to death began to regain his fitness and more, at an alarmingly rapid rate. In the space of two weeks, Chambers was running ten laps of the gym, breaking all previous records. The coach pressed his stopwatch, looked at the timing and whistled to show his amazement.

"Well, General, I don't think that time will be beaten any time soon," he enthused.

The general smiled and sauntered off to take a shower. David and McInnes watched him stride confidently away.

"I think he's ready," declared McInnes to the professor.

"Yes," replied David tentatively.

"Do you have any concerns?" enquired McInnes, picking up on David's reticence.

"Have you noticed that he is a little more reclusive than he used to be?" suggested David.

"Well, possibly," mused McInnes, "now you come to mention it. Is that a problem?"

"I don't know," admitted David. "We know so little about this drug. Sure, we are aware of the physical effects it has on the body – but what of the psychological effects?"

"You think we should keep a closer eye on him?"

"Perhaps," offered David. "The only person that I encountered who has taken the drug was a psychopath. The question that needs to be considered is: was he that way before taking the drug or did it make him one?"

David wasn't the only one to notice the general's reclusive behaviour. After the traumatising experience with the pig, Katrina was nervous around a human who had been administered with the serum. In short, she didn't trust him and kept a close eye on the general's activities. Katrina decided to take her misgivings to Slater.

"Have you noticed how the general has been keeping more to himself recently?"

"You mean since his rehabilitation?" Slater felt the euphemism was appropriate, then considered Katrina's remark. "Well, I guess so. I haven't been watching him *that* closely."

"I have," confirmed Katrina. "When he isn't in his quarters, he seems to spend much of his time either in the gym or in the computer room on the internet."

"Picking up emails?" offered Slater.

"No," replied Katrina, shaking her head emphatically, "it has to be more than that. He spends too much time there."

"You could ask him," suggested Slater.

"If he is up to no good," Katrina postulated, "how will

he react if we confront him? No, I'm not going anywhere near the guy."

"Look, it's lunchtime," concluded Slater, looking at his watch, "let's get something to eat. I'm sure you're blowing this up out of all proportion."

As they approached the canteen, Chambers, now wearing a clean set of light grey sweats, was seen to leave and head for his billet. He'd had a full morning of exercising and had eaten a big lunch before showering. Chambers would do the same again later; one of the many changes he had noticed in himself was that he always seemed to be hungry.

In his room, Chambers stripped off and studied himself naked in the mirror fixed to the back of the wardrobe door. The difference was palpable and to say that he was back to his old self was an understatement. The strict exercising regime and the presence of the serum had made his body firm and strong, far beyond his younger physical peak, and it showed in his muscle tone. He put on a white short-sleeve shirt, some dark grey trousers and sat on his bed. Picking up the two printouts he had obtained from the computer room, he began to study them. One printout was of a newspaper clipping from February 1991; its headline read: '*Police baffled by mysterious death of young woman*'. The second was a download from the *United States Geographical Survey* website – a topographic map of the state of New York. Chambers made some notes on a scrap of paper and hid it all in his nightstand drawer. Then he lay back and rested, drifting off into a light slumber as he thought of the mission to come. As far as Chambers was concerned, he was ready.

***

Black Rock Desert Testing Ground, Nevada
June 2007

The call to mobilise came two days later after Chambers had been given a clean bill of health. An entourage of three large trucks and two Humvees, each equipped with a roof-mounted M240B machine gun, rode shotgun, fore and aft of the convoy. Making its way to a top-secret destination around 250 miles north of AirForce Plant 52, for McInnes and Chambers it was a case of *déjà vu*, having made this journey twelve years earlier. This time, however, they had high hopes for a successful outcome. Despite starting out early, the journey took all morning, and when they finally turned off US Route 95 and travelled for an hour over the pale alkali flats of the desert *playa*, the entourage drew to a halt. Personnel began to disembark from comfortable air-conditioned cabins into the blistering midday desert heat and began the arduous task of setting up a base of operation. The temperature was approaching thirty degrees Celsius as Katrina watched the activity. She very quickly put sunglasses on to protect her eyes from the intense glare of the salt flats, then looked around beyond the *playa* at the mountain ranges which seemed to surround the basin, shimmering blue and grey in the heat haze. It became apparent to her why this location had been chosen: it was remote and provided a good level of seclusion.

Two hours later the team were in an anteroom where Chambers was preparing for the test flight. He had just pulled on a sage green flight suit and zipped up the front.

"Are you sure this will be adequate, Professor?" he asked doubtfully. "The previous test pilot used a space suit."

"The Germans used overalls without any problems," assured David. "They were also equipped with these."

The professor handed Chambers a pair of dark-lens goggles, who duly put them in his pocket.

"I'm not sure why," continued David, "but you'd better take them just in case they're needed."

A technician stepped up into the room and saluted.

"Everything's in place, sir, whenever you are ready."

"This is it, Sterling." McInnes smiled reassuringly. "Good luck."

Chambers looked around at the faces opposite him.

"If you could give me a minute to myself," he remarked solemnly, "I'll be out directly."

The team gave understanding nods and filtered out, leaving the general on his own. As the door was pulled to, he immediately delved into a bag by his side and retrieved a black woollen full-face ski mask and the scrap of paper which he had hidden in his nightstand. Unzipping one of the diagonal pockets on his chest, Chambers slipped the piece of paper in, then tucked the mask inside his suit and zipped it back up again. Finally, he opened the door and squinted at the brightness of the sun. Placing a pair of aviator sunglasses over his eyes, he looked around and saw, 200 yards away, the *Die Glocke* time machine, its highly polished surface in the shadow of an awning to protect it from the heat.

"Okay," he announced, stepping down with confidence, "let's do this."

After handshakes and good lucks, Chambers clambered up into one of the Humvees and was driven down to the time machine. McInnes was sitting next to him.

"Well, if you want to back out, now's the time to do it."

"I think we both know that's not an option," imparted Chambers.

The Humvee pulled up close; the two men alighted and approached the bell-shaped vessel. A soldier saluted the general and opened the hatch. Without hesitation, Chambers clambered into the seat and got comfortable before strapping himself in. Giving a cursory wave, McInnes stepped back as the hatch door was closed. Chambers paused in the semi-darkness before removing the slip of paper from his chest pocket and switching on the timer. The red holographic controls hovered in front of his face and immediately he began changing the date, time and coordinates to those he'd written down, replacing the settings that were already preset. Confident that he hadn't made a mistake, Chambers hovered his right hand over the red start button and braced himself.

Back at the base of operations, David, Slater and Katrina watched as the Humvee returned. McInnes stepped down just in time to see the spectacle of the launch. The vessel rose up, rotating at high speed until it disappeared in a thunder-like crack. A shock wave halo emanated out until it dissipated.

"Wow!" exclaimed Katrina. "That was pretty spectacular."

Slater thought back to Operation Solar Eclipse; the sight gave him a sense of foreboding.

"When can we expect it back?" enquired Katrina.

"It's set for ten minutes from now," confirmed McInnes.

The team looked at their watches and moved into the shade of the anteroom.

***

Oxford, Chenango County, Upstate New York
February 1991

Chambers' body tensed as the vessel rose up. Very quickly it became apparent why the goggles were needed as the dazzling white light began to burn into his retinas. He pulled out the goggles and quickly placed them over his eyes. The date counted down on the holographic controls as the *Die Glocke* sped back in time, and the coordinates scrolled over at speed as it accelerated through space. Barely a minute went by before Chambers felt the machine decelerate and settle on the ground with a gentle bump. Removing the goggles, he looked at the display and checked the coordinates. They were exactly as stated on his slip of paper. The date and time were spot on also, reading Sunday 17 February 1991, 2000 hours.

After adjusting his watch, Chambers tentatively opened the hatch and stepped out to look around. He had landed in a small clearing surrounded by woodland. It was cold, around one degree Celsius, and Chambers knew that with no coat he would have to move fast to keep warm. He looked up into the clear night sky; stars were twinkling like glitter and the sliver of a waxing crescent moon hung awkwardly at an oblique angle. Grateful for this, Chambers knew that a full moon would cast more light, putting him at greater risk of detection.

Closing the hatch, Chambers began to jog in an easterly direction towards the tree line. In less than five minutes, he stopped in the woodland and scanned around him.

"Good," he muttered. He was early; there was no sign of the red hatchback.

Continuing on, Chambers picked up the pace until he eventually came out onto a main road. The street was quiet, but he kept to the shadows as best he could. After a while he turned down a side street and walked up to a timber-constructed house, painted white with a stone chimney rising above its gable end. No smoke could be seen, the windows were in darkness and with no car on the drive, it was clear the house was vacant. Encouraged by this he made his way round to the back of the house and peered into the kitchen through a rear door window. He looked around to see if there was any activity, then, satisfied nobody was about, he pulled his elbow back and shattered the glass in the kitchen door. Carefully inserting his right arm through, he navigated past the jagged edges, found the key in the lock and turned it. The first thing he did when inside was to find the fuse box and turn off the electricity.

Finally, he dug out the two-holed mask from inside his flight suit and pulled it over his head. Chambers looked at the soft glow of his luminous watch; it was approaching 2030 hours. All he could do now was hide in the sitting room and wait patiently in the darkness. Around an hour later, he saw car headlights shine briefly in through the window and the intruder braced himself.

***

Denise Palmer pulled up onto the drive, switched off the lights and then the engine. She sat for a second staring into the darkness, then thumped the steering wheel with both hands and burst into tears. Tired of the fighting and squabbling, she just wanted it to end. Having just returned from yet another acrimonious meeting with her estranged husband, Blake, it seemed they were just going around in circles getting nowhere. Her frustration had been building up for weeks; he wanted to sell the house and move on, but she wanted to retain it. Denise had invested more than money into the home and was loath to give it up. The problem was, she couldn't afford to buy him out.

She pulled herself together, stepped out of the car and grappled for the door keys in her purse. Opening the front door, she stepped in and flicked the light switch.

"Shit!" she exclaimed as the room remained in darkness. Denise flicked the switch again in the forlorn hope that they might work with a second attempt.

"Crap," she muttered again, and slowly made her way to the kitchen as her eyes grew accustomed to the dark.

Putting her purse and keys down on the worktop in the kitchen, Denise was suddenly startled by a sound coming from the sitting room. She gave out a gasp and moved towards a knife block.

"W-who… who's there?" she stammered, hoping it was just her imagination.

A dark figure appeared in the doorway and stopped. Denise could make out the face mask looking sinister with just its two eye holes. Terrified, she pulled a carving knife out of the block and brandished it in front of her.

"D-don't come any closer," she screamed.

Chambers stared for a moment at the slim attractive woman in front of him with the dark permed hair which cascaded around her shoulders in gentle ringlets.

"Please," urged Chambers, "we haven't much time. You must come with me. You have to get out of this house."

"Get out. Leave me alone." In her panic, Denise refused to listen. It didn't help that the stranger's words were muffled behind the mask.

Chambers knew that he had to do something decisive, so he lunged forward to grab her outstretched arm. Denise tried to strike her assailant with the knife as she stumbled backwards away from his grasp. Still wearing her high heels, her left ankle buckled under on the smooth tiled floor. She fell sideways and back with force until her head made contact with the edge of the worktop. With a sickening crack her whole body wheeled around and she hit the floor face down. Tentatively moving forward, Chambers stared in horror at the motionless body. He gently turned her over and saw the carving knife protruding from her chest. The nine-inch blade had pushed in right up to the handle, piercing her heart. Scrambling backwards against a wall, Chambers screamed at the top of his voice and put his face in his hands as he felt tears well up in his eyes. This wasn't supposed to happen. He stared in shock at what he had caused until he began to lose all track of time. Then, snapping out of it, he realised that he had to get out quickly before he was discovered. Taking one final look at the hapless girl lying immobile at an awkward angle, Chambers picked up her car keys, pulled off the mask and quietly slipped out of the back door and worked his way around the house to the red Honda Civic sitting on the drive. There was nothing he could do now but get back to his own time, knowing that he had failed.

The vicinity was quiet as Chambers reversed off the drive and retraced his route up the road. His instincts were to put his foot down and get back to the *Die Glocke* as fast as possible, but he managed to restrain himself and keep to the speed limit. The last thing he wanted was to attract attention. His presence in this time period would take some explaining. As if on autopilot, he made his way to the woods and parked the car as close to the time machine as possible. Leaving the keys in the ignition, he got out and began to hastily walk over to the shiny bell-shaped vessel sitting ominously in the clearing. He made one last glance back at the red hatchback and it suddenly occurred to him, to his dismay, that this was exactly how and where the car was eventually found. It was like a self-fulfilling prophesy in reverse. Chambers couldn't think about this now, his mind was focused on the return journey. Inside the vessel, he settled down and reset the date, time and coordinates for 2007, placed the goggles over his eyes and pressed the button.

***

The tension could have been cut with a knife as, nervously, the team kept checking their watches and looking across the glare of the salt flats, awaiting the return of the time machine.

"Any second now," observed McInnes.

Right on cue there was the usual loud crack and the time machine materialised in a blinding flash, hovering steadily, then slowly descending to the ground. Everyone looked at each other, slightly puzzled.

"What's happened?" asked Katrina. "It's come back on time but it's much further away."

"I don't know," commented McInnes. "It must be half a mile away. Maybe more."

Slater lifted a pair of binoculars to his eyes, as did McInnes. They stared tentatively for any signs of life. There was a pause for one long minute, until eventually they observed the hatch opening.

"He's getting out!" exclaimed Slater. "He made it."

The whole team cheered and applauded in celebration of the first successful American time travel launch. McInnes, Slater and Katrina, along with a technician, jumped into a Humvee and began to drive out to meet Chambers, who had begun to walk steadily away from the vessel. The Humvee was getting close but McInnes sensed that something wasn't right. They began to hear a loud claxon sound and McInnes recognised it immediately.

"Stop!" he shouted in panic. "Back up. He's triggered the self-destruct!"

The driver skidded to a halt and began reversing just as the *Die Glocke* exploded. A mushroom-shaped fireball billowed into the air as the time machine was ripped apart. The shock wave blew past Chambers, who continued walking away as if he was unconcerned by the event. Chunks of metal casing began to rain down around the general and still he didn't flinch. A smoking piece of debris landed on the bonnet of the Humvee making a deep dent, and the driver reversed further back.

Alighting from the vehicle, the team stared in disbelief at the inferno of billowing flames and thick black smoke, now drifting high up into the sky. They could feel the heat, even from this safe distance. Still confused by what they had just witnessed, the team watched Chambers approach and continue to walk past them, as if they weren't there.

"Sterling?" called McInnes as the general continued on his way towards the control centre. "Are you okay?"

Chambers ignored him and walked on, seemingly in a daze. Turning the Humvee around, they approached him and stopped. McInnes opened the door.

"Get in," he urged.

Chambers gave him a vacant look and stepped up into the cab. Then came a barrage of questions: what happened and why? He just sat silently staring out at the wreckage, brushing off their remarks, deep in his own thoughts.

***

"How is he?" enquired Slater.

"I've checked on him a few times," confirmed Katrina, "but he just sits on the edge of his bed, stares at the wall and won't speak."

Slater looked at his watch; it was getting late.

"Look, it's time for shut-eye now. Leave him to get some rest and we'll check on him first thing. Maybe then we'll get some sense out of him."

Katrina nodded reluctantly and made her way to her room; Slater looked doubtfully at the closed door of Chambers' room and did the same.

After a long day, Slater and the others all drifted off into fitful slumbers, only to be awakened by a loud siren sounding off somewhere in the building.

Hurriedly, they all got dressed and stepped out into the corridor. A furore of activity could be seen as several soldiers armed with automatic weapons were running in the general direction of the laboratory. McInnes stopped one to find out what was happening.

"It's the armoury, sir," he bellowed excitedly over the din, "it's been broken into."

The soldier seemed anxious to be on his way, so McInnes let him go and approached David, Slater and Katrina, still looking slightly dishevelled from their rude awakening.

"Did you hear that?" shouted McInnes to all three.

"They seem to be heading for the lab," said Slater, nodding. "I think we'd better get down there."

Very soon they were pushing past infantry to get to the door of the lab. About six feet away a captain restrained their progress.

"No further, sir," he said with a grimace, "for your own safety. He's got the place rigged."

"Who?" cried McInnes.

"General Chambers, sir," replied the captain. "We don't know what he wants, he won't talk."

"Let me try," requested McInnes, "I've known him for years."

The captain looked at McInnes doubtfully for a moment then reluctantly nodded his head and allowed McInnes through.

"Okay, but for chrissake be careful."

Tentatively, McInnes made his way to the open door of the lab and stepped in. What he saw was the general still wearing the flight suit, standing behind a bench with several M67 fragmentation hand grenades gaffer-taped to his body. The ex-CIA director counted the smooth green orbs hanging like baubles on a Christmas tree and gave up at nine. He noticed that the lever safety clip had been removed from all of them and the pin to release the lever was partly pulled. Attached to every pin was a piece of string, and they all converged into the beleaguered general's right hand. McInnes realised that it wouldn't take much to activate them. Also, placed nearby were several green plastic jerry cans filled with gasoline. The general's expression was grim and determined.

"Don't come any closer!" demanded Chambers, pulling slightly on the strings. McInnes held his hands up in an attempt to placate him.

"You've been busy, Sterling?" he enquired, trying his best to keep calm. "Now, what's this all about?"

"*This* has to be stopped." Tears began to trickle down the general's cheeks. "This whole project is an abomination. It goes against all that is natural."

"Why?" said McInnes, frowning. "What happened to you?"

"Time travel is too dangerous," he bemoaned. "I created a kind of time loop from which it's impossible to escape and the only way to stop it is to destroy the time machine and the drug."

It was only then that McInnes noticed the phials piled up around him and the empty aluminium cases discarded on the floor.

"This is crazy," declared McInnes, "we've worked too hard to get to this point. Years of waiting, and you're going to destroy it all? For the love of God, tell me what happened."

Chambers stared at him for a moment before he spoke.

"I changed the setting to send me back to 1991."

"Why would you do that?"

"I went to try and save the life of a young woman who died in mysterious circumstances," Chambers revealed. "I thought that changing such a small piece of history wouldn't make *that* much difference. But the truth is we can't change anything. The past, present and future are all interlinked. I realise that now. I went back to save her, only to find out that I'm the one destined to kill her. I didn't mean to, it was an accident."

"What was so special about this woman?"

The look of anguish on Chambers' face was almost too much to endure.

"She was my daughter!" cried Chambers. His demeanour seemed to crumble under the weight of this admission. He sniffed and repeated with resignation, "My daughter."

"My God," muttered McInnes, "you killed your daughter."

McInnes took one step into the lab and the general immediately pulled the strings taut.

"One more step and I pull the pins," he cautioned.

"Come on, Sterling, you don't really want to do that, do you?" reasoned McInnes.

Feeling he had no choice but to call the general's bluff, McInnes made one more step inside. With the smallest of movements, Chambers pulled out all of the pins, which swung on their strings and swayed vertically like plumb lines. Safety levers sprang away in all directions.

"Goodbye, Alex."

Knowing that he only had seconds, a horrified McInnes turned tail and exited the lab as fast as he could.

"He's pulled the pins," shouted McInnes, running into the corridor.

The crowd had already backed off for safety but began to move further back. Five seconds elapsed and a huge explosion shook the floor, rupturing the wall and causing a fireball to erupt out of the door and fill the corridor. The blast billowed down the corridor and they had to back up further from the intense heat. McInnes was thrown to the floor, his back in flames. The captain pulled him to safety and put out the flames, then he checked McInnes for a pulse.

"He's alive," he confirmed. "We'd better get him to the medical centre."

It took several soldiers with fire extinguishers an hour to get the fire under control, before David and Slater were able to examine the damage. The laboratory was gutted from floor to ceiling. They stepped in and picked their way through the devastation. There was nothing left but a charred mess. Ceiling panels hung down dripping water and much of the floor was covered in black puddles.

"That's it," exclaimed Slater in dismay, "it's all gone."

"Maybe it's for the best," consoled David. "You heard what he said about his daughter. Maybe time travel *is* a waste of… err time."

"Where's Katrina?" replied Slater, ignoring David's observation.

"She's gone to check on Alex," advised David. "He isn't too badly burned but seems to have been badly shaken."

"When he's fit, we will need to reconvene to see where we go from here," declared Slater.

David simply nodded and the pair walked out of the laboratory with their heads down.

***

The team reconvened in the meeting room to discuss the disastrous events of the previous day. The mood in the room was sullen and nobody wanted to be the first to speak. McInnes winced as he sat down, his back sore from the injuries he sustained.

"Are you okay to be here?" asked Slater eventually.

"Can we shed any more light on this?" sighed McInnes, ignoring him.

Katrina had a folder in front of her. She opened it and pulled out a map.

"These were found in the general's room. It would seem that he downloaded this USGS map of the state of New York and this newspaper cutting," she advised. "I knew he was up to something."

"Then why didn't you alert us to it?" exclaimed McInnes.

Katrina looked furtively at Slater, who duly took the hint and owned up.

"It was my fault," he confessed. "I said it was probably nothing."

"To be fair," chimed in David, "who could have possibly foreseen this?"

His discomfort had made McInnes irritable; he was in no mood for lame excuses. He shifted awkwardly in his chair and turned his attention back to Katrina, who continued with her findings.

"From what I can make out, his daughter, Denise Palmer, died in 1991 in mysterious circumstances. She was going through a messy divorce at the time and her husband, Blake, was suspected, but nothing could be proven."

"And he went back to try and stop it?" mused McInnes.

"Yes, only to find out that he was the killer, unbeknownst to his younger self," added David. "How crazy is that?"

"Instead of destroying everything," suggested Katrina, "couldn't he have gone back a second time to stop himself?"

There was a pregnant pause as they all thought about this possibility. David was the first to break the silence.

"Clearly time travel is unpredictable and the more you mess with the time line, the more variables you add, there is more opportunity for things to go awry. God knows what chaos would ensue."

"Hmm, Murphy's Law," stated McInnes. "If something can go wrong, the chances are, it almost certainly will."

"So, what you're saying is time travel causes more problems than it solves," surmised Slater.

"Perhaps," replied a non-committal David, who then added, "I think the general had a point. What he said makes perfect sense to me. The past, present and the future are all interlinked. It's the only way a time machine could function. We fuck with them at our peril."

Everyone in the room raised their eyebrows at this uncharacteristic profanity from the professor, but it only served to confirm his strength of feeling on the subject.

"Well, since we no longer have any fuel or serum to continue with this project," declared McInnes, "the whole matter is now academic."

"What will happen to the other time machines?" enquired Slater.

McInnes shrugged his shoulders. At this moment in time, he was at a complete loss. Since Project Phoenix was now dead in the water, the meeting was adjourned and they all left in solemn silence.

"We have two injured and two dead," pointed out Katrina to Slater when the others were out of earshot. "Three if you count the general's daughter. How many more will have to die before this is all over? Is it worth it?"

Deep in thought, Slater nodded. He was only too aware how the death toll was mounting up.

"What now?" asked Katrina.

"Home, I guess," said the ex-CIA man, shrugging. "I would imagine that Project Phoenix will be put on hold for the foreseeable future. And we can only be grateful for that."

***

A week later, Slater was back in his beloved Rocky Mountains. He had made sure McInnes was fit to travel home and helped Katrina with her report before she returned to CIA headquarters at Langley. It was the end of June and the mountain was glorious at this time of year. The sun beat down, warm on his face and he breathed in the clean mountain air. Slater was glad to be back. The madness that he had been immersed in seemed a million miles away now and he hoped that that would be an end to it. Chastising himself for even daring to hope, he knew better than most that it only led to despair and disappointment. Forlorn hope can crush the spirit. It didn't help that he had promised David to keep an eye on Jessica if something were to happen to him; and Slater agreed, assuming that that day was a long way off.

The day after Slater's return and after he had settled back in, there was one more thing that he had to do. Around 9am, he was driving through the rickety old town of Evergreen. The tourist season was getting underway and the roads were busy. Pulling up outside the Lakeside Café, he stood for a short while and took in the activity on and around Evergreen Lake; it was nice to see the world going about its business, oblivious to the insane exploits with which he was involved. *And why shouldn't they?* he thought. *After all, this is what's normal, surely? Isn't it?*

As he opened the door to the café, it was teeming with customers. He saw Martha behind the counter; she looked exactly the same as when he last saw her. Bright and cheerful despite being rushed off her feet.

Every morning, Martha kept an eye on the door in the hope that this would be the day when Slater returned. This particular morning, she wasn't disappointed. The man of whom she was so fond walked in, a little weary looking perhaps, but there, large as life, with a tentative smile on his face. Before he could say anything, she picked up the coffee jug and said with a warm grin,

"Morning, Liam. The usual?"

***

After all the activity of the last few weeks, David was exhausted. His left knee was hurting badly and he desperately needed some well-earned rest and recuperation. Eventually he turned his attention to more pressing matters. Despite his arm injury he had important affairs to put in order. David was becoming more and more frustrated with the plaster cast; it was bad enough that he had to put up with a gammy leg, without this added encumbrance. With his right hand hindered, it was difficult to cut the slots into the foam which now padded out a small white plastic box. He sat on his bed, pulled open the top drawer of his nightstand and carefully removed some socks. Gently he tipped them up and extracted a phial of serum, until he had four nestled safely on a pillow. Security at the base had been tight and every drop of serum was accounted for. So, when David had smuggled out four phials, he wondered at the time how he would explain the shortfall. This ceased to be an issue when General Chambers destroyed the laboratory; it didn't occur to anyone that he might have four phials secreted in his room.

One by one, he picked them up and placed them firmly into the foam slots in the white box, closed the lid and wrapped rubber bands around to secure it. Then he lay on his bed and stared doubtfully at the box sitting on his nightstand, questioning his motives for smuggling the phials out. The destruction of the laboratory put an end to it all, surely? Alas David knew that this could never be so, not while Jessica was still alive. She had the drug entrenched in her DNA, and if she were to have children, she would pass it on. If Jessica's singular genetic makeup was discovered, her life could be in danger. The fewer people who knew the better, and that included Jessica herself. At least for the time being. And if she were to meet someone, how would they cope with her lifespan? Jessica would age significantly slower; the problems this would cause would be insurmountable. Perhaps if she could find someone to share her longevity – perhaps. No, despite his misgivings, with the serum available, Jessica would have options. It would be up to her what to do with it.

David decided to take the box and a letter that he'd typed out and open a safety deposit box account. He knew just the place to go: a bank in Sausalito just north of the Golden Gate Bridge. Then lodge the key with his solicitor, instructing him to pass it on to his daughter after his death. Maybe then he could try to forget about the whole sorry business.

Knowing the day would eventually have to come when Jessica would need to be told her true heritage, he felt guilty leaving all this in the hands of Slater, to tell her after his death – assuming he went first. He wanted his remaining years with her to be as normal as possible and resented having to divulge that her biological father was a psychopath. Thinking back to that day in 1985 when Laura introduced von Brandt to him, David marvelled how one man could blight so many lives for so long. And as Slater so reassuringly put it, he was long gone. David's one comforting thought was, at least he wouldn't have to look into the cold blue eyes of that smug, arrogant face again.

CHAPTER TWELVE

BUTTERFLIES AND MONSTERS

Berkeley, Near San Francisco, California
October 2016

After placing his cell phone back on the nightstand, Professor Nathan Harrison slumped back on his pillow and gave a gentle sigh. Sophie slid her naked body over his and he could feel her ample, firm breasts pressing resolutely and unyielding against his stomach. With her arms linked across his chest she rested her chin on her hands and beamed a mischievous grin. Sophie could make out a female voice on the other end of the phone, but didn't recognise it.

"Why, Professor," she said, frowning with mock indignation, "I hope you are not seeing another woman."

Harrison thought about his evening with Jessica and he grimaced inside. He really wasn't sure what was going on. His feelings towards Jessica were mixed, confused even. On the one hand he was attracted to her, but on the other he felt protective. More of a father figure. Harrison knew this was crazy; they were both of similar ages, but despite her education, despite her intelligence, Jessica was so unworldly and lacking in self-confidence. Ironically, not like the beautiful young woman, ten years his junior, who had knocked at his door this evening and was now sharing his bed. Harrison couldn't remember how they got to this point and couldn't help thinking that perhaps *he* was the one who had been seduced. Sophie was a woman who knew what she wanted and usually got it.

"That was Dr Phillips," replied Harrison, checking the alarm clock on his nightstand. It read 9.45. "She wanted me to come over, but it's a little late."

"Besides, you're with me," said Sophie, beaming lasciviously.

"You, madam, are going to get me fired," censured Harrison.

"I don't see why, if we're discreet," countered Sophie. "Besides, I take my finals in May and that's only seven months away."

"I hope you're not expecting any favouritism," said Harrison, frowning, suddenly worried that Sophie might have an ulterior motive for being here.

"Certainly not!" Sophie took exception to this affront.

"I shall succeed on my own merit. I don't need you to get my degree. How could you say such a thing?"

Sophie began to roll off him but Harrison held her close. He knew she was more than capable and was annoyed with himself for suggesting it.

"I'm sorry," he beseeched, "but I had to be sure. This is a big risk for me."

Sophie relaxed again and her expression changed to its usual cheerful demeanour.

"So, why does old misery guts want you to go round anyway?"

"Hey, show some respect, madam," admonished Harrison, with a playful slap to the left cheek of her behind. "She has just lost her father."

"I didn't know that," lamented Sophie, secretly enjoying being chastised, "I'm sorry. It's just that she never seems happy."

Harrison had to concede this point; Jessica rarely smiled, if ever.

"You didn't answer my question," admonished Sophie.

"What?"

"Why are you going?"

"She's asked me to meet her at her father's house tomorrow," confirmed Harrison.

"Why?"

"I don't know."

"Intriguing," quipped Sophie.

"Look, if you're staying the night, then we'd better get our heads down," insisted Harrison. "You need to be out of here early tomorrow, before anyone sees you."

"Whatever you say, Professor Harrison." Sophie rolled off him, grinning mischievously.

"Can't you call me Nathan?" requested Harrison. "Especially when we're in bed."

Sophie giggled, kissed him passionately and snuggled in.

"Yes, Professor Harrison," she simpered.

No matter how their relationship developed, he would always be the professor to her. Harrison lay back, wondering what he'd got himself into. Eventually they both fell into a fitful sleep locked in each other's arms.

***

The following morning, as Professor Harrison drove towards Oakland, he reflected on his life. The sun was shining, he had a career that he loved and had just slept with one of the most attractive girls on campus, who was also ten years his junior. Most men would have been on cloud nine, so why had a wave of melancholia swept over him earlier like a tsunami? Having expected Sophie to be wilful and reluctant to leave early this morning, he was surprised to wake up with her beautiful face close to his, beaming a wide smile. She simply bid him good morning, kissed him, got dressed and left. Her carefree manner seemed to belie a maturity which he clearly underestimated.

Harrison pinpointed his mood to David's funeral. Not because of David's death *per se*, after all he wasn't particularly close to the man, and amazingly, this *was* his first funeral. The whole experience made him think seriously about his own mortality, and these thoughts were only compounded by the fact that Sophie was so much younger, plus the knowledge that Jessica's life had been extended significantly purely by a perverse form of natural selection.

Everyone is different in their own way, but Jessica's form of uniqueness put her beyond anyone else on the planet, and it could easily find her becoming more and more lonely and isolated as her generation began to age. Harrison identified this problem almost immediately and wondered whether Jessica had too. With a morning free of lectures, he was now heading out for his rendezvous with Jessica and wondered what it was all about. Harrison pulled up onto the drive of David's bungalow beside a car which he recognised as hers; he stepped out of his car and rang the doorbell.

Jessica heard a car pull up on the drive and opened the door whilst Harrison's finger was still on the button. He smiled and was then slightly taken aback by her appearance. She was wearing a plain pink T-shirt, tight-fitting light blue jeans and white trainers. Her hair looked bedraggled, after being hastily tied up out of the way, plus she had a smudge of dirt on her left cheek. In her hand, Jessica held a duster and Harrison warmed to this less than perfect incarnation of the young woman, simply because she looked slightly dishevelled and normal. With a perfunctory smile, Jessica ushered him in.

"What are you doing here?" enquired Harrison.

"Oh, just sorting things out," replied Jessica wistfully. "I've been checking the house to make sure there are no more surprises waiting for me."

Looking around the sitting room, the professor could see that several drawers had been emptied, their contents arranged in neat piles.

"Did you find any?" asked Harrison.

Jessica looked at him with dark enquiring eyes, eyebrows raised.

"Surprises," elucidated Harrison.

"Oh – yes, well, kind of," confirmed Jessica, "in here."

Harrison followed her into the kitchen and Jessica stopped at the worktop and gestured towards a neat pile of petri dishes and, tipped on its side, an open box of hypodermic syringes. A few were displayed on the worktop, each one individually sealed in their sterile packaging.

"I've found these," she revealed. "I suppose they might come in useful."

"Is this what you wanted to show me?" quipped Harrison in disbelief.

Jessica shot him a glance of pure contempt and walked into the sitting room. She sat on the couch and delved into her bag. Harrison followed her in and sat down opposite just as she was retrieving a white plastic box. With the rubber band pulled off, Jessica placed the box gently on the coffee table, opened the lid and turned it around to the professor.

"What is it?" enquired Harrison, staring intently at the four phials set neatly into their foam inserts.

"It's the drug," replied Jessica, "the Infinity Serum."

Harrison leant forward and picked one up.

"It doesn't look like much, does it," he commented somewhat dismissively.

"I have a letter from my father here." Jessica now brandishing an envelope. "It says that this stuff is lethal unless handled correctly. It also has the formula for reproducing it, and administering it."

"Do you know how many doses there are here?" Harrison placed the phial back very carefully in its foam slot.

"Approximately 500," said Jessica with a shrug, "but it all depends on the weight of the individual."

This was huge; Harrison understood now why Jessica had phoned him when she did and why she felt the need to share it with someone she could trust. He felt foolish for not being in a position to see her the previous evening.

"I'm sorry I didn't come over last night," he declared.

"Oh, that's alright, I guess you were busy." Jessica shot Harrison a tentative smile and then gave the slightest of frowns. "Who were you with last night? Sophie, I suppose."

"What?" Harrison was mortified. It was as much an exclamation as a question.

"I'm sorry, Nathan, it's none of my business." Jessica shook her head and looked away in embarrassment.

"What makes you think that I was with someone?" he blurted, alarmed. The question unsettled him.

"I could hear someone breathing, quite close to you," revealed Jessica cautiously. "I'm assuming it must have been a woman, you wouldn't be that intimate with a man."

"You could hear her?" jabbered Harrison, his mind racing.

"Yes, my senses are very keen, I'm afraid." Jessica could see he was mortified but was not prepared to let him off the hook yet. "So, it *was* a she then."

"Yes, it was Sophie Hunter," sighed Harrison in surrender. "Look, I know exactly what you're thinking, I'm risking my career. I didn't plan it. It just… well, it just happened."

"You're a grown-up," commented Jessica. "If you want to risk your career, that's entirely up to you."

"We are being discreet," offered Harrison, though he wondered why he felt the need to justify himself. "She leaves very early in the morning, just before sun up."

"I thought that you and I…" Jessica let the sentence trail away. She slumped back on the couch, with a sombre expression on her face.

Jessica waited for a reply, but Harrison was at a loss as to how to respond, so they sat in silence until it started to become awkward; Jessica finally took the initiative.

"Would you like a drink?" she offered.

"Err, coffee, please," replied Harrison, relieved to see Jessica leave the room.

Shortly, she returned with a tray of cups and a cafetière. Placing the tray down next to the phials, she noticed Harrison studying them intently.

"Do you think David considered injecting himself?" suggested Harrison.

"Possibly," mused Jessica, "though I doubt whether he did. He would've been physically much fitter."

"What are *you* going to do with it?" Harrison enquired. "Any ideas?"

"I haven't thought that far ahead," she replied, pouring coffee into cups. "Why, have you any ideas?"

They both sat back and sipped their drinks. Harrison fixed his gaze on Jessica and then spoke.

"Inject me."

"You?" exclaimed Jessica. "Are you being serious?"

"Yes – why not?" retorted Harrison. "I want what you have."

"And what is that exactly?"

"A longer life span for starters."

"Be careful what you wish for, Nathan," advised Jessica. She said it with feeling, remembering how it affected her, growing up.

"Do you want to live your life being the only one to grow old slowly?" reasoned Harrison. "Look, I want this."

"Okay, if you're sure." This had come as a complete surprise to Jessica, but she liked the implication that they might have a future together. "When shall we do it?"

"How about this afternoon?" suggested Harrison. "There's no time like the present."

"Haven't you got lectures later today?"

"Yeah, I've got two later," replied Harrison thoughtfully. "I'll ring in sick."

***

Back at her apartment, Jessica improvised a light lunch from the supplies she had available. She carried in a tray of green salad, tomatoes, cheese and half a loaf of bread, set it down on the dining table and left to get some orange juice.

"Help yourself," she announced and Harrison began to butter some bread.

"Aren't you eating?" enquired Harrison.

"I need a shower," remarked Jessica. "Besides, I'm not hungry."

As she padded off to the bathroom, Harrison proceeded to make himself a cheese salad sandwich. She might not be hungry but he was famished. Whilst he was pouring himself a second glass of orange juice, Jessica reappeared, dressed in a white bathrobe and running a brush through her long black hair as she moved to the bedroom.

"You need to strip off and weigh yourself," she declared in a way which suggested that this was normal behaviour for guests.

"Why?"

"I need your weight as accurate as possible, to calculate the amount of serum to give you," Jessica confirmed. "I have digital scales in the bathroom, they will be accurate enough."

Harrison did as he was told and stood naked on the scales then checked the reading; it displayed 175lbs. This came as no surprise to him; he had been around this weight for years.

Jessica re-emerged from her bedroom after drying her hair, barefooted, wearing a plain white T-shirt and pink shorts. Harrison had just exited the bathroom wearing only his white T-shirt and cream chinos, his faded denim shirt draped over his left forearm. He stared at her as she walked over to her purse, lying discarded on the couch. Even without trying, she still looked stunningly beautiful. But maybe, conjectured Harrison, *that* was why he considered her so attractive. There didn't seem to be any vanity about this woman, she didn't even seem to be aware of her physical appearance.

"What?" Jessica looked up from the couch and had noticed Harrison studying her.

"Nothing," conceded Harrison, suddenly snapped out of his reverie. "What's next?"

Without answering, Jessica opened her purse, extracted the envelope containing the formulae, plus her cell phone, and moved to the table and sat down.

"How much do you weigh?" she asked.

"A gentleman doesn't disclose such things," he retorted in mock indignation, trying to keep the mood light.

Jessica shot him an old-fashioned look and waited patiently for his reply.

"175lbs," he acquiesced with a sigh, realising he should have known better than to try and jest with her.

With the contents of the envelope unfolded in front of her, Jessica began to tap numbers into the calculator on her phone. Eventually she presented Harrison with a notepad of figures.

"Check my work," she insisted, "we can't afford any mistakes."

Harrison went over her calculations and came to the same conclusion.

"This all seems in order," confirmed Harrison, "but why two calculations?"

Jessica was ready for this question. She looked at him, trying to gauge what his response might be to her answer.

"I'm going to inject as well."

"For God's sake, why?" questioned Harrison. "You don't need to."

"Call it a gesture of solidarity," declared Jessica. "If you take the drug it's only fair that I do too. My physiology is far more robust than yours, so I don't anticipate any problems. Besides, I am intrigued to see what effect the serum has on me."

"Okay," said Harrison, frowning, "where shall we do it?"

"The spare bedroom," suggested Jessica.

Nodding, Harrison followed her in and began to suddenly have doubts as to whether he'd done the right thing. Picking up on his unease, Jessica smiled and gestured for him to lie on the bed.

"It will be alright," she soothed.

Harrison watched nervously as Jessica took a phial and pushed the needle of one the hypodermics into the lid. She charged the syringe and squirted a small amount out, checked the dose was correct then turned to the professor.

"Which arm do you prefer?"

"The left."

Jessica gave his left forearm a gentle slap to make a vein stand out and pushed the needle in with expert efficiency. Then she discharged the syringe and removed it.

"How do you feel?" asked Jessica.

Before Harrison could answer, he began to go into convulsions. Jessica threw her weight onto him to keep the professor from hurting himself. Thirty seconds later the fitting stopped as suddenly as it had started. Harrison lay there perfectly still. Fumbling to find a pulse, Jessica began to panic then she reeled back in surprise as he gave out a loud gasp of breath and became conscious again. He was panting and it took about ten seconds for him to regain his composure.

"Are you okay?" implored Jessica.

Harrison didn't answer. He just blinked his eyes and assessed his surroundings.

"Yes," he replied eventually, "I feel great."

He picked up the box of syringes and began to read the small print.

"I guess I won't be needing reading glasses anymore."

"You'll find all your senses are enhanced – and your

strength," she advised, grinning with delight. "Now it's my turn."

A fresh hypodermic was unwrapped and Jessica charged it with more serum. She handed it to Harrison, laid on the bed and offered her left arm.

"Please," she implored, noticing Harrison's hesitation.

The professor had no trouble finding a vein. A prominent blue line showed up perfectly under Jessica's porcelain white skin. Doing his best to keep his hand steady Harrison inserted the needle and discharged the syringe.

Minutes went by as they waited for a reaction but nothing came. Jessica slipped her legs over the side of the bed and sat up.

"Well, that's disappointing."

"You feel no different?"

"No," Jessica looked up at him with slight embarrassment, "nothing at all."

"I guess that's better than an adverse effect," he said consolingly.

"I suppose," replied a very glum Jessica. "I thought there might be something."

As Jessica stood up, she gave out a gasp and staggered. Harrison grabbed her by the right arm for support. A seismic shift seemed to pass through Jessica's body, electrifying her nerve endings in a sudden shock wave which left her breathless for a few seconds; and then she regained her equilibrium.

"What happened there?"

"I don't know." Jessica was wide-eyed and slightly bemused. "I'm alright though. I'm okay."

"The problem is," he commented, "this is all new to us. We're like pioneers."

Jessica wasn't listening; her mind seemed to be elsewhere. Suddenly she felt the need to rest.

"Could you leave me, please, Nathan," she appealed, "I need to sleep."

"Are you sure that you should be left on your own?" he suggested, not unreasonably. "Should either of us be on our own?"

"I'll be fine," she assured, "we'll both be fine. If something really bad was going to happen, it would have done so by now."

"I don't like this," Harrison fretted.

"Don't worry," she said, smiling, "we're both at the end of a phone."

"Okay," said Harrison reluctantly, nodding, "just make sure you ring if there's a problem."

Jessica smiled weakly at him and made her way to her bedroom. His heart was in the right place, but Jessica couldn't think what possible help he might be if there was a problem.

The professor watched her settle on the bed, nodded with an uncertain smile and left the apartment to a world of new sensations.

***

After spending some time in Uptown Oakland, Professor Harrison's senses were going into overload. His newly enhanced sensory perception was becoming bemusing, and he felt the need to escape to a more sedate location so that he could hear himself think. Making his way east, Harrison pulled up in a car park at Adams Point and got out. In front of him, glistening in the sun, was Lake Merritt, a popular spot for boating and cycling. To his left were the five small islands that made up the bird sanctuary, which a man was studying resolutely with a pair of binoculars at the lake's edge. Harrison smiled inwardly, as he had no problem at all seeing the birds in detail with his heightened vision. Idly he sauntered across a footpath and found himself close to the lake's edge, where a number of large boulders had been randomly arranged. When he was sure no one was looking, he tried to move one. The rock must have been about three feet in diameter, but he had no trouble lifting it a few inches off the ground. Placing the boulder down, again he furtively looked around him to see if anyone had noticed. Happy that they hadn't, he sat down on the boulder and stared absentmindedly over the water.

Everything David and the CIA agent had said seemed to be true with regards to the effect of the drug, so he had no reason to doubt that his life expectancy had been extended also. The big question was, by how much?

His thoughts turned to Jessica and Sophie; he was becoming more and more emotionally involved with both and knew that the situation was just storing up trouble for the future. He knew at some point he was going to have to choose, but who? Sophie was vibrant, cheerful and full of fun. Whilst Jessica, despite seemingly being independent and self-reliant, was more vulnerable, and probably needed his support more. And now Jessica had taken more of the drug. What would that mean for her – for them, their future? Confused he walked back to his car and drove home to Berkeley.

After Harrison had left, Jessica dropped into a deep, dreamless sleep for a full three hours and woke up feeling normal and refreshed. She walked over to her dressing table, sat down and glanced in the mirror. As she picked up a brush, Jessica studied her reflection and her image flickered like a badly tuned television screen. Closing her eyes and shaking her head, Jessica slowly opened them to see her face just as it should be staring back at her. She dismissed the apparition and dressed to go out. Keen to reassure Harrison that she was fine, Jessica drove over to his home in Berkeley. Now that they could relate on an equal footing, she was looking forward to seeing him again. Five hundred feet from the house, however, she slowed down. Sophie was standing in the open doorway and Harrison invited her in and closed the door just as Jessica passed his apartment block. Incensed with anger and jealousy, she put her foot down and sped past, then once clear of the building, she pulled over and stopped, burst into tears and thumped the top of the dashboard with her fist. The plastic shattered under the force but Jessica barely noticed.

It was early evening when Harrison's doorbell buzzed. He answered the door to see Sophie standing there – her usual smile but a little tentative this time.

"Sophie!" exclaimed the professor. He was not expecting her and hoped to spend some more time with his thoughts. "This is a surprise."

"I hope it's okay me turning up like this," Sophie said, wincing; she didn't want the professor thinking she was getting clingy. "It's just that I was worried. You didn't turn up for classes today."

"Come in," invited Harrison and closed the door behind her.

"You don't look under the weather," commented Sophie, fishing for information. She knew Harrison had gone to see Jessica and was anxious for news.

"No, I'm fine. More than fine," replied Harrison. "I was with Jessica for most of the afternoon."

"What did she want?"

"Um," hesitated Harrison, "err… I can't really say. It's personal."

"You can tell me." Sophie had sidled up to him and pressed her firm body hard against his. Rising on tiptoe she placed her lips close to his left ear and whispered, "You can confide in me, Professor, I won't tell a soul."

Harrison felt her warm breath in his ear and nearly succumbed. With a push which was harder than he intended, he came to his senses.

"Don't pester me on this," he demanded, "I can't talk about it."

"Are you screwing her?" Sophie looked hurt and angry at Harrison's rebuff.

"I *have* slept with her," hesitated Harrison, "but that's not what happened yesterday."

"When did it happen then?" Sophie looked crestfallen.

"It was just after her father died," revealed Harrison, "before anything happened with you and me."

"Oh, a sympathy fuck then," said Sophie, smiling, regaining her composure.

It wasn't quite like that, but the professor decided to

let it go. The situation with the two women was beginning to unravel and he felt out of his depth. Completely out of his comfort zone with the subject, Harrison was keen to change it.

"I'm sorry," he beseeched, "I didn't mean to push you like that."

Again, she pressed herself tight against his body, kissed him hard on the lips and pulled away.

"That's okay," said Sophie, grinning lasciviously, "I know just the way you can make it up to me."

***

If anyone had asked Jessica how she got home later that day, she would not have been able to answer. She had driven on autopilot and now found herself not back at her apartment but at the home she grew up in: David's bungalow.

She sat in the darkness seemingly in a daze, completely unaware of the passing of time. So many memories came flooding back into her mind, mostly happy, and for the first time in her life she felt truly alone. Nathan had given her a taste of companionship – love even. To her astonishment, Jessica found that she liked it – liked him. Loved him even. Now that bitch was spoiling it all by coming between them. Wiping the tears from her eyes, Jessica wondered why she felt so threatened by this child. Sophie was hardly competition; Jessica felt that she had so much going for her, and more, that it was hardly a fair fight. And Nathan was no fool; surely he would see that. Jessica needed to know for sure and the only way to do that was to make it a fair fight. What was it Nathan had said? Sophie leaves just before sun up. An idea formulated in her mind. A crazy, insane idea, but at this moment she wasn't thinking straight. Jessica entered the garage through a door in the hallway, found what she was looking for and returned to the couch. She looked at her watch; it was nearly midnight. With six hours before dawn, she would try to get her head down and rest for a few hours.

It was still pitch black when Jessica pulled up near to Harrison's apartment block. She looked at her watch as it ticked over to 5am, switched off her engine and waited patiently, hoping that she hadn't arrived too late. Her vigil was a short one, as thirty minutes later Sophie appeared, closing the door gently behind her and looking around furtively. Jessica heard the door click shut as if it was right beside her and could see her quarry in the twilight as clear as day, even though the sun had not quite broken the horizon. Despite the fact that the streets were deserted, Jessica knew that she would have to choose her moment. So, with her headlights switched off, she followed Sophie from a safe distance back as she made her way home at a brisk pace. The opportunity came for Jessica about forty minutes later when Sophie turned off the main sidewalk and entered Euclid Walk, a footpath which passed through a small park of trees and shrubs on the edge of the college campus. Jessica parked up and moved stealthily through the trees towards Sophie. The sun was well above the horizon and Jessica knew that she would have to move fast.

Close to her digs now, Sophie was about to pick up the pace when a hand suddenly wrapped itself around her mouth from the right, whilst a left arm grabbed her waist. Wide-eyed and trying to shout through the hand, Sophie was dragged into the trees. She assumed that her assailant was a man because the whole operation was executed with immense strength. Jessica pushed the beleaguered girl up against a tree trunk hard and placed a six-inch strip of silver gaffer tape, which she had retrieved from the garage, over Sophie's mouth. Then she grabbed both arms and bound them tightly with gaffer tape behind Sophie's back. Without uttering a single word Jessica grabbed her captive by the right arm and pulled her towards the road where her car was parked. Sophie stared in disbelief as she recognised her attacker. What was going on? Why was Dr Phillips doing this? The two women broke cover from the trees and Jessica hastily looked around to see if anyone was watching. Luckily the street was still empty, so without hesitation, she opened the rear door and bundled the hapless girl in and forced her down onto the floor. Sophie watched as Jessica got into the driving seat, turn around and rip the tape off Sophie's mouth.

"What the fuck are you doing?" screamed Sophie. "You mad bitch."

"If you know what's good for you, you will keep still and keep quiet," Jessica's voice was unsettlingly calm as she spoke, "and you will come to no harm."

"But what's this all…" Sophie couldn't finish the sentence because another piece of tape had just been placed over her mouth.

Despite the journey back being short, the ride for Sophie was an incredibly uncomfortable one. She tried shifting herself to no avail and was relieved when the car stopped and the door finally opened. Jessica leaned in looking stern. More so than usual.

"I'm going to remove the tape from your mouth," she advised, "and I strongly advise you to keep quiet."

With no effort, Jessica pulled her captive out from the seat well with one hand and placed Sophie in front of her.

"I don't understand, Miss Phillips," beseeched Sophie. "Why are you doing this?"

"Just walk calmly to the door," replied Jessica unhelpfully.

When they were inside the apartment, Jessica dead-bolted the door and looked at her watch; it was 06.17. She studied the terrified and confused Sophie who now had tears running down both cheeks. As Jessica approached the girl, Sophie instinctively backed away until her evasion was impeded by the couch. With her right arm, Jessica spun the girl round and removed the gaffer tape from Sophie's wrists. In a desperate attempt to defend herself, Sophie spun around and tried to lash out at her captor. Alas Jessica was too fast and too strong; she merely grabbed Sophie by the upper arms and pushed her hard down onto the couch. Sophie made a move to stand up again.

"Stay there," demanded Jessica in such a tone that Sophie slumped back again. She rubbed her wrists and became sullen.

"You can't just go round abducting people, you know."

"Oh?" retorted Jessica, with raised eyebrows. "I think I've just proved that I can."

"Yeah, well now I'm here what are you going to do with me?" sneered Sophie. Now it was becoming apparent that she was not going to be harmed, she became more spirited.

Jessica sat on the coffee table and put her hands to her face and became pensive. Eventually she looked at the girl in front of her and spoke.

"Why did you choose Professor Harrison?" Jessica's tone was almost pleading now. "You could have any boy on campus, and you chose him."

"Is that what this is all about? Nathan?" Sophie detected the look of sadness in Jessica's eyes. "Oh my God, you're in love with him."

Jessica's eyes narrowed; she didn't like the way this conversation was going, but Sophie hadn't finished.

"Well, I'm in love with him too. You don't own him," Sophie continued defiantly, "and all's fair in love and war."

"Oh, so it's a war you want? I wouldn't fight me on this," replied Jessica with a humourless smile. "I am stronger than you in every way possible. All you have on your side is youth. It wouldn't be a fair fight."

Jessica stood up and walked around, deep in thought.

"In fact," she announced finally, "let's make it fair. And then we'll see who wins."

Sophie simply looked nonplussed; she had no idea what the woman was babbling on about.

"Stand up," demanded Jessica.

Sophie remained seated so Jessica took her by the right arm and pulled her upright.

"Alright," said a petulant Sophie, squirming, "you're hurting me."

Jessica dragged Sophie to the bathroom and pushed her in. Astounded, Sophie looked back at this mad woman, still bemused.

"Get undressed," demanded Jessica.

"What?"

"Get undressed down to your bra and panties," confirmed Jessica.

Sophie just stared in astonishment.

"Look, if you don't do it, I'll do it for you."

With shaking hands, Sophie began to unbutton her blouse. Jessica looked on with disinterest, then left her to it.

"When you've done that, I want you to step on those scales and tell me your weight," shouted Jessica from the sitting room, "and give me an accurate reading. Your life will depend on it."

Still wearing her underwear, Sophie looked down at the scales.

"149lbs," she shouted through to the sitting room.

"Get dressed," ordered Jessica and waited for Sophie to reappear.

Shortly Sophie exited the bathroom just as she finished buttoning up her blouse. Without hesitation, Jessica stood up and forced Sophie up against the wall with her left forearm pressed hard under Sophie's chin. It took no effort for Jessica to stretch out Sophie's right arm and press it against the wall also. Then to the hapless girl's horror, Jessica brought up her right arm, her hand holding a hypodermic syringe.

"What the fuck!" shouted Sophie in panic.

Ignoring the cry, Jessica squirted some liquid from the needle and inserted it into Sophie's arm. The young woman looked on in horror as she saw the fluid enter her veins. Jessica picked the girl up and quickly placed her on the couch just as Sophie went into convulsions. She held Sophie's limbs down until the fitting stopped and the girl lay there motionless. Minutes later, Sophie gave an almighty gasp and was conscious again, staring at the ceiling and wondering what hit her.

"W-what happened?" stammered a confused Sophie.

"I have injected you with a drug," replied Jessica, moving back to the dining table.

"What?" cried an outraged Sophie. "You can't do that. It's assault."

"It's no ordinary drug," continued Jessica, ignoring her. "Now you can see better, hear better. You are stronger and faster. Plus, your life has been extended. You will be no good to Professor… Nathan without it."

"What is this drug?" said Sophie, frowning as she stood up and realised she felt different.

"It's called the Infinity Serum," declared Jessica, "and you now have it coursing through your veins, altering your DNA."

Turning back to the table, Jessica picked up another hypodermic. She rolled up her left sleeve and smiled.

"I won't do anything to someone that I won't do to myself."

With that she inserted the needle into her left arm and pushed down on the plunger. Then she removed the syringe and looked at Sophie triumphantly.

"I was born with this," she announced, "it has no effect on me."

Sophie had so many questions, but right at this moment she was lost for words. She simply stared aghast as Dr Phillips injected herself. Jessica placed the syringe back on the table and before she could turn back again, gave out a cry and her legs buckled beneath her.

"What is it?" agonised Sophie, feeling helpless.

Jessica was in no position to answer; she had collapsed to the floor and lay spread-eagled seemingly unconscious. Stupefied for several seconds, Sophie put a hand to her mouth, incapable of mobilising herself into any kind of action.

"Shit!" she exclaimed eventually, coming to her senses. "Shit, what have you done?"

She knelt down at the prostrate figure and tried to find a pulse. There was nothing.

"Oh God – oh God," she panicked, looking around her. "What do I do?"

She tried compressions on her chest but Jessica refused to respond. Giving up, Sophie scooped the inert body into her arms, carried her into the bedroom and laid Jessica down gently on the bed.

"You've killed yourself, you stupid bitch," Sophie moaned, tears streaming down her face.

Her mind was racing; what should she do now? She couldn't call for an ambulance. How on earth would she explain this? No, there was only one thing to do. Try and contact Nathan. She pulled her cell phone out of her back pocket, called him and waited to hear his reassuring voice. Alas the phone went to voicemail. Of course, he was giving a lecture which she was supposed to have attended. With one last look at the immobile figure lying on the bed, Sophie picked up Jessica's car keys and left the apartment.

Half an hour later she was standing outside the lecture room, debating with herself whether to enter or not. The decision was made for her as Professor Harrison spied her through the glass window of the door. He halted his lecture and opened the door to see the ashen face of Sophie standing there, clearly in distress.

"Sophie, what is it?" he whispered. "You're late, there's only ten minutes left."

"Nathan," she moaned, "something terrible has happened."

"Can it wait 'til after the lecture?" he replied, looking around in the corridor, worried that someone might be observing them.

Sophie nodded; it occurred to her that nothing could be done for Jessica, so ten minutes wouldn't make much difference.

"I'll come in and you can finish up," she agreed.

Pulling herself together, Sophie sat down at the back of the room and half listened to Harrison wind up his talk.

"So, you see," he concluded, "contrary to what is shown in the film *Jurassic Park*, there is no evidence to suggest that *Dilophosaurus Wetherilli* had a frill around its neck or indeed that it could spit poison."

"They don't have bullet holes either," chuckled a student from the back of the room.

Everyone except the professor and Sophie chuckled and turned to the culprit, who was laughing and high fiving his friend.

"Thank you, Mr Christianson, for sharing your kind words of wisdom." Harrison was cringing inside but refused to let it show. "If only it showed in your coursework."

The laughter subsided and Harrison looked over to where Sophie was sitting. She had her head down with a hand to her brow.

"On that note we'll wind up this session," he said, frowning. "Next time we will be concentrating on pterosaurs – chapter nine in your textbooks. Thank you."

The class rose and began filtering out of the room. The professor waited for the last student to leave before approaching Sophie and sitting down in the row in front of her.

"Do you think you'll ever live it down?"

"They'll have forgotten about it by the next semester," imparted Harrison. "Now, what's this all about?"

"It's Jessica," replied Sophie, bursting into tears. "She's dead."

"What?" exclaimed Harrison. "Where? How?"

"Look, we'd better go to her apartment now," Sophie decided, pulling herself together. "I'll explain on the way."

They took Jessica's car and drove back to the apartment whilst Sophie divulged her story from the moment that she had left him in bed. Harrison listened in disbelief; the story was insane.

"What's happened to the dashboard?" said Harrison, frowning, bemused at the damage. Sophie had no answer and replied with a shrug.

They pulled up in the car park and rushed up into Jessica's apartment. Sophie opened the front door and gave Harrison a tentative glance as they entered. To the surprise of both, however, Jessica was in the sitting room, drinking a glass of water, looking feeble.

"I must've passed out," she said, rubbing her forehead.

"Passed out!" bellowed Sophie. "You were dead! That's why I've brought Nathan. I didn't know what else to do."

"I'm fine," assured Jessica, "though you did the right thing."

"Are you sure?" Harrison walked over and put an arm around her. "You look like hell."

"I said I'm fine. Please don't fuss." Jessica was getting irritable. Fine wasn't the right word for how she felt. At this moment, different was the only way that she could explain it.

"I can't believe you injected yourself again," declared Harrison.

"I survived, didn't I?" replied Jessica rhetorically.

"Why on earth did you inject Sophie?" barked Harrison. "What were you thinking of?"

"I was thinking of you, who else," retorted a sullen Jessica. "Look, I need a shower."

Harrison looked at Sophie, and sighed in exasperation as Jessica stood up and made her way to the bathroom. She switched on the shower, undressed and stepped unsteadily into the stream of hot water. Slowly she began to sponge soap over her perfect alabaster skin when suddenly she became aware of her body becoming iridescent, candescent even. A surge of power permeated her whole being and then subsided just as suddenly as it had appeared. Stepping out of the shower, Jessica grabbed a towel and wiped the steam from the mirror. She glanced at her reflection and saw an electric blue glow in her pupils shine intensely and then dim to nothing.

As Jessica entered the sitting room wearing a bathrobe, Harrison was relieved to see she looked much improved.

"How are you feeling?" he asked.

"Tired," sighed Jessica. "I can't explain it but something is changing inside of me. Some kind of metamorphosis. I need to rest."

"Look, I'm going to order a cab and get Sophie home," decided Harrison, "then I'll check in on you after I've picked up my car."

Without answering, Jessica gave him a withering look, walked into her bedroom and closed the door.

At Sophie's suggestion, they waited outside for the taxi to arrive. She wanted to talk freely.

"Do *you* believe this drug extends life?" asked Sophie.

"We shall see in due course," replied Harrison.

"We?"

"Yes, I was given the drug too."

"Willingly or…"

"I asked for the injection," interrupted Harrison.

"At least you had a choice," glowered Sophie.

"You might not like the situation now," suggested Harrison, "but I think you'll come to love it eventually. This is a rare gift."

"What do you think she meant by metamorphosis?" Sophie asked.

"Well, metamorphosis is…"

"I know what it means," interrupted an exasperated Sophie. "What will it mean for her?"

"God knows," Harrison sighed; Jessica had him worried. Was she becoming addicted?

"The question is," observed Sophie, not unreasonably, "what is she morphing into? A butterfly? A monster?"

It was a very pertinent question, to which Harrison didn't have an answer. The taxi arrived and just over an hour later Harrison was back at the apartment in his own car. He got out and looked up to Jessica's sitting room window with trepidation. Inside the apartment, all was quiet. Cautiously, he opened the bedroom door to see the beautiful woman, lying on her back naked on top of the bedding, her arms down by her side, her breasts rising gently as she lay peacefully in a deep sleep. He closed the door quietly again, put her door keys on the dining room table and left. As he walked to his car, Harrison looked up to Jessica's apartment again and thought,

Well, as Sophie so eloquently put it, what are you becoming, Jessica? A butterfly or a monster?

CHAPTER THIRTEEN

PANDORA'S BOX

Oakland, Near San Francisco, California
November 2016

There seemed to be no half awakening, no gradual sleepy-eyed return to consciousness from a fast-receding dream. One second Jessica was in a deep sleep and the next, her eyelids flipped open and she was wide awake. She stared at the white ceiling above her and suddenly became aware of the fact that she was naked. A thought entered her head: *It's 8.17 and fifty-seven seconds.* She turned and looked at the digital alarm clock on her nightstand, just as it clicked over to 08.18.

"Interesting," she muttered to herself, "it seems I have an internal clock. And an accurate one at that."

Swinging her shapely legs off the side of the bed, Jessica stood up. She felt fantastic, but suddenly became aware of faint noises in her ears. It was people talking, neighbours in the adjacent apartments, their voices blending into a jumble of incomprehensible jabbering. Bringing her hands up to her ears, Jessica concentrated hard and, to her relief, gradually tuned the irritating sounds out. With a sigh, she stepped up to the full-length free-standing mirror in the corner of the room and glanced at her reflection. As she moved her hands down over her small, firm breasts, continuing over her slim hips, she was feeling a new-found sexuality which had hitherto been suppressed. A stabbing pain suddenly throbbed on the left side of her head and she brought her hand up to ease it as she winced. Jessica felt a strange sensation in her stomach and slid her right hand over the flat surface just as a faint glow began to slowly pulse, outlining her fingers with a bright yellow light. Astonished and slightly perturbed, she removed her hand. The gently pulsing light was emanating from just below her naval and continued for ten seconds longer, before gradually fading away along with the pain in her head.

Putting it out of her mind, she padded off into the sitting room, booted up her laptop and began typing out a letter of resignation to the university, no longer feeling the need nor the inclination to continue with her work. Then realising that she was famished, Jessica walked into the kitchen and opened the fridge, only to find, to her dismay, it was empty. She expected to feel some coolness from inside the gaping abyss, but felt nothing. In fact, it occurred to her that she ought to feel a slight chill; it was, after all, the first day of November, and here she was, walking around with no clothes on as if it was the height of summer. After a quick shower, she dressed in some dark blue denim jeans, a black close-fitting V-neck top and a plain grey hoodie left open at the front. Pushing the sleeves up to her elbows, she slipped her feet into her black leather loafers, nodded her approval in the mirror, picked up the letter of resignation and left to get some breakfast.

***

Downtown Oakland, Near San Francisco, California November 2016

The waitress looked at the plates of food she was holding, and then looked doubtfully at the slight woman in front of her. Jessica looked up expressionless as the waitress placed a large plate piled up with scrambled eggs, crispy bacon, sausages and baked beans. On a smaller plate were several rounds of hot buttered toast. Immediately, she tucked in and began to devour the feast in front of her, intermittently washing it down with sips from her coffee cup. Two waitresses looked on in amazement as Jessica polished off the last morsel and poured herself another cup of coffee.

Her first port of call had been to the University of California, Berkeley, so that she could hand in her resignation. After entering the inner sanctum of the vice-provost, whose many duties were dealing with personnel, Jessica was confronted with a dour middle-aged woman who promptly told her that the vice-provost was unavailable and she could leave the letter with her. Jessica handed over her identification badge and the keys to her laboratory, and when the secretary asked if she had removed all personal belongings, Jessica pointed out that she didn't keep any belongings on site. As Jessica walked away, she heard the woman mutter under her breath, "I don't doubt it." Jessica stopped in her tracks momentarily, to alert the woman to the fact that she had been heard, and then continued on without looking round.

Placing a $10 bill down on the table, Jessica put her wallet back in her purse and promptly left, much to the amazement of the staff who wondered where she had put it all. Then she made her way to one of the many Chinese supermarkets in the area to stock up on some groceries.

The shop she chose was not particularly busy, so she grabbed a trolley and began to peruse the aisles, absentmindedly picking items off the shelves as she progressed along. An oriental woman of similar age to Jessica was approaching with a five-year-old girl, who was helping her mother push the trolley. The woman gave Jessica a glance of disinterest and continued past. The child looked back, continuing to stare, until her impatient mother badgered her to keep up. As Jessica placed a bag of rice in her trolley, however, the stabbing pain to the left-hand side of her head returned with a vengeance. She let go of the trolley and clutched her head, and the trolley continued on until it hit the shelving and stopped. The little Chinese girl watched the strange woman and started tugging at her mother's right arm. The mother tried to ignore it but the child was insistent.

"Mommy, Mommy," pestered the child.

"What is it?" said the mother, scowling.

"That woman disappeared."

The child's mother looked around to see the discarded trolley and no sight of the woman pushing it.

"Don't be silly," she admonished, "she'll be in another aisle, I expect."

The little girl frowned indignantly at her mother and held her ground in protest until finally being dragged along by her irritable parent.

"But, Mom," she beseeched, pointing behind her.

"Stop it and come on," insisted the mother.

The little girl gave one last look as they turned the corner just before entering another aisle. She peeked down the next to see if the woman was there, but the aisle was empty.

***

The ground was uneven, causing Jessica to stumble. She regained her balance and felt the warm sun and gentle breeze on her face. The rich blue sky looked massive, with a smattering of white cumulous clouds slowly drifting from the east. Jessica couldn't remember ever seeing such a large expanse of sky. The pain in her head had receded and she looked around in disbelief. She was no longer standing in a supermarket but on a plain of grassland that expanded as far as the eye could see. Gone was the built-up metropolis of Oakland, the busy streets, the roar of motorcars sounding their horns. The plain had no features on it whatsoever, apart from some oak trees dotted randomly on the horizon. As she rotated, taking in the vista, she saw Lake Merritt, clearly visible now the heavily built-up city was no longer there. Smoke drifted up lazily from an encampment close to the lake. Jessica zoomed in with her hawk-like eyes and could see activity in a small village made up of dome-shaped lodges, thatched from tule rush. She watched the activities of a number of women, barely clothed, and the sounds of children playing. This land was the territory of the indigenous Ohlone people and these natives were the Chochenyo tribe.

Panicking, Jessica spun around, trying to make sense of what had happened. The whole area looked like a scene long before the area was colonised, possibly as far back as 300 or 400 years, she reasoned. Her head whipped round to the left as she heard a small group approaching from the left at some distance. Six dark-skinned men approached, two carrying a dead deer on a pole; the others carried bows and spears. Jessica watched intensely as the group approached some 150 feet away. The men, wearing one or two feathers in their hair, were naked save for a string around their waist supporting a small flap of material covering their groin. The men stopped as they came adjacent with the mysterious female and stared somewhat puzzled by the unusual apparition. One of the men broke away from the group and tentatively began to walk towards Jessica. Slowly she began to back up, fearing for her safety. The native sensed her unease and stopped. Then he spoke in a language Jessica didn't have a hope of understanding. Again, he tried to approach but Jessica backed off even further. As Jessica's anxiety increased, the pain returned to her head, and without warning she vanished. The tribesman looked astounded and turned to look at his hunting party for reassurance. They looked just as dumbfounded. Eventually he turned away and rejoined the group to engage in a lively discussion about what they had just witnessed, then the group continued to the village by the lake, their minds filled with stories of the strange disappearing figure with which to thrill the children.

Jessica suddenly found herself in the middle of the road, back again in Downtown Oakland. An insistent wail of a car horn rang in her ears and she turned to see a car bearing down on her. At the last minute the vehicle swerved and careered into the side of an oncoming car at an oblique angle, the rear end swinging round and slamming its side against the unfortunate vehicle. The driver scrambled out unsteadily and began shouting at the cause of the accident, just as a beleaguered Jessica made it to the sidewalk. She turned and looked at the angry figure shaking his fist and berating her. Several people were beginning to gather and she looked around her, confused and panic-stricken. Jessica decided that she must get away from here and began to run. Not too fast, she reminded herself. No need to attract more attention. She stopped at a side alley and glanced down to see if it was empty. The alley was deserted, so she ran down between the buildings, concentrating very hard. Seconds later she vanished, though this time, luckily, no one witnessed the spectacle. Still running, Jessica reappeared in the alleyway so she slowed down to a stop and looked around her. It seemed like the same place but there was more trash around and discarded cardboard boxes, piled high on one side. Straightening her hair, Jessica walked out onto the main sidewalk. The sun was shining, just as before, but everything around her was different. The first thing she noticed were the fashions. Women's clothes were brighter, dresses and skirts were shorter and men were walking around in flares and platform shoes. Cars were garish colours and seemed bigger and flatter to Jessica. David Bowie's 'Rebel Rebel' could be heard emanating from a shop somewhere ahead of her. She didn't recognise the song, but guessed it wasn't current. Eventually she found a street vendor standing by a rack filled with newspapers and magazines. The middle-aged man was serving a customer as Jessica approached. Randomly, she picked up a broadsheet and studied it. The paper was the *Los Angeles Times* and the headline read, '*Nixon Admits Coverup, Expects Trial*'. Her eyes drifted back up to the date: 6 August 1974.

"Watergate," she muttered to herself.

After dispensing with his customer, the vendor now turned his attention to Jessica reading the paper intently.

"Hey, lady, you can't try before you buy," he growled. "This ain't no lending library."

Startled, Jessica turned to see the man bearing down on her, cigarette hanging from underneath a grey moustache, slightly browned from nicotine. She pushed the paper into his hands and hurriedly moved on. Jessica needed to think, to process what was happening to her. After walking around for a while, Jessica stopped at a café and entered. She found a seat close to a window and ordered a drink.

Okay, okay, this is madness, she thought, her mind racing. *It would seem that I can now time travel. But it seems to be totally random. I need to get it under control, if it's going to be of any use. Can I travel into the future? Can I travel through time and space? I need to give this a try. Will I need more serum to achieve this?*

As she absentmindedly watched the world go by outside the window, Jessica sipped her cappuccino. All these questions that needed answering. Jessica felt that she had opened Pandora's box. The time came to pay the bill and she pulled out a dollar note. A panic suddenly ran through her. *Is the present-day dollar design the same as those of this time period?* She had no idea. She studied the note for clues which might give it away, like a date, but could find nothing. Placing two notes down beside the cup, she stood up and made for the door. A waitress approached her table and picked up the payment and looked at Jessica, smiling kindly her appreciation for the generous tip. To Jessica it was a cheap cup of coffee. Walking back to the point where she had arrived, the time traveller stopped at the end of the alley and looked around. Nobody was watching so she squatted, placed both hands on her head and concentrated hard on the date which she wanted to return to – 1 November 2016. In an instant the alleyway changed back to the familiar scene, much to Jessica's relief. Tentatively she approached the entrance to the alley and peeked out. The police had arrived and two men were speaking animatedly to an officer who in turn was trying to calm them both down. A truck with a crane appeared, weaving its way through the traffic now backed up on one side, sounding horns with futile impatience.

Jessica zipped up her hoodie, pulled the hood up over her head and quickly made her escape. In the fracas, nobody noticed her slip away, so she found her car and drove home.

With a heavy sigh, she slumped down onto the couch and wiped her hands over her face.

What a morning, she thought, *and it's not even midday yet!*

A buzzing from her purse grabbed Jessica's attention; she pulled out her cell phone and studied the screen to see that she'd had two missed calls and four texts, all from Nathan. She threw the phone on the couch beside her and suddenly realised: there *still* wasn't any food in the place.

***

"How could I call you when I was 400 years away?" complained Jessica, who then smiled and quipped, "I couldn't get a signal."

Harrison had never seen Jessica so animated. He motioned up and down defensively with his hands to calm her. Customers in the pizza restaurant were turning round and smiling. The admonishment for not returning his calls was born more out of frustration than anger.

"What are you saying exactly?" Harrison didn't care that he might seem slow on the uptake, he wanted it spelled out.

"I can time travel," hissed Jessica, trying to keep her excitement in check, "though I don't seem to have control of it yet."

"So, this morning you travelled 400 years… I presume into the past?"

"Yes," replied Jessica. "I can't say for sure how far back I went but I could see Lake Merritt, and all around me the land undeveloped. Just plains of grasslands as far as the eye could see."

Jessica gave him a full account of the whole morning's events, much to the astonishment of her companion. After the encounter with the car her new appearance made perfect sense. Jessica had put her hair up in a bun and was wearing the biggest pair of sunglasses that she owned.

"Do you think Sophie and I could do this too?"

"How would I know?" said Jessica with a shrug. "I'm learning as I go along. One thing is for sure though: I'm going to have to get it under control. I can't just go popping off to some random time zone when my body sees fit."

"Something must trigger it," reasoned Harrison.

Jessica picked up another wedge of pizza and bit into it. She had suddenly become pensive, staring into the middle distance as she chewed. Harrison took the opportunity to tuck in also.

"I'm going to have to take more serum," announced Jessica, finally.

"What!" Harrison spat half-masticated tomato and pepperoni across the table. "How much more of it do you think you can take? It could be suicide!"

"I don't think so." Jessica's voice was calm, reassuringly assertive. "How much of our DNA is believed to be junk? Two thirds? Three quarters? But what if these so-called junk codons in our genetic sequence were just lying dormant waiting for a trigger to induce them?"

"Like the Infinity Serum," mused the professor, realising where Jessica was going with this.

"Exactly," said Jessica, smiling triumphantly, sitting back in her chair. Her expression became intense and she leaned forwards again. "Maybe it completes us. With my whole DNA sequence activated, who knows what my abilities will be. I could become perfect. A perfect specimen."

"A perfect specimen of what exactly?" doubted Harrison. "And why only you?"

"Because I was born with it," countered Jessica, "I have a natural resilience to the serum."

"You think it would be dangerous for Sophie and myself to take more?"

"Yes, I believe so," mused Jessica. "Aren't the benefits of one dose enough for you then?"

"I'm just trying to get my head around all this, that's all," he countered.

They finished up their meal in relative silence and made their way to Harrison's car. The parking lot was quiet and there were no cars parked close. Before he unlocked the doors, Harrison glanced over the roof to Jessica, who was patiently waiting for the bleep.

"Can you give me a demonstration?" he enquired.

"What, of time travelling?" asked an incredulous Jessica. "Here? Now?"

"Why not?" reasoned Harrison. "There's no one about, and there's no time like the present."

If ever there was an occasion when that expression was less pertinent, it was now. The irony wasn't lost on the professor.

"If I do," she warned, "I cannot guarantee when or where I'll return. That's why I want to take more serum."

"Fair enough. It was just a suggestion."

"Okay," relented Jessica, "I'll try."

She took her cell phone out of her purse and slipped it into the back pocket of her jeans.

"What's that for?"

"I don't know where I'll return to, you might need to pick me up."

Jessica sat back in the car seat and closed her eyes. She concentrated hard for nearly a minute, then to Harrison's astonishment, with no sound, no fanfare, she disappeared. He looked around and then exited the car. Fifty yards away, he could see Jessica approaching, looking no worse for wear.

"That was quick," said Harrison, beaming. "Where did you go? And for how long?"

Jessica didn't answer; she looked worried and confused. She opened the car door and sat down. Harrison did the same and put his hand on hers.

"I was only gone for a minute," she confirmed.

"Yes, but where?"

Jessica didn't answer the question. She just stared out of the windscreen seemingly in a daze.

"Jessica?" enquired a concerned Harrison.

"Just get me home," she said eventually, and clipped her seatbelt in.

Harrison did the same and they drove back in silence.

Back at Jessica's apartment, Harrison was astounded to hear about her resignation.

"What the hell!" he exclaimed. "Why?"

"My work seems unimportant now, insignificant even," contended Jessica. "Besides, it's not like I need the money."

"You will be missed."

Jessica gave him a look of surprise and sat down on the couch.

"I don't think so," she countered glumly, thinking back to the comment made by the vice-provost's secretary. "I don't think that I was particularly well liked."

"I'll admit you were never the easiest person to get along with," Harrison sat down on the couch beside her and put a comforting arm around Jessica's shoulders, "but I always liked you. Even when you were being mean to me."

"I wish I had your easy-going nature. Nothing seems to faze you." Jessica turned and looked at the man holding her close. Tears welled up in her eyes. "You have always been there for me, even now, and I love you for it."

She could see that Harrison was about to speak but she shook her head slowly and placed a finger gently over his mouth. Moving in closer, Jessica kissed him tenderly on the lips, and when Harrison responded, their kissing became more passionate.

"Should we be doing this?" whispered Jessica as Harrison began kissing her neck and gently nibbling her earlobe.

"Probably not," said Harrison, smiling. "Would you prefer me to stop?"

Jessica didn't answer with words; she stood up and led him into the bedroom. Harrison had neither the will nor the inclination to put up any resistance.

***

It was early evening; the sun was low on the horizon and the light in Jessica's bedroom had a crepuscular hue as the day made its gradual transitional ritual from daylight to night. She stared at the ceiling, listening to the gentle breathing of the man lying beside her. Harrison, in deep slumber, had rolled onto his front and was now inconveniently trapping Jessica's right arm. Eventually she looked across at him, smiled warmly and gently extricated herself from his clutches. Harrison stirred and shuffled onto his side and continued to sleep. Slipping quietly out of the bed, Jessica put on her silk pyjamas, opened the bottom drawer of the nightstand and removed a phial from the white box and a hypodermic syringe from the other. As quietly as she could, Jessica left the bedroom, closing the door gently behind her. She walked into the kitchen and charged the syringe with a double dose of serum. Then she placed the phial in a drawer and walked into the sitting room. Placing the syringe down carefully on the coffee table, she switched on a side lamp and drew the curtains. Jessica sat and contemplated the wisdom of what she was about to do.

Her mind went back to earlier in the day when she demonstrated her new ability for Nathan. Jessica had lied to him. It was more like ten minutes that she was away for, not the minute that she had stated. The place she had travelled to was like nothing on earth, at least nowhere that she was familiar with. She didn't seem to rematerialise fully and felt suspended between two worlds, as if hermetically sealed in a bubble. Her surroundings were dark and cool, and in front of her were massive pillars of a sandy colour rising up and disappearing into the heavens. She tried to move and found that she couldn't. Jessica was suddenly startled by the sound of men speaking in the distance and getting closer. The voices were deep and resonated through the vast chasm in a language which Jessica didn't recognise. As the voices got closer, she was able to see several figures coming her way. To her utter amazement what she saw was a small group of men, who stood over eight feet tall and, even more astonishingly, some of them had wings. They all looked very regal in black full-length gowns, ornately decorated in gold. Their long hair and beards were braided in multicoloured beads.

The men stopped abruptly and stared in her direction. They could see a ghostly image looking distressed and trapped. It became apparent to Jessica that the men could see her but they looked puzzled. They spoke frantically to one another and one tried to address her. Alas she couldn't make out what he was trying to say. Panic got the better of her, so she closed her eyes and concentrated. Instantly she was back in the car park about ten yards from Harrison's car. He was confused as to why she had returned to a slightly different spot and Jessica was in no frame of mind to offer an answer. The thought of being transported to a place that appeared to be not of this world disturbed Jessica immensely. All the more reason to get this ability under control.

With a sigh of apprehension, Jessica picked up the syringe, ejected some serum and inserted the needle into a vein in her left forearm. She pulled back the plunger to aspirate some blood into the barrel of the syringe, paused for five seconds and determinedly pushed the plunger down, discharging the full double dose into her bloodstream. Knowing that it takes around fifty seconds for blood to circulate the body, Jessica sat back and awaited a reaction.

As she expected, nothing happened for thirty seconds, then without warning, an unseen force bent her back double. Jessica's chest and abdomen were thrust outwards and her head was forced back. The pain was excruciating and she gave out a cry. Her eyes rolled back in her head to reveal the whites and she could no longer see. She was not aware of it but Jessica had begun to float about a foot off the couch. The room was becoming electrically charged, the bulb blew out in the side lamp, throwing the room into darkness and Jessica found herself being slammed hard against the wall above the couch. Opening her eyes Jessica found that she could now see despite the fact that only the whites were still showing. It was becoming difficult to breathe as the room became a maelstrom of objects flying around at speed. Ten feet away from her a small white dot appeared and quickly spiralled out larger with arms of multicoloured light. A rapid pressure drop in the room caused the window to crash inwards, taking the frame and curtains with it. Glass fragments were flying around with all the other paraphernalia in the chaos. Still Jessica was fixed steadfastly against the wall, mesmerised by the hypnotic abyss rotating in front of her, which had now grown to about six feet in diameter.

The mayhem woke Harrison up with a start and he leapt for the door and tried to open it. He turned the handle with all his might but it wouldn't shift. Then it began to splinter and rip away, and Harrison had to hold on to the doorframe to prevent himself from going with it. Helpless, the professor could only watch the devastation, until he had to cover his eyes as shards of glass flew perilously close to his face.

Jessica refused to allow herself to be sucked into the powerful eddy and gave out an almighty cry of defiance. The wall where the window once was crashed in along with the joists in the ceiling, cracking the plasterboard as the spinning, spiralling vortex collapsed in on itself and disappeared. Air pressure returned to normal in the room and Jessica dropped unceremoniously to the floor in a crumpled heap onto broken glass and bricks. Harrison stepped into the room in bare feet, trod on some glass, then, realising that he was naked, hurriedly stepped back into the bedroom and got dressed. When he returned, Harrison found the room completely wrecked, with a gaping hole where the window once was. Jessica was lying on her side, her legs pulled up into a foetal position, seemingly unconscious. There was dust everywhere and Harrison began to cough as he tried to rouse Jessica. He checked her body over but could find no cuts or contusions. Picking Jessica up, Harrison carried her to the bedroom and just as he laid her down, Jessica began to moan. Slowly her eyes opened and she saw Harrison gazing at her anxiously.

"What happened?" she said, wincing.

"You tell me," declared Harrison, "the living room is destroyed."

Jessica suddenly came to her senses; she sat up and dashed to her wardrobe.

"We've got to get out of here," she exclaimed, "before the authorities arrive."

Hurriedly she packed some clothes into a bag, along with the white box of phials, plus the box of syringes, and dragged Harrison out into the hallway. A number of residents were standing in their doorways, some in the corridor, wondering what all the commotion was about. But before they could say anything the two culprits forced themselves past and disappeared into the parking lot. As Harrison fired up the engine, he turned to Jessica.

"What in God's name happened in there?"

"I took more serum," replied Jessica, holding her forehead. "A double dose."

"You've got to be shitting me," exclaimed Harrison in disbelief. "Why?"

"I can handle it," retorted Jessica, not really answering the question.

"Where to?" sighed the professor.

"Your place," asserted Jessica. "Where else?"

Harrison pulled out onto the main road, wiped dust out of his eyes and made his way home. He looked at Jessica for some kind of explanation but she had fallen into a deep sleep.

***

As the lamps rotated on the emergency vehicles, blue light intermittently highlighted the grim face of Robert McQuillan as he took in the pandemonium around him. Two fire tenders and four police squad cars were crammed into the parking lot as the residents, who had been evacuated for safety, along with other bystanders who had simply turned up to gape, looked up at the damage to Jessica's apartment.

Despite his scruffy appearance, McQuillan was an exceptional investigative journalist. He was a middle-aged man of short stature, with grey thinning hair, brushed untidily over his scalp and thick-lens glasses which seemed to magnify his eyes, giving him the appearance of a startled tarsier. His mouth was an untidy gash of rubbery lips which concealed teeth stained by tobacco. Not that anyone ever saw them since McQuillan was not given to grinning.

His demeanour meant that more often than not, he was underestimated, and that suited McQuillan just fine. It enabled him to pursue the job – which to him was more of a vocation – with more efficacy. He seemed to have a natural gift for identifying a scoop where lesser journalists would fail. McQuillan's nose would twitch like a sixth sense when he perceived something big, and, as he continued to observe the activity around him, his nose was twitching like a rabbit sniffing out a fox.

It wasn't the first time today that his nose was twitching. Earlier, an accident had been caused by a mysterious disappearing woman, who was yet to be identified. Some witnesses were able to give a description of the woman but nobody seemed to know who she was. The police had as usual been circumspect and generally unhelpful, but it put McQuillan in mind of another strange case which, to his chagrin, he was unable to get to the bottom of. The case of the death of a family dog in Los Angeles nine years ago. Lieutenant Detective Kiefer had clammed up, muttering something about the security services, and even Detective Jacks, who normally could be relied upon to spill the beans for a backhander, had become uncharacteristically reticent. McQuillan hated loose ends; he liked to wrap up a story, forget about it and move on to the next, but this one had lingered in the back of his mind, gnawing at his subconscious. And this was the second strange event to happen in the course of a few hours; McQuillan was keen to see if they were connected.

When he thought the moment was right, he approached Captain Frank Coghill of the San Francisco Police Department just as he was finishing up talking to the fire chief.

"I should've known you'd be the first on the scene," sneered the captain.

"What caused it?" asked McQuillan, ignoring the jibe. "Earthquake? Gas leak?"

"Doubt it, there is no evidence of an explosion," said Captain Coghill, frowning. "No tremors were felt either. It's like a tornado hit. And if you look at that wall, only one apartment was affected. It's chaos inside. I can't for the life of me begin to understand what happened. The Fire Department are puzzled too."

"Were there any casualties?"

"No, the apartment is empty but two adults, a man and a woman, were seen fleeing by other residents."

"Do you know who lives here?" pressed McQuillan.

Captain Coghill hesitated for a second, questioning the wisdom of revealing this information. But he knew McQuillan and reasoned that he would find out anyway, so relented.

"It's the woman seen fleeing," Coghill revealed, "Dr Jessica Phillips."

"Description?"

"About five feet seven inches, slim build with long straight black hair," continued Coghill. "She sometimes wears glasses but has recently taken to leaving them off."

Looking at his notebook from earlier, McQuillan saw that this description fitted that of the disappearing woman. It was too vague to be certain, however, the information was a little sketchy; it could be anyone.

"Could I go up and take a look?" McQuillan knew he was pushing his luck, but thought he would give it a shot anyway.

"I think you know the answer to that one," said the captain, grimacing.

Turning around, distracted by the fire chief, Coghill exchanged a few words but when he turned back to address McQuillan again, he had gone. The devious reporter, seeing his opportunity, managed to sneak into the building undetected.

One step in, and the devastation became apparent. McQuillan switched on the flashlight on his cell phone and scanned the room with the light. The sitting room was covered in broken glass, bricks and dust. Furniture and ornaments were in complete disarray and McQuillan trod carefully as glass cracked under his feet. He glanced into the bedroom and saw a few drawers which had been removed and placed on the bed. He walked in and casually picked through the items. Pushing undergarments aside, he found an envelope and opened it to reveal some incomprehensible formulae. Furtively looking around him, McQuillan photographed the pages. He found a few pictures of Jessica and took photos of them also. Then he placed the envelope in the inside pocket of his jacket and moved into the kitchen. Like the bedroom, drawers had been pulled open. He shone his flashlight into one and his attention was brought to a small container at the back of one drawer containing a clear fluid, obviously missed amongst the cutlery. McQuillan picked it up and slid it into the top of his left sock.

The fire chief looked up to see light moving about from the damaged wall. He nudged Coghill.

"Someone's up there."

"McQuillan," asseverated Coghill, who immediately ordered two officers to go and extricate him.

The intrepid reporter was unceremoniously

frogmarched out of the building and shoved in front of the police captain.

"What did I freaking well tell you?" shouted the captain rhetorically.

"I've got a job to do," said McQuillan, wincing, trying to break himself free from the clutches of the officers.

"Search him," ordered Coghill.

The two police officers began to rifle through his pockets and quickly found the envelope. McQuillan wasn't duly concerned; he had taken it as a decoy. The men patted him down to his knees and stopped, satisfied he was clean of any more contraband.

"What do you think you were going to do with this?" asked Coghill, triumphantly waving the envelope in McQuillan's face. "It's incomprehensible."

The reporter simply shrugged; indeed, it didn't make any sense, but you never know.

"Get outta here," ordered Coghill finally, and McQuillan, happy with his night's work, made his way through the crowd. He kept his head down and didn't notice the strange figure in a black suit who was quietly observing the proceedings from the opposite side of the road. The mysterious figure watched the dishevelled man remove something from his sock before getting into his car. The enigmatic man made a note of the registration. Before he drove off, McQuillan studied the phial, then glanced at the formulae pictures stored on his phone and wondered whether they were connected. And was it the same fluid which killed the dog? It was a leap but definitely needed to be checked out.

***

"How are you going to explain this?" Harrison was angry and struggling to keep his voice down.

"I don't have to explain it," said a nonplussed Jessica, shrugging. "When asked, I'll just feign ignorance. But they're going to have to find me first."

"Great," replied Harrison, thinking ahead. "If they can't find you, they'll start checking out your friends and family. That will involve me and possibly Sophie…"

Right on cue the doorbell buzzed and Harrison answered. It was Sophie grinning from ear to ear, holding up a bottle of wine. Harrison let her in and Sophie's initial smile in anticipation of a booty call was confounded by the presence of Jessica. The smile quickly disappeared as Sophie detected the atmosphere in the room.

"What's going on?" she remarked, looking from Jessica to Harrison.

The professor sat her down and related to Sophie recent events, to bring her up to speed. Sophie's jaw dropped wider and wider until she put a hand over her mouth, unable to conceal her incredulity.

"Time travel?" retorted Sophie, looking at Jessica, who merely nodded a reply. Her antipathy towards the young woman was palpable.

"What do we do now?" asked Sophie. "The cops might come after me and Nathan."

"So, what if they do?" reasoned Jessica. "They know nothing about the serum. Or our abilities for that matter."

"I think they might be getting some idea of your abilities," countered Harrison.

A sudden look of shock came over Jessica's face. She put her hand to her mouth.

"What now?" asked the professor.

"The serum and the formulae," gasped Jessica. "I left a phial in a kitchen drawer. The formulae are in my nightstand."

"That's just great," seethed Sophie, standing up and walking around with her head in her hands.

"Wait a moment," said Jessica decisively and standing up. She closed her eyes and concentrated. Seconds later she disappeared, to Sophie's amazement.

Jessica materialised in the familiar surroundings of her bedroom; even in the pitch black she could see that the room had been searched. She could hear activity in the parking lot and checked the front door to ensure it was closed. Anxiously she made her way to the kitchen drawers and to her dismay saw that they had been searched also. With a cry of despair, she saw that the phial had been taken and felt a panic attack well up inside her. She breathed deeply and calmed herself down so she could think rationally. Then, she closed her eyes and concentrated back to the previous hour. In her mind's eye she watched as firemen and then police officers went through her apartment seemingly, to her, ransacking the place. She continued running the events through her mind until a shabby little man entered the flat surreptitiously looking around. Jessica observed him photograph the formulae, then move into the kitchen to eventually find the phial.

"Okay, McQuillan, you've had your fun." Two officers had entered the building to drag the reporter away.

So, you have it, thought Jessica, *McQuillan. What are you? A newspaper reporter?*

She had seen enough; Jessica closed her eyes and disappeared.

Whilst Harrison and Sophie waited patiently for Jessica to reappear, Sophie began to think ahead, what all this might mean for them all.

"Do you think we will need to go on the run?"

"That seems a little overly dramatic, don't you think?"

"Don't you think this whole situation *is* a little dramatic?" fumed Sophie. "We might have to leave the country."

"Passports might prove a problem," mused Harrison, giving this idea serious consideration. "They may be checking for us at ports and borders."

"Leave that to me," cogitated Sophie, "I have an idea."

At that moment, Jessica returned; she looked troubled. The other two were initially taken aback. Jessica's materialisation was going to take some getting used to.

"The whole apartment has been checked over by the police. The bad news is, the phial and the formulae are gone."

"So, the police have it," seethed Harrison. "What do we do now?"

"No, I think they're in the hands of a journalist," confirmed Jessica, "unless the police searched him. Anyway, it's unlikely he'll put two and two together, so we've got some time."

"We need to get it back off him before he hurts himself," insisted Harrison.

"It'll be his own stupid fault if he does," retorted Jessica.

"For crying out loud, Jessica, listen to yourself," shouted Harrison, finally losing his temper. "It's time you took responsibility for your actions."

Jessica made a move to protest, but was cut dead by Harrison in full flow.

"You could've killed us by what you did in your apartment," he bellowed. "Christ! You could have destroyed the whole block and killed innocent people."

"I don't know what happened in my apartment," countered Jessica, in tears and shouting in retaliation. "Not all of that was my fault. That vortex thing, I didn't create that."

"You don't know what you're doing." Harrison had calmed down a little seeing Jessica in distress. "I'm worried that you're becoming addicted to the drug."

Sophie took the wise decision to stay out of this fight, as Jessica stared in disbelief at Harrison's accusation.

"So, you think I'm a junkie now," she fumed again.

"I can only go by what I see," retorted Harrison, much calmer.

"Well, to hell with you," declared Jessica. "I don't need to stay here and listen to this."

Without awaiting a response, Jessica closed her eyes, screwed up her face in frustration, and disappeared once again, leaving Sophie and Harrison confounded.

"Like you said," commented Sophie, once she was confident Harrison was calm enough to converse with, "what do we do now?"

"Looks like we're left holding the bag," surmised Harrison. "For the time being I suggest that we keep our heads down."

"I can't stay," announced Sophie suddenly.

Harrison raised his eyebrows as she stood up to leave. Sophie gave him a kiss on the lips and smiled.

"Things have changed. Booty call is going to have to wait."

"Where are you going?" cried Harrison.

"I'll be in touch," smiled Sophie. "See you soon."

The two women in his life had left him on his own, so Harrison slumped on the couch and wondered how long it would take the cops to make the connection with him and Jessica. Finally, Harrison picked up the bottle of wine and walked into the kitchen to find a corkscrew. He felt like getting drunk, but wondered whether the drug would allow it. In that moment he couldn't care less one way or the other.

CHAPTER FOURTEEN

A NEEDLE IN A HAYSTACK

Lower East Side, Manhattan, New York City
November 2016

The temperature was around nine degrees Celsius as Jessica materialised in amongst the trees surrounding the East River Park Amphitheater, which overlooked the East River estuary and the Brooklyn Navy Yard beyond. She had chosen this spot because, she surmised, quite correctly, that at 0900 hours, it would be deserted. Autumn had well and truly shown its hand with a display of red and golden leaves, highlighted by the low yellow orb poking through a break in the clouds and struggling to warm up the chill in the air.

Jessica walked up the arc of steps which provided seating, then looked back and down at the concrete stage with its arched roof. Turning her attention inland again she was confronted by FDR Drive and its rush hour traffic. Jessica was no stranger to busy traffic but to her this looked like gridlock. She turned north and made her way in the general direction of the Williamsburg Suspension Bridge, one of three bridges which link Manhattan with Brooklyn. By the time she had walked into the centre of the Lower East Side, the streets were coming alive, and as she turned into Second Avenue, the shop she was looking for was open for business. The frontage of the boutique she had chosen to visit looked tatty, and a black and white sign which desperately needed repainting read simply: '*The Vintage Clothes Shop*'. Wondering whether she had made a mistake, Jessica opened the door to the peal of a bell and stepped in. The interior was a cornucopia of racks festooned with clothes of all colours and styles. Mesmerised by what was on offer, and not being sure exactly what she was looking for, Jessica decided to seek some help from a member of staff.

The only sign of life was a well-tanned man in his mid-twenties, tall, slim and wearing a baggy multicoloured silk shirt and tight black skinny jeans. His hair of vertical short spikes was bleached white, giving him the appearance of someone in a constant state of shock. He sized up the young woman in her jeans and hoodie, with barely concealed disdain, as she approached the counter.

"Can I help you?" he asked in a tone which suggested he seriously doubted whether this was possible.

"I hope so," replied Jessica awkwardly. "I'm looking for period costumes."

"Oh, okay." The man's tone perked up a little. "Which period are you looking for?"

"I would say late 1920's," offered Jessica.

"My dear," announced the man in a camp tone, clapping his hands together, "I have simply oodles."

Leading Jessica down one of the aisles, he put a forefinger to his mouth and looked Jessica up and down again.

"A size six methinks."

"Yes," said Jessica, nodding.

"Evening or day wear?"

"Day wear," Jessica replied, thinking on her feet. "Yes, definitely day wear."

He pulled various items off the racks and returned with them to the counter. The salesman offered a few dresses to Jessica.

"Nothing too flamboyant," dismissed Jessica, regaining some confidence, "I don't want to stand out."

Nonplussed the young man offered a maroon silk knee-length skirt and a black cotton top with black lace across the shoulders.

"This is more like it," she enthused. "Can I try these on?"

"Yes, yes," fussed the man and ushered his customer to a changing room.

Minutes later, Jessica emerged wearing the clothes and her white socks. The salesman put his hand to his chin and thought. Then without a word he briskly walked around the shop picking up items as he went.

"Take your socks off," he demanded on his return and offered her a pair of black shoes with a two-inch heel and T-bar strap.

Jessica did as she was told and put them on. Then he offered her a maroon felt cloche hat with a black ribbon above the brim. The shop assistant studied her some more and then gave her a black belt to finish off the look. Standing in front of a mirror, Jessica studied her new outfit. The style suited her slim build perfectly.

"Darling, you look simply divine," gushed the young man and dashed off yet again. He returned with a black knee-length coat with a black fur-lined collar. "This should finish off the look."

Jessica slipped the coat on and studied her new look in the mirror.

"Perfect, simply perfect," he effused.

"Yes, this will suffice," said Jessica, nodding, echoing his approval.

With two carrier bags and $400 lighter, Jessica had one more errand to undertake before returning to the same spot where she had arrived, and within the blink of an eye returned to her father's bungalow in Oakland, California.

***

The Brandenburg Gate, Berlin, Germany
August 1930

That same day, Harrison had phoned to warn Jessica that the police had been round to question him about her whereabouts. She let it go to voicemail, still angry at being accused of being addicted to the serum. He'd been woken up, with a mild hangover, by the insistent buzzing of his doorbell. After a difficult half hour trying to convince them of his non-involvement in the damage to his colleague's apartment, he insisted, in all honesty, that he had no idea where she was. He needed to be at work, and to get rid of them, eventually gave Jessica's father's address as a possible location. Jessica had not long returned from New York, when she found herself having to hurriedly put on her period clothes, and check that the serum was in her purse. Also, she verified that a limited amount of Reichsmarks – a mixture of coins and banknotes dated between 1927 and 1929, procured from a coin dealer on Fifth Avenue just south of Central Park – were in her purse and all US currency was removed.

It was a very flustered Jessica who emerged early in the morning between the Doric pillars of the Brandenburg Gate, after making the time jump just as the San Francisco Police arrived outside the bungalow. She stepped out from the shadow of the tall pillars and looked around her, marvelling at the *Quadriga* statue mounted above the gate. The chariot pulled by four horses and bearing the figure of Victoria, the Roman goddess of victory, brandishing the Standard with its Germanic Cross and topped with an eagle, displayed a powerful image of Teutonic grandeur. It looked so much more impressive in real life.

Jessica decided to walk into the centre of the city, not really knowing where to start. By the time she had made it to the Berliner Dom Cathedral, with its three green domes and ornate Gothic architecture of the *Kaiserzeit* period, people were milling about, on their way to work. Jessica was pleased to see that she blended in perfectly and drew no attention to herself. She sat down on a bench, pulled out a black and white photograph from her coat pocket, and studied it wistfully. The image of a young, good-looking man wearing a Waffen-SS uniform stared back at her.

"Well, Father," she sighed, "finding you is going to be like looking for a needle in a haystack."

She continued to wander aimlessly, taking in the sights and trying to avoid the ubiquitous *Sturmabteilung,* the SA Brown Shirts who seemed to be marauding like packs of dogs, bullying anyone who got in their way. Jessica had to make a detour as she inadvertently stumbled upon a group of Brown Shirt thugs kicking and beating with sticks an elderly man who was lying on the pavement endeavouring to protect his head. She wanted to intervene, but knew that there was nothing she could do. It was shocking for her to see these men acting with impunity, knowing that there was no one who could stop them.

Enjoy your moment in the sun, she thought. *Your day of reckoning is only a couple of years away.*

By mid-afternoon, Jessica found herself on Potsdamer Platz, a traffic intersection in the centre of Berlin. To her it looked like chaos as trams, buses, cars, bicycles and even horse-drawn carriages all vied for right of way. The traffic light tower in the centre of the square, the first in Germany, tried to maintain order, but to Jessica seemed to be fighting a losing battle. She found a café and sat down at an outside table with an awning stretching out above her head. After ordering a coffee, she pondered her situation. It was hopeless, the man she was looking for could be anywhere; she hadn't even seen any Waffen-SS soldiers in the streets. Then later as the day turned into night, she had some glimmer of hope. Whilst walking down a side street north of Potsdamer Platz, she spied a group of three men wearing the distinctive black uniform of the Waffen-SS. She decided to follow them as they laughed and cavorted their way down the street until they stopped and entered a building. Jessica stopped and studied the building as she reached it, and saw that it was fairly nondescript apart from a dimly lit sign which read: '*Der Katze und Maus Klub*'. Tentatively, she entered through the open door and made her way down a darkened staircase. At the bottom was a door which appeared to be guarded by a tall man in a dark grey pin-striped suit. He looked her up and down with indifference and opened the door to allow her inside.

The interior opened out into a spacious room, festooned with small round tables draped in white tablecloths, each with a dimly lit table lamp. Groups of people sat drinking and laughing, some watching the show and others wrapped up in their own little world. Beyond the tables were a small orchestra pit and a stage lined with plush maroon velvet curtains, and to Jessica's shock, performing on stage was a line of chorus girls, completely naked, dancing the can-can. She glanced away, but not before spotting the three young men sitting at the front and harassing a waitress who was trying to serve them. She noticed that all the waitresses were topless, brazenly baring their breasts for everyone to see. As she moved away from the centre of the room, Jessica stumbled into a table occupied by a small group of men and women. To her they looked upper class and one of the men drunkenly grabbed at her but lost his balance as she pulled away. The woman sitting next to him did the same but Jessica backed away as they laughed at her, then they turned back to their table and seemed to forget that she was even there.

In one corner was a bar which arced round from one wall to the other. High stools were positioned around it and the barmaid, a pretty young woman heavily made-up, with blonde hair, watched with interest as Jessica stumbled ineptly in her direction. Jessica reached the bar and the scantily clad girl leant over and grinned mischievously.

"You're not German, are you." It was more of a statement than a question.

"American," confirmed Jessica, still flustered.

"I can always tell," said the barmaid, beaming. "This is a fabulous position to people watch."

A topless waitress approached and completely unselfconsciously stood next to Jessica and ordered drinks in German. The barmaid expertly dealt with the order, said something back in German and turned her attention back to the young woman in front of her.

"What would you like to drink?"

Jessica looked nonplussed and didn't know what to ask for. The barmaid decided to help her out.

"Champagne," she announced, taking the decision from her.

After paying for the drink, Jessica propped herself up on one of the stools and considered the girl in front of her.

"You're British," observed Jessica. "How did you end up here?"

"I must've taken a wrong turning," the barmaid laughed, "though I can think of worse places to be, and the money's not bad."

"What is this place? I've never seen anything like it," replied Jessica as she glanced around at the den of iniquity.

"Welcome to Berlin Cabaret," announced the girl with a flourish of her arms.

The attention of both was drawn to the stage as the chorus girls danced their way off stage to great applause, whistles and caterwauling. A figure entered the stage from the opposite side, heavily made-up, wearing evening dress of top hat and tails. Squinting, Jessica studied the bizarre figure and couldn't tell if it was a man or a woman. The master of ceremonies spoke a few words in German and the crowd laughed, then he or she spoke again and as he held out his hand, he announced with a big grin, "… Elsa and Mirko!"

The MC moved off the stage as a little man came running on – a scantily clad midget with a pot belly hanging over a black leather thong. The only other attire he wore was a bowler hat and both eyes were heavily made up with mascara. Jessica looked on askance, then looked at the barmaid, who was grinning from ear to ear. The time traveller was unable to look away as the weird little figure ran around the stage to sped-up music from the house band. The midget stopped dead front-centre of the stage as the tone of the music changed to something more ominous. The expression on the little man's face turned to mock fear as a taller figure entered the stage behind him and walked into the light.

A woman, who might have been more attractive if she hadn't slapped on so much makeup, walked forwards to make herself known in six-inch black stiletto shoes and black silk stockings. She had shoulder-length wavy fair hair, was petite and skinny and wearing a tight-fitting black leather bodice with straps down its front and stopping short just under her exposed tiny pointed breasts. In her right hand was a whip which she tapped menacingly on her left hand, grinning lasciviously at the audience.

The SS soldiers who Jessica had followed in were heckling the woman. She calmly stepped down from the stage and sauntered up to one of the men and sat astride his legs facing him; she wrapped the whip around the back of his neck and pulled his face towards her bare breasts. Then before he could react, she swiped the cap off his head with a flourish, placed it firmly on her head and ran back up onto the stage. She faced the audience and gave a Nazi salute, turned and goosestepped around the stage, in an exaggerated parody, much to the delight of the audience. Then she began to crack her whip at the midget who ran around the stage trying to avoid its sting. While this was going on the soldier who had lost his cap moved to the back of the room to visit the lavatory. When he reappeared, the woman was sitting astride the midget, smacking his behind to giddy him up. Turning his head to the left, the soldier noticed the woman sitting on a bar stool sipping champagne. Oblivious, Jessica was agog as she watched the antics on stage and didn't notice as the SS man approached her.

The man stumbled into Jessica in a drunken sprawl, spouting German and getting far too close for her liking. She pushed him away but he came at her again, refusing to take no for an answer. The affray was beginning to get out of hand; Jessica knew that she dared not use her strength so tried to protest in the strongest possible way. Over in an opposite corner a figure hidden by shadow quietly observed as these proceedings transpired. When the shadowy figure decided that enough was enough, he placed his cap squarely on his head, picked up his swagger stick and marched briskly over to the bar. He grabbed the inebriated man's right arm, pulled it out straight and twisted it into a hammerlock behind his back. Jessica looked on in shock as the stranger pulled up on the hapless soldier's wrist until he screamed out in pain. Pushing him against the bar the stranger put his swagger stick under the soldier's chin and pulled his head back, causing him to cough and splutter. When his arm was released, the man, who had now sobered up somewhat, spun around to confront his assailant only to stop dead in his tracks and stand to attention. His attacker was a *Rottenführer* in the Waffen-SS and he was only a *Schütze* or private. He gave the Nazi salute and stood very still. The officer studied the man, looking him up and down, and then pushed the tip of his swagger stick up under the private's chin again, forcing his head upwards.

"Your uniform seems to be incomplete," sneered the officer.

"M-my cap, sir," stammered the private, pointing, "it's up on the stage. The girl has it."

"Then I suggest you go and retrieve it, before it is lost." With that the officer removed the stick and motioned for him to go.

"Yes, sir, thank you, sir," conceded the private and began to move away.

"And when you have reclaimed your cap," ordered the officer, "you and your friends will leave. Is that understood?"

The private nodded and made his way to the front of the theatre. The officer turned to a mesmerised Jessica, clicked his heels and bowed.

"Baron von Brandt, at your service, madam," he kissed her hand and smiled, "but you can call me Gustav."

Unable to speak, Jessica simply sat rooted to the spot, not knowing how to react. This was why she was here; this was what she was looking for. But now she had found her father, she was dumbstruck. The barmaid, who was also impressed by von Brandt, held out her hand.

"I'm Gabby," she said, beaming.

"A bottle of champagne, if you please," he replied, ignoring her. "Have it brought over to my table."

He led Jessica over to the secluded corner and held out a chair for her to sit, then walked round and sat opposite.

"My name is Jessica," his guest trembled, trying to regain some composure, "Jessica... err Harrison." Instinctively she felt it prudent not to use her real name. In a fleeting moment of wishful thinking, she used Nathan's surname. He may well remember this encounter and she didn't want to compromise this man's meeting with her mother. Jessica's very existence could well depend on it.

"Well, Jessica Harrison," smirked von Brandt, "out of all the many clubs in this city, luckily you chose this one."

"Of all the gin joints in all the towns..." commented Jessica, trying to sound smart and sophisticated, but then realised that her reference would mean nothing, since the film that she was quoting from wouldn't be released for another twelve years.

Ignoring the comment, von Brandt expertly opened the champagne, poured out two glasses and lifted one with a charming grin.

"Cheers," he saluted.

"Good health," reciprocated Jessica, picking up a glass, having regained her composure.

Sitting back in his chair, von Brandt quietly sipped

his champagne and studied the beautiful woman in front of him. Just when he felt that she was beginning to feel uncomfortable, he leant forwards, placed his drink on the table, then fished out a cigarette case from his inside pocket. He offered one to Jessica, who politely declined. After lighting one for himself, he inhaled deeply and let the smoke exhale from his nostrils and gave a grin which could easily have been a sneer.

"So, what is an American doing here?" Von Brandt gestured to the room, suggesting that he was referring to the club as much as the country.

"I'm on vacation," lied Jessica, "and I stumbled in here by accident."

"It would seem that your misfortune is my good fortune."

"You speak very good English," observed Jessica.

"My father insisted I learn from a very young age," revealed von Brandt, "plus I spent a considerable time in England."

"Why didn't you stay?" enquired Jessica. "I would have thought that England would be more preferable to Germany right now."

"I could ask you the same question," reasoned von Brandt. "I had to leave England in a hurry."

"Oh?" replied Jessica, eyebrows raised.

"Let's just say it was a harrowing experience," said von Brandt, grinning mischievously, "and leave it at that."

"I'm surprised a man like you needs to frequent a place like this."

"Nobody needs to come here," corrected von Brandt, "it's more a question of want."

Von Brandt stubbed out his cigarette in an ashtray and poured himself another glass of champagne, then topped up Jessica's.

"No matter what predilection or sexual proclivity," he continued, "it is all catered for in clubs like this. Drugs, sex or just come to observe. Nobody judges, because nobody cares."

"And that's what you do, is it? Observe."

"I come for the girls," he replied candidly. "For a small fee I can have any one of them for the night."

"You prefer to go with prostitutes!" exclaimed Jessica.

"Don't be so shocked," said von Brandt, smiling. "As relationships go, it is a more honest one. Unlike a relationship born out of something as specious as love, it is an equitable arrangement. With a whore there is no pretence. You know exactly what you're getting."

"There may be tolerance here, I don't see much tolerance in the streets," mused Jessica. "The Brown Shirts are particularly cruel."

"Ah the *Sturmabteilung*, the Storm Detachment," said von Brandt, nodding pensively. "Many of them are soldiers who returned from the Great War. They hate the Weimar Republic and all it stands for. They feel betrayed by the Republic for signing the Treaty of Versailles. After all, Germany was never occupied, and they don't believe the Fatherland was defeated. Many of them blame the Jews for undermining the country towards the end of the war, hence their hatred of them. These men fear the Communists in this country, fear that they may get a foothold. And fear makes men do desperate things. They expect change, and they want revolution, and feel that the National Socialist Party is the only group who will satisfy their needs."

"I think they will be disappointed," commented Jessica.

"Indeed," said von Brandt, smiling.

"And what about you?" enquired the time traveller. "Do you hate them?"

"I don't care about the Jews one way or the other," dismissed von Brandt, "but then I don't really care about anyone much. I am… apolitical."

"And possibly amoral also," Jessica suggested.

"Politics – morals," von Brandt laughed heartily, "I have no use for either."

Jessica's attention was distracted by a performer who had just begun to sing. The figure was elegant, wearing a full-length silver evening gown and white elbow-length opera gloves. Under the black bob hairstyle, yet again she couldn't tell whether it was a man or a woman, as the figure sang in a husky voice and gesticulated with a long cigarette holder. Whilst Jessica was distracted by the performance, von Brandt took the opportunity to break off the tip of a small glass ampule and pour the contents into her drink. Jessica's ears pricked as she heard the snap of glass but didn't perceive its significance.

"What is he… err she singing about?" Jessica enquired, turning back to her host. "It seems so passionate."

"The song is called '*Das lila Lied*'. The Lavender Song," von Brandt declared. "It is a song lamenting the plight of inverts."

"Inverts?" enquired Jessica.

"Homosexuals," confirmed von Brandt.

He watched intently as Jessica picked up her glass and took a long sip. She looked up at the man opposite her, with enquiring eyes. The champagne tasted different.

"Is everything alright?" asked von Brandt.

"Yes," frowned Jessica, unsure, "I think so."

Thirty minutes later, Jessica began to feel drowsy, the room was swimming and she stumbled in an attempt to stand up. Von Brandt summoned the doorman.

"Can you order us a taxi," he beckoned, "I fear the lady has had too much to drink."

The doorman nodded and by the time von Brandt was manhandling her into a taxi, Jessica was out cold. Her assailant gave the address to the driver and the vehicle sped away into the night in the direction of von Brandt's rooms in the district of Spandau.

***

Jessica woke up and groaned. She was lying on a double bed, fully clothed, with a dull ache throbbing inside her skull. She looked around at her unfamiliar surroundings. The room was old-fashioned but tastefully furnished with antique furniture, even for this time period. As she endeavoured to push the fog from her mind, she wondered how long she had been here. Her mind became clearer and she instinctively knew from her internal clock that it was 22.27 hours. Swinging her legs off the bed, she slipped her feet into her shoes and buckled them up, then tried to stand. After a few unsteady moments, she gained her balance and made her way into the drawing room. Jessica could see von Brandt rifling her purse. To her alarm he had removed the white box of ampules and put it to one side on the couch as he studied a curious object in his hand. He turned to the doorway, startled to see her awake so soon. Her captor stood up, clearly surprised.

"You're awake!" he exclaimed. "How? You should've been out for hours."

"What did you give me?" replied Jessica, ignoring the statement, and walking towards her father. "Give me that."

Von Brandt moved his right arm to avoid her grab for the object.

"Just morphine, enough to knock a bull out," he said, frowning, then turned his attention to the object in his hand. "What is this?"

Jessica couldn't believe that she was so stupid as to leave her cell phone in her purse. And now this brute had managed to light up the screen with the phone's blue and purple wallpaper.

"I've never seen anything like it," continued the Nazi officer. "Please explain."

"I said give me that." Jessica moved closer, desperately trying to grab the phone. "How dare you go through my things."

Grabbing Jessica around the waist, he pulled her close. Adrenaline was pumping through her veins and she was panting. As she began to try and struggle free, taking care not to use too much force, von Brandt threw the phone on the couch and swiftly withdrew a silver stiletto from inside his jacket. As he brought the razor-sharp tip up under Jessica's chin, she could feel it sting as the blade depressed her skin. She stared at him wide-eyed, keeping very still; von Brandt grinned at her, certain that he had the upper hand. Slowly Jessica brought her left hand up and gripped his right wrist. Glancing at this manoeuvre, von Brandt was shocked to see her pull the stiletto away with ease. Jessica placed the palm of her right hand over the tip of the blade and stared intently into her father's eyes. Then she pushed down hard on the tip. Her left eye flinched a little as the blade went through, much to von Brandt's astonishment. Jessica slowly slid her hand down the blade, until it reached the hilt and then she wrapped her fingers around von Brandt's hand. She began to squeeze, not too hard at first, then gradually building up the pressure. The expression of the man in front of her changed from astonishment to a grimace as the pain began to shoot through his clenched hand. Jessica piled on more pressure and von Brandt was now on his knees. Jessica held the pressure as he started to gasp for breath.

"Stop it!" he cried out, sweat forming on his brow. "You're crushing my hand."

With her left hand, Jessica picked up the hapless man and threw him onto the couch with such force it shifted several inches. Von Brandt had let go of his stiletto and Jessica was left with it hanging from her hand. As von Brandt nursed his bruised fingers Jessica took her other hand and slowly pulled the blade out. She studied the wound with great curiosity as it already began to congeal and heal. By the time von Brandt had turned his attention back to her, the wound was all but gone, save for a red patch on the skin to either side. He foolishly made a move to stand up but Jessica threw the stiletto at the couch. It buried itself in up to the hilt, between his legs, much too close for von Brandt's liking.

"Don't move," she barked, "don't move a muscle."

"Who the hell are you?"

"Someone who made a mistake," Jessica could feel her eyes welling up, "the mistake of coming here."

"What do you want with me?" von Brandt's voice trembled with fear and anger. "Do you expect me to beg for my life?"

"To grant you something you will never learn," Jessica's voice was charged with contempt, "and that's mercy."

Not wanting to show that this man, her father, had got to her, she picked up her belongings, and put her coat over her arm.

"Men are such disappointments," she quipped as a parting shot, and left the flat without a goodbye.

Von Brandt pulled himself together and reached for a side drawer and found his holster. He winced with pain as he withdrew the Luger and made his way to the front door. Opening it, he dashed into the corridor, expecting to hear his assailant on the stairs, only to be greeted by silence. He looked down the stairwell for any signs of her, but the mystery woman was gone.

***

For the second time today, Jessica found herself flustered in amongst the Doric pillars of the Brandenburg Gate. She had no recollection of the journey but guessed that she must have travelled through space but not time. A few people were out and about, but nobody seemed to have noticed her sudden appearance. She was shaking from her encounter with her father. Everything Slater had told her about the man was true, but she had to find out for herself. As her emotions got the better of her, Jessica slid down the pillar until she was sitting on the ground. With both hands over her face, she sobbed. Thoughts raced through her mind but her overriding fear was, *Am I like him? Am I evil too?* Emotionally drained, the time traveller stood up. It was late and she had had enough. It was time to go home.

Jessica hid amongst the pillars, closed her eyes and concentrated hard. Moments later she opened them to see that she was not where she expected to be. Through gaps in stone pillars surrounding her, she could see the sun just dropping below the horizon and the cloudy sky getting darker, beyond them an expanse of green fields. She looked around her and then in panic spun around, taking in exactly where she was. It couldn't be, surely, but there was no mistaking the massive circle of vertical stones, capped off with horizontal stones forming a circle. Closer to her was a smaller U-shape circle of taller stones thirteen feet high, and between these two circles, another circle of much smaller stones rather like headstones.

Jessica recognised the monument instantly: it was Stonehenge. The only difference being that unlike the ruins that she and everyone else were familiar with, this one was intact. Completely intact.

"Okay, so I'm in England," she reasoned to herself, "but how far back in time have I come?"

She surmised that the monument *she* was standing in must be at least 5000 years back in time from 2016. And here she was, slap bang in the middle of it. Some distance away, Jessica could just about make out some movement. Shadowy figures keeping their distance and speaking in an ancient tongue.

In an attempt to get a closer look at them, she began to step forwards but found that she was transfixed. The monoliths began to change; quartz crystal within the stone began to shine with bright blue dots, like stars in the firmament. Again, Jessica tried to move, but now her whole body was immobile and she was firmly rooted to the spot. A droning sound started to emanate from the stones and they seemed to crackle with electricity. With a sudden crack the lights linked up with electric blue sparks in a random web formation, like synapses in the brain. The energy in the air built up to an oppressive amplitude and hundreds of blue lights shot into the centre of the henge like spokes of a wheel. Jessica was bathed in blinding blue light from head to toe; she could no longer see anything and she screamed, but heard nothing. Then just as the sensation was beginning to become unbearable, Jessica vapourised, and the monument once again was silent and calm. One of the shadowy figures in a long robe approached the stones, flung both arms into the air and uttered an incantation that only he understood, then dropped to his knees in double genuflection.

CHAPTER FIFTEEN

WHEN THE DEVIL DRIVES

*University of California, Berkeley, Residence Halls Unit 4
November 2016*

As Sophie lay soaking in the bath, she dismissively allowed
the book that she was reading to casually slip from her
fingers and drop unceremoniously to the floor. The book
was *The Catcher in the Rye*, and after struggling to engage
with the plot, she decided to persevere until page one
hundred, and, if she still wasn't into it, then she'd give up.
With an intake of breath, she slid under the water and
began to count. By the time she had reached 450, Sophie
surfaced again, not because she needed to, but because
she was getting bored and felt that perhaps she should. It

did make her wonder, however, just how long she could stay underwater before needing air. It was something that needed to be looked into; not now though. Sophie had other things on her mind.

With a towel wrapped around her torso, she padded into her bedroom, threw the book on the bed and absentmindedly brushed her wet hair in a mirror. Then she moved over to the bed, allowing the towel to drop to the floor. Flopping on the bed, Sophie lay on her front, and gasped a long drawn-out sigh. Baths always made her feel concupiscent and right now she yearned for the intimacy of the professor. Instead, she picked up her cell phone and scrolled through the contacts, stopping at one, with her finger poised. Just as she was about to select a name, the phone rang and startled her.

"Hey, Professor," she greeted, regaining her composure.

"Hi," responded Harrison. "I just thought I'd check that you're okay."

"I'm okay," confirmed Sophie, with hesitation, "just a little worried is all."

"You and me both," agreed Harrison.

"Any sign of Jessica?"

Harrison paused before responding, long enough for Sophie to deduce what his answer would be.

"She seems to have disappeared off the face of the earth," he replied eventually. "Her phone is unobtainable and her landline goes straight to the answering machine."

"I shouldn't worry too much about her," retorted Sophie sardonically, "I suspect that she can look after herself. It's you and me that I'm worried about."

"What do you have planned?" enquired Harrison.

"It's just an idea," evaded Sophie. "It may come to nothing. Leave it with me."

"I think our best bet is to continue as normal," suggested Harrison, "keep to our regular routines. The police might be watching us."

Sophie hadn't seen Nathan for over twenty-four hours but had to agree that, for the moment, this was the best course of action.

"I miss you," beseeched Sophie.

"I… I miss you too," faltered Harrison, "but I'll see you in class tomorrow, right?"

"Maybe," replied Sophie. At this very moment, she couldn't make that promise.

The conversation ended on an irresolute note and Sophie turned her attention back to the task from which she had been distracted. Selecting a contact, Sophie waited patiently for a reply from the other end.

"Hey, Sophie! How ya doin'?" came the familiar voice. The tone was cheerful and relaxed, putting Sophie at ease. "Long time no see."

"I know, it's been a while," agreed Sophie. "Look, Tuck, can we meet up?"

"Sure thing, when did you have in mind?"

"I was thinking tomorrow morning, if that's okay."

"No problem," confirmed Tuck. "You know, like, where I live, right?"

"Yeah, I remember," quipped Sophie. "Tomorrow then."

They hung up and Sophie took a white cotton shirt, pulled it over her head then slipped into bed. She picked up the book that she was struggling with and opened it to where she had left off. Unable to concentrate, she slammed it shut, tossed it over the end of her bed and tried to put everything out of her mind as she settled down to sleep.

***

Wayne Tucker was known to just about everyone as 'Tuck'. So much so in fact, that very few people actually knew his Christian name. He was tall and skinny, with pointed features. His unbrushed ginger hair and stubble gave him a general scruffy, unkempt appearance. As he pulled back the curtains of his living room to observe the tatty red Mini convertible pull up outside his ground-floor apartment, he felt a slight tang of sadness for what might have been. The figure of a girl alighted from the Mini and approached the building, the hood of her black hoodie firmly pulled over her head. Allowing the drapes to drop back into position, Tuck moved to the front door to let his visitor in. He opened it to see Sophie standing, uncharacteristically, with a troubled look on her face.

"Hey, Sophie," he greeted. "Come in."

Sophie stepped through and walked into the living room. She glanced around at the dishevelled, unsanitary surroundings. Unwashed dishes, magazines, empty beer bottles all competed for space with discarded clothes draped over random furniture as if they were dropped just where they had been removed by the wearer. With the badly fitting curtains closed, the room was in semi-darkness and light was struggling to force through the partially covered window in strong, dust-laden beams. The anxious girl turned as Tuck entered the room; his demeanour was no better. Sophie noticed that he had lost weight since she last saw him, and he was skinny back then. His sunken eyes had black rings around them and didn't seem to shine the way Sophie remembered.

"You should look after yourself better," she said finally, hugging him. "Are you still dipping into your stock?"

Tuck pushed her away with slight indignation.

"Just pills and blow, I don't touch dope," he replied petulantly. "What's it to you anyways?"

"It's why we split up." Sophie gestured around the room with her right arm. "I didn't want to end up like this."

"Don't hassle me, man," Tuck said, grimacing, flopping down on the couch and putting his head in his hands. "If that's why you came round…"

"Sorry." Sophie cut him off, worried that she might have gone too far. She sat on the couch next to him after removing a couple of empty beer bottles. "I'm worried about you is all."

"Why are you here, Sophie?" responded Tuck with a pleading look in his eyes.

"I'm hoping you might be able to help me," she declared.

"So, that's why you're here," stated Tuck sardonically.

"Look, I could be in trouble," revealed Sophie. "Do you know anyone who makes false passports?"

"Oh, so you think just because I'm a drug dealer, I'm gonna know about other dodgy dealings."

"Well, do you?"

Tuck put his head in his hands for a long minute, rubbed his face and finally turned and looked Sophie straight in the eyes.

"As a matter of fact, I do."

"Can you take me to him?" Sophie observed the doubtful look on Tuck's face. "Please."

"I'll call him, but I'm not promising anything."

"You're a sweetheart," said Sophie, smiling and kissing him on the cheek. "I'm going to need three."

"Three!" exclaimed Tuck.

"Will that be a problem?"

"I guess not," Tuck conceded, "but it's gonna cost ya. And you'll need photos."

"No problem," confirmed Sophie, "I'll find a photo booth later."

"He'll want a deposit."

"How much do you think?" enquired Sophie.

"A thousand bucks, at least," declared Tuck.

"Okay, I'd better get going then and sort things out," decided Sophie. "I'll call you later."

"Are you sure you want to do this?" asked Tuck, wondering what the hell she had got herself into. What she was getting *him* into.

"Needs must," replied Sophie with a wry smile, "when the Devil drives."

***

"It's okay, he's expecting you," encouraged Sophie's passenger. "Just say Tuck sent you."

Sophie gave him a doubtful, hesitant look as she stopped the car in front of the self-storage facility on Almeda Island, just south of Oakland. The island, being the largest in San Francisco Bay, hugged the mainland closely, separated by the narrow tidal canal.

Stepping out of the car, Sophie looked up just as an airliner roared low overhead, taking off from Oakland International Airport. The noise startled her initially, primarily because she was nervous. She gave Tuck a withering look, perturbed by the fact that he wasn't going to accompany her, then proceeded to enter the large building. As she walked the corridors, Sophie checked off the numbers on the shutters lining both sides, until she came to the one that she was looking for. Sophie knocked gently on the metal and waited. A metallic clang echoed down the corridor as the shutter was pulled up and a man appeared.

"Tuck sent me," announced Sophie, summoning up as much confidence as she could muster.

The man immediately ushered her in and closed the door behind him. Looking around the compact lock-up, Sophie saw a myriad of tools and equipment, necessary for this man to ply his trade. He was well dressed in clean denim jeans and light green shirt, plus he looked clean and well groomed, wearing a pair of horn-rimmed spectacles. The moon-like face was somewhat podgy, being neither handsome nor ugly, and Sophie felt that if she saw him in the street, she would not have given him a second glance. He gave Sophie a quick appraisal and then sat down.

"What can I do for you?"

"Didn't Tuck say?" Sophie was a little taken aback by this question.

The man didn't answer and awaited a reply.

"I need three passports," stated Sophie succinctly.

The man remained silent, continuing to appraise Sophie until she became uncomfortable. Sensing her unease, he finally spoke.

"It will cost you six grand." His tone became businesslike. "Can you manage that?"

"No problem," confirmed Sophie.

"And I'll need a deposit."

"I have a thousand on me."

"Good enough," confirmed the counterfeiter. "Now down to details. Are all the passports for you?"

"No, one for me and one for two other people."

"I'll need their details and photos as well."

Sophie dipped into her purse and pulled out a strip of four photos which she had taken earlier in a photo booth. They showed her with her blonde hair pulled back tightly on the scalp and tied in a ponytail. She handed them to the man, who studied them intently.

"Could you alter my hair? Different colour or style maybe?" she enquired.

"No problem," confirmed the counterfeiter. "I can Photoshop that. What about the other two?"

"I haven't got a photo of them but I thought you could use their picture from the university website."

After giving him the website details, the man found the Berkeley University page and looked at Sophie for further instructions.

"Their names are Professor Nathan Harrison and Dr Jessica Phillips," she advised.

"I can use these," he confirmed. "I might have to tweak the smile off the professor's face but the other one is fine. Have you any name preference?"

"No, I'll leave that up to you."

The following ten minutes were taken up with Sophie giving the counterfeiter all the details necessary to create the passports and then she passed him the deposit. He smiled and put the wad of notes down on his bench.

"Aren't you going to check it?"

"My work is built on trust," he replied, smiling for the first time. "It wouldn't be in your interest to try and cheat me."

"When will they be ready?"

"Come by this time next week," he confirmed, "with the balance, of course."

Sophie nodded and said goodbye, then ducked out of the shutters and was gone. Tuck was waiting patiently in the car with his eyes closed. Hearing her open the car door, Tuck glanced across.

"Okay?" he asked.

"Yeah, all okay," confirmed Sophie, with a sigh of relief. She put the key in the ignition, started up the engine and they sped away.

***

Five Miles South of Huntington Lake, Sierra National Forest, Fresno County, California
November 2016

The black SUV thundered up the forest road towards its destination, a substantial chalet-style log cabin secreted in a secluded spot in amongst the dense pine firs, which loomed ominously like silent sentries in the darkness. The car hit a pothole and jerked, causing the body in the trunk to stir and moan. Hearing the noise from behind them, Thaddeus and Bartholomew looked at each other impassively and remained silent as they continued on their journey along the track.

The two Apostles had been tasked with following Robert McQuillan the investigative journalist, and the order had been received from Jude to bring him in. They had watched as he broke into the bungalow in Oakland now owned by Jessica, which was, at this moment, clearly vacant. The two men waited for the reporter to exit the house before ambushing him. McQuillan was bludgeoned unconscious by the grip of Bartholomew's handgun before the reporter knew what was happening. Now he was hogtied and gagged in the back of the SUV, slowly beginning to regain his senses.

After receiving a text to say that they were on their way back with an extra body on board, Jude walked out through a sliding door, onto the wooden balcony. He shivered in the cold night air, waiting eagerly for the SUV to return. The balcony wrapped itself around the extensive property, built on the side of a slope to take full advantage of the forest views and the jagged white peaks of the Sierra Nevada mountain range beyond. A glimmer of headlights flickered between the tall trunks of evergreens, and Jude pulled his coat in closer as the sharp wind began to cut into him. The car turned into the grounds and drove up the long, steep tarmacked drive. It made a slight turn to the right and flooded the balcony with light from its front beams. Jude squinted as the vehicle emerged onto the level ground in front of the two dark green garage doors. The balcony fell back into semi-darkness and Jude began to make his way down to greet them, opening a garage door just as his accomplices were lifting the tailgate. With his bindings removed from an efficient slice of a blade, McQuillan's captors effortlessly lifted the diminutive man, confused, frightened and with a pounding head, out of the trunk and dumped him on his feet, still gagged. Leading him through to the back of the garage, the three men passed through a door into a hallway and straight down some steps which led to a basement. The stumbling prisoner, still groggy from his ordeal, was forced into a chair and bound around his chest with gaffer tape. After adjusting his spectacles back into place, McQuillan surveyed his surroundings. The basement was well lit with fluorescent striplights, showing a room well fitted out as a workshop. At one end of the twelve-feet by fifteen-feet area was a workbench running the full length of the wall and fitted with a vice. Tools of various types were arranged in an organised fashion, either on the wall or on the bench, and at the other end various garden implements were laid upright against the wall. Although his head was still pounding, McQuillan was fully *compos mentis* now as he observed the rest of the Apostles – Matthew, Simon and James – enter the basement to complete the complement. Jude took another chair, swung the back around and sat down, his elbows leaning on the back of the chair and his hands clasped together. The two men stared at each other from a distance of about four feet, then Jude nodded and the gag was removed.

"What the fuck are you doing?" spat McQuillan, without hesitation. "You won't get away with this."

"You are here to help us with our enquiries," revealed Jude impassively. "I believe your friends call you Scottie. May I?"

"Do I have a choice?" said McQuillan, grimacing.

"The relationship between captor and interrogator is such an intimate one," said Jude, smiling, "I feel a more casual approach will be more… beneficial."

McQuillan could see that he was in a desperate position; not one of these men, whoever they were, had bothered to conceal their identity. It didn't look good. He was frightened, and for good reason.

"Why should I tell you anything?" he exclaimed. "You're going to kill me anyway."

"So many people talk about the quality of life," sighed Jude, "but only the old and infirm think about the quality of death. I'm afraid now is the time for you to start thinking about your quality of death."

"I don't know anything," stated McQuillan, trying to brave it out.

"Why have you been snooping around those apartments and that bungalow?" asked Jude with a frown.

McQuillan remained silent, staring defiantly at his interrogator. Jude gave him thirty seconds to answer and then motioned to Simon, who took the reporter's left hand and put his little finger in the vice. Slowly but steadfastly, he wound the vice tighter until his victim began to wince with pain. Simon glanced at Jude, who nodded his consent and the torturer continued winding in the vice. The beleaguered reporter began to scream out in agony as his finger began to be crushed. Sweat formed on his forehead and he began to drool as the pain shot through his hand and up his arm. Bone began to crack and shatter, the skin splitting open, allowing an outpouring of blood onto the floor. The vice was wound back permitting the finger to be released.

McQuillan pulled his arm away in an attempt to nurse the injury. His finger, still bleeding badly, was beyond repair.

"Now, I'll ask you once again." Jude's voice was calm and controlled, completely unfazed by the violence he had just witnessed. "What is your interest in these properties?"

McQuillan appeared not to be listening, concentrating on his injuries. Simon grabbed his hand again and moved it towards the vice.

"Stop! Alright, I'll tell you," cried McQuillan, who paused to catch his breath. "The apartment in Berkeley belongs to a university professor called Nathan Harrison. He is somehow connected to Dr Jessica Phillips who also works... worked at the same university. Since the destruction of her apartment in Oakland, she now lives at her dead father's bungalow, the one where you caught me."

Jude remembered the bungalow well. Baby Jessica had hurt his finger there thirty years before. The irony of the current situation wasn't lost on him.

"We know about Jessica Phillips," divulged Jude. "What were you expecting to find?"

"I don't know," railed the reporter. "Something, anything that might help to make sense of all that's been happening."

"And did you?"

"No," replied McQuillan with unequivocal finality. His hand was throbbing and he began to feel nauseous.

"What about Dr Phillips' apartment?" pressed Jude, ignoring his victim's obvious distress. "What happened there?"

"I got there after the event," confirmed McQuillan.

"Yes, but you managed to spend some time in the building."

"It looked like an earthquake had hit, but it was different. As though the room had imploded."

"Did you remove anything from the scene?"

"No, no, not at all," protested the reporter.

"That's not what one of my men reported back to me with," replied Jude. "He observed you remove an object from your sock just before getting into your car. Then you spent a few minutes studying your phone."

"Maybe I was texting," reasoned McQuillan.

"Check his pockets," ordered Jude.

James moved forwards and did so, finding the man's cell phone in his inside jacket pocket. He passed the device to Jude.

"Pin number, if you please," he asked. McQuillan complied and Jude was able to access the phone. He scrolled through the pictures and stopped at one.

"What's this?"

"It's some sort of formula," muttered McQuillan. "I don't know what for, I'm no scientist."

"What did you remove from your sock? Clearly you smuggled it out of the apartment."

The injured man remained silent; the last thing that he wanted was for the phial to fall into the hands of these thugs. Jude motioned to Simon to go to the back of the room. Thaddeus dragged the chair-bound reporter closer to the bench and pulled his left elbow up onto a block of wood. Simon returned, dragging a sledge hammer, which he lifted without hesitation, and slammed it down hard on McQuillan's forearm. The radius and ulna snapped with a sickening crack, causing McQuillan to stiffen and gasp in shock, wide-eyed and mouth gaping. His head fell forwards and he vomited violently before passing out. Jude stood up and walked over to the unconscious man, slapping his face in an attempt to revive him. Slowly McQuillan's head began to loll and he moaned as the pain in his arm returned to his consciousness.

"What did you take?" shouted Jude, endeavouring to get through to him.

"Phial," muttered the reporter. He no longer cared. He just wanted the pain to stop. "In my drawer."

"What's in the phial?"

"I... I don't know for sure," he muttered. "I think it's some kind of drug, looking at the bottle. It might be connected with the death of a dog that swallowed some nine years ago."

"Were there anymore?"

"Yeah, one," said McQuillan, wincing. "It was confiscated by the CIA and US Air Force."

Checking McQuillan's pockets again, Jude found his keys. He gave them to Bartholomew and instructed him to find the phial. McQuillan lived over a hundred miles away, so Jude knew it was going to be a while before he could confirm that the phial was in their possession.

After leaving McQuillan in the basement, the remaining Apostles made their way upstairs to wait. Jude lit a cigarette and walked out onto the balcony; he needed some air. His mind was working overtime. Was this the Infinity Serum that Kaplow so desperately wanted? They had been following McQuillan's reports; it would seem this Dr Phillips was connected with the strange disappearance which caused a traffic accident. And what did this professor have to do with it? Was he the man seen exiting the damaged apartment with Dr Phillips?

James joined Jude out on the balcony and shivered. The temperature had dropped significantly.

"This could be the drug the Air Force are looking for," he stated.

"I've been thinking that myself," replied Jude.

"It must be connected somehow with the time machine," suggested James.

"It's got to be the drug that Colonel Pearson is looking for," confirmed Jude, leaning on the balcony railings and staring into the trees, deep in thought, "which would mean it's highly likely that we now have the two things the Air Force need."

"The Infinity Serum and Liquid Chrome," said James, nodding.

"Let's see what Bartholomew brings back," concluded Jude.

Just under three hours later a text came through from Bartholomew; he had the drug. Jude looked at his watch; it was just gone midnight. He walked back down to the basement, followed by the other four, to find the reporter with his head slumped forwards, his eyes closed. He put his hand under the man's chin and pulled it up.

"Water," rasped McQuillan.

"Pass me that water bottle," ordered Jude.

He gave the injured man a good draught of water until it began to overspill out of his mouth.

"Now, Scottie," McQuillan was barely conscious and Jude had to hold his head up, "do you know what this drug does?"

"It's dangerous," mumbled the reporter, "that's all I know."

"In what way? What did it do to the dog?"

"It… it dissolved its insides."

The six men looked at each other in astonishment and McQuillan's head slumped down again; all he could think about was the intense pain in his arm.

"I think we've got all that we can from him," declared James.

"One more thing," concluded Jude. "What do you know about a time machine?"

At this extraordinary question, McQuillan's senses revived a little. He lifted his head and frowned.

"A what?" he muttered, in total bemusement.

"Time machine," repeated Jude.

McQuillan simply shook his head before dropping it again.

"I don't think he knows," observed Simon.

Jude sighed and nodded his agreement. He walked round behind McQuillan as he pulled out a handgun from his waistband. He screwed on a silencer, pulled back the slide to load a bullet into the chamber and put the muzzle to the back of McQuillan's head. A muffled sound and a spray of red exited the poor man's left eye, flinging his glasses several feet across the room. James picked them up, shaking off some blood and brain.

"Well, wadya know," he said, grinning, holding them by the temples and squinting through the thick lenses, "they didn't even break."

"We need to clean this mess up and bury the body before dawn," advised Jude getting businesslike again.

By the time this was done, Bartholomew had returned with the phial. Jude held the innocuous-looking fluid up to the light.

"We have the Liquid Chrome," he declared to the room, "now it looks like we have the Infinity Serum."

"What's our next move?" enquired James.

"We need to find out more about this drug and what it does," replied Jude. He pondered for a moment longer and confronted his men.

"Dr Phillips," he announced, "she's the key to all this. She is our next priority."

***

Almeda Island, San Francisco Bay, California
November 2016

"I don't know what I'm doing here," complained Tuck.

Sophie had asked her friend along for moral support with the transaction. She wasn't used to such nefarious activities and felt uncomfortable simply dealing with this man.

"I just feel better knowing you are here," she explained.

Exactly one week to the hour, Sophie's little red Mini convertible pulled up outside the storage facility and she grabbed her purse before stepping out.

"I won't be long," she assured him.

Nervously she made her way down the aisles until she found the lock-up that she was looking for, stopped, adjusted her hoodie and knocked. The shutter opened and the forger allowed her into his inner sanctum. Without a greeting or smile, he got straight down to business.

"You got the money?"

"Sure," replied Sophie, slightly taken aback, "but I'd like to see the goods first."

The man smiled and turned to his desk and opened a drawer. He removed three dark blue booklets and passed them to his client.

"Did you have any problems?" asked Sophie, opening one at random.

"They're getting tougher to fake as technology improves," he revealed, "but I manage okay."

Sophie leafed through all three until she was satisfied with her purchase.

"All good?" the man enquired.

"Yeah," confirmed Sophie, "all good."

In fact, they were perfect and she was particularly pleased with the way she had been changed in her photo.

"That will be five big ones then," announced the forger, "and if you'd like to give me a little something extra, I can think of something you can do."

He pushed Sophie up against the wall with some force and pressed his body tight against hers. A faint whiff of armpit sweat wafted into her nostrils. Lesser mortals may not have noticed but Sophie found it repugnant. She pushed the man off her and he flailed across the room and sprawled across his desk. Sophie looked at her hands; she was shocked at how little effort it took to push this not inconsiderable man across the room with force.

"Oh, so you want to play, do you?" said the forger, beaming, running a hand through his hair and lunging back at her. Sophie was too quick for him and the man slammed into the wall. She flipped him round like a rag doll so that he was facing her again. With her left hand pushing him tight against the wall, she slowly moved her right hand down to his groin and squeezed gently.

"Seems to me you're the one who wants to play," said Sophie, grinning.

"God, you're so hot," leered the man.

Feeling a stirring in his loins, Sophie squeezed harder, then harder still, until the grin became a grimace and her adversary began to whimper. Gripping even tighter the man began to cry out and Sophie lifted him up off the floor by his genitalia until the man's head hit the ceiling. Watching this jerk sweat and wince in pain amused her until she felt that he'd had as much as he could take. She threw him across the room and he fell in a heap, almost knocking the computer off his desk. Without even looking at him, Sophie put the three passports in her purse and pulled out the $5000. With a casual flick of the wrist she flung the notes at him. They flew out of the envelope and fluttered down around the prostrate figure, sprawled across the floor.

"You bitch," he hissed, trying to regain some dignity.

"It's all there," rejoined Sophie, stepping out of the door. "Consider yourself lucky to still be alive."

Walking back to the car, Sophie was grinning from ear to ear. She was beginning to enjoy her new abilities and silently thanked Jessica for the gift. Not that she would ever give her that satisfaction.

Settling down into her Mini, Tuck was anxious for news.

"Got what you wanted?" he asked. "No problems?"

"No problems at all," chuckled Sophie and drove Tuck home.

Back at Sophie's lodgings, she took her false passport and hid it in the bottom of a large knapsack, with her real one, in her wardrobe. She also checked that the $30,000, her entire savings, was still in the side compartments. After taking a shower and changing into a white T-shirt and some black denim dungarees she drove out to The Smokehouse burger joint and ordered a charbroiled burger and fries with a strawberry milkshake. Sophie didn't realise how hungry she was and ate with gusto, wondering whether it was the adrenaline rush of the afternoon or the drug itself which gave her such an appetite. Thoughts of Nathan wandered into her mind. She hadn't seen him for a few days and looked forward to meeting him later. By the time she had finished her meal, it was dark. She put on her jacket and drove towards Nathan's apartment, wondering what else this day might have in store for her.

***

At his wits' end the past week, Professor Nathan Harrison had found it difficult to concentrate on work. Sophie had a point; the publicity created by the destruction of Jessica's apartment threatened to expose them all. The only option was to lay low and hope it all blew over. Though he felt that perhaps this notion was a little optimistic, even for him. The thought of having to leave the country just to safeguard the secrecy of the Infinity Serum now seemed like a reasonable idea. And where was everyone? Harrison felt abandoned and useless whilst the other two were getting things done, whatever that might be. He had some inkling of Sophie's whereabouts, but where the hell was Jessica?

Snapped out of his train of thought by the sound of the doorbell, Harrison hoped it would be one of the two. He sighed with relief at the sound of Sophie's voice and buzzed her in. She entered the apartment and walked straight up to the professor and embraced him, holding on as if her life depended on it.

"Oh, it's so good to see you again," she sighed. "I've missed you."

"I've missed you too." Harrison said it with feeling, simply because it was the truth, but then, he was missing Jessica also.

"I've been busy," declared Sophie.

"Doing what?"

Delving into her purse, Sophie pulled out two passports and handed them to Harrison. He thumbed through them noting the false names, checking for obvious mistakes which might give their lack of authenticity away. He could find none.

"They're perfect," she assured. "I checked mine with my real one."

"Isn't this my university website picture?"

"Yes," confirmed Sophie, "though he had to take the grin off your face, they're not allowed in passport photos."

"How…" Harrison was cut short as Sophie anticipated his next question.

"I've got contacts. The guy proved to be a pain, but I handled it."

"This couldn't have been cheap," considered Harrison. "Can I give you some money?"

"Don't worry," replied Sophie, shaking her head, "it's all been taken care of."

There was a pregnant pause and Sophie sat herself down on the couch.

"I've opened a bottle of wine, would you like some?" offered the professor.

"Yeah, fine."

She watched as Harrison disappeared into the kitchen and returned with two glasses and a bottle.

"It's red, is that okay?"

Sophie nodded and he poured out two glasses. As she sipped the deep maroon liquid, she became pensive.

"Have you heard from you know who?"

"I presume you mean Jessica," he replied in a slight disapproving tone, "and no, I have not."

"Do we need to stick around and wait for her to turn up?"

"We can't leave her behind." Harrison was outraged by the notion. "She deserves *some* loyalty, don't you think?"

"Why? All this has been forced on me."

"True," declared Harrison indignantly, "but you and I wouldn't be together now if you hadn't been injected too."

Sophie fell into a sullen silence, as if she had been reprimanded by a parent. Harrison felt the need to lighten the mood.

"Are you staying the night?" he asked with a mischievous grin.

Sophie delved into her purse and pulled out a toothbrush, also with a mischievous smile.

"I'll take that as a yes, then," he chuckled.

Later that evening the pair were fast asleep in bed together when Sophie was awakened by a sound. Startled, she sat up and looked at the luminous dial on the professor's alarm clock: it read 2.30am. Sophie shook Harrison rigorously to rouse him. Stirring, Harrison rubbed his eyes.

"What is it?" he asked.

"Listen," whispered Sophie, "I can hear someone trying to get in."

Harrison concentrated his hearing, and, sure enough, the faintest of scratchings could be discerned emanating from the front door.

"Quick, get dressed," hissed Sophie.

With great haste, the pair put on some clothes and tentatively made their way into the sitting room. In the darkness, they could both make out shadowy figures standing still. Suddenly the light was switched on and they had to squint while their eyes adjusted. Surrounding them were six men in black suits, five pointing semi-automatic carbines at them, while the sixth was standing casually with his hands in his pockets.

"What is this? What's going on?" shouted Harrison. "Who are you?"

Sophie didn't wait for an answer; with lightning reactions, she leapt at one and wrestled the rifle off him. Before she could bring the gun to bear, however, four muzzles were pointing close to her head. Reluctantly, she handed the carbine back to a slightly dazed Apostle. Jude stepped forwards.

"We're looking for Dr Phillips," he announced, ignoring Harrison's outburst.

"Jessica?" he exclaimed. "What do you want with her? We haven't seen her for a week now."

"You were with her when her apartment was damaged, were you not?"

"What difference does that make?" he replied, trying to bluff it out. Harrison was perturbed by how well informed this man was.

"And you," frowned Jude, turning his attention to Sophie, "your performance just then was quite remarkable. Quite remarkable indeed. If I didn't know better, I would say you had some superhuman powers. Maybe we don't need Dr Phillips after all."

Sophie and Harrison looked at each other furtively but remained silent.

"Bring them," ordered Jude, then turned his attention to his prisoners. "We will be taking you unshackled in separate vehicles, but if either one of you tries to escape, the other will be shot on sight. Do I make myself clear?"

Again, Sophie and Harrison glanced at each other and acknowledged Jude's statement with a resigned nod.

"Good," said Jude, smiling. "It's time to go."

The prisoners were led out into the parking lot where two black SUVs were waiting. Each was bundled into a separate car with their head covered in a black hood. Harrison heard the muffled cry of Sophie shouting, "Nathan!", before being bundled into the back of the lead vehicle. He was manhandled into the following car and heard a handgun being primed by a man getting in beside him. With three Apostles in each SUV, one driving and two holding guns to their heads, the convoy moved off into the night for the long drive back to the Sierra National Forest.

As the journey continued, Harrison had only one thought in his mind.

Where are you, Jessica? Where the hell are you?

CHAPTER SIXTEEN

RIPPLES ON A POND

Jessica opened her eyes wide and looked around. She couldn't see her body; in fact, she couldn't see anything except a blanket of white. Despite this disembodied sensation, she felt an odd awareness of floating, though there seemed to be no up or down nor sideways. With an overriding desire to reach out, Jessica endeavoured to touch the all-pervading blanket of white, but found that it constantly seemed to be just out of reach. Deprived of her senses, all Jessica had to determine her existence were rational thoughts, her self-awareness, though she felt her mind slowly starting to unravel in this sterile environment.

Completely bereft of any notion of time and space, Jessica had no idea where she was or how long she had been here. Was she dead? *Is this the afterlife? If it is*, she scoffed to herself, *then there are an awful lot of people in for a big disappointment.* Struggling to maintain some mental composure, Jessica tried to remember where she was before this surreal state manifested itself, and just as an image of Stonehenge came into her mind, she heard a disembodied voice.

"Jessica," the voice was deep but sounded calm and reassuring, "open your mind, Jessica."

"What? Who is this?" She had no way of knowing whether she had said this out loud, but her voice appeared to be heard.

"Empty your head of all your previous conceptions, perceptions and prejudices. Allow your mind to see."

Not really knowing what was required of her, Jessica emptied her mind of all thoughts and concentrated hard. Very gradually, her white confinement began to fade into a translucent mist, and as her eyes adjusted further, the haze dissolved and Jessica found herself lying at the centre of a smooth, golden structure very similar to Stonehenge but half the size. The floor where she was sprawled felt cool and smooth, with alternating stripes of gold and dark metallic blue radiating from the centre like a dartboard. Jessica stood up and suddenly realised that she was naked, but before she could react to this embarrassment, two females approached, both holding out a robe. She stared aghast at the two figures, their jet-black hair braided with multicoloured beads and with dark, tanned skin, each scantily clad in a shimmering white dress. They were classically beautiful, with high cheekbones, large dark eyes and a full sensual mouth. Their bodies were petite, with slim hips and small but shapely breasts which gave the creatures a girlish quality. But what astounded Jessica was the pair of wings which both girls displayed, with feathers of iridescent colours. Jessica held her arms out to allow the red and gold robe to be placed around her before taking the belt and tying it securely.

"Are you angels?" enquired Jessica, not unreasonably. She was annoyed with herself; the question seemed so childlike, but she couldn't help but ask.

The two creatures placed a hand over their mouth and a giggle echoed in the hall beyond as they turned and fluttered away. Tentatively, Jessica stepped out from inside the henge and looked around her. The point where she was standing was slightly elevated, and it gave her a view of the large hall. Square sand-coloured pillars flanked both sides, and the walls and ceiling were bedecked with star charts and murals. Hanging plants drooped from the ceiling, displaying a multitude of colours. Jessica studied them and didn't recognise any. Two men stood patiently at the back of the hall waiting for their guest to emerge. She recognised them immediately as the men she had witnessed when demonstrating her ability for Harrison. Just like the previous occasion, they were robed in black and gold, with their beards and hair braided with beads.

"Come, Jessica," beckoned one of the men, "come so we can know you."

Still unsteady on her feet, Jessica proceeded down the six arced steps and approached the two men. She had to crane her neck to look them in the eye, estimating them to be around eight feet tall. Their facial features were striking, with skin of light bronze. The high-bridged Roman nose was set below a heavy brow causing the dark eyes to look somewhat sunken. The overall effect gave the two men a statue-like countenance of authority and strength. As Jessica opened her mouth to speak, one of them raised a hand to quell her.

"All your questions will be answered, and more in due course," he declared, "but first you will need to be purified."

"Excuse me," uttered Jessica, taken aback by this statement.

"You will need to be cleansed, body and soul," advised the man. "It is a prerequisite for any who abide here."

The two winged girls appeared again; taking Jessica under her arms and giggling, they manoeuvred her out of the hall and into another smaller room with a large sunken pool. The liquid in the pool was gold in colour. Jessica turned to one of the girls.

"You certainly like the colour gold here, don't you," she said, frowning.

The girls smiled.

"Gold is pure," said one girl.

"Gold is incorruptible," said the other.

"And yet it corrupts," commented Jessica cynically.

"People are corrupt," echoed the girls. "Gold is just gold."

Relieved of her robe, Jessica was encouraged to walk down some steps into the dubious-looking fluid. Sensing her reluctance, one of the girls walked in first, followed by the other. Together they led Jessica down into the bath until only her head was exposed. With a mischievous grin they pushed Jessica's head under and she floundered for a few seconds in the murky solution. When she finally resurfaced, the two creatures had left. Jessica began to relax a little; the fluid was warm, soothing and a little more viscous than water. She found that floating was easy and she began to let her tensions flow out. Jessica revelled in the comforting sensation; it was like having loving arms wrapped around her. Having no idea how long she had been in the bath, Jessica's internal clock seemed to have deserted her, and when the two girls were back at the edge of the bath holding out a white towel, reluctantly she swam over to the edge. Feeling the steps with her feet, Jessica ascended from the fluid into the outstretched towel. This, she surmised, was to preserve her modesty because it became apparent as she was clear of the liquid that neither her hair nor skin were wet. Both the winged creatures smiled kindly again; one gestured to a stone bench, over which garments were draped. Jessica thanked them and they fluttered away again.

Dressing herself, Jessica found a full-length mirror fixed to a wall. The dress, similar to the robe, was red and gold with an intricate ornate pattern. It had no sleeves and buttoned up to the neckline. The waist was close-fitting and the skirt flared out and stopped short halfway down her thighs. The sandals she had been provided with were flat, with fine straps coloured gold. As she studied herself in the mirror, Jessica found that she was pleased with the result. The dress was perhaps shorter than she would have chosen, but she had a shapely pair of legs and had to admit, for the first time in her life, that she looked rather good. The overall look, however, did make her wonder whether she had stumbled onto the set of a Roman film epic. She caught herself in the mirror, smiling at the thought of this and turned away to re-enter the hall. Only one of the men was waiting for her return and he was standing beyond the pillars, out on a veranda, looking out at the vista beyond. Without turning round, he spoke.

"Come here, Jessica, and observe."

Jessica walked over to the stone railings and looked out at the amazing view below. The city was expansive – a mixture of low buildings interspersed with a large area of perfectly manicured lawns and flower gardens. Either side of this were huge truncated pyramids with horizontal stripes of dark blue and gold. Down the centre of one side of each pyramid ran a flight of steps from top to bottom, which put Jessica in mind of the ruins of South and Central America. A large cigar-shaped silver vessel hovered into view and landed on the flat plateau of one of the pyramids. Bright blue static electricity formed around the craft, and to Jessica's astonishment it disappeared without a sound. She noticed other smaller craft flying to and fro at a lower level and small dots – people – milling about at ground level. Jessica glanced up to the sky; it was cloudless, pale green, with a distant sun burning low on the horizon. Jessica looked up at the tall man, who seemed to her to be in a meditative state.

"What happened to my clothes?" she said, frowning.

"That's your first question?" chuckled the man incredulously. "You are transported to a different planet and your first concern is for your clothes."

"They cost me $400, and I had them for less than a day!" she complained. "Besides, I liked them."

"They didn't make the transfer," explained the man. "The portal that you came through wasn't designed for a person without the protection of a special suit. We couldn't be sure if you would even survive."

"You mean you risked killing me!"

"It was a calculated risk," revealed the man, still looking out at the sky. "We know that your physical makeup is much stronger than that of other humans."

"I've seen you once before," said Jessica, frowning. "I tried to time travel, but something went wrong."

"You are a very elusive creature, my dear. It was an attempt to bring you here. We tried to bring you in with a portal in your domicile, but you managed to resist us."

"So, Stonehenge was designed as a portal?" mused Jessica. "But it's in ruins now."

"Indeed, one of many all over your planet," confirmed the man. "It was dismantled thousands of years ago, when we left."

"You've been to Earth?" vociferated Jessica, aghast.

"I think it might be clearer if I start at the beginning," decided the tall figure, "but where are my manners? You must be hungry and thirsty. Please, follow me."

Jessica was led to a banquet table in the hall where a feast was laid out especially for her. The food looked very much like what she would find on Earth. She sat down and filled a plate, whilst a servant girl filled a glass with white wine. Jessica tucked into fruit and salad, plus a delicious meat with a taste very similar to chicken. The man watched for her approval as she raised the glass and sipped some wine.

"I trust it is to your liking."

"It's delicious, thank you," replied Jessica through mouthfuls.

"Let me introduce myself," announced the man finally. "My name is Tammuz. I am one of the elders of this world, the planet Nibiru. We are known by many civilisations on your planet as the Anunnaki. It translates as 'Those who from the heavens came'."

"I have heard of the texts relating to the legends of the Anunnaki," pondered Jessica. "Didn't the Sumerians chronicle your time on Earth? But I assumed it to be just a legend."

"Many civilisations wrote about us," confirmed Tammuz. "Have you heard of the Book of Enoch?"

"Wasn't it a scripture excluded from the Old Testament for being too fantastic, even by biblical standards?"

"Quite so," said Tammuz, smiling. "It writes of a group of angels who descended to Earth called the Watchers." Tammuz paused for effect. "We are those Watchers, Jessica, and since we left, have been watching Earth with great interest. And more recently, we have been watching you and your development with concern and fascination."

"How long ago did you visit Earth?"

"Five hundred thousand years ago," revealed Tammuz. "We set up the portals, to allow us to come and go at will. And we dismantled them when we finally left. We had to drag you back in time to a point when the portal was operational, just to bring you here."

"How far back did I go?"

"Twenty thousand years."

"I didn't know Stonehenge was that old."

"Alas, your archaeologists have got it wrong," smirked Tammuz.

"So, you could planet hop at will?"

"Not just planet hop," declared Tammuz, "universe hop."

"This is an alternative universe?" exclaimed Jessica with a gasp.

Tammuz patted his lips with a napkin, pushed his chair back and stood up. He gestured to his guest.

"If you are replenished, perhaps you would like to take a walk."

Jessica nodded, stood up and followed the strange tall figure through a corridor and into another room. She looked around in awe. The room was massive, circular in shape with a domed ceiling. It was lit from an indeterminate source and illuminated what looked like thousands upon thousands of small circular star charts. At the centre of the room was a low, stout pedestal, its highly polished surface reflecting light.

"What is this place?" whispered Jessica as she craned her head and looked around. Her voice echoed in the cavernous space.

"We call it the Univarium," said Tammuz, smiling with pride. "Each of those circles represents a universe. Not an alternative universe as you mentioned, but a completely different one."

"And I am now in a completely different universe?" Jessica was now walking around taking it all in.

"Indeed you are."

Tammuz gestured with his hand at one of the circles and it floated towards him. He guided it over the black pedestal, where the orb, only twelve inches in diameter, now hovered, seemingly fixed in position. He placed his hands either side and moved them outwards away from the rotating globe. As Tammuz's arms widened, the orb grew to around six feet and a multitude of galaxies could now be discerned. He spun the image gently with one hand and stopped, zoomed in further and further then stopped again.

"This is your universe," he announced, pointing at a swirl now at the centre of the orb, "and this is your galaxy."

"Yes, I recognise it," replied Jessica, wide-eyed.

Zooming in still further, Tammuz took Jessica into the Milky Way and then into the Orion Spiral Arm, where the solar system containing planet Earth seemed to be orbiting an insignificant star.

"Yours is just one universe." Tammuz gestured at the ceiling. "Even we haven't discovered them all. And the laws of physics that apply in your universe do not necessarily apply in others."

"What was the purpose of your visit to my planet?"

"We set up a base to mine gold. I'm sure you must have noticed that we use it extensively."

"Yes, I have noticed," replied Jessica laconically.

"But that wasn't our primary objective," confessed Tammuz. "We visited your planet to accelerate the evolution of hominids."

"What! You took a primitive human species and manipulated its genetic makeup?"

"We are genetic engineers," quipped Tammuz. "It's our *raison d'être*."

"You created *Homo Sapiens*." Jessica spoke in a hushed tone as the notion sank in.

"We took the species known by you as *Homo Heidelbergensis* and helped it along. They were the ideal template for what you became. They stood upright and used simple tools," said Tammuz, smiling. "Without our intervention, you would still be using flint tools right now."

Tammuz sent the image of the universe back to its place on the ceiling and turned his attention to the pedestal. With a wave of his hand, he summoned up another holographic image. Jessica stared intently as the scene unfolded. What she saw was a grassy plain with a series of upright stones, set out in a circle and embedded in the ground. It became obvious to Jessica that the stones were part of Stonehenge, currently under construction. A large stone came into view, seemingly being levitated in a horizontal position by a futuristic vessel flying just above it. The stone was lowered into position on top of two stones, aided by, to Jessica's astonishment, several figures over twenty-five feet tall.

"They're giants," she exclaimed.

"Hybrids, engineered by us to help with the construction of this portal," confirmed Tammuz. "They are mentioned in a number of your religious texts and are referred to as the *Nephilim*."

"Yes, I've heard of them," declared Jessica. "Doesn't the Book of Enoch state that they are the progeny of angels and humans?"

"Is it so surprising? Any primitive creature who encounters advanced technology will look upon such visitors as gods. We came from the stars and bestowed knowledge and wisdom. To them we were gods."

"What happened to the giants?"

"They were a simple creation, who, once they had outlived their usefulness, were... dispensed with."

"And what about us?" said Jessica, frowning. "Will we outlive our usefulness?"

"That, Jessica, depends entirely on your kind."

Tammuz placed a hand in a pocket of his gown and removed a grey stone. It was perfectly round and smooth.

"Observe." It seemed to Jessica to be more of a command than a request.

She did as she was told and watched him raise the stone. Holding his arm out, Tammuz allowed the object to fall from his hand. It landed on the pedestal and the resounding clunk echoed through the chamber, and they both watched as a ripple spread out down the pedestal, along the floor and up the wall, causing a tsunami-like wave through the multitude of universes displayed on the ceiling. Jessica picked the stone up, studied it and then passed it back to the tall figure.

"This small stone represents the time machine used recently on your planet," explained Tammuz, "and every time it is deployed, it creates a ripple through not just your universe, but every universe."

"What is the significance of this?"

"It means that the people who invented the technology are aware of its use and have identified the source. It was confiscated from them, and they want it back." Tammuz's tone had become stern. "Dark forces are moving towards your planet, Jessica, and only *you* can do something about it."

"But... but what can I do?" stammered Jessica.

"It's been a long day," Tammuz said, smiling, his tone becoming kindly again, "and you've had an arduous journey. You should rest now, and we shall speak more of this on the morrow."

"I must admit, I am tired," conceded Jessica.

She was led to a bedroom with a huge double bed and left to rest. Jessica undressed and slipped under the sheets. They were smooth on her skin and cool to the touch. Very soon she fell into a troubled sleep.

***

It seemed to Jessica like a perfect spring morning. The air was fresh and cool and the sun was rising on a cloudless day in the pale green sky. She had woken up refreshed, then washed and dressed in a frock, similar to the previous one, except the colour was green and gold. Studying herself in a mirror, Jessica preferred this colour combination; it seemed to suit her eyes and complexion better. Now she was overlooking a large walled garden from her bedroom balcony, with trees filled with blossom. She could also see borders of flowers creating a cornucopia of colour and perfectly manicured lawns. Birdsong filled the air, and to Jessica it seemed as though she had stumbled into some kind of paradise. As beautiful as her surroundings were, however, Jessica was troubled. Her home seemed light years away, but it was so much more than that: light years away in a different universe. She felt a pang of anxiety sweep through her like a person stranded on a desert island who has come to realise they have no hope of rescue.

A sound of movement echoed in the high-ceilinged bedroom and Jessica turned her back on the view and re-entered to see whom it might be. One of the winged girls had come fluttering in with a tray of food. She giggled as Jessica entered, and placed the tray on a table. Just as she was about to leave, Jessica spoke.

"Tell me, what is your name?"

"My name is Aruru," giggled the girl.

Jessica was beginning to find this girlish nonsense irritating. She needed serious answers to serious questions, but conceded that this flighty will-o'-the-wisp would have to do.

"Am I a prisoner here, Aruru?"

"Goodness me, no," assured Aruru, appalled at the very notion, "you are quite free to come and go, just as you please."

"Where would I go in any case?" commented Jessica, more to herself than anyone else.

"The gardens are most pleasant at this time of day," advised Aruru, ignoring the comment. "You can access them by a staircase just outside this door."

"Thank you," said Jessica, smiling. "I might just do that."

Aruru gave a final giggle and left Jessica to eat. The tray was filled with bread and fruit and a cool, sweet drink which tasted like nothing she had ever encountered before.

Just as Aruru had said, a wide staircase wound its way down to ground level and she was able to enter the gardens through tall arches. The sun was higher in the sky now, warming up the air, though a gentle breeze kept it fresh with the aroma of blossom from all the plants and shrubs. Absentmindedly, she wandered deep in reflection as she wondered about Nathan and Sophie. She was concerned for them and felt a strong desire to get back home. As she ambled further, two figures studied her from the balcony: Tammuz and another man named Ugazum.

"We can't delay much longer," sighed Ugazum.

"Indeed," agreed Tammuz. "There is much for us to do; much for her to learn."

Hearing voices, in a language that she didn't understand, Jessica looked up to the balcony to see Tammuz beckon her back into the building. She approached the tall men, who looked at her with steely-eyed determination.

"It is time, Jessica," announced Tammuz, "for you to fulfil your destiny."

She was led into another large room, though this one was much more austere and clinical-looking. Walls, floor and ceiling were a pale grey and in the centre was a large object which looked to Jessica rather like some kind of scanner. It comprised a white slab around eight feet long and four feet wide. Above and either side of this were huge tunnels fixed to the walls and facing each other. They jutted out into the room, looked to be about twenty feet in diameter, with a gap between them of about fifteen feet.

"What are you going to do to me?" exclaimed Jessica, who was alarmed now.

"Relax, child," comforted Ugazum, with a reassuring smile, "we only intend to finish what you have begun."

"And what's that?" said Jessica, frowning.

"The manipulation of your DNA," revealed Tammuz. "You have already guessed, quite correctly, that the serum you've been taking is unlocking your latent potential."

"Oh no, the serum." With all that had happened, Jessica had quite forgotten all about her purse.

"The serum is gone," replied Ugazum. "It went the same way as your clothes. But this is of no consequence, we do not need it. We have been engineering genetics since the beginning of time."

"When we created *Homo Sapiens*," added Tammuz, "we put certain restrictions into your genetic makeup to limit your ability. If you used all your DNA, the human race would be something akin to what one of your philosophers called an *Übermensch,* and we don't think you are anywhere near ready for that."

"So, you are going to unlock my DNA?"

"Isn't it what you were striving for?"

"I suppose," conceded Jessica.

"It's a very simple process," assured Ugazum, leading Jessica over to the machine. "Alas you will have to remove all your clothes."

"What, here? In front of you?" complained Jessica.

"We have female assistants to help you," said Tammuz, smiling. "We have no interest in your form."

The two female assistants were summoned to help Jessica out of her garments and onto the slab of the machine, whilst the two men left the room. A head restraint was fixed in position, and her naked body was held firmly in place by another slab which descended from the ceiling, its hollowed-out underside fitting perfectly to the shape of her body. The two slabs made a perfect seal and as Jessica was made immobile, she began to feel claustrophobic. There was a pause of less than a minute, then she felt a sting of several needles entering her body at various points from head to toe. So many, in fact, it was impossible for her to discern just how many injections were administered.

After a short pause the slabs with the bemused girl were raised into the air by an ascending post, stopping in a central position between the two circular objects, which immediately began to rotate. The slabs separated themselves from Jessica; one lowered back to the ground, whilst the other raised up to the ceiling. Now suspended in mid-air at the centre of the large contraption, Jessica could see that she was between two tunnels made up of several rings, each one rotating and contrarotating alternately. They started slowly at first, and then began to speed up until they became a blur. Jessica could no longer see the rotating rings as a dim light slowly intensified. The room was invisible to her as she was blinded by white light, shooting from one tunnel to the other, like a jet stream. Jessica heard herself cry out a blood-curdling scream as it all became too much for her to bear. She seemed to be no longer in the room but floating in space. In that moment, she opened her eyes to see her body giving off an intense yellowy white light, her body burning like the hottest sun. In her mind's eye she saw the universe, her universe. Nebulae, galaxies; she saw stars being born and stars dying, the whole spectrum of her existence. Of all existences.

"I see it all," she gasped, "not just my universe but all universes. It is magnificent and beautiful. Frightening, wondrous and awe-inspiring. Everything makes sense now; I understand it all. The whole of existence is sentient, omnipotent and self-aware. I see it – oh God, I see it all."

At that moment everything went black and Jessica slumped into dreamless oblivion.

***

Before she was fully conscious, Jessica became vaguely aware of more than one presence on the bed that she was tucked up in. Startled awake, she sat up abruptly and saw the two angelic creatures sitting either side of her. The childlike giggling seemed to have gone to be replaced by what to Jessica looked like adoring smiles. Each girl took one of Jessica's hands, and in that moment, she remembered her experience between the rotating tunnels. Was it real? It felt so profound, so overwhelmingly exquisite. Jessica burst into uncontrollable sobs as tears streamed down her cheeks.

"There," soothed Aruru, putting an arm around her, "it's alright to feel this way."

"I feel like I've seen something no mortal should see," replied Jessica through sobs and wiping her eyes.

"What makes you think that you are mortal?" said the other girl, smiling.

Jessica looked at her astounded, stumped for words.

"Don't you see it? Don't you feel it?" she continued. "You shine, Jessica, more intensely than the brightest star."

"Yes, I do feel it," replied Jessica, "it's just so difficult to accept. Like I don't deserve it."

"The very fact that you feel this way is proof that you do," affirmed Aruru, placing her right hand to Jessica's cheek. "Now it's time to prepare you."

"I didn't ask you your name," said Jessica, turning to the other girl.

"My name is Aea," replied the girl.

"Aruru and Aea," mused Jessica, relaxing a little. "That's really sweet."

The two girls led her away to a large sunken bath where she was washed. Under normal circumstances, she would have been appalled at the very idea of being washed by two females she hardly knew, but it seemed at that moment to be perfectly natural. And besides, who was she to say what was normal anymore? After Jessica had dried herself off, and with the towel wrapped around her, Aruru and Aea proceeded to braid her hair with multicoloured beads.

"Is this really necessary?" said Jessica, wincing.

"Of course," smiled Aruru, "you are like us now. You must look the part."

It seemed pointless to argue and Jessica gave in and allowed them to continue. Finally, Aea disappeared and returned with a white gown which shimmered in the light. Jessica stepped into it and the girls laced the garment up the back. The dress was full length and flowed across the floor. Though the styling was simple, being sleeveless with a V-neck, the shimmering material more than made up for it. Jessica was led to a mirror and had to admit that with her hair now braided and the dress, the effect was simply dazzling.

The two girls led her by the hand down the spiral steps into the garden. In the centre of the lawn, a feast was laid out on a low table on Jessica's behalf. The three girls sat on the grass, breakfasted and chatted about everything and nothing, until Jessica lost all track of time. Then a shadow cast itself across the table and Jessica glanced over her shoulder. Tammuz was standing there, his head eclipsing the sun, its corona framing his solemn face like a halo. He held out his hand and smiled.

"Jessica, I'm afraid the moment has come."

"Just when I was getting used to it here," sighed Jessica with resignation.

She was led into the great hall where Ugazum was waiting, and she glanced uncertainly at the portal at the end of the hall. The girls bowed their heads, smiled at Jessica, gave her hands a gentle squeeze and left the room.

"Come, Jessica." Tammuz's tone, compared with the girls', was now cold, more formal. "We need to speak and time is short."

"What you experienced in the tunnel, whatever that may have been, came as a complete surprise to us," revealed Tammuz.

"Indeed, it was most unexpected," concurred Ugazum.

"I feel so different." Jessica found it difficult to articulate her feelings. "What I experienced was… was divine."

"The very existence of your universe, and possibly others, is in grave danger of being ripped asunder. We cannot allow this to happen," declared Tammuz, placing an arm on Jessica's shoulder.

"I understand," said Jessica, frowning, with a tinge of sadness in her voice. "I understand everything. I know what I must do."

"Then you are ready," announced Ugazum.

Jessica nodded solemnly and the two men led her up the arced steps to the portal. At the top, Tammuz clasped both of Jessica's hands in his. He looked down at the young woman, the way a father would a child.

"Fix this, Jessica, the very future of your planet depends on it."

"Good fortune," said Ugazum with a nod.

The two tall figures stepped back down again and bowed in deference.

"It's a shame," lamented Jessica, holding out the material of her gown with both hands, "I really like this dress."

On that final note she turned and walked into the centre of the henge and closed her eyes.

CHAPTER SEVENTEEN

ECHOES OF THE PAST

Meadows Field Airport, Bakersfield,
Kern County, California
November 2016

Colonel Thomas Pearson was a tall man who hated travelling in all its forms, the principal reason for this being, with extraordinarily long legs, he could never get comfortable. It was the reason why he had chosen to take advantage of his rank, and use the Beechcraft U28A Huron twin turboprop utility aircraft that was at his disposal. The fifty-mile journey barely took twenty minutes, but as far as he was concerned, better to abuse his privileges than endure an hour plus drive by road. As the aircraft taxied off the runway, and pulled to a stop, the colonel turned to the slightly younger man sitting next to him by the window – Major Owen Wells.

"It looks like we're going to be early," declared Colonel Pearson.

Major Wells looked at his watch with apprehension; the time was 1015 hours, three quarters of an hour early to be exact. He was uncertain how the meeting that had been set up was going to unfold. He hoped it wasn't going to get ugly, which is why a public space was chosen for this engagement. That way, proceedings *should* remain civilised.

"Yes, sir," replied the major simply, his mind still preoccupied. He unbuckled his seatbelt and stood up.

Both men stepped down into the mid-morning sunshine and placed sunglasses over their eyes. They were wearing plain navy-blue suits, white shirts and black ties. There was nothing about them which might suggest that these men were United States Air Force. Even the aircraft from which they had just alighted, with its white and grey livery, betrayed little of its identity. Only the words United States of America printed in black above the passenger windows and the stars and stripes on the tail fin suggested that perhaps this aircraft might be official.

They exited the terminal to find a taxi waiting for them. The two men stepped into the back seats and removed their glasses.

"Where to?" asked the cab driver over his shoulder.

"The Courtesy Inn," replied Major Wells. "You know it?"

"Sure," declared the driver, offended at this slight and pulling away to enter the traffic.

The Courtesy Inn was only two miles away, close to the intersection with State Route 99 and 65, but the journey seemed to take almost as long as the flight. The architecture was hacienda in style, having cement-rendered walls painted a bright sand colour and terracotta pantiles undulating their way over the pitched roof. Well-kept shrubs lined the entrance drive and tall, randomly placed palm trees swayed gently against a bright blue backdrop in the autumnal breeze.

The two men walked into the hotel and approached the receptionist. They were greeted by a personable young woman who smiled brightly from behind the counter.

"My name is Colonel Thomas Pearson. We are expected for a meeting here at eleven."

"Ah yes," said the girl, beaming, "I have been told to expect you. You're a little early. If you would like to take a seat in the lobby, I will ring through for you. Would you like some coffee?"

"Coffee would be fine, thank you," replied Colonel Pearson.

The lobby was fairly plain and spartan, having smooth off-white floor tiles, and white walls with a few typically nondescript pictures. They sat down on one of the plain grey couches and thanked the receptionist as she placed a tray laden with cups, cafetière and cookies.

"They're on their way down," she advised them.

"Thank you," retorted Colonel Pearson.

Whilst they waited, Major Wells poured two cups and handed one to the colonel. They sat quietly sipping their drinks as two tall men in black suits approached with a confident stride. Both officers stood up to face the approaching men. They shook hands and introduced themselves.

391

"I'm guessing that you're Jude," declared Colonel Pearson astutely.

"That's correct, Colonel." Jude wasn't sure whether to be flattered or perturbed by this. Clearly the man saw something in him that he recognised, an air of authority perhaps. "And this is one of my associates, James."

Jude assessed the two men as he sat down opposite them. They were both, he surmised, in their early to late fifties, physically fit with short brown hair and brown eyes. Neither had any distinguishing features of note and had average good looks. Meanwhile Colonel Pearson sized up the two men in front of him. They were both around six feet tall, clearly very fit and seemed to him to be clones. They both had bright blonde hair, and the colonel wondered whether it might have been dyed. The only thing which seemed to set them apart was Jude's perceptible air of authority.

"Our apologies for being early," beseeched the colonel. "Oh, and help yourself to coffee."

"No apology necessary," assured Jude. "We are as keen as you to conclude this business."

"When you contacted the base and spouted on about a time machine," chuckled the colonel, shaking his head, "I have to admit, no one took you seriously. Then you mentioned Liquid Chrome... and I have to admit, that certainly got our attention. Especially me. You caused quite a stir, that's for sure."

"I thought that the mention of the gravity-defying metal might be the clincher," agreed Jude. "I trust it didn't cause any security problems."

"None that we couldn't plug," retorted Major Wells.

"We don't know how you came by this item and its

significance," cautioned the colonel, "but you can imagine how highly classified this is."

"We have kept this secret for a very long time," confirmed James. "You can rely on our utmost discretion."

"We also know of its value," chipped in Jude, feeling that polite preamble had run its course.

"What proof do you have?" asked Colonel Pearson.

James delved into his inside jacket pocket and produced his cell phone. He tapped the screen a few times and passed the device over to the colonel. Glancing at the screen, Pearson saw a dimmed image of a silver sphere about three inches diameter in a perspex box, floating in mid-air.

"If you scroll across," continued Jude, "you will see an image of a document given to us, written in Russian. We've had it translated and it explains how to replicate the substance. And that should make it priceless."

"How did you come by it?" enquired Major Wells.

"We are not prepared to name names," disclosed Jude, "but what I can say is that it came to us indirectly, via a renegade Russian colonel."

"And where is this colonel now?" asked Pearson.

"He is dead, not by our hand, you understand, but dead nonetheless."

"Very convenient," mused Pearson, "and what's to stop us arresting you for extortion?"

"This isn't extortion, Colonel," said Jude, smiling, not in the least bit intimidated, "it's a simple business transaction. Besides, if anything happens to us, you will never see the Liquid Chrome again."

"How much do you want?"

Jude pulled out a piece of paper from his jacket. He had

already anticipated this moment and had a price written down. He passed the slip over to Pearson, who looked at the figure and raised his eyebrows.

"You think it's worth $20 million, do you?" he barked. A few people turned around at his outburst and he hushed his tone. "This is a fortune."

"Take it or leave it, Colonel," chimed in James.

"We'll take it," sighed the colonel after a long pause. "What are your terms?"

"We would like five million paid up front into an OFC in the Cayman Islands," confirmed James, taking the initiative, "just to show good faith."

"OFC?" enquired Major Wells.

"Offshore financial centre," explained James, "then we will meet to make the transaction and then both go our separate ways – happy. The account details are also on that slip of paper. Both payments will be made via untraceable links through the Dark Web."

"I trust this is acceptable," offered Jude.

"There is one other thing," added the colonel. "We need a drug, it's powerful and dangerous. Called the Infinity Serum. Are you familiar with it?"

"We know of the serum," confirmed Jude, "but we have never procured any."

"That's a shame, we would pay handsomely for it."

"We are currently watching a journalist who is poking his nose into some unusual places," pondered Jude. "Let us get back to you on that. We will need a contact number for you, Colonel."

The colonel produced a notebook, scribbled a number on it and passed the torn-off page to Jude. He entered the number into his contacts, then duly passed the note to James.

"As soon as we see the money in our account," smiled Jude, "we will be in contact."

The four men wound up the meeting, shook hands again and the two officers left. The major turned to his superior as they waited for a taxi.

"We were too eager to meet their terms," he said, wincing. "They could've easily asked for more."

"And I would have paid it," said Pearson, grimacing, "especially with the knowledge on how to replicate it."

Jude and James followed them out, just as a taxi took the two officers away.

"That went better than expected," commented James.

"Yeah, let's follow them to the airport," muttered Jude, with a frown. "I want to see them take off."

Thirty minutes later, the two Apostles watched the twin-engine aircraft rise into the sky and disappear into the distance.

"We could've asked for more," declared James. "They agreed too readily."

"This deal isn't over yet," mused Jude. "Contact Thaddeus and Bartholomew. It's time for them to bring McQuillan in, let's see what he knows."

***

Oakland, East Bay, Near San Francisco, California November 2016

It came as no surprise to Jessica as she slowly emerged from unconscious torpor, that, yet again, she was naked. But if spending any time on Nibiru had taught her anything, it was to feel at ease with her body and indeed her soul. For the first time in her life, Jessica actually liked herself. Raising her head, she looked around at her surroundings. Immediately it became clear that she was sprawled on the floor next to a bed, in her father's bungalow. Jessica looked at the bed in disdain and then up to the ceiling.

"Close, but no cigar!" she exclaimed to anyone who might be watching.

Clambering onto the bed, Jessica plumped up a pillow and placed it behind her. She drew her legs up close, wrapped her arms around them and leant her head on her knees. Tears began to roll down her cheeks as she remembered her time with the Anunnaki. She felt it would be no exaggeration to say that her sojourn was a revelation which had left her emotionally overwhelmed. Jessica knew she had a task to perform and she also knew that she was the only one who could execute it, to prevent more damage to the fabric of space and time before the situation became irredeemable. The notion of free will entered her mind as she considered the possibility that *she* might just be a pawn in an intergalactic struggle to which planet Earth was oblivious. If she had no free will, was her future all mapped out? Was she nothing more than a character in a story dreamt up by some demented writer, playing God with their creations? Shaking her thoughts free from solipsistic contemplation, she padded off to the bathroom.

Jessica showered, dressed and made herself some coffee – black, because in the six days that she had been away, the milk had turned. She wandered into the sitting room, absentmindedly drinking from her cup, when ghostly images began to play out in front of her. Jessica recognised the woman in the room instantly; it was her mother, Laura. She watched aghast as the spectral figure opened the front door to let in several men wearing black suits. No, she hadn't let them in, they seemed to force their way in. Standing in the centre of the room, Jessica watched in horror as her mother's demise was played out with brutal efficiency by these strange men, who finally put her body to bed and departed. Jessica knelt by the bed and stared at her hapless mother as she slipped slowly into a coma and eventual death. Hopelessly, she held out a hand to her as tears fell down her cheeks.

"Oh, Mother," she cried helplessly.

A wail from behind her caused Jessica to whip around to see herself as a baby crying in her cot. Jessica knew that if she stayed much longer, she would witness David discovering the body, and that would be too much to endure. She put her hands up to her ears and closed her eyes, willing the apparition to disappear.

"Make it stop!" she cried at the top of her voice.

When Jessica finally opened them again, the vision had gone. Wiping her eyes, she picked up her keys and the cash which she had removed from her purse when she time-travelled back to Germany, and left the apartment in a state of great exigency, the faces of the six strange men burned into her memory.

***

It was late afternoon when Jessica returned to the bungalow, and the heartache of what she had witnessed earlier descended on her like a storm cloud. After a busy day shopping and eating, she flopped on the couch to catch her breath, shopping bags around her feet. Realising that she was thirsty, Jessica walked into the kitchen to get herself a glass of water. With her back to the room, however, Jessica sensed that she was not alone. In panic she swung round to see a short scruffy man, with thick-lens spectacles, looking in drawers and then cupboards. He seemed oblivious to her presence and Jessica realised that she was witnessing another past event. This one, however, was less ethereal and she surmised this to be because it had happened more recently. As she followed the man from room to room, she watched him carefully checking everything, leaving no stone unturned. Jessica recognised the man instantly. It was the reporter, McQuillan. Finally, the apparition left the bungalow, only to be ambushed by two men in black suits. Jessica frowned; she recognised them but was puzzled as to why they hadn't aged in thirty years.

With her attention turned towards Nathan and Sophie, Jessica was concerned; she felt an overwhelming desire to find them, and to protect them. Taking her shopping into the bedroom, Jessica changed into the new clothes that she had just purchased. She stood in front of her full-length mirror and appraised the result. She had bought herself a tight-fitting black body suit of lycra and spandex. It had a crew neck, full-length sleeves and leggings, giving the overall effect of a Ninja. For her feet she had chosen a black pair of flat ankle boots with a side zip. As Jessica studied her reflection, she felt that something was missing. In a moment of inspiration, she delved into the bottom of her wardrobe and found a discarded present which she never thought she would ever use: a wide black leather belt with two small pouches that hung off her hips either side. With her hair still braided with beads, she had to admit the overall effect was copacetic, and she mentally gave her appearance the thumbs up, and even allowed herself a smile.

Forty minutes later, Jessica stepped out of her car close to Harrison's apartment. It was early evening and as the sun set, dusk slipped swiftly into night. She hoped to find him at home, but alas these hopes were soon dashed as she walked across to the parking lot only to see a vision of two SUVs. They looked so real, so solid, Jessica felt as though she could touch them. The event she was witnessing must have been very recent. Jessica watched in shock as Nathan and Sophie, clearly in distress, were each bundled into a separate car and driven away. It came as no surprise to her that the culprits were, yet again, the men in black suits. The last thing that she witnessed as the two vehicles drove off was hearing Harrison's thoughts echo through her mind: *Where the hell are you, Jessica?*

Knowing that she had to act fast, Jessica got back into her car and drove home. She needed to locate where they had been taken, and so, striding into her bedroom, she sat down cross-legged on the centre of the bed and breathed in deeply. With steady breaths she calmed herself down, decreased her pulse and closed her eyes. Focusing on the point of abduction, Jessica traced the route of the SUVs to their destination. The moment of reckoning was at hand and Jessica's eyes snapped open, then squinted as she uttered one simple word…

"Gotcha!"

***

Five Miles South of Huntington Lake,
Sierra National Forest, Fresno County, California
November 2016

Through the night and the following day, there was not one moment when at least two Apostles didn't have submachine guns trained on their captives. Nathan and Sophie both knew that if they tried to escape, at least one of them would be killed. Neither was prepared to take the chance. Their prison, however, could have been much worse. The living area that they were being held in was elevated to take advantage of the views. All four walls had large picture windows or French doors opening out onto the wraparound balcony. And now that it was daylight, Harrison could see that they were in the middle of nowhere. The room was comfortably furnished and the prisoners had been forced to spend the night on a long couch, placed against a wall under one of the large windows.

By midday, Jude took over guard duty with James. The Apostles appraised their prisoners with indifference, whilst Nathan and Sophie looked upon their jailors with fear and contempt.

"Well, what do you want with us?" hissed Harrison. "If you were going to kill us, you would've done it by now."

"No, we're not going to kill you," sighed Jude. "You may have some value. After all, you do have the drug running through your veins."

"What value?" asked Sophie.

"Time will tell," said Jude, smiling. At this point he wasn't sure what value they were, but sensed instinctively that they might be a useful bargaining tool.

Jude handed the professor two printouts from McQuillan's cell phone. Harrison recognised them straight away as the formulae Jessica used to inject them all. He decided to feign ignorance.

"What are these?"

"Come, Professor," smirked Jude, "don't try and kid a kidder. These pictures were taken in Dr Phillips' apartment. When you were injected, do you honestly expect me to believe that you didn't see them?"

"Okay, so I saw them," conceded Harrison, "but I don't understand them. I'm a palaeontologist, not a biophysicist. Besides, they're useless without the drug."

"Oh, we have the drug," assured James.

"If your intentions are to sell to the highest bidder," contended Sophie, "let them work it out."

The two Apostles didn't respond to this pertinent point, and realisation dawned on Harrison.

"Of course, you don't want to pass it on until you've been injected yourselves," sneered Harrison. "Well, the only person who can do that is Jessica and she's gone missing."

By late afternoon, James was able to catch Jude alone, getting some air out on the balcony. He approached his boss.

"Why are you holding off?" he enquired. "We have everything we need and more."

"I know, but I thought if we could capture Dr Phillips, it would be a real coup for us and could pay dividends."

"It has nothing to do with taking the drug yourself then?"

"Think of it, James, you and me," Jude's eyes were wide, almost manic, "just think of what we could achieve."

"What about the others?" asked James.

"The others," declared Jude, "are expendable."

This revelation shook James to the core. For the first time since they had formed this team, he felt disloyalty creeping in. Even though Jude was including him, he feared for his safety.

***

Mid-evening, James took Jude to one side. He needed to talk to him, to convey his concerns. He found him in the kitchen making coffee.

"The others are getting fidgety," imparted James. "They don't understand what the delay is for."

"If any of them have a problem, then they should come and see me." This didn't come as a surprise to Jude; he was expecting some dissension. He needed just a little more time.

"Yeah well, they elected me as spokesman," added James. "They see me as your number two."

"Look…"

Jude didn't have a chance to finish his response, as power shut down throughout the house. The two Apostles hastily made their way into the sitting room where the other four Apostles had been relaxing with Harrison and Sophie. Since the two prisoners showed no intention of trying to escape, they had relaxed their guard.

"What's happening?" exclaimed Jude, straining to see in the pitch black.

"I think the fuses must have gone," replied Simon.

Five of the Apostles drew their handguns automatically, their instincts telling them that something was seriously wrong. A wind seemed to come out of nowhere, whipping round the room, and knocking over ornaments. Then just as suddenly as it started the wind stopped, power returned and a figure stood in the centre of the room dressed in a black tight-fitting lycra suit.

"Jessica!" exclaimed Harrison.

Her sudden appearance shocked them all, not least the six Apostles, five of whom trained their handguns on her in response. Jessica ignored Harrison's remark; her eyes were fixed on the man in front of her – Jude.

"The wind wasn't really necessary," said Jessica, grinning, "but I so wanted my entrance to be… dramatic."

"If you want to stay alive, then I suggest you join your friends over on the couch," sneered Jude. He felt the need to assert his authority; Jessica's sudden appearance was, to say the least, unsettling.

Jessica said nothing; she bent her knees, with her arms close to her sides and bowed her head. Slowly, she brought her arms up until they were stretched out on either side. The five Apostles, still bearing guns on her, burst into flames, and five pillars of fire blazed up to the ceiling but left no mark. The men were engulfed in flames but no heat appeared to be emanating from the intense apparitions. As Jessica straightened up, she stared directly at Jude, her eyes full of red and yellow flames.

"I feel in this moment that I should say something witty or urbane," she smiled, "but meh, I've got nothing."

With that she flung her arms out again and the five infernos were flung backwards at great force, each one smashing through a window, continuing over the balcony and plummeting down to the grounds below. Sophie and

Harrison ducked as a fireball flew over their heads, glass shattering and falling around them.

"Whoa," cried Sophie, "that's so badass."

She clambered out of the window onto the balcony and looked over, expecting to see flames, but there was nothing but the still of the night. Harrison was dumbfounded. He couldn't believe what he had just seen. Neither could Jude, who scrambled for his firearm, a look of sheer horror on his face. His whole team had just been taken out by one small gesture and he was shaking.

"Hey, Jude," said Jessica, smiling as she casually approached the man, who had just managed to bring his gun to bear, "don't be afraid."

"Sorry," she added, "I couldn't resist that."

Sophie, who was now back in the room, leant over to Harrison and whispered,

"When did Dr Phillips get a sense of humour?"

"When did she get so hot?" responded Harrison, staring at the slim but shapely body in the tight-fitting suit, and her hair in braids. He barely recognised her as the Jessica he'd known for the last decade.

"I know, right," said Sophie, gawping, "I'd do her."

Jessica was so close to Jude now, that she could smell his fear. He tried to point the gun at the woman, her eyes still blazing with fire.

"You think you can kill me with that toy," sneered Jessica. She twisted the gun out of Jude's hand before he knew what was happening, and placed it up against his forehead.

"If you're going to kill me," sneered Jude, "then just do it."

"Don't tempt me," sneered Jessica. "You've got some balls, I'll give you that."

Jessica allowed the magazine of bullets to drop to the floor then threw the gun to one side.

"You know nothing about me," bellowed Jude.

"Oh, you are so wrong," replied Jessica, with just a hint of compassion in her voice, "I know everything about you. Your brutal upbringing, how you had to run away as a young boy to avoid it. Being groomed by drug dealers and your eventual transformation into a hired killer. You've made quite a career for yourself, but alas, it's a career which is about to come to an end."

Grasping Jude by the throat, Jessica picked him up off the floor. She held him there with his legs kicking as he struggled to breathe. Then she threw him with force where he hit the wall and slid to the ground. Turning her attention to Harrison and Sophie, Jessica approached them and smiled, the fire in her eyes gone.

Knowing that she had left Harrison under the cloud of an unresolved argument, she looked at him furtively to see if he was still angry with her.

"I am so sorry, Nathan," she beseeched, "you were right to be angry. Can you forgive me?"

After a slight pause, Harrison smiled and gave her a hug; he wrapped his arms around her tightly and pulled Jessica in close.

"Just this once," he teased.

"Are you two okay?" Jessica asked, finally, wiping tears from her eyes.

"Err... yes," stammered Harrison. "Where have you been?"

"Out of town," disclosed Jessica enigmatically.

"How did you find us?" enquired Harrison.

"We have a special connection, you and I," declared Jessica. "I followed you here."

"Is he dead?" asked Sophie, spoiling the moment and pointing at Jude. She didn't like the intimacy that she was witnessing between the two.

"No, he's just unconscious."

"Love the braids," said Sophie, smiling, giving Jessica's hair a flick. "Did you do that?"

"No," replied Jessica impassively, "angels did."

"Say what…" quipped Sophie, not quite believing what she had just heard.

"What do we do now?" asked Harrison, in an endeavour to stay focused on their present predicament.

"Our first priority is to find a small wooden box," revealed Jessica, "and a phial of serum. It will be somewhere in the house."

"What's in the box?" enquired Sophie.

"A substance called Liquid Chrome," replied Jessica, who, anticipating the next question, added, "It's fuel for a time machine."

"Okay," uttered Sophie incredulously, "my life just gets weirder and weirder."

"Right, we'd better start looking," announced Harrison.

It didn't take long to find the wooden box. Harrison found it in a bag under one of the beds, along with the phial of serum and two sealed syringes. Harrison looked at Jessica appalled.

"They were going to inject themselves."

"No," corrected Jessica, turning to look at the

unconscious man who was beginning to groan, "only one was."

"What are we going to do with him?" enquired Sophie.

"Give him what he wants, of course," proclaimed Jessica. "We're going to inject him."

"Are you serious?" shouted Sophie. "This man's a killer."

"He won't kill you," reassured Jessica, "and I feel this man still has a part to play in all this."

Jude slowly began to come to his senses and Jessica picked him up by the scruff of the neck and dragged him to the couch. She pulled his jacket off and rolled up the sleeve of his left arm. Taking a syringe, Jessica filled it with a measure of serum.

"Hold it," advised Harrison. "Shouldn't we find out his weight first?"

"I know his weight," responded Jessica. "You two hold him secure while I inject him."

As Sophie and Harrison reluctantly held Jude tightly, he became aware of what was happening.

"What are you doing?" he cried out, in a pointless attempt to break free of their grasp.

After being injected, the whole process took less than five minutes and Jude found himself sitting up and feeling indominable. He felt the surge of energy course through his whole being which only the serum could bestow. Looking at his hands, he then picked up one of the machine guns and bent the barrel through ninety degrees as if it was rubber. Jude grinned mischievously at the other three.

"You've become like we are," announced Jessica, unimpressed. "You're one of us."

"One of you," sneered Jude. "How do you know that I won't kill you all?"

"Yes, it's possible that you could kill Nathan and Sophie," pondered Jessica, smiling menacingly at Jude, "but it would be the last thing you'd do. You have no dominion over me."

Picking up his jacket, Jessica rummaged through the pockets and found Jude's cell phone; she tossed it to him.

"It's time for you to earn your thirty pieces of silver," declared Jessica. "Make your call to Colonel Pearson."

"How do you know all this?" implored Jude. Despite the drug, he still felt at a disadvantage.

"Just do it," insisted Jessica, struggling to conceal her contempt, "and, with everything here, the serum plus us three, I'm sure you'll be able to up the price to fifty. Don't you think?"

A few minutes later, Jude disconnected his call and looked up.

"They're on their way."

"Wait," uttered Harrison. "Who's on their way?"

"The United States Air Force," replied Jessica, moving over to the wooden box.

Carefully she opened the lid and removed the perspex box inside. Harrison and Sophie approached for a closer look. Jessica opened the sealed lid to the perspex box and Jude placed a hand on her arm.

"Be careful," he declared, "this stuff is lethal. I have a Russian document which states that it dissolves all organic matter except plastic."

"Okay," smiled Jessica, "let's find out."

Without hesitation, Jessica placed her left hand into the silver liquid, until it was fully immersed. The substance crept up her arm under the sleeve of her suit and reappeared around her shoulders, neck and finally her head. The other three stared open-mouthed at Jessica's gleaming silver face. The perspex box was empty now and Jessica removed her silver hand, inspecting it like a curious child. She smiled at them and closed her eyes, then gradually Jessica's skin returned to normal.

"Now, if the Air Force wants the Liquid Chrome, they're going to have to take me."

"They've been awaiting my call," confirmed Jude. "We should expect them within three hours."

***

The four occupants heard the small convoy before they saw the headlights flitting through the trees – two Humvees front and rear, escorting a canvas-covered truck. Jessica watched impassively from the balcony with her arms folded as the three vehicles pulled up in front of the garage doors. As she saw Jude walk out to greet the two officers who had alighted from the lead Humvee, she turned and walked back into the living area.

"They're here," she announced, quite unnecessarily.

Before Harrison and Sophie could respond, Jude had reappeared with Colonel Pearson, Major Wells and six soldiers all carrying M4A1 carbines.

Jude made introductions and hands were shaken, except for Jessica, who resolutely stood firm with her arms folded.

"If we could see the goods now," declared Colonel Pearson.

"Has the money been deposited?" asked Jude.

"Check your account," said Major Wells, frowning. "This had better not be a double cross."

Walking into the kitchen, Jude opened up his laptop and tapped in his bank account details. He smiled at the amount showing in credit. In excess of $50 million. He walked back into the living area to an expectant Colonel Pearson.

"I have the serum and the Liquid Chrome," asserted Jude, "but there is a problem."

"Oh, and that is?" said Pearson, frowning.

"She has them both," revealed Jude, pointing at Jessica.

Colonel Pearson approached Jessica and stood very close to her, looking down in an attempt to appear intimidating.

"Then I suggest you pass it over to us," barked the colonel.

"She seems to have absorbed the Liquid Chrome," said Jude, wincing, knowing how fantastic this notion was.

"Absorbed it?" exclaimed Pearson, keeping his stare firmly fixed on Jessica. "Don't be ridiculous."

Jessica smiled and allowed her whole face to turn from skin colour to shiny chrome. Pearson took two steps back in shock and looked at Jude and then the rest of his men, just to confirm that they'd seen it also. The expressions of shock on their faces confirmed he wasn't hallucinating.

"You see, Colonel Pearson," declared Jessica, letting her face return to normal, "the Liquid Chrome and I are one. I will not relinquish it until we reach your base."

Colonel Pearson looked at the three strangers, then looked at Jude.

"Where's the serum?"

"Here," said Jessica, smiling, patting the left pouch on her belt.

The colonel couldn't help but feel that he was being manipulated, but decided he had no choice.

"Bring her," ordered Colonel Pearson, "bring them all."

"No, I'm staying here," insisted Jude. "That wasn't part of the deal."

"Things are different now," revealed Jessica, "you're different now. I'm afraid events are out of your hands."

Realising that Jessica could make him do whatever she wanted, Jude conceded defeat and allowed himself to be taken with Jessica and the two people who he now realised were never really his captives. It began to dawn on him that he was never in control, and he didn't like it one bit.

Jessica and her entourage were bundled into the back of the Humvees and taken on a short journey south to a clearing just north of Shaver Lake. Here an AgustaWestland AW139M was awaiting them. Colonel Pearson, Major Wells, Jessica and the other three were taken aboard, with two soldiers sitting at the rear. With Sophie at her side, Jessica stared out of the window as the single-rotor helicopter rose into the air and headed south. As the flight continued Jessica placed her hand on Sophie's and squeezed it gently.

"I'm sorry that I got you into all this, Sophie," she beseeched, sensing Sophie's unease. "I was wrong to involve you."

"That's okay." Sophie wasn't sure how to react. An act of contrition was not what she expected from the woman sitting beside her.

"Just remember," confided Jessica, still holding Sophie's hand, "whatever happens, I will always be with you."

"What do you mean?" said Sophie, frowning.

Jessica didn't answer; she was no longer listening to the confused girl. She had turned away and was now looking out into the blackness of the night, contemplating her future. All Jessica could see was the ghostly image of herself reflected in the window. She smiled grimly, and the ghostly image smiled back.

CHAPTER EIGHTEEN

SANTA CLAUS AND THE
PIZZA BOX

International Space Station, Expedition 50/2,
Low Earth Orbit over the North Atlantic Ocean
December 2016

As the International Space Station orbited at a speed of just over 17,000 miles per hour, the view of Earth looked spectacular, and for many an onlooker, never gets old from 220 miles up. Cosmonaut Fidir Ruslanavich, however, felt that he could reach out and touch the beautiful light blue orb with its smattering of dappled cloud cover, from where he was suspended. It looked to him like a giant hand could pick it up and shake it like a snow globe and then set it back in place again. If those Flat Earth meatheads could just see the world from where he was standing, thought Ruslanavich, it would soon change their minds. Or maybe not.

He was attached by his feet to the end of the Orbital Boom Sensor System, a long straight tubular arm, which in turn was attached to the articulated Canadarm2 robotic arm, used to facilitate maintenance on the station. As extravehicular activity went this had been a lengthy one, being nearly nine hours' duration in space. In that time, they had circumnavigated the planet six times, but Ruslanavich always relished the opportunity of a spacewalk, just to break up the monotony of his normal routine. The task in hand was to repair a rip in one of the panels of the photovoltaic solar arrays. The massive 108-feet-long by 30-feet-wide panel stretched out in front of him, one of four that formed part of module S4. He had just finished stitching up a rip in panel 3A close to its tip, though why the panel had torn was open to speculation, a small meteorite or a piece of space junk which plagues the outer atmosphere being the most likely culprits.

"Are you nearly there yet?" The question was posed deliberately in that childlike fashion to keep the moment light, though in reality the owner of the voice was becoming a little fed up.

The voice over Ruslanavich's radio came from US astronaut Margaret Stephens who had been watching diligently from the post which rotated the solar panel towards the sun. Her task was to make sure that Ruslanavich didn't make contact with the panels and run the risk of an electric shock. Since this was a real and present danger, it was important that she relay this information back to the crew who were controlling the arm from inside. This enabled the cosmonaut to concentrate on the job more efficiently, without having to worry about his positioning.

With very little to do, however, Margaret was getting bored, and after nine hours was keen to get back inside. To her there was only so long that you can marvel at the splendour of the planet.

"I'm just finishing up," replied Ruslanavich with his strong Russian accent. He was tired and keen to get back inside also.

"Good, I'm famished," retorted Margaret.

"Me too," agreed Ruslanavich, with feeling. "Let's get this arm back."

Margaret gave the command and the long articulated Canadarm2 began to swing back towards its resting position. Just as it was halfway across, however, there was a sudden flash of light behind them and a shock wave that hit both astronauts in the back. Margaret was sent flying until her safety tether was taken up. She flayed about on the end of the line like a fish on a hook. The robotic arm was sent swinging away out of control, with the cosmonaut skimming a hair's breadth from the surface of the solar panel as it swept its way across on a long arc. The arm jerked to a halt and the cosmonaut's left foot became detached and he began to flail, praying that his right foot would remain secured. Luckily for him the restraints held and the articulated arm was gradually brought back in again.

After finally getting herself back under control, Margaret turned slowly to see what might have caused the flash of light. She strained her eyes in the darkness, then gradually a shape began to form, very gradually getting closer. The shape was indistinct, being bulbous with jagged edges, like badly put-together Lego, and painted dark grey. On its lower half was an array of aerials of different lengths, splaying outwards, giving the object the overall look of a catfish. It had no discernible lights or windows, but as the object came within a quarter of a mile range it became apparent to both astronauts that this was some kind of spacecraft.

"Are you getting this?" shouted Margaret, nervously, checking her GoPro camera was still running.

"I see it," bellowed Ruslanavich, "but I don't believe it."

"We need to get back inside asap," ordered Margaret. "Santa Claus is back in town."

"What?" came a somewhat surprised voice from inside the station. "Can you repeat."

"Just get me back," shouted Ruslanavich.

"Copy that," came the confused response.

Margaret hastily made her way along the integrated truss structure, which ran along the length of the space station, forming its backbone. She met up with Ruslanavich, just as he was detaching himself from the arm, now having been manoeuvred to its resting place. Together they made their way to the living quarters of the Russian orbital segment until they reached the Pirs docking compartment for Soyuz spacecraft, which also doubled as an airlock. The two spacewalkers took one last doubtful look at the massive craft which had moved uncomfortably close, and then they entered the docking compartment, closing the hatch behind them.

"What the fuck is that?" panicked Ruslanavich, removing his helmet.

"Whoever they are," replied Margaret, switching off her GoPro and hoping that she had some film of the object, "let's hope to God they're friendly."

***

Vandenberg US Air Force Base,
Santa Barbara County, California
Joint Space Operations Center (JSpOC)
December 2016

Private Gracie Turner turned her head as she saw a figure appear to her right, in her peripheral vision. She was sitting in front of a monitor tracking the path of the International Space Station as it continued its orbit across the North Atlantic. Both recruits were wearing shirt tunics and pants in USAF T5 digital camouflage, which was predominantly green with flecks of beige. Gracie whipped her head around with such force that her ponytail flew over her left shoulder. She was twenty-seven, attractive and felt that she needed a greater challenge than the one with which she was currently saddled. To make matters worse she had been ordered to oversee some induction training for new recruits, and today it was to be the turn of a young rookie by the name of Private Kayden Landry. Already he had made a name for himself for being an overconfident loudmouth, the type of recruit she tended to avoid like the plague in her down time.

"Private Kayden Landry reporting, sir."

"You don't need to call me sir," quipped Gracie, looking across the top of her large dark-framed spectacles, "we're the same rank."

"What are we looking at here?" he enquired.

"*I* am monitoring space junk, in low Earth orbit," she revealed.

"I've got some junk here," said Kayden, grinning, grabbing his groin and giving it a gentle shake. He sniggered lasciviously.

"I'm not interested in the microscopic stuff," said Gracie, wincing. "Now sit down, shut up and you might just learn something."

"Yes, ma'am." Like a scolded child, Kayden did as he was told and sat down beside her. He took a moment to look around the darkened room. There were rows of people sitting at banks of monitors and larger screens fixed to the walls. The room was a hive of activity and looked somewhat daunting to the new recruit.

"If you follow this trace, you can see on the screen the path the ISS is taking as it orbits the Earth," stated Gracie getting down to business. "My task is to keep an eye out for anything, especially space junk, which might collide with it and cause serious damage."

"And what if you see something?"

"Well, I report it of course," she turned away from the screen to look at the rookie, "then Houston can manoeuvre the space station out of harm's way."

"How does it show up on the screen?" asked Kayden, frowning. "Is it like that large white blob that's just appeared?"

"What?" snapped Gracie, turning her attention back to the monitor. "Where did that come from?"

"It just popped up as you were talking to me."

Both watched transfixed as the radar trace of the object slowly moved over the trace of the ISS, to become one large Echo.

"Shit, it's massive," declared Gracie, her brow deeply furrowed, "and well inside the Pizza Box."

"The Pizza Box?" queried Kayden.

"Oh, it's an area of space thirty-one miles square by about half a mile deep. It looks like a pizza box and slap bang in the middle is the ISS," revealed Gracie, "and if anything comes into this area, it's considered too close for comfort and has to be monitored closely."

She picked up a receiver on her desk, looked nervously at Kayden and pressed a button.

"Captain Hatfield," announced Gracie excitedly, "Private Turner here. Could you spare a moment? I think we might have a situation."

The captain, a man in his late forties, arrived within a few minutes. Kayden stood up and saluted.

"At ease, soldier," he said, smiling, and turned his attention to the young woman staring at the screen. "What have we got, Gracie?"

"We've got a large object that has just suddenly appeared on the screen, sir. It appears to be sitting behind the ISS and keeping pace with it."

"That's way too big for space junk," mused the captain. "It looks like it's hiding behind the ISS."

"Yeah," chuckled Kayden, forgetting himself, "like an elephant hiding behind a mouse."

The other two looked at him, Gracie in disdain and the captain with contempt. Kayden shrank into himself.

"I don't think it's hiding, the object is way too big for that," reasoned Gracie, "but it could be using the ISS as a shield."

"That's clever," added Kayden with excitement, hoping to redeem himself. "Whoever it is, or whatever it is, will know that if we try to take them out, we will take out the ISS too."

"That's a good point," agreed Captain Hatfield, "but that would suggest that this is something intelligent."

"Yes, sir," said Gracie, wincing. "What do you suggest?"

"Go through the usual procedure, contact TOPO and inform them. Assuming they don't already know. In fact, scratch that, I'll do it personally."

Captain Hatfield strode away and Kayden leant forwards when the officer was out of earshot.

"What's TOPO?" he whispered.

"It's the Trajectory Operations Officer at Houston," confirmed Gracie. "We report anything irregular to him."

"Well, he's about to hear about the mother of irregularities, by the looks of things."

"Ain't that the truth," agreed Gracie, still frowning at the huge blip on the monitor.

***

Lyndon B. Johnson Space Center, Houston, Texas
Mission Control Center, ISS Flight Control Room
December 2016

The EVA had been a long one, approaching nine hours, and Barbara Morris, the ISS flight director, was anxious to see the two astronauts safely back inside. The procedure had been successful and she watched with relief as the Canadarm2 began to move back towards its resting place on the large monitor fixed to the wall above her.

Suddenly there was a flash and the picture went haywire, with spiralling images of space, the Earth and the space station flashing over the screen. Either astronaut Margaret Stephens' GoPro was loose or she was out of control on the end of her safety tether. A sudden glimpse of the robotic arm swinging away could be seen for a second, cosmonaut Fidir Ruslanavich's arms waving about as his left foot became detached.

"What was that?" shouted Morris, standing up and walking down closer to the screen.

Since no one in the control room was any the wiser, her question fell on deaf ears. Morris looked around the room at the controllers' reactions, dumbfounded and panicking.

"Find out what's going on," she demanded.

Before her command could be carried out, however, a picture came up on the screen: a faint image of a large object, slowly moving closer. There was a short conversation between the astronauts and the screens went blank. All communication with the space station was cut off.

"Did I hear right?" fretted Morris.

"Margaret used the code word 'Santa Claus' before we lost contact," replied one of the controllers.

"Can we run that piece of film again and get a better look. I thought there was something just before we lost transmission. It might have just been shadows." She was talking as much to herself as anyone else. Everyone in the room knew what Santa Claus meant: an unidentified flying object had been spotted. The term had been in use ever since the Apollo moon landings, and the majority had been false alarms, but there were still a few which were unexplained. They watched the film again, but it was all too brief, too indistinct to be certain.

Another controller approached, his furrowed brow betraying his concern.

"We just had notification from Vandenberg," advised the controller excitedly. "They've picked up something big on their radar. They say it seems to be tracking the ISS. What do you propose we do?"

"We wait," pondered Morris. "This might just be a blip. I'm not going to go public on a false alarm."

The blip, as the flight director had put it, was still in effect one hour later when Morris was approached yet again.

"We've got Hopkins University on the line. They've been pointing the Hubble telescope at Mars."

"How does that affect us?" quipped Morris irritably; the last thing she needed at this juncture was distractions.

"You'd better speak to them."

Morris sat in front of one of the few screens still operating in the room. A middle-aged man looked back at her. His balding head was round and he wore a tweed jacket with matching bow tie. His face didn't show its usually cheerful demeanour; he looked concerned.

"Hello, Professor Dawkings," greeted Morris. "What's this about Mars?"

"Hello to you, Barbara," reciprocated the professor. "We have been watching Mars for quite some time now and it appears that something big has begun orbiting the planet."

"Like what?" Morris was almost afraid to ask.

"Well, it certainly isn't natural, that's for sure," insisted the professor. "Dare I say it looks like a spacecraft. I'm sending some images over to you right now. Let me know what you think."

Five minutes later, Morris and a few others were staring at a high-resolution image of Mars, and just above its equator was a long thin black line. It could easily have been mistaken for a smudge or a fault, but the blow-up sent through with it showed quite clearly some kind of structure which was obviously not natural. The beleaguered flight director studied the images on the screen.

"It looks massive," mused Morris with a frown.

"What are we going to do?"

"I don't know," fretted Morris. This was totally unprecedented and she didn't have a procedure to cover it. For the moment, she decided to sit tight.

Just over sixty minutes later, Professor Dawkings was back on the line. Morris rolled her eyes. *What now?* she thought.

"Hello again, Barbara," greeted the professor. "I don't know if this is relevant, but I thought I'd better report it anyway…"

"Yes, Professor," she interrupted, wishing he'd just get to the point.

"Well, we tracked a pulse of light from space, that hit the Earth a few minutes ago."

"Is this relevant, do you think?"

"Well," said the professor with a frown, "it appears to have come from the same position that the ISS is currently orbiting."

"Where did this pulse of light hit?" Morris was getting increasingly nervous.

"Our best guess is somewhere in the Tahoe National Forest in California."

"And that's all you've got?"

"For now, yes," said the professor, nodding apologetically.

The call ended and Morris went back to her workstation and leaned on the desk, her head down, deep in thought.

"Have you made a decision?" pressed one of her staff.

"Like I said," she announced, looking up at the blank screens, "we wait. I don't want to cause a panic unnecessarily. That pulse of light may well have been a meteor." Even as she said it, Morris knew that this was almost certainly wishful thinking.

The flight director could feel the eyes of the room burning into her. Clearly, they felt that she was making a mistake.

"Get back on to Vandenberg," she ordered. "We're relying on them now. For the moment we're flying blind."

***

Tahoe National Forest, California, Nevada Border
December 2016

The final day of angling had been a particularly successful one for the three fishermen as they made their way laughing and joking back up the slope from the Yuba River. They were in high spirits after netting several rainbow trout, which were difficult to catch in these waters, and a brace of salmon. The sun had just set and the forest was almost completely dark when they finally reached their metallic red Ram 1500 pickup truck, which was silently waiting on a track high above the river. They were cold, damp and keen to get back to the cabin which they had rented for the weekend. All three looked forward to the roaring fire and a snort of whisky that awaited them.

As they piled their equipment into the tailgate, one of the men saw a flash of red light out of the corner of his eye. Despite the fact it made no sound, the close proximity made him jump.

"Hey, did you see that!" he hollered.

"Yeah I saw something," responded the second.

"Let's go check it out," suggested the third. "It can only be about a hundred yards away."

"I dunno if that's a good idea," replied the first man nervously.

"Hey, relax," chuckled the third man. "It's probably just a meteor."

Reluctantly the first man picked up a rifle and the three anglers began to make their way through the undergrowth until eventually a red glow could easily be discerned pulsing gently, partially obscured, through the shrubs.

Tentatively they approached the glow to find a ball of red light about two feet in diameter, with what appeared to be white veins running through it. They looked at each other not knowing what to make of the strange object, when suddenly it began to unfurl itself. The three men stood transfixed as the shape altered and rose slowly to become a red humanoid figure over six feet tall. The apparition had similar proportions to a human but apart from a heavy brow and deep eye sockets, no obvious facial features could be seen. The whole body had a translucent look, enabling a network of white veins and vague shadowy shapes of organs to just about be distinguished. As it stood staring at the three men, one of them tried to raise his rifle but found that his limbs wouldn't move. Suddenly a figure stepped out of the body of the creature and stood beside the first to the right. It didn't glow as brightly, but stood impassively looking at the three men. A second figure stepped out of the original and stood to the left and now all three identical creatures glowed equally at a slightly dimmed level.

After a short pause the three apparitions stepped up closer in unison to the three hapless fishermen until they were virtually face to face. The men, seemingly hypnotised, stood wide-eyed and terrified as a wisp of what appeared to be red vapour began to flow out of the mouths of each figure and into the open mouths of the men. This process continued for another minute until the apparitions were gone and the men were completely taken over. With the transmigration complete, the three men turned and began to make their way back towards the car without a word; the only evidence of them ever being there was a discarded rifle on the ground.

***

The vehicle made its way out of the forest and eventually picked up State Route 49 for the long drive south. To avoid drawing attention to themselves the driver kept the speed to fifty miles per hour, staring through the windscreen zombie-like into the total blackness of the night. They hadn't been driving for more than an hour when a noise, strange to them, could be heard outside and coming from behind. The driver looked in the rear-view mirror to see a single white headlight flanked by lights, red and blue, flashing alternately, as a California Highway Patrol motorcycle wailed up behind and overtook. The police officer stopped in front of them, preventing their progress. The pickup pulled to a halt about twenty-five feet back and the three possessed men looked at each other.

Sergeant Blake Ryan wearily swung his left leg over the black and white Harley-Davidson Electra Glide motorbike and stood looking at the car that he'd pulled over. He couldn't believe that anyone could drive this road in pitch black without any lights on. He was about to approach the vehicle when the driver stepped out.

"If you could just step back into your car, sir," he ordered nervously, "I'll check your details."

The driver ignored his request and began to walk towards him slowly but deliberately.

"I must insist you get back in the vehicle, sir," he repeated, somewhat rattled this time.

The apparition continued forwards, picking up his pace a little. Sergeant Ryan drew his handgun, and pointed it directly at his would-be assailant.

"Stop or I'll fire," he demanded.

The figure bearing down on him took no notice and continued on. At the halfway point, the police officer discharged three bullets into the chest of the man. He watched the man flinch and drop lifeless to the ground. To his horror a red figure rose out of the corpse and stepped to one side, staring intently at the police officer. With his gun still raised he discharged the rest of his magazine into the creature. The bullets had no effect, but simply passed straight through the glowing figure.

The alien stepped up to Sergeant Ryan, who now found that he too was immobile and unable to escape. The red face drew up close to the policeman and studied it with what seemed like curiosity and then red vapour from his mouth seeped into the officer's mouth and he felt his own sense of being begin to fade as a new soul possessed him completely.

Alighting from the pickup, the two passengers approached the driver, who removed the helmet from his head and threw it into the bushes at the side of the road. Then he dragged the lifeless body of the angler until it too was out of sight, whilst his cohorts took the motorcycle and wheeled it off the road and into the bushes. With a hard push the bike freewheeled for a short distance until it lost momentum and fell with a clatter of metal on its side.

Not a single word was said between the three possessed men as they walked back to their pickup and stepped aboard. Taking more care this time, they fastened their seatbelts and fired up the engine. The driver looked around at the controls and found the light switch. He turned on the lights and they continued on their journey south.

The 350-mile journey was, for the rest of the way, uneventful, and took them into the small hours of the following morning. They abandoned the pickup in the desert a few miles from their destination, stepping outside into the cool dry air and all-encompassing darkness. Standing abreast, the three aliens looked at the men still sitting strapped into the vehicle, the driver with his hands still gripping the steering wheel. With their eyes staring blankly out of the windscreen, only the complete lack of animation gave any indication to suggest that all three were dead, unable to endure the stress of metempsychosis. As the aliens moved away, they left their victims to their silent vigil in the still of the night, in the middle of nowhere.

After moving for one hour over and through the rocky terrain the sky was still pitch black, with only a partially waxing moon and a blanket of stars to illuminate the way. The three creatures finally stopped at a high-rising rock face. They paused in front of it, and satisfied themselves that this was the correct point. Then in unison, they strode purposely towards the near-vertical surface that rose high above them.

CHAPTER NINETEEN

NIL AD INFINITUM

*AirForce Plant 52, Death Valley, Mojave Desert, California
December 2016*

The staccato chopping sound of rotor blades was heard long before the helicopter heaved into view, prompting Sergeant Conrad to pick up his clipboard and step outside. The lights of the chopper hovered above him, the downdraught threatening to sweep him off his feet. He looked at his watch and put a hand over his cap to keep it in place as the aircraft descended and settled on the ground. It was just gone midnight and he smiled inwardly, pleased that the occupants were bang on time.

One by one, the passengers stepped onto the tarmac

and Sergeant Conrad approached Colonel Pearson, stood to attention and saluted.

"A Humvee is ready and waiting for you, sir," he confirmed. "If I could just take the names of your, err… guests."

Whilst Pearson was dealing with this, Jude looked around at his surroundings. Clearly it was a military installation, but which one?

"Where the hell are we?" he enquired to no one in particular.

"Edwards Air Force Base," retorted Major Wells.

"Why here?" enquired Sophie.

"We're not staying here," revealed Colonel Pearson, turning back to the group. "If you would all follow me, please."

They were led to a beige Humvee M998, a troop-carrying variant with a matching colour canvas top. The rear flap was down and Colonel Pearson stood beside it and invited the others to step up inside. Sophie, Harrison and Jessica looked at each other doubtfully, a reaction which didn't go unnoticed on the colonel.

"It's going to be a little bumpy," he said, wincing, "but the journey won't be a long one."

"Where are you taking us, Colonel?" asked Jude.

"Please, all will be revealed in due course."

Jessica decided to take the initiative and stepped up first, followed by Major Wells who sat opposite her. Then Sophie and Harrison stepped in and sat next to Jessica, finally followed by Jude and the colonel. A driver and a guard climbed in the front and the Humvee roared into life.

As they passed stationary aircraft, it wasn't long before they left the perimeter of the base, its lights gradually diminishing as they progressed. Very soon the road became more of a track, and the Humvee began to rock and bounce as their route became more uneven. Harrison glanced at Sophie as she nervously took his hand in hers. He gave her what he hoped was a reassuring smile, but guessed that it wasn't very convincing. Jessica noticed the gesture but remained impassive, staring resolutely in front of her. Eventually, Major Wells noticed Jessica gazing directly at him. He felt like her eyes were burning into the back of his skull and it made him squirm. Jessica's unflinching gaze became too much for him and he averted his eyes. When he looked up again, Jessica was staring out of the open rear of the truck. Jude, also, was studying the lie of the land which they were leaving behind them, and noted the fact that they were now well into desert terrain, with rocks and shrubs littered either side of the track.

Forty minutes later the Humvee began to slow down, the driver spoke into an intercom and the passengers suddenly heard a loud metallic creak as the front of a small mountain began to part on either side. Slowly the vehicle passed the gaping mouth, and the doors with their castellated edges interlocked when they came back together behind them with a satisfying, echoing clunk. The truck drove into the underground base for about one hundred yards and parked up. Alighting from the front, the driver and the guard moved swiftly round to the rear and dropped the flap, enabling the colonel and Harrison to step out first. The professor couldn't believe his eyes; the area was vast. A few trucks, SUVs and Humvees were littered about and a skeleton night staff in white overalls paid little attention to the new arrivals as they continued with their duties. Soldiers in T5 camouflage uniform stood discreetly, strategically placed round the perimeter of the huge vestibule. The floor was smooth with a grey semi-gloss sheen and the walls merged into a high ceiling which arced slightly, braced by steel girders. Harrison turned to the colonel, a look of total bemusement on his face.

"What is this place?" he enquired.

The colonel smiled, pleased at the impression the installation had made.

"Welcome to AirForce Plant 52," he announced with pride, "and yes, it's top secret."

"Not anymore," commented the professor with a wry smile.

Jessica gave a cursory disinterested look round and stood next to Sophie, Harrison and Jude.

"What do you think goes on here?" asked Sophie.

"That's anybody's guess," said Jude, shrugging, "but I think we'll be finding out pretty soon."

Colonel Pearson and Major Wells left the group and approached two soldiers wearing full combat uniform and holding M4A1 carbines. Both soldiers had been fully briefed and knew what was expected of them. They saluted the two officers who, assuming they were out of earshot, addressed the men.

"Gentlemen," said the colonel, "those four people over there will need to be watched very closely. Don't underestimate them, they are strong and potentially dangerous."

"Especially the woman with the braided hair," confirmed Major Wells. "I want you to keep a particularly close eye on her. Is that clear?"

"Sir, yes, sir," came the chorused response.

"Good," declared the colonel. "Let's get moving."

Jessica and her three cohorts heard every word and all looked at her as she was mentioned. Inwardly, Jessica was amused by their assessment of her, but remained stolid. They were herded over to a large door, which opened at the press of a button to reveal a large service elevator. One soldier stepped in, followed by the others and finally the second soldier. Inserting an ID card into the control panel, Colonel Pearson pressed a button, and Jessica and the others watched as the lights on the panel gradually descended to settle at level five. The doors opened automatically and the group stepped out. This level was of no surprise to the military men but yet again, Harrison looked around astounded.

The hangar was massive, being oval in shape with steel girders lining the walls and rising high above them, converging at the centre of the domed ceiling one hundred feet above. To the left of centre, was a smooth concrete apron with a strange bell-shaped object, ominously sitting in the centre of a slight depression, forty feet square. Its polished shiny surface reflected the lights which illuminated the whole cavernous space, and it displayed the Air Force insignia below a large black number 2. As Harrison scanned his eyes around further, he could see a metal gangway to the right above him and steps leading down. Further beyond that, nestled silently against a back wall, were another ten bell-shaped objects, just like the one in the centre, all with their own identifying number. Sophie and Harrison looked at Jessica.

"They are time machines," she revealed matter-of-factly.

Nobody could take their eyes off the bell-shaped craft as they were ushered round to the right and into an anteroom. Pearson invited everyone to sit at the large table and the two soldiers stood either side of the door, carbines slanted across their chests. Harrison sat with Jessica to his right and Sophie to his left. Jude sat next to Jessica. Opposite, were Major Wells, Colonel Pearson and one other, a man who followed in behind them all, wearing an olive-green flight suit.

The man was tall, slim, clearly physically fit, with short brown hair and light brown eyes. He looked alert, intelligent, though a little anxious. Placing himself next to Colonel Pearson, the man locked his hands together on the table and gave the people in front of him a steely stare.

"This is Major Devin Avery," introduced Pearson. "He will be our test pilot in *The Bell*."

"And will this be a precursory test run?" enquired Jessica. "Or do you have something more purposeful in mind?"

"That's none of your goddamn business," growled Major Wells aggressively, getting out of his seat.

"Sit down, Owen," advised the colonel, placing an authoritative hand on his shoulder. "There's no need for that."

"We've paid good money for those items," continued Major Wells, who had barely calmed down, "and we ain't seen squat yet. We're not answerable to these jerks."

Delving into the left-hand pouch on her belt, Jessica pulled out the phial of serum. She held it between her forefinger and thumb, for everyone around the table to see.

"You'll have your drug, Colonel, and the Liquid Chrome," she assured them, "but I must insist you tell me of your intentions. And be warned, I'll know if you are lying."

Colonel Pearson looked at Major Avery and then at Major Wells, who was still glowering across the table.

"This is bullshit," Wells asseverated.

"Okay," sighed the colonel, placing both hands on the table, "we intend to send Major Avery to the outskirts of Berlin."

"Berlin?" said Harrison, frowning. "Why?"

"What year?" pressed Jessica.

"Mid-October 1836," revealed Pearson.

"The nineteenth century," confirmed Harrison. "For what reason?"

"To assassinate Karl Marx," announced the colonel. "We know that he matriculated into the Humboldt University of Berlin, in late October of that year, though then it was called the Frederick William University. And if we could err... take care of him before he formulates his theories on communism, then we feel certain that the world will be a better, safer place to live in."

"This is madness," cried Harrison, standing up. "Do you honestly think that you can destroy an idea just by killing one man?"

"That's why this operation includes the elimination of Trotsky, Lenin and Stalin, all before they reach the age of twenty. Our aim is a systematic destruction of the very foundations of communism."

"You can't do this," cried Harrison again. He began to pace the room, thinking on his feet. "It will turn history upside down."

"Exactly," sneered Wells, "with no Pinkos there will be no Korea, no Vietnam, no Red China and no USSR. Hell, think of the lives we'll save."

"So, with no Marxism," considered Harrison, taking all this in, "there would be no revolution. The monarchy will prevail, Stalin will never come to power, Russia could potentially be a weaker country and, as a consequence, the Nazis will beat them in World War II. My God, if the war was to be extended by just a few years longer, the Third Reich could win. You can't do this. You're sending us headlong into anarchy, a new dark age."

"We have weighed up the odds," replied Colonel Pearson, "and we feel the means justify the end."

"Jessica, you can't allow this," beseeched Harrison.

"I'm sorry, Nathan," said Jessica, grimacing, "it's out of my hands."

She turned away from a shell-shocked Harrison and addressed the colonel.

"Jude has the formulae for the drug on his cell phone. If you have the weight of Major Avery, we can inject him."

"Excellent," said the colonel, standing up. "Let's get started then."

One of the soldiers opened the door and everyone followed Pearson and Wells out of the room. Harrison was finally speechless; he realised that nothing that he might say was going to change their minds.

***

As Major Avery slipped both arms back into his flight suit and zipped up the front, Jessica consulted her inner clock. It was 01.34 and she realised that time was becoming short.

"How do you feel?" she asked the test pilot.

"Just great," said Avery, grinning and flexing his arms. "Let's get this done."

"I will need a plastic container to decant the Liquid Chrome," advised Jessica, addressing the colonel.

"We've got one ready," he replied, and made a motion to Major Wells who left the room. A few minutes later he returned with two technicians dressed in orange plastic bio-suits, with white plastic boots and white rubber gloves. Their faces were protected with goggles, a full-face visor, and one of them carried a circular, clear perspex container, the lid of which was airtight. The top twisted off with a pop of air and the container was placed on a table. Now all eyes were fixed on Jessica. Approaching the table, Jessica looked at the throng staring at her in anticipation as she placed her right hand into the clear box. She closed her eyes and concentrated. As her hand turned to silver, Liquid Chrome began to drip rapidly from her fingers. Jessica's silver face slowly began to fade back to normal as the last of the silver liquid dripped from her forefinger tip. She gave it a final shake and the process was complete.

"Jeez, what is she, some kind of mutant?" sneered Major Wells. "Where the hell did she come from, space?"

"What she is and where she came from can wait," replied the colonel. "We'll deal with that another time."

One of the technicians approached the table, replaced the lid and stood awaiting orders.

"Prepare *The Bell* for take-off," ordered Colonel Pearson.

"Jessica, there's still time," beseeched Harrison. "You can stop this."

"I'm sorry, Nathan, I told you, there's nothing I can do."

As the technicians exited the room with the Liquid Chrome, Harrison gave up in exasperation. Sophie put a consoling arm around him and Jessica followed the men into the main hangar area.

"I don't understand what she's playing at," lamented Harrison, reluctantly following her out.

Everyone watched as the orange figures set to work preparing *The Bell* for its launch, and Harrison found a chair, sat down and put his head in his hands. Jude pricked his ears as muffled noises could just be discerned emanating from somewhere above. He walked around the hangar trying locate its source.

"Can you hear that?" he asked anyone who might be listening.

"I don't hear a goddamn thing," said Major Wells, frowning, straining his ears. "You people are freaks."

"Yes, I hear it," replied Sophie, picking up on the faint noise. "It sounds like gunshots."

"It won't be long now," announced Jessica, gazing up enigmatically.

Major Wells turned to Colonel Pearson; he felt that these civilians had no place there, now that they had everything they needed.

"I'm getting pissed with her," he growled, following Jessica's eyes. "The bitch talks in riddles."

"We wait until after a successful mission," declared Colonel Pearson. He too looked up to the ceiling but heard nothing.

***

Five floors above, two soldiers, close to the entrance, got the shock of their lives as three bright red figures suddenly stepped through the metal construction of the closed doors. Casually they continued into the centre of the floor and looked around them.

"What the fuck!" exclaimed one of the men as he finally came to his senses. He raised his M4A1 carbine, switched it to fully automatic and sprayed the three figures with 5.56mm bullets. Without even flinching, the three aliens watched as several rounds passed through them and two technicians had to dive for cover as bullets zipped past their heads. The second soldier joined in, giving a long burst from his automatic.

"Stop," ordered the first soldier. "We're just shooting the place up."

"What are they?" panicked the second. "They just walked through the wall."

"Jesus, they're turning toward us," cried the first.

The three aliens studied the men and one approached the first soldier, gazed down on him with his featureless face and slowly entered the body of the hapless soldier. After a moment, he turned to his comrade, lifted his gun and whacked him hard against the left-hand side of his head. The soldier dropped, unconscious before he hit the floor.

A technician began to back away as the possessed soldier approached him. He finally pressed up against a wall and looked around, his expression imploring for help. Paralysed with fear, he stood motionless as the soldier came close and pushed the barrel of his gun hard up under the terrified man's chin. Barely noticing the discomfort, the wide-eyed man began to sweat.

"W- what do you want?" he screamed, the sound echoing through the vestibule.

"Time machine." The soldier's voice was impossibly deep and guttural.

"W- what?" He noticed that several staff and guards had moved in slightly closer as the two remaining aliens held their ground.

"Where?" came the deep booming voice again.

"It's five floors below us," came a voice from behind. The possessed soldier turned slowly to address its owner.

"Five floors down," he repeated, a little more uncertainly this time, and pointing downwards with his finger.

The creature stepped out of his host, who duly collapsed against the technician and slid to the floor. Then he casually rejoined his companions. Two technicians ran to the man's aid only to establish that he was dead.

"You killed him," one of them shouted, "you murdering bastards."

The aliens gave no response; they stood three abreast and, to everyone's astonishment, simply sank through the floor.

"Quick, get on to Edwards," demanded one of the technicians. "This is an emergency. We've been infiltrated."

Several men, including soldiers, dashed to the reception area. The girl behind the desk looked up at them in dismay. After witnessing the apparition of the aliens, she had tried to send out a distress call.

"I can't get through," she panicked. "Nothing's working."

"What about the door?" bellowed another man. "We've gotta get out."

"I've already tried," said another voice from the back. "It won't open. We're trapped in here with no means of communication."

The small group looked at each other, every one of them hoping that someone, anyone might have a solution.

"What in God's name is going to happen now?" declared one of the technicians rhetorically.

***

Colonel Pearson approached Major Devin Avery, who had just changed into period clothes to enable him to blend in with mid-nineteenth-century appearances. The off-white collarless shirt, dark grey pants and jacket were a little tatty, as were the black boots. With a flat cap to finish off the deception, the overall effect was of an unremarkable working-class man to whom nobody would give a second look. The colonel was pleased with the result and smiled.

"Have you got your handgun?" he enquired.

"Yes, sir," replied Major Avery, opening the left-hand side of his jacket to reveal a shoulder holster, and a Beretta M9 nestled securely within. "I've got a box of cartridges too." He patted his jacket side pocket to indicate the fact.

"Good luck," said Pearson, smiling and shaking his hand. "It's a grand thing that you are doing. You'll return a hero."

Major Wells shook his hand also, and the test pilot breathed in deeply and walked out to the centre of the hangar where the *Die Glocke* awaited him. He was about to be helped into the vessel by the two orange-clad technicians when all eyes turned to the wall behind him. Three red alien figures appeared from nowhere and stood side by side, looking around like tourists.

"What the…" gasped Colonel Pearson, mouth gaping.

Major Wells stood stunned in silence, as did the others. Only Jessica watched unsurprised and impassive. After regaining their senses, the two soldiers moved forwards in an attempt to block any approach, but before they could open fire, two of the aliens moved quickly upon them and they entered the men's bodies in a wisp-like vapour. After this process was complete, they stood motionless for a few seconds and then looked at the M4A1 carbines in their hands. Having no use for them, however, they tossed them away and the guns hit the floor with a metallic echoing clatter. Approaching the two soldiers, the third alien stood between them. The possessed men turned around and all three walked closer, slowly. They looked at the time machine, and then the red glowing alien approached Jessica and looked down on her in an attempt to look intimidating.

"I've been expecting you," she said finally, with a wry smile.

"Judas H priest," exclaimed Colonel Pearson. "What's happening here? Are they ghosts or something?"

"Not ghosts, Colonel," Jessica's attention had turned from the alien to the throng in front of her, "but people from another world. Here not in body but in spirit."

"Are you telling us that these things are the souls of aliens?" quipped Major Wells, regaining his composure.

"That's exactly what I'm saying," responded Jessica. "Is it so surprising? After all, aren't we all God's creatures?"

"What do they want?" said the colonel, frowning, fearing the answer.

"They've come for their property."

"Property?" shouted Major Wells. "What property?"

"Why, this of course." Jessica waved her right hand in a sweep around at the *Die Glockes*. "The time machines and the serum belongs to them. And they want them back."

"So, they think they can take it, just like that," sneered Major Wells.

Jessica ignored the major's diatribe, and turned to look at the alien, who was no longer bearing down on her. Then she addressed the two possessed soldiers who were standing slightly to the rear.

"You arrived just in time," she declared. "Observe, your invention is about to be demonstrated."

All three figures turned their attention to the time machine and the test pilot who was awaiting his orders. The red glowing creature returned his gaze to Jessica and nodded slowly.

"Well, Colonel," said Jessica, smiling, "it's up to you now."

Looking around him, unsure how to proceed, the colonel realised that there was no one that he could look to for reassurance. Finally, he sighed and nodded.

"Proceed with the launch," he ordered nervously.

Major Avery entered through the side hatch and closed it behind him. There was a pause, and then a metallic creaking sound as the forty-feet-square depression, which the *Die Glocke* sat on, began to slowly descend. Finally, twenty-five feet down it stopped with a booming shudder.

After a pause of one minute, everyone was on tenterhooks. A drone began to echo out of the hole, reaching a high pitch, and the *Die Glocke* rose out, continuing on its ascent, high into the hangar. At about twenty-five feet from the concrete apron, it stopped, reached its optimum speed and disappeared with a thunderous crack. A halo-like shock wave emanated out and over their heads. Just as the colonel was about to congratulate Major Wells on a successful launch, the machine was back, still in the air, but something was wrong; the image of the craft was faint and distorted. Again, the time machine disappeared only to flash back again, this time looking more substantial. Yet again, it blinked away only to return in a blinding flash, to collapse in on itself with a mighty crack, causing all present to cover their ears. All that remained were a few small blue-white orbs that seemed to be juggling around each other, then suddenly they pulled together fast as though they were magnetised. Then they too collapsed into a small roaring trumpet-shaped funnel. The mouth seemed to be hovering twenty-five feet off the ground and, little more than six inches in diameter, light was sparking around its edges and the apparition was making a loud sucking sound.

"What is that?" shouted Colonel Pearson over the noise. "What's happened?"

"Call it what you will, Colonel," declared Jessica stepping towards the apparition, "black hole, dark matter, anti-matter perhaps, it's of no consequence. This particular time-travelling attempt has rented a schism between time and space. Take a glimpse into nought times infinity, the closest thing to hell that you will ever witness in this life."

"But this didn't happen before," declared Major Wells.

"Including my own jaunts," revealed Jessica, "this is the fifteenth attempt. It was only a matter of time before something cataclysmic would happen. The delicate relationship between time and space has been ripped asunder."

Turning to look at the aliens, Jessica wanted to gauge their reaction to what she had just explained, but with no facial features, it was impossible to tell. The two possessed soldiers and the red glowing alien simply stared blankly at the rip in time.

"That bitch is responsible for this," bellowed Major Wells, pointing at Jessica. He lifted up his dark blue tunic just below the front buttons and retrieved a handgun from a small plastic waist holster and, wide-eyed, pointed it at Jessica. She stood unflinching as he took aim.

"For heaven's sake, Wells, are you crazy?" growled Colonel Pearson as he tried to grab at the major's right arm. "Lower your gun, that's an order."

At that moment Major Wells pulled the trigger as the rest looked on with alarm. Harrison was the only one to react and leapt in front of Jessica.

"No!" he cried as the bullet hit him in the right lung.

Harrison was knocked back and fell at Jessica's feet.

Colonel Pearson grabbed the gun off the bemused major and pistol-whipped him across the face. Reeling back, the major put a hand to his face and glowered petulantly.

"Nathan!" shouted Jessica in shock and horror, kneeling down to cradle his head in her lap. Blood was oozing from the wound and Jessica pressed it to try and stop the flow. Harrison coughed and blood trickled from the side of his mouth.

Sophie screamed and dashed over to Harrison's side. She could see that he was in a bad way and desperately needed help. Looking up, tears streaming down her face, she could see Jessica was sobbing also.

"You bastard," she screamed at Major Wells and, without warning, leapt at him with great speed. Grabbing him under the arms Sophie threw Major Wells with all her might in the general direction of the launch site.

A dazed Major Wells went tumbling along the ground, until he reached the drop from which the time machine had risen. Before he could stop himself, Wells slipped over the edge and began to fall. He only plummeted five feet before his body was suspended at the Lagrangian Point, the position where an object will be held in suspension by two equal gravitational forces. He hovered there for a moment, then his head and his body began to stretch. With a blood-curdling scream, his eyes ripped out of their sockets, disappearing into the gaping maelstrom. The skin on his face was beginning to stretch away from his head and that too ripped away to reveal an eyeless skull with sickly red sinews and gaping white teeth. Finally, the pull of the vortex became stronger and he was lifted up and sucked into the abyss.

As if nourished by Wells' body, the vortex suddenly quadrupled in size, its shape becoming uneven; the chasm was becoming unstable. A powerful wind seemed to appear from nowhere, turning the hangar into turmoil. Loose objects were being picked up and thrown across the room in a whirlwind. Looking at the chaos around her, Jessica looked desperately at Harrison.

"My love, you must leave this place," she sobbed.

"I'm not going anywhere," coughed Harrison. "I wouldn't make it anyhow."

"Nathan," cried Sophie, "you've got to."

"No," countered Harrison, struggling to breathe. "I'm staying here with Jessica."

"But what about us?" she continued. "We could be so good together."

"I'm sorry, Sophie, but you must get out of here," urged the professor. "It was always Jessica, I realise that now."

In the pandemonium, Jude had retrieved one of the discarded carbines. He ran over to where Harrison was lying and crouched down.

"Get her to safety, Jude," beseeched Harrison.

Jude looked at Jessica who nodded in agreement. He tugged at Sophie's arm, but she resisted, shaking her head in defiance.

"Sophie, you must go with Jude," insisted Jessica. "It's your only chance."

Still shaking her head and tears streaming down her face, Sophie allowed herself to be pulled away by Jude.

"The lift isn't working," he urged, then, looking at the steel gangway, "our only hope is up there."

Glancing back at the scene of Harrison lying on the floor, Jessica kneeling at his side, Sophie was dragged up the steel steps, both her and Jude struggling against the maelstrom. They ran along the top to the entrance door which could only be opened with a six-digit code.

"It's locked," cried Jude, banging the door in frustration with the butt of his carbine.

Jessica looked up, closed her eyes and concentrated. Buttons on the keypad lit up in sequence and the door clicked open. The gangway was beginning to buckle as Sophie and Jude exited the hangar. Coming to his senses, Colonel Pearson saw his opportunity and made a dash for the staircase. He made it to the top but before he could get to the entrance, Jessica closed her eyes again and slammed it shut. Before Pearson could react any further, the gangway was ripped from the wall. He and twisted metal were sent hurling towards the vortex. Jessica watched dispassionately, then turned to the aliens. There were three glowing figures standing there now. Behind two of them were the inert bodies of the soldiers which they had just discarded, lying dead at their feet.

"Do you see now?" vociferated Jessica. "Do you finally understand?"

The creatures gave no response but stared resolutely at the abyss.

"The universe is an intelligent entity," Jessica motioned to the vortex, "and this is the universe saying, enough is enough."

Continuing with their eyeless stare, Jessica had no way of knowing whether she was getting through to them.

***

The door slammed shut behind Sophie and Jude, its boom resounding down the short corridor and up the stairwell. They ran to the foot of the stairs, where Jude stopped and tried the buttons on the elevator.

"Nothing's working," he fretted. "How many levels did we come down?"

"Five, I think," offered Sophie. "Yes, definitely five."

"We'd better get moving."

They leapt up to the fourth floor without encountering anyone, so continued to level three. As they reached the landing, a guard came round the corner. He had heard some commotion below and was on his way to check it out. Without hesitation, he brought his M4A1 carbine to bear. Jude was too quick for him; he grabbed the gun and threw the soldier down the stairs with such force that he barely touched the steps. He landed at the bottom in a crumpled heap, out cold.

"I hope we don't encounter too many of them," remarked Jude, looking at the two carbines that he was now holding. "We must keep going."

They didn't encounter any more guards until they got to level one, where two soldiers were halfway down the staircase which led from ground level. Sophie and Jude had just reached the bottom, when both soldiers raised their carbines to confront them.

"Lower your weapons," ordered one soldier.

Jude ignored the command and pressed on, whilst Sophie stopped at the foot of the stairs. Without waiting for them to make the first move, Jude sprayed a short burst into the chests of both men, who fell back onto the steps and slid down to a halt near the bottom. Picking up one of the dead men's carbines, Jude flung it to Sophie who caught the weapon and looked at her accomplice in dismay.

"Take it," he ordered. "I think you're gonna need it."

They reached the ground-floor level, only to be confronted by a hail of gunfire. Bullets zipped around them and they were forced to take cover behind a vertical beam, fixed to the wall. Jude scanned the area, weighing up their options.

"Can you drive?" he shouted over the noise of gunfire.

"Yes, of course," replied Sophie, pressing herself hard against the wall. Being shot at was a new experience for her and she was terrified.

"If you can get to that Humvee over there," he suggested, "I'll give you covering fire."

Sophie looked across to where the vehicle was waiting for them. It was parked about fifty feet away.

"When I say go, you run like your life depends on it, because it does. Okay?" he bellowed. "Then reverse it back over here."

Sophie nodded with uncertainty and waited for her cue.

"Go," shouted Jude.

As Sophie leapt forwards, Jude sprayed the area with bullets and Sophie made it to the Humvee in seconds. Opening the door, she sat in the driver's seat and looked around the dashboard, frowning.

"I don't know how to start it," she shouted back to Jude.

"There's a switch to the left of the steering wheel, pointing to '*Eng. Stop*'," he advised.

"Okay, I've got it."

"Turn it to '*Run*' and wait for the light to go out."

"Right."

"Now turn it to '*Start*'."

The Humvee roared into life, and a volley of bullets hit the right-hand side of the car's bodywork. Sophie eventually found reverse and swung the vehicle out and round to where Jude was returning gunfire in the general direction of his adversaries. The Humvee pulled to a stop about three feet away from him and Sophie leaned across and opened the passenger door. Wasting no time, Jude leapt in and ducked as bullets hit the front and peppered the hood.

"Move it!" he ordered, and Sophie put the Humvee into gear, then put her foot down. They sped off down the middle of the vestibule, wheels spinning, running the gauntlet of bullets that were hitting the Humvee from all directions.

The vehicle covered the distance to the entrance very quickly and both occupants could see the doors looming up on them. Jude scrambled across the centre tunnel which separated them and grabbed the handbrake.

"When I say," he shouted, "you turn that wheel to the left as hard as you can. Okay?" Sophie nodded.

"Now!" bellowed Jude.

Sophie swung the steering wheel anti-clockwise and Jude pulled the handbrake up hard. The Humvee squealed as the rear came round and they broadsided up close to the doors. Before the soldiers could react, Jude pulled Sophie across and out of his side of the car. Now they had the Humvee for cover. Keeping low, they inspected the door and found the point where the two halves came together.

"I'll cover you," said Jude, "and you see if you can push this door open."

"You're shitting me, right?" said Sophie, looking up at the massive construction.

"Look, you're strong, remember," encouraged Jude, "and it's our only hope of escape."

Jude began firing back at the soldiers shooting at him and noticed a few moving to different positions, to get to a better vantage point. Sophie managed to get a purchase on the gap in the doors and, with a grimace, she pulled. The door moved by about four inches. Turning round, Sophie pushed as hard as she could, putting her shoulder into it. She shouted as she did so over the roar of machine gunfire, bullets ricocheting off the metalwork around her. The gap between the doors was eighteen inches and Sophie could feel a cool breeze wafting in from outside. She had to hold the door at this point, as she could tell that if she let go, it would slam shut again. Sophie needed help, but Jude was busy trying to give her cover. He had run out of ammunition on two of the guns and had just picked up the last. Turning to Sophie with a desperate look on his face, a splatter of blood leapt up from his left upper arm as a bullet nicked his skin. Jude slid down for cover and shouted,

"Get that fucking door open!"

"I need your help," responded Sophie. She had put her back into the gap and was now holding the door open with her feet pressed up against the opposite edge.

Jude jumped across and joined her in the gap; he also was pushing with his back to the door. With their joint effort, the gap began to widen, but because of the castellated interlocking teeth, there was still not enough gap for them to effect an escape.

"Push," encouraged Jude, grimacing as he strained under the pressure of the door. Struggling to help Sophie whilst firing his carbine at the same time, Jude flinched as a bullet hit him in the chest. Soldiers had worked their way to one side of the Humvee and were firing at an oblique angle. Another hit him in the stomach and he began to waver. He gave one final shove with his legs and the gap widened just enough for Sophie to slip through.

"Go," he urged. Jude's voice was weak; his eyes glazed over. "I'm hit. I won't make it."

Looking at him in dismay, Sophie hesitated, so Jude pushed her hard, causing her to tumble outside into the cool night air. Sophie scrambled to her feet just as Jude took a bullet to his forehead. Blood sprayed, and his head was thrown back, then Jude's legs slipped down, and the door slammed shut on him with a sickening squelch.

Tentatively, soldiers began to approach the door when they realised there was no more returning fire. They looked at each other in shock as they saw Jude's right arm sticking out of the interlocking join, the machine gun hanging from his fingers and a pool of blood expanding on the floor.

***

After pulling Harrison to the edge of the hangar, away from the whirling maelstrom, Jessica propped him up. She smiled at him lovingly, placing her right hand on his cheek. Harrison was hot, sweating and struggling to breathe.

"If you were quick," he said, grimacing, "you might just escape."

"No, no," soothed Jessica, "that is not an option."

"There's nothing you can do now," coughed the professor.

"This thing can't be left unchecked," said Jessica, frowning, "it will only get bigger and more powerful, until it swallows the planet. And then the solar system. And so on, until the whole universe is consumed."

"And then what?" asked Harrison, his curiosity piqued.

"It will implode in on itself, until it is just a single atom and then explode out again."

"Like a second Big Bang!" spluttered Harrison.

"Well, another Big Bang, at least," corrected Jessica.

"Maybe another universe would be better than this one," choked Harrison, in an uncharacteristic moment of cynicism.

"Or maybe it will be worse. Better the devil you know, my darling," suggested Jessica.

Blood was steadily oozing from Harrison's chest and his front was one sodden mass of dark red. His breathing became laboured.

"I'm scared," he gasped.

"I've been scared all my life," declared Jessica, "but I've realised that only when facing up to our fears do we know when we're truly alive."

Harrison gave her a feeble grin; Jessica's pearls of wisdom counted for nothing right at this moment.

"Look, I am going to have to leave you for a moment," Jessica continued, "but I promise that we'll be together again very soon. I love you."

Before Harrison could respond, Jessica stood up and moved to the centre of the hangar. She looked around and realised that they were the only two still living apart from the three aliens. They were still standing watching the swirling chaos around them, completely unperturbed. They glanced at Jessica as she approached, turned and then walked away.

"Well, bye then," retorted Jessica sardonically, then turned her attention to the vortex, which had grown frighteningly huge.

Stepping up as close as she dared, Jessica confronted the vortex. It was taking up about a third of the height of the hangar and dwarfed her. The edges were flashing light and constantly changing shape. Jessica stared into the centre of the vortex; its caliginous emptiness was unsettlingly hypnotic.

A glow began to emanate from Jessica's stomach, a phenomenon that she had noticed once before, in front of her bedroom mirror, only this time it was much more intense. The yellow glow increased in size until it was a ball about two feet in diameter. Yellow streaks began to fly off the glowing ball of light and orbit it like neutrons around an atom. The manifestation lifted her off the ground until she was level with the gaping mouth of the abyss. Suddenly she knew exactly what she had to do. Jessica threw her arms out and flung her head back. She could feel the energy building up inside her.

"The darkness shall not prevail," she cried out as loud as she could. And then, almost to herself, she whispered, "For I am the light."

At that moment the yellow orb rapidly increased in size, the orbiting beams engulfed Jessica, and everything became white.

CHAPTER TWENTY

SOUL SURVIVORS

Death Valley, The Mojave Desert, California
December 2016

Outside the entrance doors, Sophie, her hands to her mouth, looked on in horror as she witnessed Jude die in front of her as the doors slammed shut. Alone in the still of the night, she realised that she owed it to everyone who had sacrificed themselves, allowing her to get to this point, to make good her escape. Turning, Sophie ran as fast as she could, trying to put as much distance between her and the base as possible. She barely got one hundred yards away when suddenly night time turned to day and then blindingly white. Instinctively she turned to look at the light but was blown off her feet by the searing heat of a shock wave. Having no idea how far she had been thrown, Sophie was only aware of the agony that she was suffering. Her skin felt like it was on fire and her dungarees were in flames. She hit the ground hard, rolled and came to a halt.

Through half-open eyes Sophie could make out her smouldering clothes and the stars in the night sky. Unable to move, she watched as the white glow gradually died down and disappeared. All was dark and peaceful for several minutes and then she saw three red glows emerge from the ground where the mountain used to be. The aliens came to within fifty feet of where she lay; they looked around them but appeared to be oblivious to her presence.

The three figures slowly merged into one and became a brighter red glow. Then the single figure began to curl up into a ball which seemed to hover inches from the ground. A bolt of light flashed down from above at lightning speed and the ball was gone, leaving no trace. The pain that Sophie was experiencing was beyond anything that she or anybody had ever endured. Sophie prayed for the luxury of death, just to be free of this agony, but it did not come. Unable to move her body, Sophie rolled her eyes around; it appeared that she was in a shallow ditch. Finally, Sophie's injuries got the better of her. Slowly she closed her eyes fully and, mercifully, everything went black.

***

Lyndon B. Johnson Space Center, Houston, Texas
Mission Control Center, ISS Flight Control Room
December 2016

Flight director Barbara Morris looked forlornly at the clock on the wall, which had just struck 0300 hours. It had been a long night of anxiety, and she should have been exhausted, the only thing keeping her going being coffee and adrenaline. She sighed and sat down at her workstation, staring accusingly at the blank screens, willing them to burst back into life. To Barbara they seemed to be mocking her. She looked around at the others in the flight control room; all eyes seemed to be upon her like expectant puppies. An overweight middle-aged man called Milton approached with a mug of coffee and placed it on a coaster in front of her.

"If I pour any more caffeine inside me," declared Morris, looking up at him, "I'm going to be bouncing off the ceiling."

"You'll need to be alert for when you report this," replied Milton. "It's been over nine hours now. How much longer do you think that you can keep a lid on this?"

Barbara leant forwards and picked up the mug and put it to her lips. The strong liquid felt good; its comforting warmth helped to soothe her dry mouth and throat.

"Still no update from Vanderbilt, I suppose?" she asked hopelessly, knowing what the answer would be.

"Nothing," replied Milton succinctly.

"What about Hopkins?" she added.

"Still no change. Professor Dawkings is knocking on a bit now. Don't you think that he might be tucked up in bed?"

"With an alien interstellar juggernaut orbiting Mars," she retorted, "would you?"

Realising that there was nothing he could do to ease her suffering, Milton slinked away to leave the flight director to her anguish. She looked at the clock again; it now read 03.07. With a sigh, Barbara picked up the phone and began to punch in some numbers; it was time to make the call. At that moment all the screens burst back into life and Barbara dropped the receiver.

"Mission Control, are you there?" came a familiar Texan voice. "We lost you there for a few seconds."

"Can you repeat that?" asked Barbara, feeling a little dizzy. "Did you say a couple of seconds?"

"Yes, ma'am," the astronaut replied. "We had a bit of a blip, but all seems okay now."

"Can you look out of the Cupola? And tell me if you can see anything."

"Can I ask why?"

"Could you just do it," urged Barbara.

One of the astronauts made his way down to the Cupola, the seven-window viewing point, on the underside of the space station. As they waited patiently for news, a member of staff stood up and addressed Barbara.

"Vanderbilt has just been on," he quipped excitedly. "They say the echo trace has gone and all seems normal."

"There's nothing but a beautiful view of Earth," advised the astronaut. "What's this all about?"

Milton had returned and was back beside her, frowning.

"What is it?" she asked.

"Professor Dawkings is on the line."

"We'll get back to you," said Barbara, addressing the ISS again.

The flight director moved over to another screen to see the jolly face of the professor. He seemed excited, agitated even.

"I hope you've got some good news for me, Professor."

"Indeed I have, Barbara," he said, beaming. "That object orbiting Mars, well, it just disappeared. One second it was there, and then it was gone. I'm sorry to have troubled you with this, but I fear it may have been a false alarm."

"Not at all, Professor," said the flight director with a smile. "Maybe we can all get some shut-eye now."

Barbara signed off and walked back to her workstation; suddenly she felt exhausted and slumped in her chair. Feeling a compulsion to keep checking the screens, she needed constant reassurance that all was running as it should.

"You ought to get some rest," advised Milton, "you look done in."

"I will soon," she replied. "Just a blip huh? They've no idea. When do you think we should tell them that they were out of our control for nine hours and twenty-two minutes?"

Milton shrugged dismissively; luckily for him, it wasn't his decision.

***

Edwards Air Force Base, Kern County, California
December 2016

Katrina Hart sat opposite a desk in the office of General Walter Long, patiently waiting for the absent man to arrive. When she had signed in to CIA headquarters this particular Monday morning, she was expecting to continue with the previous week's paperwork. The last thing she expected was to be immediately sent out on an assignment; though under the circumstances, she understood why.

Lucas Foster, the director of operations, had summoned Katrina personally to inform her that there had been a major incident close to Edwards Air Force Base and he felt she was the person best placed to check it out. This could mean only one thing as far as Katrina was concerned. Something must have happened at the top-secret facility out in the Mojave Desert. Having arrived just after midday, she luncheoned in the canteen and was now keen to get on. Katrina had always felt that there was unfinished business at the base, and in these nine long years, despite the numerous tricky assignments which she had been sent on, it rarely strayed far from her thoughts.

Katrina looked around the office; she had a theory that you could get the measure of a person by the things with which they surrounded themselves. On the walls were several pictures of aircraft of all manner of vintage. The desk in front of her was tidy, as she would have expected from a military man, but there was little to suggest his private life, save for a photo of a good-looking young man in flying gear, smiling in front of a North American P51 Mustang. Below was inscribed Captain T. Long, England, 1944. On the other side of the desk was a shiny chrome model of the same aircraft displayed on a stand, fixed to a polished wooden base. There was little else to suggest his private life – no wife and no children – and Katrina wondered whether the general was a confirmed bachelor, and all that implied. Outside the window behind the desk, she watched with indifference as a huge transport aircraft took off from a runway and disappeared into clouds, leaving a trail of exhaust. The door opened behind her and a middle-aged man stepped in to greet Katrina, holding an iPad. She stood up as he walked round to his side of the desk.

"You must be Katrina Hart from the CIA," he announced brusquely, without smiling. "My apologies for keeping you waiting, but there was something important that needed my attention."

They both sat down and the general placed the tablet on the desk in front of him. Whatever needed his attention Katrina guessed was on that device. She appraised the man in front of her. The moment she saw him enter, Katrina was impressed by his appearance. General Long was African American, tall, slim, with short greying hair and brown eyes, and clearly took care of himself. His face, with its broad nose, showed little signs of vanity save for a grey moustache, kept perfectly trimmed above his wide mouth. She could see also a striking resemblance to the man in the photo on his desk. It was his demeanour, however, that perturbed Katrina; it was perfunctory and she couldn't tell whether this was because she was a woman or a CIA operative. Picking up the picture on his desk Katrina smiled.

"I'm guessing this is your father. He is very handsome," she said, in an attempt to endear herself.

"Yes, he was a Red-Tail Angel," said the general with a smile, warming to her slightly, "a Tuskegee Airman."

"Did he survive the war?"

"Indeed," replied General Long, placing the photo back on his desk, "and Korea too. My mother made him retire from active service at the earliest opportunity. She wanted her children to grow up with a father."

"Well, you can't blame her for that," declared Katrina.

"No." The general mentally shook his thoughts out of the past and picked up the iPad. "This was brought to my notice while you were waiting."

He moved his right forefinger over the screen and passed it to the CIA agent. Taking the tablet, Katrina frowned.

"What is it?" she enquired.

"Press play," urged the general.

Doing just that, Katrina saw an image of a metallic red pickup truck in the half-light of dawn. The video was a little shaky as it moved in closer and traversed around the rear of the truck to the cabin. Inside were three men: two in the front and one in the back. They sat staring blankly out of the windshield and if it had been a still photo, it could easily have been a shot of the men driving along.

"They're all dead," chipped in General Long.

"How?" asked Katrina. The video was showing a close-up of the interior now, and it was beginning to creep her out a little.

"We don't know," he revealed, "there isn't a mark on them. An autopsy has yet to be been done. Obviously, it is hoped that it will tell us something. Another mystery is the driver. If you check out his uniform, he's a highway patrolman. His name is Sergeant Blake Ryan."

"Yes, I see that," confirmed Katrina.

"When he didn't report back after his shift on Saturday evening, a search was sent out," added General Long. "His bike was eventually found discarded off State Route 49 with what we believe to be one of the original occupants of the truck. He was shot three times in the chest, we think with Ryan's handgun. Though ballistics should confirm this."

"How do you know that the dead man was one of this group?" challenged Katrina pointing at the video.

"Because they were all wearing similar clothing," he confirmed, "and items found in the back suggest that these three men were on a fishing trip. We have identified the owner of the vehicle and expect to have some confirmation soon."

"So," said Katrina, frowning, thinking out loud, "they're stopped by this cop, he shoots one, then drives them miles south to the desert and then all three just die, mysteriously."

"That's about the size of it," summed up the general.

"It doesn't make any sense," declared Katrina.

"No, but they were found near the top-secret facility and I… we feel it might have some connection to the incident, though God knows how."

"When can I see AirForce Plant 52?" asked Katrina.

The general reeled inside; he didn't like this CIA agent using its correct name, in fact he didn't like anyone knowing about it, full stop. His disinclination to be more forthcoming wasn't lost on Katrina. She didn't like being taken for a fool and wasn't going to allow this man to fob her off.

"Don't forget, General, I have been to this *facility*, as you call it," she asserted, "and I am aware of some of the top-secret activities conducted there. Two of those activities were joint operations with the CIA, remember. So, let's dispense with the pretence."

General Long gave her a steely glance; it had been quite a while since anyone had had the balls to talk to him like that. He decided that he liked this young woman and resolved to cut her some slack.

"Last night, four guests were taken to AirForce Plant 52."

"Do you have their names?" asked Katrina, taking a notepad and pen out of her purse.

"I have names and descriptions," confirmed the colonel, reaching into a drawer for a sheet of paper. Jotting down the information, she raised her eyebrows at the description of a woman with her hair braided with beads, but continued writing. Realising that this raised more questions, she placed the notepad back in her purse and sat back on the chair feeling a little more relaxed.

"Do you know who they were and why they were brought in?"

"That I don't know," replied General Long, with conviction. "Colonel Pearson kept his activities at the base close to his chest, and to be honest I didn't *want* to know."

Katrina smiled thinly and nodded. On this point she believed him.

"Right, if you're ready, we'll get going," he added. "We'll take a chopper. You'll want to see it from the air."

"Very good," replied Katrina solemnly, and both stood up and left the general's office.

***

The noise from the AgustaWestland AW139M helicopter made conversation difficult, though this suited Katrina just fine. It gave her an opportunity to survey the area below. The terrain, as she expected, was desert for miles around, dotted with shrubs and bushes. Rocky outcrops heaved into view and suddenly a hive of activity could be seen on the ground, with several military vehicles randomly parked. She noticed that most of the men were wearing yellow hazmat suits and holding a device, which she surmised, quite correctly, to be a Geiger counter.

As the chopper passed over the yellow men, it slowed and banked to the left. Then she saw it: a massive crater sunk deep into the ground. The general spoke to the pilot and he made a circuit of the indentation. Katrina glanced at the general, in shock.

"That's where AirForce Plant 52 used to be," he shouted.

She couldn't believe it; all that construction, all those levels, all those people, just gone, to be replaced by a hole in the ground. Nobody could survive that, she thought. The chopper made one more pass and then landed on a clear piece of ground fifty yards from an army mess tent shelter – a khaki canvas roof supported on poles, which had been erected to provide shade.

Alighting from the aircraft, the general led Katrina over to the shelter. She had to close her eyes as dust from the rotor blades threw up sand as the chopper took off and roared away in the direction it had come. They ducked into the tent, grateful to be out of the sun. Inside were a couple of tables, several canvas chairs and a woman, a little older than Katrina, in her late thirties. She was of stocky build and average height, wearing sand-coloured army boots and desert camouflage cargo pants. A scuffed, baggy white T-shirt covered her ample round chest and her hair was tied back in a ponytail under a plain black baseball cap. Without a hint of makeup, her face was not so much pretty as easy on the eye and she smiled warmly as she saw Katrina and the general step under, into the shade.

"General Long, it's good to see you at last," said the woman with a smile, and then turned her attention to Katrina.

"This is Professor Dorothy Reynolds," announced the general.

"Katrina Hart," Katrina smiled, offering her hand. "I'm representing the CIA here."

"Yes, they said someone would be coming from the agency." She looked Katrina up and down, appraising her attire. Katrina was wearing her stock dark grey trouser suit and white blouse with low-heeled black shoes. "You're not exactly dressed for the occasion. I'll see if I can find you something more appropriate."

"It's all been a bit of a rush," said Katrina, wincing. "When I turned up for work this morning I wasn't expecting this."

"I don't think anyone was," said the professor, grinning, "least of all me."

"What have you got here, Professor Reynolds?" enquired Katrina.

"Please, call me Dee, everyone else does."

Turning to the tables behind her, Dee motioned to an array of rocks laid out on display.

"These were found close to and around the crater." Dee picked up two pieces of rock and handed one to each of her visitors.

The rocks fitted easily into the palms of their hands, and had a green quartz-like appearance.

"What are we looking at, Dee?" asked the colonel.

"Trinite," revealed the professor enigmatically.

Both stared blankly back at her.

"It's a glassy residue," she informed them. "It was first found in the Jornada del Muerto Desert of New Mexico in 1945, after the Trinity test of the first atomic bomb. Basically, sand is thrown up into the fireball and drips back to earth to form this. The glass is scattered all round the crater."

"Are you telling us that a nuclear device has been detonated here?" asked an incredulous Katrina.

"We think not," confirmed Dee. "Our tests have shown that only background radiation levels have been detected and even inside the crater radiation levels are normal."

"So, what could have possibly caused such, such… devastation?" stammered the general.

"That's the 64,000-dollar question," said Dee with a shrug, "and one which no one has an answer to."

The professor took the rocks off them and returned both to their place on the table.

"Would it be possible to get a closer look at the crater?" asked Katrina.

"Surely," enthused Dee, "but first I'll see if I can find you some boots and suitable pants. Those wouldn't last five minutes."

"I'm going to stay under here," commented General Long, struggling to lower himself into one of the canvas chairs. "I can't take the heat like I used to."

Both women smiled at him and left the tent, in search of a change of clothing for Katrina.

***

Professor Reynolds smiled at Katrina's reaction. They were standing at the edge of the massive crater, looking down. Katrina had been kitted out in slightly oversize army boots, overlong desert cargo pants, and a khaki boonie hat to keep the sun off her face. Despite feeling ridiculous, no one had given her a second glance.

"There used to be a mountain here," she uttered.

"Impressive, isn't it," said the professor, grinning. "We've surveyed the crater and it is 2150 feet in diameter. That's just under half a mile."

"What about depth?" asked Katrina, still staring down.

"Over 500 feet, at its deepest."

"It's all gone," whispered Katrina, almost to herself, then she turned to the professor. "All seven levels, gone. Vapourised, I guess."

"You were familiar with the installation?" said Professor Reynolds frowning.

"Yes, that's one of the reasons I'm here," she replied, "though I only got as far down as level two."

"What went on down there, Katrina?"

"I'm not authorised to tell you," declared the CIA agent. "You must know that the base was top secret."

Kicking herself for asking such a stupid question, Professor Reynolds decided to change the subject.

"The flash was seen in LA and Vegas," she revealed, "over fifty, sixty miles away. We've had a hell of a job keeping reporters at bay."

"And radiation levels are normal?" Standing so close, Katrina was keen to get this reaffirmed. "What kind of bomb could do this?"

"Everything about this suggests a nuclear detonation took place, but without radiation…" Reynolds let her sentence trail off, then added, "The official line is that a meteor landed here. It's similar to the Barringer Crater in Arizona."

A young man in uniform could be heard scrambling his way up the slight incline to the edge and the two women turned around to see who it was. The young soldier in front of them looked ashen.

"They've found something, ma'am," he announced. "If you would like to follow me."

Struggling to keep up with the soldier, Katrina and the professor were led away from the crater and over to a small group of men, about 500 yards away, staring down into a shallow ditch. Both women approached and followed their gaze.

"Oh my God," declared Katrina, putting a hand to her mouth and turning away.

A badly burned body was lying inert on its back, its clothes partially scorched away exposing the full extent of the damage. One singed trainer was still on the left foot and the legs, torso and head were red raw and blistered. Most of the hair was singed away, leaving wispy tufts still clinging to the blistered scalp. A man in a hazmat suit was running a Geiger counter over the body, but was getting nothing significant.

"The radiation levels are normal," commented a man, standing next to the two women, "but I've seen photos like this before."

"Yes, Hiroshima," replied Reynolds, stepping down for a closer look.

Plucking up the nerve to turn back again, Katrina watched Professor Reynolds study the body. A wave of nausea came over her and Katrina fought to keep her lunch down.

"Well, our Jane Doe here is clearly female," assessed Reynolds, "and judging by what's left of these dungarees, she was a civilian."

Dipping into her purse, Katrina pulled out her notepad. She looked at the girl's remaining hair and saw that it was blonde.

"It's possible her name's Sophie Hunter," advised Katrina.

"You poor love," simpered Reynolds. "She must've gotten caught in the blast. That alone would've been enough to kill her, and she's got third-degree, possibly fourth-degree, burns to ninety percent of her body. She stood no chance."

Looking up at the crowd which had gathered, Reynolds put her hand to her eyes, shielding them from the sun.

"Can we get the ambulance over here pronto, please," she beseeched, "and we'll need to make a sweep of the area. There may be more casualties."

A khaki Humvee M997 ambulance with a large red cross on its side arrived, and two medics got out and removed a gurney from the rear and placed a stretcher with a black body bag on top. They wheeled the gurney to the edge of the ditch and brought the stretcher down and placed it by the body. Carefully they lifted Sophie's immobile body onto the stretcher and into the body bag.

Then they lifted the stretcher up and placed it on the gurney. Professor Reynolds took one last look at the horrendous sight and then nodded to the medics.

"Okay, zip her up," she sighed.

The medics complied, but just as the zip reached her chin, Sophie's head moved slightly and she gave out a weak moan. The two men stepped back in shock.

"Good God, she's alive," cried Reynolds. "That's impossible."

She stepped forwards and placed a finger on her neck.

"There's a pulse but it's weak." Her mind was racing, then she snapped to her senses. "Get her in the ambulance. We've got to get her to hospital."

"I'm going with her," insisted Katrina; she had a bad feeling about this girl and needed to find out more. She followed the medics to the front of the vehicle and as she was about to step up, she turned to the professor. "Let me know if there are any new developments."

"Wait," requested Reynolds, holding up a hand, "one moment."

The professor turned and disappeared into a tent and quickly returned with a bundle in her arms.

"Your clothes," she said, beaming.

"What about these?" asked Katina, gesturing to the outfit that she was wearing.

"Keep them, they won't be missed," smirked Professor Reynolds, then she addressed the driver, "Take it steady down the track, that girl is in a bad way."

"Thanks," said Katrina with a smile. "I'll keep you posted."

The ambulance kicked up dust as it sped off down the track towards Edwards Air Force Base. Professor Dee Reynolds watched it disappear in the mid-afternoon heat haze, and wondered, knowing that the CIA was involved, whether that would ever happen.

***

Huntington Hospital, Pasadena, Los Angeles, California
December 2016

The hospital room was in semi-darkness when Katrina quietly opened the door and stepped in. A young man in blue scrubs followed in and stood beside her. They both considered the red, blistered head poking out from the sheets, a drip attached to her arm.

"I expected to see her in ITU connected up to all manner of machines," quipped Katrina.

"There's no need," replied the doctor. "Believe it or not, she's stable. Her pulse is normal, blood pressure is fine, and she is breathing without assistance. This young woman is one tough cookie."

"It's a miracle," added Katrina.

"Miraculous is the word," agreed the doctor, then he frowned. "She has a fractured right clavicle, two fractures to her cervical vertebrae, C3 and C7, plus a fractured skull. The burns alone should have killed her, but here she is, sleeping like a baby." His expression became mystified. "The puzzling thing is, though, we can't identify her blood group."

"Pardon me?"

"It's nothing like anything we've encountered," he revealed. "Under different circumstances, I would even say it's not human."

"Have you sent her blood for further testing?"

"Not yet," confirmed the doctor.

"Then don't, at least not for the moment," pondered Katrina. This was beginning to look all too familiar.

"May I ask why?"

"This girl is a CIA and military asset," Katrina replied. "I need to keep this contained. Also, I'm going to post two of my men on the door."

"Is that really necessary?"

"You don't know what we're dealing with," said Katrina with a grimace.

The CIA agent departed the room, leaving the doctor contemplating this very point.

***

Five days went by and Sophie found herself drifting in and out of consciousness. A patient-controlled analgesia device had been set up so that she could administer pain relief at the press of a button, any time that she felt as though it was needed. The first time she'd awoken in hospital, it felt like her whole body was on fire and she could barely move. She welcomed the pain relief then, but now found herself using it less. Amazingly, the pain in her neck and shoulder seemed to have gone and despite the fact that her neck was restricted by a brace, she found that movement of her shoulder was getting easier.

One evening, at 2319 hours, she was suspended in soporific torpor, when she was jolted back to a higher level of consciousness by a voice.

"Sophie." The voice didn't seem to be in the room, but in her head. And it sounded familiar.

"Sophie," came the voice again, a little more urgent this time.

"Who is it?" she croaked through a dry throat.

"Sophie, it's me. Wake up."

Opening her eyes, Sophie could just make out a shadowy figure sitting in a chair at the far side of the room, with shoulder-length black hair, wearing faded blue jeans and a pink T-shirt.

"Jessica?" quipped Sophie, incredulously.

"Why do you dwell with the sick and infirm?"

"I'm hurt," retorted Sophie. "Can't you see?"

"You must leave this place," urged the shadowy figure, "and leave it now."

"You're kidding me, right?"

"Get up, Sophie, now." This time the voice was commanding. "You cannot stay here. You know that."

"Yes, I know that," Sophie conceded, losing her patience, "but can't I stay just a little while longer?"

"You have the inner strength," the figure told her, "use it."

Sitting up, Sophie swung her legs over the side of the bed and glared at the chair. The figure had gone and Sophie was beginning to wonder whether she had been hallucinating.

"Shit, Jessica," she complained, staring at the chair like a petulant teenager, "why are you still screwing with me?"

Slowly, she began to detach herself from all encumbrances. First of all, she carefully ripped the plaster from her shoulder, then she removed the neck brace and finally detached the intravenous PCA device inserted into her left hand. Standing up, she rotated her shoulder and then her neck. They both felt good, if a little stiff. Realising that she was wearing only a hospital gown, Sophie realised that she needed to get some clothes, and quick.

She tiptoed over to the door and placed her ear up close. The gentle rhythmic breathing of someone on the other side came through to her and as she listened further, the unsynchronised breathing of another person could easily be discerned.

Two of them, she thought.

Looking around the dark room, the only thing that she could see of any use was a large vase of flowers, sitting on the nightstand by her bed. She picked it up and stood behind the door and then knocked. The guards outside looked at each other in surprise, then one shrugged and opened the door. As he entered, the first thing he noticed was the empty bed. Before he could react, however, something hard and heavy came smashing down on his head. The guard outside heard the shattering vase and immediately spoke into his left cuff.

"Miss Hart," he declared, "we need backup now."

Katrina was one floor below, in the reception area, and was just considering trying to get some sleep, when the call came through.

"I'm on my way," she reassured him.

The second guard entered the room to see his companion prostrate on the floor, pieces of broken vase around him. He didn't get a chance to draw his gun from its shoulder holster; Sophie had taken the first man's gun and pistol-whipped him hard across the back of the head. The man dropped to the floor, next to his colleague, out cold.

Katrina rushed up to the first-floor corridor just as Sophie was exiting her room. She saw the injured girl pocketing one of the handguns whilst keeping a firm grip on the other. Under different circumstances, Katrina would have laughed at the sight in front of her. Sophie had stripped one of her men of his suit, shirt and shoes and was wearing them like a bad impression of Charlie Chaplin. The two women stopped and sized each other up in the corridor. Katrina was the first to speak.

"What do you think you're doing, Sophie?"

"I'm getting outta here," she said, grimacing, "and you're going to help me."

"That's what I'm here for," reasoned Katrina, "to look after you."

"Don't patronise me," sneered Sophie. "I know exactly what the CIA wants."

"Sophie, look at you," pleaded Katrina with genuine compassion. "You're in no fit state to leave."

"What and stay here," sneered Sophie again, "and become a guinea pig? I don't think so."

"You took the serum, didn't you?" accused Katrina. "Have you any idea how special you are?"

"Nobody can have it. I'm going to make damn sure of that."

"What happened in the base, Sophie? What went wrong?"

"Everything," shouted Sophie, losing her patience. "You're lucky to be alive, everyone is. It's fixed now, thanks to Jessica."

"Who is Jessica?" Katrina recognised the name from her notebook. She feigned ignorance, hoping to get more out of Sophie. "Is she the other woman in your group?"

"We're wasting time," snapped Sophie, ignoring her question.

"If you use that gun, you'll just raise the alarm."

Approaching Katrina, Sophie swivelled her round, frisked her and stuck the gun in her back.

"I don't need this gun to kill you. Sound the alarm and I'll snap your neck like a twig."

"Where are we going?" asked Katrina nervously.

"The fire escape," replied Sophie. "Now move."

It didn't take long to find the staircase that led down to an emergency fire exit, and Sophie herded her captor to the bottom and around a corner. The grey double doors of the fire escape loomed in front of them.

"This is a waste of time." Katrina tried to reason with the girl. "You'll only trigger the alarm."

Sophie ignored her and looked around. She discovered a red alarm on the wall and jumped up, grabbed it and ripped the alarm off, leaving bare wires dangling limply. Leaning on the push bar, one side door swung open and they were out into the dark, cool air. It felt soothing on Sophie's exposed skin.

"Where is your car?" demanded Sophie.

"It's around the corner, in the car park."

Pushing Katrina forwards, they moved round to the front of the large hospital building, until rows of cars came into sight.

"Get your keys out," demanded Sophie again.

Complying, Katrina dipped into her purse, found her keys and zapped the car. A white sedan bleeped with orange lights and Sophie urged her captive forwards.

"You drive," ordered Sophie as they both opened doors and slipped inside. Katrina started up the engine and looked at Sophie and the gun pointing at her stomach.

"Where to?"

"West on Freeway 210," said Sophie succinctly.

They pulled out of the hospital grounds and picked up the freeway. Katrina glanced at Sophie. She was concerned for the girl.

"How long do you think you'll last?" she muttered. "You look rough."

"Shut up and drive." Sophie looked at a signpost and had an idea. "Head for Angeles National Forest."

Soon they were on a quieter road and leaving the residential area behind them. As the trees became denser, the road ahead became pitch black.

"Okay, pull over here and get out," ordered Sophie.

She led Katrina over to some trees, well away from the road, and stopped.

"You won't get away with this." Katrina was scared. "Killing me will bring a ton of crap down on you."

"Kneel down," snarled Sophie.

"Please, Sophie," pleaded Katrina, bending to her knees.

Walking behind her captive, Sophie gripped the handgun by the barrel and brought her arm back. Lights flashed through the CIA agent's brain and she slumped sideways onto the ground.

"Kill you?" exclaimed Sophie. "What do you think I am?"

CHAPTER TWENTY-ONE

THE SOJOURNER

Angeles National Forest, California
December 2016

Glancing at the clock on the dashboard, Sophie retraced her steps back to the northern suburbs of Los Angeles; it read 0045 hours. If she picked up Interstate Route 5 northbound, which would bring her close to the Bay Area of San Francisco, Sophie calculated that she would arrive by dawn if she kept her speed to sixty-five miles per hour. The evening's exertions had taken their toll and her immediate problem now was trying to stay awake for the six-hour drive. Sophie's body was sore, her blistered skin still burning, and her right shoulder was beginning to ache, but she knew that resting was not an option if she was to make a clean getaway.

In an attempt to help keep her awake, Sophie turned on the radio. The first song that she heard was 'Street Spirit' by Radiohead. She smiled inwardly, remembering the last time that she heard the song, when looking at the dinosaur bones with Nathan back in the summer break. Like the *Dilophosaurus* it seemed a million years ago now. A tear rolled down her cheek as it brought back the fact that he was dead and she was now alone, only a single CIA handgun for company. Before leaving Katrina, she had changed out of the ridiculous-looking, oversized suit of the CIA agent, into the desert cargo pants and boots which she had found in the trunk of the car. They were a better fit and made driving easier.

The road was long and tedious, with only the beams of occasional oncoming vehicles to shake her out of her stupor. As Sophie stared out at the gloom beyond the headlamps, she struggled to keep her eyes open, fighting the fatigue which threatened to overcome her.

The sun had still not shown itself above the horizon when she picked up Interstate Route 580 but the sky was beginning to lighten behind her and Sophie knew that very soon dawn would break. The road ahead looked more like home to her now as she headed west towards the coast and the familiar skyline of San Francisco. In less than an hour she would be in Berkeley, and she realised that her first port of call must be to pick up a travel bag from her digs at the university hall of residence.

Parking the car close to Residence Halls Unit 4, she checked the clock on the dashboard. It was 06.34; she had made good time. If she was quick and quiet, hopefully she would get in and out again before anyone was up. It would be bad for her and any of the residents to see her looking like this. Stealthily, Sophie made her way to her rooms and realised that she didn't have a key. She winced slightly as she gave the door a firm shove and it gave way with a crack of splintered wood. The first thing that she did was go straight into the bathroom to check herself out in the mirror. It was the first time that Sophie had seen what she looked like and instantly regretted it. Most of her lovely blonde hair was gone, leaving wisps of straggly filament which she tried to flatten against her red raw scalp. Her face was still very red, with blisters on both cheekbones and her lips were cracked and painful. Not one square inch of her skin was unaffected. She looked at herself with dismay.

"Oh, Sophie," she lamented, "what's become of you?"

Snapping out of her malaise, she returned to the bedroom, pulled out a knapsack, checked that the money and both her passports – the real and the false – were inside, then she proceeded to pack some clothes. Finally, she undressed herself and tried not to look at her body which, to her distress, was much the same as her face. Slipping a sports bra over her head was agony, but felt better once she had it in place. Then panties and socks and the loosest-fitting pair of joggers that she could find. To finish off she found a loose-fitting black T-shirt emblazoned with the Ramones logo, black and white Converse and, finally, a plain black hoodie which zipped up the front.

Picking up her knapsack, Sophie gingerly opened the door and looked out. The corridor was still deserted, so she stepped into it, closed the door behind her and made her way out of the university campus. The question now was, where to? In Sophie's mind, she had only one option. It would mean a five-mile walk; she didn't dare use the car from now on, and Sophie hoped that she would have the strength to make it. Pulling the hood up close around her, she hung her head down and began to stride out as fast as she could. The streets were still quiet, something for which she was eminently grateful.

It took three painful hours to reach her destination, and by the time she was knocking on a tatty front door, Sophie was ready to drop. A tall bleary-eyed young man opened the door, and stared uncomprehendingly at the figure in front of him.

"Hello?" he faltered, automatically suspicious of the mysterious hooded figure.

"Tuck," Sophie said, grimacing, wavering slightly, "can I come in?"

"Sophie?" he exclaimed, recognising her voice. "Is that you?"

Ushering Sophie inside, Tuck was in shock at the sight of his friend.

Sophie tried to hide her face, but Tuck pulled the hood down to expose her injuries.

"Jesus, what happened to you?" he beseeched, jumping back in shock.

"Not now, Tuck, please," she said, wincing. "It's been a long night and I need to sleep."

"Is there anything I can get for you? Food or drink?"

"Just water," responded Sophie. "I'm so thirsty."

Tuck watched as Sophie drank three glasses of water

down, barely coming up for air, and Sophie could see the concern on his face.

"Shouldn't you be in a hospital?" he asked, not unreasonably.

"I'll be okay," she reassured him, "if you could just let me rest up."

"Sure thing," agreed Tuck, and led her to his bedroom.

"Thanks, Tuck." Sophie put a blistered hand on his arm and tried to smile, but it was too painful. "You're a good friend. In fact, my only friend."

"Oh and Tuck," she added, "nobody, but nobody must know I'm here. Is that clear?"

Smiling wanly, Tuck closed the bedroom door to give Sophie some peace. It was just gone 10am and he wondered what else the day might have in store for him.

***

Awaking with a start, Katrina sat up and realised that she was frozen. The sun had just broken above the trees and was yet to bathe the area in any kind of warmth. Her head was pounding and she rubbed the back of her scalp to find some blood on her fingers. Sophie had placed the clothes that she had changed out of over her unconscious body the night before, in an attempt to keep her warm. Katrina suddenly realised that she was also holding one of the handguns which Sophie had taken. Katrina gave out a short chuckle.

"Well, you may be on the lam, Sophie," she muttered to herself, "but you ain't no killer." She was annoyed with herself for even thinking it in the first place. The car was gone and she was stuck in the middle of nowhere. Katrina needed to contact her team and frantically began to search for her cell phone, in her purse. Finding it in the inside pocket of her jacket, Katrina sighed with relief.

"Good girl, Sophie," she muttered again, and prayed that there would still be some battery left. She switched the device on and sighed again, when the screen lit up.

It took over an hour for one of her team to find a car and track Katrina to her location. Time that Katrina knew all too well they couldn't afford to lose. A black SUV turned up and a man in a light grey suit alighted and approached the dishevelled agent.

"Thank goodness we've found you, ma'am." He looked a little sheepish knowing that he'd screwed up.

"Smith, we need to get going," replied Katrina, ignoring his comment. "I have Anderson's clothes here."

They both stepped up into the SUV, strapped themselves in and drove back to the hospital.

"Sorry about last night, ma'am," Smith beseeched.

"Don't beat yourself up about it," consoled Katrina. "You were no match for her. None of us were."

"What's our next step?"

"Where would a young woman go if she was on the run?" thought Katrina out loud.

"Friends' maybe?" suggested Smith.

"Perhaps," mused Katrina, "but she's going to need clothes. No, our first stop is her crib. We need to find out where she is staying. That will give us a good idea where to start."

Katrina jumped suddenly as her phone began to ring. *Crap*, she thought, recognising the number, *I'm going to have to explain how I lost her.*

***

University of California, Berkeley, California
Residence Halls Unit 4
December 2016

After being chewed out by Lucas Foster, the CIA director of operations, he finally had some intel for them. Katrina hung up and Smith, who had heard everything, gave her a withering look.

"Right," she said, decisively, "pick up Anderson, and let's head north for the Bay Area. I know where she's staying."

"Do you think she'll be there?"

"Who knows," said Katrina with a shrug. "For the moment, it's all we've got."

Six hours later, as they pulled into the university parking area, Katrina smiled as she noticed her white hire car sitting neatly in a parking bay.

"My car's here," she said, pointing, "maybe *she's* still here."

Smith looked at her doubtfully, and deep down Katrina knew it was a forlorn hope. But hey, she reasoned, stranger things have happened. The door was open when they got to her rooms and Katrina knew that Sophie would have flown the nest some time ago. With a cursory look into the bedroom, Katrina noticed a neat pile on the bed. It was the cargo pants and desert boots that the fugitive had borrowed. In between the pants she found the handgun and the keys to her hire car. With the way Sophie was acting and what she had told her, Katrina was beginning to question who exactly were the bad guys in all of this. She began to empathise with her quarry, and Katrina wasn't sure whether that was a good thing. After a thorough search, no passport was found, so Katrina felt it prudent to put an APB out to all ports, just to be on the safe side.

Later she found herself walking through a wide gate with a green ornate archway, emblazoned with the name '*Sather Gate*'. At its peak was an oval motif, surrounded by oak leaves. In its centre was a star, radiating shards of light and below this were the Latin words '*Fiat Lux*'. As Katrina passed through the gate, she could just make out the white obelisk of Sather Tower, protruding high above the trees, its pointed spire giving the impression of a rocket ready for take-off. Here she had agreed to meet the chancellor of the university. The middle-aged woman looked lean and stern as Katrina approached, but smiled kindly and offered her hand.

"It's a lovely campus you have here," complimented Katrina. "Tell me, though, what does *Fiat Lux* mean? My Latin is a little shaky."

"It means 'Let There Be Light'," revealed the chancellor, then with a frown enquired, "Now what business does the CIA have here?"

Katrina smiled inwardly; after recent events the motto seemed eminently appropriate.

"I need to speak with anyone who knew, or is friends with, a certain Sophie Hunter, who is enrolled here."

"Oh, Sophie," exclaimed the chancellor, "I know her, bright girl."

"She's gone missing," urged Katrina, "and it's imperative we find her."

"Is she in some kind of trouble?"

"Not as such. But she needs hospital attention."

"Follow me," responded the chancellor, pausing to think for a minute. "I'll point you in the right direction."

After interviewing several students, the one thing that Katrina established was the fact that Sophie was a popular girl. Going through the list of possible people that might be harbouring her was going to be exhausting. Another connection Katrina made was when the chancellor pointed out that one of their staff, a Professor Nathan Harrison, had gone missing also, and he in turn was connected to a Dr Jessica Phillips. Katrina's ears pricked up when she heard the names Jessica Phillips and Nathan Harrison being mentioned. Both names were on her list. The dots were beginning to join up. Shaking these thoughts from her mind, Katrina met up with her team. She looked at the list of names in her notebook and frowned.

"It's time to head out," commanded Katrina, opening the front passenger door to the SUV, "we've got some legwork to do."

***

Sophie woke up suddenly and cried out. She had slept solidly for fifty hours, and Tuck, who had been checking in on her, had been getting more and more concerned. Her cry made him jump and he rushed into the bedroom.

"Are you okay?" he bawled.

Sophie was sitting up looking slightly bemused.

"How long have I been asleep?"

"Two days," replied Tuck, sitting on the end of the bed. "How are you feeling?"

"Terrible," said Sophie with a grimace, tentatively touching her face. "How do I look?"

"Well, you don't look no worse," Tuck ventured forwards for a closer examination, "but yes, now I see it, there is some improvement."

Sophie wasn't sure whether he was telling the truth or just being kind, trying to boost her morale. Tuck had a tendency to say the things which he thought people wanted to hear – an error of judgement which often got him into trouble.

Not wanting to take his word for it, she swung her legs over the side of the bed in an attempt to stand up. Sophie grimaced as she got her limbs moving again, and finally straightened up wearing only her sports bra and panties. Tuck noticed that they were stained a yellowy red colour from her weeping sores, her body completely covered in red raw skin and blisters.

"Jeez, Sophie, what happened?" said Tuck, frowning. "You look like you've just been pulled out of a fire."

"You're not far from the truth. Let me have a bath," she pleaded, "and something to eat, then I'll tell you what I can."

Taking her undergarments off proved to be agony as she endeavoured to peel them off her skin. They had stuck themselves to her wounds and she had to release them with great care. Once naked, Sophie inspected herself in a mirror and was surprised to see that her skin had in fact improved slightly. Her face wasn't quite so red and the blisters were much diminished. Sophie prayed that there would be no scarring if and when the healing process was complete. She ran a bath and looked around at the clutter, looking for something resembling bubble bath. She didn't hold out much hope; Tuck wasn't renowned for his hygiene. After much rummaging, she finally found a suitable bubble bath. Sophie smiled to herself; she recognised it as one that she had left here a few years ago, still hardly used. Pouring some into the tepid water, Sophie sloshed it around until she had a flotilla of foam bobbing about on the surface.

Slowly she eased herself in and allowed her body to soak in the warm soapy water. She didn't know whether this was the correct thing to do, but Sophie didn't care, the water felt good, bathing her body in a warm comforting envelope. Eventually she arose from the tub and wrapped a towel gently around her torso; already she was feeling a whole lot better.

Opening the door, Sophie was hit by the smell of bacon frying and realised that she was famished. She padded to the bedroom, rummaged in her knapsack and found a long loose-fitting nightgown. By the time she returned to the kitchen, Tuck had made sandwiches for them both. Sitting down at the table opposite Tuck, Sophie ate heartily.

"Well, your appetite hasn't been affected," he chuckled.

"This is the first thing I've eaten since..." She stopped and thought for a moment. "I can't remember when I last had some food."

"Are you ready to tell me what happened to you?" pressed Tuck, standing up to make some coffee.

"Just water for me, please," insisted Sophie. "I'm not ready for hot drinks yet."

Tuck carried their drinks into the sitting room and he cleared some space on the couch for them both to sit down.

He took a sip from a stained, cracked mug and looked at the injured girl expectantly.

"I can't tell you much, it's safer that you don't know," considered Sophie. "What I will tell you, though, the reason that I'm still alive is because I'm not like other people."

"What do you mean," Tuck looked puzzled, "not like other people?"

"I was injected with a drug that alters your DNA. It has made me more resilient, more robust than other people. I'm stronger, faster and all my senses are heightened. And it would appear that my ability to heal is accelerated too. That's something I didn't know."

"So, are you like a superwoman then?"

"I guess so," replied Sophie, giving it some thought.

"Whoa," whistled Tuck, his mind racing. "I could make a fortune out of a drug like that."

"You don't want to be anywhere near this," cautioned Sophie. "Too many people have died for this thing. It's a curse."

"Are you the only one?"

"I believe so, I think so," she considered. "The drug is all gone too, so you can put all those thoughts out of your head."

"Why did you come here? You'd be much better off in hospital."

"I can't," Sophie shifted awkwardly on the couch, "the CIA are after me."

"What!" bellowed Tuck.

"Look, I'm sorry, Tuck, but I had nowhere else to go. And if they catch me, they're going to try and harvest my DNA to get the drug back again. No way can I let that happen."

Tuck sat back, reeling from the implications of spooks turning up at his crib. He looked at Sophie, how desperately, hopelessly lost she looked, and he knew that he couldn't just throw her to the wolves.

"I know what you're thinking, Tuck," she said, placing a hand on his.

"Oh, so mind reading is another one of your powers, is it?" he said sarcastically.

"Don't be silly," Sophie admonished gently, "but we do need to hide my things."

Giving this some thought, Tuck stood up.

"Get your stuff together and bring it back in here."

Doing as she was told, Sophie returned with her knapsack to see Tuck had shifted the couch to one side, lifted a rug and pulled up several loose floorboards. She looked into the hole to see packs of cannabis all neatly stacked in clear plastic bags. Tuck was on his knees systematically removing them.

"There's space further back where we can hide it," he said, smiling and looking up at her.

"Quite the little industry you have here," declared Sophie.

"It's a living," quipped Tuck. "Besides, cannabis is legal in California now."

"Yeah, just," admonished Sophie, "but dealing isn't."

Tuck gave Sophie a 'don't hassle me' look, so she dropped the subject.

With the knapsack stowed away and the plastic bags returned, Tuck dragged the rug and the couch back into place.

"What now?" he asked.

"You continue as normal and I, hopefully, will get better soon. Right now, I can't think beyond that." She switched on the TV and sat down on the couch, happy to immerse herself in the mind-numbing banality of daytime television.

***

Seven days of vegetating in front of a television screen, and Sophie was beginning to get restless. The serum in her DNA was continuing to work its magic, as her body seemed to repair itself at a rapid rate. The blisters were gone and Sophie's deep red lesions were looking less angry, feeling less sore.

Tuck, sensing her listlessness, placed a chessboard down on the table.

"It's time you started engaging that brain," he announced. "See if you can beat me. I warn you, though, I'm good."

In her ennui Sophie lacked the spirit to argue and slumped in the chair opposite him like a petulant teenager. She stared down at the chessboard in front of her. With a look of shock on his face, Tuck gently lifted her chin.

"Have you seen your scalp?" he exclaimed.

"No, why?" Sophie was nearly panicking at Tuck's manner. She dashed to the bathroom and looked at her scalp closely in the mirror. Running her hands over the spiky stubble she turned to Tuck, half grinning, half in tears.

"My hair's growing back," she burst out.

"You're really on the mend now," he affirmed, giving her a gentle hug.

Within a few days, Sophie's hair was three millimetres longer, giving her scalp an even velvety sheen. The one thing that she was most relieved about, however, was the fact that the healing process was leaving no scarring. It was the one thing she dreaded most. Her skin was feeling much better now and she decided to risk a warmer bath. It was early one evening after she had put some water in the tub – deep so that she could immerse herself fully – and lots of bubble bath, threatening to overflow over the side, that a sudden knock at the door startled them both.

"Are you expecting anyone?" hissed Sophie.

Tuck shook his head.

"I'm getting in the bath," uttered Sophie. "Strip down to your T-shirt and shorts, and pretend the bath is for you."

Stepping into the water, Sophie gasped from the heat, then she inhaled deeply before slipping down below the bobbing soap suds. Static apnoea was something she had tried only once briefly, and Sophie prayed that she could stay under long enough. Opening the door, Tuck was greeted by three people wearing grey suits: one woman and two men.

"Wayne Tucker?" asked the woman, glancing at the scruffy man in his underwear.

"Who wants to know?" countered Tuck.

"CIA," replied Katrina, producing some identification. "May we come in?"

"Well, it's a bit awkward right now," bluffed Tuck. "I was literally just about to take a bath."

"That's okay," asserted Katrina, refusing to be fobbed off. "We won't keep you."

The CIA agents pushed past him and entered the apartment. Katrina produced a colour photograph and showed it to Tuck.

"Have you seen this person recently?" she enquired.

"That's Sophie. Sophie Hunter," bluffed Tuck again. "I ain't seen her in years, why?"

"She is a person of interest. That's all you need to know." Katrina motioned to her men. "You won't mind if we take a look around."

Before Tuck could protest the two henchmen were checking out the bedroom. He glanced at his watch anxiously. Sophie had been under the water now for at least three minutes. The men eventually came out of the bedroom shaking their heads and proceeded to start searching the sitting room, shifting the dirty clothes and debris with mild disgust.

"Don't you ever clean up?" winced Katrina. "It stinks in here."

"It's my life," said Tuck with a shrug, glancing nervously into the bathroom.

"You were about to take a bath, huh?" Katrina had noticed his slight agitation, and strolled into the bathroom. She looked down at the foam covering the entire surface of the water. Pensively she ran her fingers through the suds, and just as Tuck thought that the game was up, there came a call from the sitting room.

"Ma'am, I think we've found something," announced Anderson.

Distracted, Katrina looked at Tuck and then joined her cohorts. Anderson was pressing a creaking floorboard with his foot. He looked triumphantly at his boss.

"Move that couch," ordered Katrina, gauging Tuck's nervous reaction at the same time. "Let's see what's under there."

The loose floorboards were finally removed to reveal the bags of cannabis neatly stacked.

"Well, well," said Katrina, grinning, "we have been a busy boy."

"It's just for my own use," lied Tuck.

The two men began pulling bags out and stacking them on the floor, until it became apparent that there were only about fifty.

"It's just cannabis, ma'am, nothing else."

"Cannabis is legal now, and this is just for me," assured Tuck, "and I don't touch hard drugs."

"Look, I don't care what you do," declared Katrina, sitting on the couch, "I'm not here for that. Though don't try and kid me all this is for personal use. Cannabis may be legal now in California, but it's still a felony to deal without a licence. We might just pay you a visit another time."

Tuck looked at his watch; fifteen minutes had gone by and still Sophie remained submerged. He thought she had either drowned or was going to come bursting up for air any minute.

"Are we keeping you from something?" enquired Katrina, who had noticed Tuck glance at his watch.

With a nervous shrug, Tuck sat down. Katrina gazed back into the bathroom but all was still, so she turned her attention back to her suspect.

"Have you any clue as to where she might be or where she might stay?" asked Katrina. "You see, we're running out of options. You are our last resort."

"I told you, I ain't seen her since we split up three years ago."

"Yes," commented Katrina doubtfully. She wondered why someone like Sophie would even look at such a dishevelled loser.

They sat for a while in awkward silence until, eventually, the two men approached and shook their heads.

"Nothing?" Katrina was exasperated.

"Just the drugs, ma'am," replied Smith.

Standing up, Katrina produced a business card and handed it to Tuck.

"If you hear anything, be sure to contact me." Katrina stared into the bathroom one last time. The water was as still as a mill pond; she glanced at her watch. "Goodbye, Mr Tucker – for now."

As Tuck closed the door behind them, Katrina addressed her men.

"Anderson, I want you to keep a watch on the house for another twenty-four hours, just in case she turns up."

"Just twenty-four?" enquired Anderson.

"Yeah," replied Katrina, thinking out loud, "we can't afford to waste any more time than that. The holidays are coming up, so we'd better put a stakeout on her parents' house. Though I don't think she'll be that stupid. She might just call them, though, so let's put a tap on their phone."

Watching anxiously from behind the drapes, Tuck was willing them to move off. *Why don't they just go?* he thought. Eventually the three shadowy figures drifted away and Tuck looked at his watch. It had been over thirty minutes since Sophie had dipped her head under, and he rushed to the bathroom to rescue her.

As a hand grabbed her upper arm, Sophie thought that she'd been caught. Reluctantly she surfaced and gasped for air, panting as a wave of foamy water spilled out over the end of the tub.

"It's you, thank God," she gasped. "I take it they've gone."

"I thought you were a gonna for sure," he said, nodding. "I guess it was the drug."

"Yeah, though I don't think I could've stayed down there for much longer," commented Sophie, finally getting her breath back.

As Tuck left the bathroom, Sophie stepped out and wrapped a towel around herself. She wiped steam off the mirror and studied her reflection. Could she get away with leaving soon? Her position here was becoming untenable.

***

Modesto Transportation Center, Modesto, Stanislaus County, California December 2016

Sophie wondered whether the old beaten-up Honda Civic would make the one hundred-mile round trip, and as Tuck turned into the coach station, with its Spanish-style architecture, sand-coloured rendered walls with a plethora of tall arches and pantiled roof, Tuck glanced at Sophie with a thinly disguised look of dismay.

Two days earlier, Sophie had made the decision to leave as soon as she looked presentable. Tuck had been the perfect host and it wasn't fair to compromise him any further. With makeup, her face looked presentable now and she actually liked the close crop that her hair had grown into.

"Where will you go?" asked Tuck, pulling into a parking bay.

"As far away as possible," replied Sophie enigmatically. "Anyway it's better you don't know."

"Yeah, but do you have to take the Loser Cruiser?"

"Greyhounds aren't that bad," retorted Sophie, "and besides, I want to keep things on the down low as much as I can. They'll be watching airports."

They alighted from the car and Sophie approached the ticket office. She was nervous and worried that someone would notice her injuries. The girl behind the screen barely acknowledged Sophie, giving her a look of indifference. With the Christmas holidays looming, many routes were full and Sophie had little choice in her destination. She passed over $300 in cash, took her tickets and approached the man who had been her safe haven for the last two weeks.

"I'm not going to see you again, am I?" he lamented.

"I'm sorry, Tuck." Sophie's voice was trembling with emotion. She knew that she would find it impossible to keep it in check. "There aren't enough words to say how much I appreciate what you have done for me."

Tuck hugged her and wiped away a tear.

"I'd do anything for you," he said, smiling, "you know that."

Pulling away, Sophie nodded, sniffed and tried to pull herself together.

"Now, I've left two envelopes on your bed. One is for you and one is for my mom and dad. Could you post it for me?"

"Sure, but what have you left for me?" quizzed Tuck.

"It's the title for my Mini," she said, smiling. "I won't be needing it and I want you to have it. It's all signed over to you. Just leave it a while before you pick it up. At least a month."

"I don't know what to say," blurted Tuck.

"There's no need," sniffed Sophie, "it's the least I can do."

At just gone 11.15, Sophie's bus pulled up and she turned and gave Tuck one last hug. A line of people were already boarding and Sophie was concerned that she wouldn't get a decent seat.

"Goodbye, and thanks again." Sophie picked up her knapsack and stepped into the Greyhound bus.

"Look after yourself, you hear," called Tuck.

Sophie nodded and walked down the aisle. She needn't have worried; the coach was only half full. Finding a seat near the rear, she sat down, and as it pulled away, she waved as Tuck began sullenly walking back to his car. Glancing at her itinerary, Sophie discovered that there would be two transfers: one in Los Angeles and one in Dallas. The whole journey was going to take forty-eight hours including stops along the way, so she pulled her hood over her head, slinked down on the seat and watched the world go by through the window.

***

Jackson, Hinds County, Mississippi
The Eve of Christmas Eve 2016

Stepping down from the Greyhound bus, and relieved to be able to stretch her legs, Sophie looked around at her surroundings. The bright blue old Greyhound bus station had a classic Art Deco style about it, with rounded corners and windows which wrapped around two sides, more like an old cinema; it seemed to her to be a little incongruous in its surroundings. *Well,* she thought, *I'm in the Deep South now, better get used to things being different.* The journey had been quite a trek and she was relieved to be able to smell fresh air rather than the musty aroma of the bus. It seemed to invade her oversensitive nostrils and refused to go. She breathed in deeply; the early winter air was fresh and cool.

Jackson proved to be a bustling city and Sophie began to get a positive vibe from the place. She found herself walking close to the State University and it occurred to her that this might be a good place to look for cheap lodgings.

Her assumption was correct, and within an hour, Sophie had found a perfectly acceptable room with a bathroom across the hall. Paying up front for three weeks, she was relieved to have established herself so quickly. The room was nothing special but it would do.

Looking at her face in the mirror, Sophie carefully applied makeup remover to examine her skin. There were still some red blotches, but nothing that couldn't be concealed. Flexing her shoulder and neck, she was relieved to feel that the fractured bones were healed. Flopping on the bed she ran her mind over the events that had brought her to this moment. It had been quite a rollercoaster, then it hit home that she was completely alone and it may have to be that way for the rest of her life. The thought of this saddened her and it took all that she could muster to fight back the tears. She had to forget about her parents, about Nathan, and learn to become emotionally and financially self-sufficient.

After a short nap, Sophie took a stroll to get her bearings and a better feel for the city which she had just adopted. The state capital proved to be a sprawling metropolis; a perfect place for someone, who didn't want to be found, to lose themselves. The city was a mixture of period architecture and new, with skyscrapers rubbing shoulders with buildings like the Mississippi State Capital, which, to Sophie, looked remarkably similar to the one in Washington and the classical design of the Mississippi Supreme Court.

Sophie eventually found herself a burger bar and came to the conclusion that she had chosen well. Jackson would suit her just fine.

***

Christmas and New Year were a wretched time for Sophie; she had never felt so lonely, so isolated in her life. The owners of the guesthouse took pity on her and she was invited to Christmas lunch. This proved troublesome, however, as she had to fend off awkward questions, and by the end of the day, she was glad to be back, alone in her room.

By early January of the new year, Sophie was ready to start looking for work. Her face was more or less healed now and her hair was long enough to need combing. She had found an advertisement for a job in a warehouse close to the River Pearl and decided to apply. The foreman looked her up and down and laughed when she turned up for an interview. But when Sophie demonstrated her strength, he hired her on the spot.

This became her life for the following months. Work, eat, perhaps a film or a wander through the city and sleep. She shunned any form of socialising, not wanting to form any bonds with anyone. Sophie was desperately lonely but knew that it could be no other way.

One late afternoon, after her shift, Sophie was sitting in a diner that she often frequented. She had her head down eating some apple pie and ice cream, oblivious to the fact that she was being appraised from the counter.

"Who's that girl over there?" asked a man in his early forties, slightly overweight, with a shock of curly dark brown hair. He motioned to the lone girl sitting at a table with a jet-black pixie cut hairstyle.

"She comes in now and again," replied the middle-aged woman behind the counter. "Always orders apple pie and ice cream. Nothing else."

"Perhaps I should go over and introduce myself," declared the man, "she looks lonely."

"Aw, leave the poor girl to eat her pie in peace," censured the woman. "Ain't she a little young for you, anyhow?"

"Give me two more coffees," replied the man, ignoring her.

With a sigh of exasperation, she reluctantly passed two steaming mugs across the counter and the man picked them up and sauntered confidently over to the solitary girl. He sat down opposite Sophie who barely acknowledged his presence.

"Hello, little lady," he proffered. "I thought you would like a cup of coffee."

"Oh yeah?" Unbeknownst to him, Sophie had heard every word spoken at the counter. Without looking up she pulled the cup towards her and started to stir the brown liquid.

"Yeah, I thought you might like some company."

"Oh, and why did you think that?" asked Sophie, still concentrating absentmindedly on her cup.

"Where do you work?" The man had noticed her grubby overalls, and decided to try a different tack.

"Warehouse near the river," came the curt reply.

"I'm a pilot," revealed the man. It was the ace up his sleeve, when all other chat-up lines failed, and it usually got results. "I work out of an airfield near here."

Sophie's coffee stirring stopped in its tracks at this piece of information, and the man could see that it'd had the desired effect. He had her hooked; now to reel her in.

"My name's Wesley Hodges," he said, smiling, holding out his right hand. "Pleased to make your acquaintance."

Suddenly Sophie was interested in this man. Access to an aircraft could prove useful in the future. She let go of the spoon and finally looked up at Wesley with a big grin.

"Well, Wesley Hodges, glad to meet you," Sophie responded, shaking his hand. "My name's Natalie – Natalie Young."

CHAPTER TWENTY-TWO

DAMAGE LIMITATION

Amazon Rainforest, South American Subcontinent
March 4217 AD

Being a control freak had its disadvantages. If Fabian Spyke had not insisted on accompanying the team on this loathsome expedition, he would not be overheating, drenched in sweat and generally exhausted in this intense heat and humidity. For a man in his mid-forties, Spyke prided himself on his physical fitness, but the two weeks they had been in this wretched hellhole had taken their toll.

Fabian Spyke was the CEO of Spyke Industries and took a particular interest in the bio-weapons research division of his company. Ever since the colonisation of Mars 300 years earlier, plus other outposts in the solar system, the need for an effective security force had become imperative. World leaders had put the contract out to tender and Spyke thought that he might just have the upper hand with the idea that his assistant, Roberta Townsend, had presented him with. It had come to her attention from old declassified CIA files that a certain Sophie Hunter, aka Natalie Young, had escaped into the Amazonian Rainforest and had eluded capture ever since. In fact, she had disappeared without a trace. Long believed dead, Sophie Hunter's escapades had attained legendary status and were known only to the cognoscenti. Spyke thought that if there was any chance, however slight, that she might still be alive, even after all this time, then all this discomfort would have been worth it.

The team consisted of Spyke, his PA, Roberta Townsend, anthropologist Dr Patrick Floyd, jungle expert, survivalist and adventurer Bruno 'Viper' Jordan, plus two ex-SAS soldiers on loan from the British Army. Centuries of economic sanctions and political bickering plus the Fifty-Years War of 3899, between the superpowers of China, Russia and the United States, had taken their toll, and both the New Empire of the United Kingdom and the Germanic Republic of Europe had risen supreme as the only viable superpowers in the last hundred years. It was a miracle that the various conflicts had remained non-nuclear.

Spyke removed his boonie hat, extricated a red patterned hankie and wiped it around his face and neck. He knew it was a pointless exercise but felt the need to do it anyway. Slapping the right-hand side of his neck, Spyke looked at the palm of his hand to see an insect squashed and motionless.

"Goddamn mosquitos," he growled. "After all this time you'd think we'd have some kind of deterrent."

"They're attracted to carbon dioxide," said Viper Jordan, grinning. "Stop breathing and they'll stop coming."

The adventurer looked at his employer. Spyke was a tall lean man with short red hair and a meticulously groomed red goatee beard. His face was long with pointed features and green eyes that seemed to be constantly on the move. The look gave him the impression of a predatory animal, an image that he had deliberately cultivated. From the moment Viper had first shaken his hand, he had taken an instant dislike to the man.

Looking all around him, Dr Patrick Floyd observed the huge deciduous trees disappearing into the canopy above. He had hoped to find some evidence of human activity by now, but since entering the rainforest they had encountered no one. Glad as he was that the rainforests had recovered to their former glory after the bad old days of deforestation, he knew it was only going to make their job all the more difficult.

Howler monkeys were making a cacophony in the trees and were following the team through the branches. The roar of a jaguar could be heard intermittently and Floyd wondered whether they were being stalked. They had heard the big cat but not once had it been seen.

Roberta Townsend approached a tree trunk, attracted by a beautifully coloured frog. Its skin was an array of different shades of blue. Moving her right hand towards it, she pointed with her forefinger close to the amphibian.

"Look at this," she observed, "it's stunning."

"It will do more than stun," drawled Viper, pulling her arm away, "that's a poison dart frog."

"Isn't there anything in this place that's safe?" she moaned. The previous day she had inadvertently sat on some bullet ants and received several painful stings to her buttocks.

"Just remember, we're the intruders here," advised Viper.

He held his hand up for the team to stop. A line of several giant bundled liana were slung across their path making it difficult to proceed. The creeper was a thick mass of twisted roots, like steel cables draped along the forest floor and climbing up tree trunks in the constant forest fight for sunlight. The two SAS soldiers switched on their guns and aimed at the creepers. A pale laser beam shot out and cut through the plants like butter, enabling them to continue.

An hour later, light was beginning to fade so Viper stopped and assessed the area around them. He could hear a river nearby and the small clearing they were in was surrounded by lupuna trees with their massive trunks, deeply fluted near their base as the roots entered the ground.

"It's getting dark," announced Viper. "We'll camp here tonight."

"Another night of not much sleep," whinged Townsend, slipping her rucksack off her back.

After an encampment had been established, Viper and one SAS man, known as West, headed off in the direction of the river. The others sat on canvas stools around a small fire nervously listening to the sounds of the forest. A flutter of what sounded like thousands of birds being disturbed resounded not far away.

"What was that?" asked Townsend. Her nerves were a little frayed after two weeks of this and she was ready to call it a day.

"Vampire bats," replied the SAS man, known only as Fox, looking up into the canopy.

"Great, so now we're going to get our blood sucked," moaned Townsend.

"That's not what you should worrying about," he said, grinning mischievously, "it's the rabies they carry."

Lost for words, Townsend didn't reply and pulled her jacket in closer. The group fell silent, deep in their own thoughts, around the fire. It wasn't long before Viper and his compatriot were back. Viper approached the fire and tipped out several blue-grey fish, about six inches long, from a canvas bag.

"What are they?" asked Spyke doubtfully.

"Piranha fish," smiled Viper. "They're good eating."

"You've got to be kidding me," declared the beleaguered woman.

Much to her surprise, Townsend actually enjoyed the meal and retreated to her tent exhausted, both physically and mentally. Floyd looked at Viper, who was staring intently at the fire. The flames were reflecting off the well-defined muscles in his arms and face, glowing red and glistening with sweat.

"Where do you think we are?" he asked.

"I would say we've passed over the border into Peru," Viper mused.

"How can you tell?" enquired Spyke.

"The fish," revealed Viper. "They were Peruvian piranha."

This seemed reasonable to Spyke, though how a fish would recognise a border created by humans was a mystery to Dr Floyd.

"Do you think you'll find what you're looking for?" asked Dr Floyd, addressing Fabian Spyke.

"I know it's a longshot," he replied, "but I'm a gambling man. Sometimes it pays off, and sometimes…" He let the sentence trail away as he cast his mind over his triumphs and failures. His performance hadn't been too successful of late and the company investors were baying for blood. If he could pull this off it would put him back on top again.

The following morning, the group breakfasted and made their way down to the river. It was flowing fitfully, sparkling in the early morning sunlight.

"If you want to freshen up," announced Viper, "make it quick, but watch out for caimans."

"Caimans?" asked Townsend, with raised eyebrows.

"Alligators to you," said Viper, smiling.

"Of course, what else," came her sarcastic reply.

Refreshed and with water bottles filled, they hitched their rucksacks onto their backs to begin the next part of their exploration. They had barely re-entered the forest, however, when Viper and the two SAS men dropped to the ground and remained motionless.

"What are they doing?" chuckled Townsend, failing to comprehend what had just happened.

Floyd knelt down beside the men to see a dart with a red plume on its end hanging from each man's neck. Before anyone could respond to this news, he witnessed Spyke and Townsend drop with a dart to their neck. He also felt a sting and everything went blank.

Several Amazonian natives stood over the prostrate bodies. They were naked and holding long blowpipes in their hands, their only adornment being a thin wooden stick pushed through their septum and a string of beads draped around their waist. One tribesman gave an order and the team were picked up and spirited away further into the interior of the forest.

***

Waking up with a groan, Fabian Spyke looked around him to see light seeping through the thin canvas of his tent. A quick check confirmed that his rucksack was present, so he scrambled out on all fours, stood up and stretched. The sun was high in the sky and he guessed that it must be close to midday. Surveying his surroundings, Spyke observed a large clearing with a number of grass huts and a group of natives looking on with curiosity. Floyd, Viper and Roberta Townsend were already up and talking animatedly together. He approached the gathering.

"Good morning, Mr Spyke," said Townsend, frowning. "I trust you're alright."

"Good morning, yes I'm well," confirmed Spyke. "What's going on?"

"I sent Fox and West out to recce the area," revealed Viper.

"And?" replied Spyke succinctly.

"They haven't returned."

Before Spyke could respond to this disturbing news, they were approached by a young woman and two young men. The girl was of average height with light brown skin and looked to be in her early twenties. Her hair was jet black, straight and hung down to her shoulders. Her fringe was low on her forehead and cut straight across, just above her eyebrows. With large dark eyes and full lips, she was very striking, not least because she was completely naked save for some beads around her waist and a single red macaw feather in her hair. The men were slightly taller, but below the height of an average man. They too were naked except for small red feather headdresses and beads around their waist. The two young men were also holding spears in a relaxed vertical position, though it was clear to Viper they were there for the girl's protection. Neither one of them seemed self-conscious about their nudity, and the girl stepped forwards and smiled, her small firm breasts standing proud.

"My name is Vaanta," she announced. "Welcome to our village."

Vaanta's English was excellent with only a hint of an accent. This revelation raised eyebrows amongst the group, who clearly weren't expecting it.

"Your English is very good," said Dr Floyd, smiling. "Do you all speak it?"

"Some speak a little, but only I am fluent," she revealed.

"Where did you learn it?" enquired the fascinated anthropologist.

"More to the point where are my men?" interrupted Viper, dispensing with niceties.

"They are indisposed," declared an unflustered Vaanta.

"Is that a euphemism for dead?" quipped Viper.

"If they were dead, I would have said so. They are quite safe," countered Vaanta. "You will notice that you have all been relieved of any potential weapons. We are a peaceful tribe and as long as you behave in a correct manner, you will not be needing them. They will be returned to you when you leave."

"Why did you bring us here?" asked Spyke.

Vaanta gave him a steely stare.

"Are we not what you are looking for?" she said eventually.

"Maybe," replied Spyke. Now he was here, he didn't really know what he expected.

"Come, you must be hungry," said Vaanta, smiling again. "We have prepared some food for you."

The group were led over to some straw matting on the ground laden with fruit and wooden pitchers of water. They were all hungry and readily sat down and began to tuck in. Young children came closer, curious about the strangers. Floyd offered one some mango; they giggled and ran away. Townsend watched the unadorned children retreat, laughing and cajoling, playing to their audience.

"Do they all have to be so... so naked?" remarked Roberta Townsend with disdain.

"Don't forget this is their world," censured Floyd. "We're the odd ones here."

"Have you any idea which tribe this is?" asked Spyke.

"No," replied Floyd, "but there must be quite a few that still need to be identified. Look at these huts," he continued, "they are very rudimentary. If I'm not mistaken, this tribe is nomadic."

As the group continued to eat their fill, they were studied from a larger hut, to one side of the clearing, by eyes that were old and saddened by the presence of these interlopers.

***

Having eaten and drunk their fill, the group stood up. Immediately a throng of young women came running over, laughing and giggling, as if awaiting their cue. They grabbed Roberta Townsend around her arms and whisked her away.

"What are they doing? Where are they taking me?" she panicked.

Chuckling as she saw the girls disappear with the distraught woman into a hut, Vaanta turned to the men.

"They mean her no harm," she said, grinning. "They're fascinated by her pale skin and fair hair."

"What are they going to do?" enquired Floyd, grinning. He could see the beleaguered woman protesting as she was being stripped of her clothes.

"She is quite safe," laughed Vaanta. "She is going to have what you call in your culture, a makeover."

"Enough of this!" exclaimed Spyke, losing his patience. "This is wasting time, we're supposed to be on a mission here."

Vaanta studied the man for a few seconds, then turned, walked over to the large hut and entered. Almost immediately she returned again and approached the three men. With a solemn look she spoke.

"Shimigitsi will see you now."

"Shimigitsi?" enquired Floyd.

"It loosely translates as 'Our Mother'," said Vaanta, smiling. "If you would follow me."

They entered the hut and as their eyes became accustomed to the dimmed light, they saw a shadowy image, wearing a full-length white cotton dress and a garland of orange marigolds around her neck, sitting upright in a cane and straw chair like a queen on her throne. The three men were shocked by the sight. Here was the figure of a frail and wizened old lady. Her skin was well tanned and deeply rutted like the bark of a tree. The skin around her bony fingers was taut and sinewy, the nails long and cracked. The woman's cheekbones were sunken and her lips thin and stretched over yellowing teeth. Wispy white hair was brushed back over her scalp and draped halfway down her back, but her eyes burnt brightly in sunken sockets, showing that she was alive, alert and lucid.

"Are you Sophie Hunter?" asked a wide-eyed Fabian Spyke.

"It's a long time since I heard that name used," croaked the old lady, after a long pause. Her movement seemed like an automaton. "Such a long time."

"So, it's true," continued Spyke. "The serum, it really works."

"The serum," hissed Sophie with utter contempt. "Yes, I was young for a long time, but I have been old for a long time also. And being old has few merits."

"You have no idea what a miracle it is to have found you, Sophie," enthused Spyke. "If you return with us, we can make your final days very comfortable. Your DNA would help create a bright new future as we forge ahead into the further reaches of space. Just think of it, Sophie, an army of supermen policing the universe, bending all to our will. And you… you would have made it happen."

"I have lived here for over two millennia," uttered the old woman. "It would seem little has changed in the world of men. Avarice, greed and violence still prevail. Men like you will never understand. I have hidden myself away to escape the likes of you and the warmongers. Great men make peace not war."

"But so much has been achieved since you've been away," assured Spyke. "Animal conservation has never been better. Many creatures have been brought back from the brink of extinction. And with conservation of the rainforests, they cover more area than ever."

"Conservation," snapped Sophie, losing her patience, "it's nothing more than damage limitation."

"But you can't possibly want to stay in this…" Spyke gestured around him, "… this godforsaken place, surely?"

"Look at my children, they live in peace in this godforsaken place as you call it. To them it's paradise and they care nothing for your malevolent petty ambitions."

"You must have been dreading this day," declared Dr Floyd. He understood all too well Sophie's point of view.

"No, I thank you for coming. I always knew someone would eventually. Sooner or later. Oh, I wish it had been sooner," sighed Sophie. "You see, your arrival seals my death warrant. I cannot allow you access to this abomination inside me. I have been clinging to dear life for so long, and now I can finally let go, rest in peace with a clear conscience. A funeral pyre will be constructed and my ashes will be scattered. I have told them my time is near. This is why they place this garland around my neck. Like the Mexican tradition of *Día de los Muertos*, they believe that these marigolds will keep my spirit close to them."

"The Day of the Dead! Of course," exclaimed Dr Floyd. "I will not allow this to happen. You don't need to be alive to help us. We all have GeoSat implants in us. I can summon a recovery craft here in less than an hour."

A wave of anger surged through Sophie's body and she stood up with a force which shocked everyone, including Vaanta. Sophie's eyes blazed with rage.

"Does your hubris know no limits? Haven't you listened to a single word I've said?"

Stepping forwards, Fabian Spyke grabbed Sophie by the upper arms; Vaanta gasped, nobody but nobody ever touched Shimigitsi.

"Please, Sophie, listen to me." Spyke began to shake the old lady.

"No!" shouted Sophie, and pushed herself away with such a force that she tripped over her chair and rolled sideways onto the floor with an exhalation of air. All was quiet for a moment as they stared at the motionless old woman, lying face down. Then Vaanta cried out,

"Mother!"

She picked up Sophie's frail body and laid her on a bed, also made of cane and straw. Gently Vaanta held the old woman's head close to her chest, tears streaming down her face.

"Shimigitsi," she sobbed.

"Don't mourn for me, child," whispered Sophie weakly. "In many ways it has been a fulfilling life. Now I am ready to go. There's nothing tragic about my passing. The real tragedy is that I lived so long."

With one last long exhalation of breath, Sophie closed her eyes and her head lolled to one side as her life slipped away in Vaanta's arms. The young girl gently placed Sophie down and wiped the tears from her eyes. Her breathing became heavy, like a snorting bull, then she turned and with a blood-curdling animal scream, launched herself at Fabian Spyke. He had no chance to react; Vaanta landed on him, wrapping her legs around his waist. The momentum sent Spyke backwards, but before he hit the ground, Vaanta grabbed his head with both hands and yanked it round with a resounding crack. Landing upright on her feet, Vaanta let the dead man slide to the floor between her legs. She looked at his inert body, panting and glaring at the two remaining men staring back, wide-eyed in stunned silence. Vaanta screamed again and stormed out of the hut, making her way over to where Roberta Townsend was being attended to.

"What do you think is going to happen now?" said Dr Floyd, grimacing.

Viper simply shook his head and frowned. This didn't look good.

With a semi-naked Roberta Townsend protesting profusely, Vaanta dragged her over to the men and pushed her into them. With her clothes in her arms Roberta proceeded to hurriedly get dressed.

"Well, you look different," commented Floyd, trying to lighten the situation. Roberta had been adorned in multicoloured face and body paint with a red feather in her hair.

"Shut up," she sneered and began pulling up her cargo pants. "What's happened?"

"The shit's hit the fan," grunted Viper, "that's what. Spyke is dead."

"What! How?" spluttered Roberta.

Before he could reply, they were distracted by a moan which emanated from the tribe, and to the three onlookers, it could mean only one thing. They had just heard the news about Sophie. A mournful chanting welled up and the natives emerged from the edges of the forest and began to advance on the outsiders. As they edged ever forwards, Viper and the other two began to back away. Not one of them saw blowpipes being lifted but all three suddenly felt the sting of a dart penetrating their neck. Their bodies were dragged to the tents and unceremoniously dumped. Vaanta looked over to the large hut. There was much to be done.

***

The first to awaken was Viper. Seeing that all their possessions had been returned, he rummaged through his rucksack and found a canteen of water. He took a long slug, then stood up and stretched. Looking around he saw that the village was deserted. To make sure, he began checking huts but all were uninhabited. Returning to the other two, he saw that they also were beginning to come round.

"All our gear is here," he declared. "They've even left our weapons."

"I thought we were dead for sure," said Roberta, wincing, rubbing her neck.

"It makes you wonder who the savages really are," quipped Dr Floyd.

Presently they were all on their feet and looking around the village. The smell of burning came from just beyond the perimeter and they followed a light trail of smoke as it drifted to the heavens. It led them to another clearing where at its centre was a large oval-shaped area of burnt ground. Clearly the site of some kind of bonfire.

"I'm going to look for Fox and West," declared Viper, then he moved off, back into the village.

Idly kicking about in the smouldering embers Floyd sighed.

"Do you think this was a funeral pyre?" asked Roberta.

"I know so," confirmed Floyd. "They certainly did a good job, it's… she's all gone."

"What's that?" said Roberta, pointing.

Floyd looked in the direction that she was indicating and walked over to an object at the edge of the ashes. It looked like a burnt book. Floyd bent down for a closer inspection.

"It looks like some kind of journal."

"Do you think Sophie kept a diary?"

Dr Floyd tried to pick up the singed papers, but as he did so they crumbled through his fingers and blew away on the breeze in a flurry of black ash. All that remained was a small segment. He looked at the writing and then looked at Roberta.

"What does it say?" She squinted as ash flew past her face.

"It seems to be a piece of verse." Floyd proceeded to read it out:

… And all my days are trances,
And all my nightly dreams
Are where thy dark eye glances,
And where thy footstep gleams
In what ethereal dances,
By what eternal streams…

"I know this poem, we read it at university," declared Roberta, thinking hard. "I believe it is by one of the ancient American writers. Yes, that's right, Edgar Allan Poe."

"What's the poem called?" asked Dr Floyd, his curiosity piqued.

"Ahh," confessed Roberta, in frustration, "it's on the tip of my tongue."

They walked back into the village as Viper was returning with two very sheepish SAS men.

"Where were they?" said Dr Floyd, smiling.

"I found them at the bottom of a very deep pit," chuckled Viper.

"Are they hurt?" asked Roberta.

"Just their pride," said Viper, grinning.

The adventurer and the soldiers walked off to find their rucksacks, leaving Roberta and Floyd to their own devices.

Minutes later Viper shouted back to them.

"We'll be picked up in thirty minutes."

"We must leave and never come back," concluded Dr Floyd. "We don't belong here."

"Do you think that's possible? Someone is bound to pick up from where Spyke left off."

"I think not, Sophie Hunter is gone. Her ashes scattered to the four winds. What is there to come back for?"

"The tribe of course. As an anthropologist, you must be fascinated by them," reasoned Roberta.

"Did you notice there were no old people here?"

"What are you implying?" said Roberta, frowning.

"Maybe they are the children of Eden," mused Floyd, "and the meek *will* inherit the Earth. After all, they have something that we'll never have."

"Oh, and what is that?"

"Time," said Floyd earnestly, "time to flourish. Time to…"

They were both suddenly distracted by the high-pitched whine of a large craft heading their way. It was only a dot but was approaching at speed.

Walking over to where Viper and the soldiers were packing up, Floyd and Roberta gathered their belongings together, and hitched the rucksacks onto their backs.

"I can't believe that Spyke is dead," pondered Roberta. "I thought this tribe was supposed to be peaceful."

"We all have the potential for rage," declared Floyd. "It just needs the right trigger is all."

"Where do you think they've buried him?"

"Probably an unmarked grave somewhere," surmised Floyd. "Not much of an epitaph, don't you think? His days were numbered in the company, and I doubt whether the board of directors will mourn his loss. This whole exercise was about damage limitation. Sophie was right about that. The desperate act of a desperate man."

"Hey," shouted Roberta as the large bulbous recovery craft hovered over them, "I've just remembered the name of that poem."

"Oh yes?" replied Floyd. "What is it?"

"It's called, *To One in Paradise*."

"What?" bellowed Dr Floyd over the roar of the hovering vessel.

"Forget it," said Roberta, wincing in the downdraught. "It's not important."

The End

ACKNOWLEDGEMENTS

I would like to thank the following people for their continued support and encouragement. In alphabetical order:

Philip Beal, Dee Bixley, Carole Bratby, Michael Bratby, Patrick Budden, Ian Crease, Darren Garner-Richards, Margaret Graham, Aimee Primrose Gunn, Jason Gunn, Roger Gunn, Rab Hopkins, Trevor Loxton – the Thai connection, Paul O'Connell, Luis Antonio Collinao Pizarro – the Chile connection, Bob and Sara-Jane Pollock, Joyce Purslow, Mark Russell, Rob Salt, Scottie – 'The Reporter', Rob Smith – for keeping it real, Jim Stringer, Ted Swan, Michael Sweet – the American connection, Lyndsey Tennant, Steve Tennant, Thapa Top, Martin Tricker, Gary Watson, Jeremy Wilson – the Canadian connection, and last but not least, Laura Wyllie.

 Matador

For exclusive discounts on Matador titles,
sign up to our occasional newsletter at
troubador.co.uk/bookshop

CPSIA information can be obtained
at www.ICGtesting.com
Printed in the USA
BVHW040442160321
602547BV00032B/463

9 781800 462656